Winner Takes All

Stunned, Eleanor was completely incapable of movement. Everything still whirled around her: the race, the close call at losing, the speed that continued to resonate in her body, Ashford's mastery of the phaeton. She was all sensation, barely capable of thought. There had been those agonizing minutes when she thought she'd really have to serve as Daventry's prize—and then she and Ashford had won. Exhilaration had surged through her.

And then . . . the earl kissed her.

For a moment, shocked inertia locked her in its vise. His mouth pressed to hers. His arms and torso were solid around and against her. Her own grip surrounding his shoulders loosened slightly. But her body understood what her mind could not.

Ashford was kissing her. And like hell would she waste this opportunity . . .

By Eva Leigh

FOREVER YOUR EARL

Coming Soon

SCANDAL TAKES THE STAGE

Eva Leigh

Forever Your Earl

The Wicked Quills of London

AVONBOOKS

An Imprint of HarperCollinsPublishers

This is a work of fiction. Names, characters, places, and incidents are products of the author's imagination or are used fictitiously and are not to be construed as real. Any resemblance to actual events, locales, organizations, or persons, living or dead, is entirely coincidental.

AVON BOOKS
An Imprint of HarperCollins*Publishers*
195 Broadway
New York, New York 10007

Copyright © 2015 by Ami Silber
Excerpt from *Scandal Takes the Stage* copyright © 2015 by Ami Silber
ISBN 978-0-06-235862-2
www.avonromance.com

First Avon Books mass market printing: October 2015

Avon Trademark Reg. U.S. Pat. Off. and in Other Countries, Marca Registrada, Hecho en U.S.A.
HarperCollins® is a registered trademark of HarperCollins Publishers.

Printed in the U.S.A.

10 9 8 7 6 5 4 3 2 1

To Zack. Forever.

Acknowledgments

Thank you to Nicole Fischer and Kevan Lyon, for making all this possible. And special thanks to the unwavering support of Rachel Jones.

FOREVER YOUR EARL

Chapter 1

Though London presents itself to the world as the apotheosis of all that is moral and upstanding, it might shock our readers to learn that the appearance of virtue can be a very clever disguise. It is the opinion of this humble periodical that wickedness and deception are far more common than our readers may apprehend. Thus the necessity of this most respectful scrap of writing—that we may, through the revelation of the scandalous activities of our Town, provide necessary guidance. But leading a life of probity may be difficult, especially when presented with temptation . . .

The Hawk's Eye, May 2, 1816

London, 1816

A man rich in wealth and scandal walked into Eleanor Hawke's office.

Eleanor was no stranger to scandal. Anything immoral, disreputable, shocking, or titillating made its way into the pages of her newspaper—particularly if it involved the wealthy and elite of London Society. She detailed all of it for her thrice-weekly publication, *The Hawk's Eye.* Nobody wanted to read about ordinary shopkeeper Mr. Jones who might or might not be spending time with the humdrum widow Mrs. Smith.

No, *The Hawk's Eye* sold strictly on the basis of its publishing the latest scandalous doings of Lord This and Lady That. All, of course, under the pretense of decrying the lack of morals in this fair city, and that publishing these lurid activities served as object lessons to the young and impressionable.

And it was Eleanor's job as owner and publisher to see to the moral education of London.

Which was utter rubbish, naturally.

But scandal put bread on her table and kept the rain off her head, and she readily immersed herself in it—the spirit of free enterprise, and all that.

Still, when Daniel Balfour, the Earl of Ashford himself, walked into the offices of *The Hawk's Eye* on a Wednesday afternoon, blocking the gray light as the door opened and closed, it was both shocking and inevitable that he should do so. Unsurprisingly, he clenched several copies of her paper in his hand.

Lord Ashford marched through the cramped warren of rooms, and writers, bent over their desks, lifted their heads to watch in openmouthed amazement as he passed. Eleanor's private office lay at the end of the corridor, giving her an ample view of the scene as it played out before her.

The earl stopped in front of Harry Welker's desk. The young writer stared up at Lord Ashford, the men separated not just by the expanse of battered oak but by circumstance and birth as well.

"H-how might I help you, my lord?" Harry asked, his voice cracking.

"Tell me where Mister E. Hawke is." Lord Ashford had a deep voice, rounded by generations of excellent breeding and *noblesse oblige*.

"*Mister* Hawke, my lord?" There was patent confusion in the young man's voice.

Lord Ashford pointed to one of the papers he carried. "It says here that *The Hawk's Eye* is owned and published by one E. Hawke. Where will I find him?"

"Nowhere, my lord," Harry answered. "There's no *Mister* Hawke here."

The earl scowled, clearly not used to being denied. "This scurrilous rag cannot publish itself."

"It doesn't," Eleanor announced, setting aside her quill and standing. "If you're looking for *Miss* Eleanor Hawke, I'm right over here."

Lord Ashford looked directly at her, and for the first time, she had a sense of what a rabbit might feel like when sighted by a wolf. But she wasn't the only one at a disadvantage. The earl couldn't hide the shock in his expression when he discovered that the publisher and owner of the paper was, in truth, a woman—which gave her a small measure of gratification.

He turned from Harry without another word and walked straight toward her. And she could only stand, pinned by his gaze, as he approached.

The closer he got, the more she realized how dangerous the earl was. Perhaps not in the traditional sense—though she'd heard and written about the duels he'd fought and won—but certainly in the realm of masculine allure. Her few times seeing him had been from a distance: the theater, the races, at a public assembly. She knew him by sight, but he didn't know her, and they'd never met. And in those instances, her vision had been good enough to recognize that he was a fine specimen, well-formed, handsome—everything a rich and notorious nobleman should be.

But Lord Ashford up close was rather . . . appalling. It didn't seem right that a man so blessed by fortune and title should also be so attractive.

His dark brown hair was fashionably cut and artfully tousled, as if he'd recently risen from a lover's bed. Given his reputation, that was most likely possible. He had a broad forehead, a coin-clean jawline, thick brows, and eyes that, even with yards between her and him, stunned her with their blue clarity. Naturally, he had a mouth that looked very adept at kissing and . . . other things.

He moved with a long-limbed ease that betrayed his skill as a sportsman. His ink-blue coat fit the broad width of his shoulders, and his cream waistcoat, embroidered in gold, defined the shape of his torso—his tailor on Jermyn Street produced excellent work. Snug doeskin breeches were tucked into polished Hessians that came from Bond Street.

Truly, he was quite alarming.

"*Miss* Hawke?" he asked sharply, coming to stand in front of her paper-cluttered desk. "I wasn't expecting a female."

"Neither were my parents," she answered, sitting, "but they learned to adapt. How might I help you, my lord?"

Though she felt an obligation to ask the question, she braced herself for what was sure to be a scorching lecture.

He removed his hat and set it aside. Then he held up an issue of *The Hawk's Eye* and began to read.

"'Lord A—d, a figure well-known to our assiduous and genteel readers, was lately seen in the company of a certain Mrs. F—e, whose late husband made his considerable fortune through the manufacture and sale of a woman's garment we blush to mention in these virtuous pages.'" He tossed one of the issues to the ground. "Wrong."

"You cannot deny—"

But he wasn't done. Holding up another issue of the paper, he read again. "'It may or may not stun our honorable readers to learn that the notorious Lord A—d has not amended his ways following the duel over Lady L., from Y—shire, and has been espied with another married lady of questionable character, at the late-night revels hosted by the equally rakish Mr. S—n. Yet it was noted by our keen-eyed intelligence that this married lady was not the only female vying for the earl's favors.'" This paper he also cast to the floor. "Wrong."

She herself had written those pieces, and while they weren't matchless examples of English prose, she was still rather proud of them, as she was of all her labors. To have her hard work thrown to the ground like so much garbage was rankling.

"I assure you, my lord," she said bitingly, "*The Hawk's Eye* strives for the greatest of accuracy." She had a network of sources, which she used regularly to provide information. Many members of the aristocracy were in dire need of funds, and they gladly turned on each other in order to maintain the pretense of effortless wealth. Eleanor always paid her informants to keep them returning.

Whether or not they lied to her just to collect payment wasn't her concern, but she always preferred it if she could validate their statements. Sometimes that meant going out and conducting a few investigations. But she was a very busy woman—writing articles, editing countless others, managing the paper's finances—and didn't always have the time.

She had to earn a living, after all. And men like the earl didn't.

Continuing, she said, "That's exceptionally conceited of you, my lord, to assume that *you* are Lord A—d." Leaning back in her chair, she gave a thin smile. "I could be writing about Lord Archland. Or perhaps Lord Admond."

"Lord Archland hasn't left his country estate in a decade," the earl answered, "and Lord Admond's days of scandal happened when red heels and powdered wigs were in fashion. The man written about is undoubtedly, nauseatingly, me."

So much for that defense. "Oh, but you're far from nauseating, my lord. In fact, you're enthralling—to my readers," she hastened to add.

Lord Ashford shook his head. "It amazes me that the citizens of London have such paltry lives that they'd care a groat what I did."

"The provinces, too," she added. "I have a thousand subscribers throughout the country."

He threw up his hands. "Ah, that improves the situation immeasurably. I cannot fathom what my concern was."

"As my paper states," she said, "you are London's most notorious rake. Of course people care what you do."

He crossed his arms over his chest, a movement that emphasized that the width of his shoulders didn't come from the work of a tailor's artful needle.

"One might think that your readers would be far more interested in the food shortages that have resulted from recent crop failures," he fired back. "Or perhaps they might be intrigued by the East Indian volcanic explosion. Maybe, just maybe, they'd be concerned with Argentina declaring its independence from Spain. Did none of that ever cross your mind, Miss Hawke, rather than reporting spurious gossip about a figure as inconsequential as myself?"

Though she was momentarily shocked that a man as infamously dissolute as Lord Ashford would be so well informed, she quickly recovered.

"I'd hardly call you inconsequential, my lord," she countered. "Your family name goes back to the time of Queen Elizabeth. If memory serves, your ancestor Thomas Balfour won himself an earldom as a privateer to the queen—though others merely called him a pirate with a government charter. It seems as though scandal runs in your blood. How could the public not be fascinated?"

It was his turn to look surprised. He likely didn't expect her to be so knowledgeable of his ancestry. But Eleanor was nothing if not thorough. She had *Debrett's* memorized the way others knew their Bible verses.

"Because I am merely one man," he answered. "Granted, a man with a somewhat extensive wardrobe—"

Of mistresses, she silently added.

"But hardly worth page after page of precious paper and ink," he concluded.

"You belong to a gentleman's club, do you not?" she asked pointedly. "White's, if memory serves. And what do you do there?"

"Drink."

"You appear quite sober now," she said, "and you always take your luncheon there. Given the hour, you likely were at White's, then came here. As I cannot smell the reek of alcohol on your breath or person, I highly doubt that drinking is the only activity in which you engage at your club."

"Ah, you have me figured out. In fact," he said, lowering his voice conspiratorially, "I spend most of my time there plotting how to live off the blood of the lower classes."

"I strongly suspect that if that had been your ambition, I and my commoner brethren would be drained dry by now."

"Perhaps I need to strengthen my motivation," he replied. "You're doing a rather bang-up job of it."

"What a proud day for me," she said. "To have driven an earl toward thoughts of vampirism. But come now, you're being deliberately obtuse. What else—besides imbibe and plot the agony of the lesser classes—do you do at your club?"

"Read the newspaper," he answered.

Ah! Finally. "And for those gentlemen who haven't the connections or wealth to be members of a club, there are always the coffee houses. They stock newspapers for their customers, too."

"Perhaps it's time to get a quill sharpener," he said acidly, "because I fail to see your point."

She came around her desk and leaned against it, so that a distance of only a few feet separated them. "My point, Lord Ashford, is that there are countless sources for the news you cited. Most of their offices can be found within a quarter mile of here. Those papers are for *news*. But *The Hawk's Eye* provides something that the *Times* and other papers do not."

"Paper for lining birdcages," he said.

"Moral guidance."

He gave one single, harsh laugh. "I ought to fetch the attendants from Bedlam, because you're clearly in the grips of a powerful delusion. Like our own dear monarch, God save him. Shall I bring you a mitre and crook and declare you pope?"

She pressed her lips together. This wasn't the first time she'd come under attack for her paper's practices, but seldom by someone as articulate and intelligent as the earl. It didn't help that he had a most distracting physical appearance. How could a man possess such a pair of spectacularly blue eyes? Like the glint of sapphires washed in autumn sunlight.

"It's right here beneath the paper's name," she said, picking up an issue lying on her desk. "*Consilium per stadium.* 'Guidance through observation.' If you led a more moral life, you wouldn't appear in my paper at all."

He looked at her with patent disbelief. "What unbounded cheek, for you to judge me. You, who profit from feeding on carrion, like some quill-wielding hyena."

Eleanor considered herself someone with a thick skin and a decent amount of composure, but for some reason, the earl's words struck her with a strange sensation she hadn't experienced in a long while. If she had to guess, it was a mixture of pain and . . . shame.

She quickly shook the feeling off. Shame was for those who could afford it. And she couldn't.

"I don't judge," she fired back, "only report the facts as I know them."

He snorted. "They aren't facts. Just half-truths buried in terrible prose."

"My writing is *not* terrible," she muttered. "Have you read the *Examiner* lately? *That* is some execrable hack work."

"And yet here I stand," he said flatly, "in *your* office."

"So you do. But, my lord, you may rail and complain and whine like a petulant child—"

He sputtered.

"—but you're a public figure. As such, that makes you fair game. The rest of the world lead fairly dull lives. We get up—"

"As do I."

"Eat our breakfasts."

"I do the same."

"Go to work."

Here, he was silent.

She continued, "Most of us cannot afford to go to the theater or gaming hells or have the social connections to attend private assemblies. But you can, and you do. You are what we all aspire to be, my lord."

He laughed ruefully. "Perhaps you and your readers ought

to set your sights higher. There are people of, how would you put it, far greater *moral* character worth mirroring."

"Maybe so," she answered candidly. "I can list dozens of men and women, all of greater purpose and ambition than yourself, that I would much rather see held up as an example to emulate. Teachers or philanthropists."

He looked insulted. "I donate generously to orphanages and veterans' assistance organizations right here in London."

"Do you?" She should make a note of that later. None of her sources had ever uncovered that aspect of the earl's life, but it would make for a surprising and rather delicious counterpoint to his rakish public behavior. It also spoke well of Lord Ashford that he did not attempt to make public his charitable endeavors. But it was rather easier to do her job if she didn't think *too* highly of him.

"Regardless of the content of your character, my lord," she went on, "you live a life only a minute fraction can ever hope to attain. As such, that makes you an object of fascination. And the truth of it is, you cannot stop me or anyone on my staff from writing about you."

"A miserable fact of which I'm well aware," he answered.

She strode back around her desk. "Then I believe we've said all we can to one another, delightful as this exchange has been. Good day, my lord." She started to sit. "I'm rather busy, but I can have Harry show you to the door if you require."

But Lord Ashford didn't move. Stood exactly where he was, with his arms still folded over his chest. "If you are going to use me as your subject, the least you can do is proper research."

She hovered over her chair. "Forgive me for not being Cambridge-educated, but I'm not certain what you are suggesting."

Unfolding his arms, he braced his hands on the edge of her desk, leaning slightly forward. Despite the expanse of the desk separating them, she felt compelled to lean away.

"What I am suggesting, Miss Hawke," he murmured, "is

that you accompany me. Day and night. That way, you can see exactly what I do with my time. You see," he continued, a slow smile unfolding, "I don't want you to stop writing about me at all. I want you to get it right."

Daniel still hadn't quite recovered from his shock at learning that E. Hawke was, in fact, *Eleanor* Hawke. She also wasn't the sort of slattern he might expect in this Grub Street milieu. Miss Hawke resembled a prosperous shopkeeper's wife—granted, a pretty shopkeeper's wife, with her wheat-blonde hair, bright hazel eyes, strong but feminine features, and nicely curved figure. She looked to be about his age of thirty-two years, as would befit someone who owned and operated their own business.

A female in a field almost entirely dominated by males. If there were any other women in her line of work, he'd never heard of them. She must have inherited the paper from some male relative—a father or husband, perhaps. Maybe a deceased husband. Certainly she hadn't founded the periodical herself.

Still, here she was, surprising in her respectability. She wore a modest peach-colored dress, and her hair was neatly pinned back. The only sign she worked for a living was the ink staining her fingers.

He hadn't counted on a woman being E. Hawke. But it was actually perfect. His suggestion would be all the more enticing to her. A journalist and a woman were the two most inquisitive creatures on earth. Combine them, and only a cat could rival her for curiosity.

He'd turn her attention away from the activities that had been consuming him these past two weeks and distract her from his true purpose. While he had her gaze focused elsewhere, he could continue on with his true goal—finding Jonathan.

His proposition clearly intrigued Miss Hawke. She continued to hover over her chair.

Despite her interest, she asked suspiciously, "Why would you *want* me to write about you?"

"As you said," he explained, "I cannot stop you from penning these absurd articles about my life. And if I can't stop you, the very least you can do is be accurate. What better way than to have you come with me each day and night and record my activities? Unless you don't feel up to the task of late-night revelry and observing firsthand how the elite of Society fill their wicked hours."

This was most assuredly not the truth. But he wasn't about to explain that Jonathan Lawson, his closest friend since childhood, had been missing for nearly a month. The situation was even more dire, because soon after Jonathan's disappearance, his elder brother had died. Now Jonathan was the heir to one of England's oldest and most esteemed dukedoms—and no one could find him. Before his disappearance, he'd been seen with low, rough company. Men who slunk around the alleys of the East End and lived like rats. If the truth ever got out about Jonathan's vanishing— especially in the newspapers—the family could be utterly ruined.

But Daniel, as Miss Hawke had so thoroughly argued, was a public figure. She documented his every movement. He had to turn her shrewd gaze away from the hunt for Jonathan. Providing specifically engineered distractions was exactly the strategy that was needed. So he'd open himself up to her scrutiny—because he owed it to Jonathan. A minor inconvenience was nothing compared to the failure to honor the unspoken promises of friendship.

And Daniel had failed Jonathan's friendship spectacularly.

Miss Hawke dropped into her chair, swiveling the seat back and forth as she mulled over his offer. Her brow furrowed, and she steepled her fingers, pressing them to her bottom lip. Were he a painter—which he assuredly was not—he'd paint the scene and title it *Study in Wary Contemplation*.

Finally, the swiveling of her chair stopped, and she faced him. "I don't trust you," she stated baldly.

No one except Jonathan and his friend Marwood spoke to him so candidly. Yet Miss Hawke addressed him as if she had every right to be so blunt. As though they were equals. On every level.

He waited to feel a hot wave of outrage or anger. None came. It was . . . refreshing. To be talked to like he was . . . himself. Not the Earl of Ashford, a nobleman that required flattery or coddling or toadying deference. But an ordinary man.

"Why should you?" he answered frankly.

His own candor seemed to catch her by surprise, which felt like a small victory. She wasn't the only one capable of shocking someone.

"I've no reason to," she replied. "We've clearly established ourselves at cross purposes. You've already observed two salient facts about me. I'm the owner of this enterprise. And I'm a woman."

"Both facts have been noted by me, yes." The unfortunate truth was that had he seen Miss Hawke on the other side of a ballroom, he would have sought to claim a dance—if not more. She was distractingly attractive. Worldly, clever. Slim and curved. But his intent was too important to let something like her prettiness throw him off his course.

She couldn't know his motivations for being here, or what prompted him to offer up such an outrageous proposition. And if she rejected his offer . . . No, she had to accept. The reputation of an influential family depended on it. Even more important, Jonathan's life lay on the line.

Miss Hawke continued, "Neither condition has inclined me to have faith in others, particularly men."

That caught his attention.

Before he could press her on that interesting admission, she continued, "And yet . . ." She steepled her fingers together again. "I'd be a fool to refuse your proposition. After all, what's to stop you from going to one of my competitors with the same offer?"

He didn't mention that none of the other scandal sheets

reported on him as regularly and with such underlying glee as *The Hawk's Eye*.

"Nothing," he said. "Only my own inclination."

Her brow still lowered in thought, she stood and began to pace the length of her office—which wasn't very far, so she caromed back and forth like a snooker ball.

"We could make it a regular feature," she murmured, mostly to herself. "Advertise it in upcoming issues leading up to the series. Drive up sales. And we'll call it . . . we can call it . . ."

"*The Adventures of Lord A.,*" he suggested.

She threw him an exasperated look, as if disappointed with his efforts. "Not nearly titillating enough."

"Forgive me if I'm not familiar with the ways of lurid prose."

"You'll never make it as a journalist," she fired back.

"Thank the heavens," he replied.

As she paced her tiny office, she continually brushed past him. He caught her scent of ink, oil from printing presses, and cinnamon. Daniel had no desire to press himself into the corner like a frightened dog, so he remained where he stood, despite the disconcerting proximity of Miss Hawke.

Suddenly, she stopped, and her face lit up. Inspiration had struck, and it turned her from pretty to extraordinary in an instant.

"*To Ride with a Rake,*" she pronounced.

He winced. Of all the names he'd been called in his life—"rogue," "prodigal," "libertine"—*rake* had always been one of his least favorite. It implied a certain leering, cheap smuttiness. "We don't need to use that word."

"Oh, but we do," she answered, face shining. "Other than the word *duke,* nothing intrigues potential readers more than *rake*. You do want people to read the columns, don't you?"

Given his preferences, his natural inclination was to say no. But these were extraordinary circumstances, and he needed as many eyes fixed on his activities as possible. "Yes," he said through gritted teeth.

She beamed at him. "Excellent. *To Ride with a Rake* it shall be."

A sudden thought bloomed in his mind. "My exceptionally keen powers of observation have noted that you are, in fact, female. Keeping company with me will harm your reputation."

Her laugh was husky, honey over polished stones. "I'm a writer, my lord. I *have* no reputation."

Most of the women of his acquaintance guarded their names assiduously, fearfully. They lived in a world where a woman's social standing meant everything. But this strange Miss Hawke seemed to dwell in a fringe realm, unconcerned about what anyone thought about her. As if she were a man. Or, at the least, a man's equal.

How very intriguing.

"Then we're agreed, my lord?" she pressed. "I'm to accompany you on your sundry activities, and write about them for *The Hawk's Eye*?"

This was it. His last chance before throwing wide the doors of his life and making himself the object of public examination. He'd been scrutinized before, but never to the extent that he proposed now. The very thought made his chest tighten and his fists clench, ready to defend himself and his privacy. Gentlemen never did anything for notoriety's sake. They were discreet, elegant, reserved.

There was nothing discreet, elegant, or reserved about appearing like a circus attraction in the pages of Miss Hawke's scandal sheet. Yet he had to. For Jonathan's family. More importantly, for Jonathan himself.

"We're agreed," he said.

She stuck out her hand. Offering it to shake. He stared at it for a moment. Ladies didn't shake hands—they presented them to be bowed over, or else the women curtsied. But here was more proof that Miss Hawke was unlike any other female he'd ever known.

His handshake was his bond. This final gesture would seal his fate.

Finally, he took her hand in his. He still wore his gloves, but through the delicate kidskin he could feel calluses lining her fingers—she worked for a living. Her hand was warm, too, even through the thin leather of his gloves. A tropic current pulsed through him. What would it feel like to have their bare palms press against each other, skin to skin? He'd known the feel of many women, but none like her.

She gazed down at their joined hands, a faint frown nestled between her eyebrows. As if trying to puzzle out an enigma.

He'd have to be on his guard around her. She was the kind of person who would never give up on a mystery until every aspect of it was uncovered. If she unearthed his true motive for this proposition, the consequences would be ruinous.

Abruptly, she broke the grip between them. Her hand pressed against her skirts. She cleared her throat. "We should fix a schedule. When shall we begin?"

"As soon as possible."

She narrowed her eyes. "In a hurry, my lord?"

Using years of a nobleman's training, he made his voice smooth and unaffected. "Don't want to keep your readers in the dark for too long." Which wasn't an answer, but he wasn't about to give her one.

"Tomorrow will suffice," she answered, "if that suits you."

"It does," he answered. "I'd been planning on spending our evening at Donnegan's."

"I'm not familiar with it."

"This gaming hell isn't exactly sanctioned."

"A gaming hell." She practically bounced on her feet in eagerness, then stilled. "Do they allow women?"

"No—so I might have to come up with a new plan." All this time, he'd been planning that E. Hawke was a man.

"I can get my hands on some masculine attire," she said. "A disguise." Far from looking daunted by the prospect of wearing men's clothing and infiltrating a haven of male vice, Miss Hawke looked as excited as a child given free rein in a toy shop. A very immoral toy shop.

"How?"

"I have friends in the theater," she answered.

"Naturally—one employment of disrepute gravitates toward another."

"And yet titled men lead lives of such incomparable virtue."

"We *are* fond of the theater," he said drily. "Feeds our appetite for dissipation."

"Well, my dissipated friends at the Imperial Theater will give me access to their costumes and wigs."

He lifted his brows. "The Imperial. They're known for their rather . . . unconventional theatrical offerings." His friend Marwood almost never missed a night at the Imperial. Marwood especially loved the burlettas of Mrs. Delamere, which inevitably skewered the upper classes.

Miss Hawke's quick, wide smile caught him between the ribs. "When one doesn't have a patent, one has to be a bit inventive in order to bring in patrons."

He set his hat on his head. "Tomorrow night, then. I'll pick you up at the Imperial."

"Tomorrow night."

After a pause, he turned and left, all the while aware of her gaze on his back as he strode from the office.

He'd no choice—this had to be done. He'd have to see this through, whatever it might bring. Yet he couldn't forget the feel of her hand in his. Slim and warm and strong. As he stepped out onto the street, where his carriage waited for him, a thought whispered that he'd just agreed to a bargain with a very pretty devil.

Chapter 2

*For all our era's claims to probity and integrity—
some of which are true—it may shock and appall this
paper's virtuous readers to learn that there is a high
degree of insincerity, nay, outright concealment, that
lurks beneath the surface of our society. Those who
represent themselves as a certain thing often prove
entirely different beneath the surface. Or else they
wear disguises of one form or another, all to obscure
purposes at which this modest publication can only
guess . . .*

The Hawk's Eye, May 4, 1816

As Eleanor entered through the side door of the Imperial Theater late the following afternoon, she found everything in the usual state of colorful, barely organized chaos.
Kingston, the stage manager, ran hither and yon, clutching
his ever-present sheaf of documents and shouting at anyone
and anything that crossed his path. Rehearsals were inevitably pandemonium. Costumed dancers wafted off the stage,
complaining in the foulest language about the choreogra-
pher's impossible demands. There were only so many joints
in the human leg, after all. As the dancers left the stage,
they were replaced by a comedic duo in loud trousers and
waistcoats, clearly hoping that if their jests didn't amuse the
audience, their outrageous outfits might.

The air smelled thickly of lamp oil, sweat, and grease-paint. Chatter and music filled the air. Eleanor stopped in the wings and took a deep breath. Ah, these were her people. She'd lived her whole life on the very fringes of respectability, rubbing elbows with theater folk, musicians, writers, confidence artists, and the generally disreputable. It was her other self—publisher, businesswoman—that sometimes felt more unfamiliar.

A world apart from Lord Ashford.

As she stood in the wings, watching the comedic duo torture puns, a dark-haired woman crossed her path, then stopped.

"Here to murder one of my plays, Eleanor?" She planted her hands on her hips.

"You manage that all on your own, Maggie," Eleanor answered.

Maggie drew her arm through Eleanor's. They slowly ambled through the anarchy backstage. "Did you see the review for *Love's Revolution* in the *Times*? 'It is the humble opinion of this reviewer that Mrs. Margaret Delamere's latest theatrical opus, while adequately entertaining, suffers from a surfeit of radical sensibility. Once again she challenges our notion that the social orders should remain distinct, a notion that could lead to a revolt not unlike what transpired in France. I can only imagine that such naiveté must be a result of her gender.'"

"How dare you challenge hundreds of years of rigidly enforced hierarchy, madam!" Eleanor said haughtily. "Surely you must remain content with your lot, particularly as a woman."

"Indeed, I should." Maggie sighed. "Or tell 'em all to go to blazes and just keep writing what I want to write."

Both women chuckled. The life of a writer was never one of ease and accolade—or money—but both Eleanor and Maggie had, from birth, been marked by the same curse. Womanhood. It was nigh impossible for their work to be judged of the same value as their male compatriots'. Or, worse, they would be shoved into writing about "proper" and "domestic" topics such as babies and other homespun dramas—things that interested neither Maggie nor Eleanor.

But Maggie was brave and published her work under her own name, rather than using a masculine pseudonym. Eleanor hid behind her first initial, never outright claiming her gender or refuting it, either.

Because the Imperial did not have a royal patent, like Drury Lane or Covent Garden, it could not perform anything that was strictly spoken word. Few theaters could compete with this two-sided monopoly. But the Imperial had gotten around this proviso by having music accompany every piece they put on. The works were a cross between operas and plays—known as "burlettas"—and often addressed subject matter that other theaters wouldn't dare touch.

Maggie had found a home here for her writing because Drury Lane and Covent Garden—and the Haymarket during the summer—hardly ever put on original plays. Yet due to the Imperial's outsider status, Maggie had been welcomed. She and her iconoclastic work were the star attractions.

"Oughtn't you be back at the office, stringing up another aristo on the pillory of public opinion?" Maggie asked as they continued to stroll around clumps of actors and dancers.

"You're mixing your metaphors," Eleanor noted. "And it's one aristo in particular who brings me here." As quickly as she could, she told her friend all about the arrangement she and Lord Ashford had made.

"*The* Lord Ashford?" Maggie pressed. "The selfsame one who caused two actresses here to get into a full-out brawl, hair-pulling and biting included?"

"The same," Eleanor answered, filing the idea away. She'd need to see if *The Hawk's Eye* had reported that little incident. If not, they were surely remiss in their duties.

"I've seen him sitting in the boxes." Maggie pointed out into the theater, where the boxes reserved for the wealthy arrayed themselves like red velvet jewelry cases. During performances, the occupants would be displayed like a veritable treasury of silk, satin, and gems. "Always surrounded by a cadre of toadies. And women, of course. He's got one of those faces I call a corset-tightener. You look at him, and suddenly air becomes a little more scarce."

"To me," Eleanor said, "he's nothing more than a means to sell more papers."

"Methinks the lady doth protest too much," Maggie murmured. "You know my history with aristo rakes. They're as trustworthy as boats made of paper."

"At least I know how to swim." It was a shame she and Maggie saw each other as infrequently as they did. But between Eleanor's deadlines and Maggie hammering away at a new play, their schedules seldom aligned.

"If your arrangement with Lord Ashford begins tonight," Maggie pondered, "what are you doing here? Shouldn't you be at home, pretending not to dress up for him?"

"I *do* need to dress for him," Eleanor said, "but my ensemble involves buckskins and beaver hats, not décolletage and diadems."

Maggie excitedly pressed her hand to her mouth. "A breeches part! But this is too wonderful! Let me fetch Madame Hortense and Mr. Swindon. They will be beside themselves with glee—we haven't had a decent breeches part since my *Countess's Deception*."

Her friend hurried off, and as she progressed through the theater, she grabbed anyone passing by to eagerly explain Eleanor's upcoming transformation. Thrilled squeals rose up from the crowd—theater people were always pleased to pull someone into their mad, idiosyncratic world, and the cast and crew at the Imperial were no exception. Soon, Eleanor found herself surrounded by nearly a dozen chattering figures, pulling her this way and that, deciding just what kind of man she'd be: dark, fair, dandy, rough. She felt like so much clay in the hands of countless giddy sculptors. Far at the back stood Maggie, laughing into her hand.

What would Lord Ashford make of such a scene? Though

he kept company with a good many actresses, he likely wasn't as familiar with this aspect of theater life.

Madame Hortense, the angular, middle-aged woman in charge of makeup and wigs, and Mr. Swindon, the heavyset costumer, shoved their way to the front of the crowd. They both surveyed her critically.

"So this is what a fish at Billingsgate feels like," Eleanor mumbled.

"Come with us." Madame Hortense led Eleanor down several flights of stairs, with Mr. Swindon and a whole entourage trailing after them. At last they reached a dressing room, lined with mirrors and tables, costumes draped over every available surface.

"Shoo, all of you!" Mr. Swindon waved his fingers at the crowd. Naturally, this command was met with a host of histrionic cries of despair.

"Let Maggie stay," Eleanor pressed. If she had to suffer under the eager hands of Madame Hortense and Mr. Swindon, she needed an ally nearby.

"Very well," sighed Mr. Swindon.

Maggie squeezed her way through the crowded door and shut it behind her. More lamentations followed, muted by the closed door.

Madame Hortense pushed Eleanor into a chair and smiled with calculation. "Now, it begins."

"God help me," whispered Eleanor. The things she'd do for a story.

There was no sense of peace like the peace one found at White's. Daniel entered the gentleman's club and was immediately met by a silent footman, who took his coat, hat, and gloves before fading discreetly away. A butler appeared, solemn as a high priest, and greeted him with muted reverence.

"Is there anything I can fetch you, my lord?"

"Brandy, and the latest issue of *The Hawk's Eye* if you have it."

"I will have to check to see if we stock that particular . . . periodical. If not, I'll send one of the footmen out to purchase a copy."

Daniel nodded and moved on to the main parlor. Large, comfortable leather chairs were like oysters, holding pearls of British aristocracy. In the heavy, prosperous quiet, men perused newspapers, each with a glass of spirits close at hand, or they murmured amongst themselves, discussing racehorses or the fate of the nation.

Pausing at the doorway to the parlor, Daniel inhaled the scents of his birthright—leather, furniture wax, tobacco. All familiar aromas, and comforting in their way. He'd been coming to White's since he'd reached his majority, though he'd expressed an interest in Brooks's, as its political leanings were more in keeping with his own Whig tendencies. His father, of course, had forbidden it. Now that his father had passed on, it was habit that kept Daniel coming back to White's.

Not just habit. He used to meet Jonathan here, where they'd talk of the events of the day, or sit in companionable silence, content to simply exist without pressures and demands and societal roles.

Daniel kept returning, a strange hope always tugging at him that he'd walk in and one day simply find Jonathan in his favorite chair, looking well and free of the shadows of war. Every time, Daniel was disappointed. His friend was never there.

Right now, a little calm before tonight's storm would serve Daniel well. He had no idea exactly what this evening with Miss Hawke would bring. Oddly, whenever he thought of it, of her, a hum of excitement would pulse through him. When was the last time anything other than a night's carousing truly excited him? There was his clandestine, crucial mission. Yet the eagerness he felt now seemed far different from that objective.

He needed a drink. But before he took more than three steps into the main parlor, two young gentlemen hardly back from their Grand Tour appeared and clung to his side, like well-dressed barnacles.

"Ashford!" the blond one exclaimed. Lord George Medway, heir to the earldom of Newholm. "Missed you at the Lashams' rout last night."

"It was deuced fun," said the other young man. The Honorable Fred Willsby, second son of Viscount Swinhope. "Danced all night."

Daniel thought of the rows and rows of white-clad girls, all eager for a dance and the possibility of any matrimonial intentions, and the sly-eyed widows and wives, searching for a way to break up the monotony, and he felt very, very tired. It wasn't the sort of evening that interested him. He'd once preferred wilder nights, but that had changed when Jonathan had disappeared. Now, everything felt thin, hollow.

"I had another engagement," he said distractedly.

The two lads perked up. "Tell us, do," pressed Medway.

What the hell—he had enough status to be honest. "I was ensconced in front of my own fire, reading about Herschel's latest astronomical discoveries."

The two young men looked baffled. They exchanged glances, as if trying to confirm whether or not Daniel was having them on. After all, it was the height of the Season, certainly not the time to stay at home with a book when there were so many other pleasures to pursue.

But after leaving Miss Eleanor Hawke's office yesterday, Daniel had found himself oddly restless. Edgy. The thought of attending a ball, or the theater, or any of the countless other social gatherings—both respectable and less so—had felt strangely flat and shrill. He'd actually enjoyed his badinage with Miss Hawke yesterday, and the brief glimpse into another world. One far away from routs and assemblies. Odd—before Jonathan's vanishing, he'd always loved those things.

Dedication and ambition had shone in Miss Hawke's

eyes—things he seldom saw outside of Parliament. And of the females he knew, most were looking for husbands, protectors, or lovers. None of them was so extraordinary as to own and publish a newspaper.

In his peculiar, dissatisfied mood, Daniel had rejected all potential amusements last night. Even Edinger, his butler, had been shocked to find him at home. Instead of going out after meeting with Miss Hawke, Daniel had indulged himself with his favorite pastime—the scientific arts. And he'd found the night far more enjoyable than he'd expected.

Did Miss Hawke care about the sciences? Or was she too involved in the world of scandal to take note of the planets or electricity?

"But you'll be at the Fallbrookes' ball tonight, surely," Willsby enjoined.

"That's tonight?" The Season was overstuffed with a surfeit of gatherings and entertainments, most engineered to match girls with potential suitors. He ought to employ a secretary to manage his social calendar, but he had a man of business as well as stewards for his estates. Hiring a man just to tell him what parties to attend seemed like a phenomenal waste of everyone's time. "I have another engagement scheduled for this evening."

"What is it?" Medway asked eagerly. "Perhaps we might attend, as well."

"Alas, I already have company for the night."

"Company of the female variety, undoubtedly." Medway grinned—an attempt at ribaldry.

"Of a sort," Daniel answered distractedly. Was Miss Hawke at this very moment donning her masculine disguise? He smiled to himself. Her theatrical friends would have to work very hard indeed to turn her into a convincing man.

"We could—" Willsby began, but Daniel had long grown weary of these two pups. They were too young, too far from the real troubles of life.

"I've got my newspaper and my brandy waiting, chaps.

On occasion, one does have need of intellectual and spiritual stimulation."

"Of course," the two young men agreed readily, unaware of Daniel's disguised insult.

He left them chattering, and proceeded to his favorite chair near the fire.

Jonathan's empty chair stood beside him, silent and accusatory.

The moment he sat, the butler appeared with not only a glass of excellent brandy but also the most recent issue of *The Hawk's Eye,* freshly ironed to keep the ink from staining his fingers.

"Your . . . reading material . . . my lord."

Daniel took the paper and nodded his dismissal of the servant. The man evaporated like so much mist. Generally, Daniel only read *The Hawk's Eye* when a friend pointed out mention of him in its pages, and then only to scoff at the—generally—inaccurate reporting of his activities. Though sometimes the scandal rag got it right, such as his arrangement with one of the theater's latest ingénues last winter, or the substantial winnings he'd collected one night at a gaming hell.

But today, with no mention of him at all, he permitted himself to give the paper an actual read. He prepared himself to be appalled at the quality of the writing—hackneyed phrases, purple prose, shrill jokes.

As he sipped his drink and read, surprise crept over him. He wasn't a critic, not by any stretch, but this little paper . . . wasn't so bad. In truth, there were parts of it that were actually well written. It had a sense of wit and self-deprecation, and here and there, buried amongst the insinuations about who was having an affair with whom, genuine bits of art showed through.

Did Miss Hawke write those parts? Or were they penned by someone on her staff? She had control over all the articles. Whether she was the author of the pieces or not, it showed that she did have an eye for quality writing.

As he shifted in his chair, a strange sensation crept through him. Something odd and bright. It was . . . respect.

How could he respect a newspaper that reported scandal, or the woman who published it?

Yet . . . it was there. Buried like coal that was starting to burn. Surely more time in her presence would smother that. He couldn't truly admire a woman who lived like a parasite off the lives of others. Could he?

Regardless, she was a necessary part of his plan, and he had to endure her company for as long as it took to get the job done and find his missing friend.

"**Y**ou are squirming like a grub!" Madame Hortense snapped. The more cross she became, the more her accent slipped away from Lyons and toward Lambeth.

"Forgive me," Eleanor replied, fighting to keep her own tone level. "My daily toilette doesn't consist of being poked and prodded as though I were a cow at an agricultural fair."

"Bloody hell . . . I mean, *mon Dieu*!" Madame Hortense tossed down her makeup brush. "I have never had to work under such conditions."

"Me, either," said Eleanor. For hours, she'd been undergoing the torturous process of being transformed—superficially, of course—from a woman to a man. She couldn't breathe, due to the heavy linen strips binding her breasts, while Mr. Swindon had forced her to don an undergarment that came supplied with its own masculine *equipment*. Then he'd treated her as his very own pincushion as he'd tailored a male ensemble to fit.

Eleanor wasn't a wealthy woman. Not by anyone's standards. She'd never undergone the unique, exhausting torment of being fitted for a custom garment. All her clothes were bought secondhand, and any alterations were done by her own needle. But if this afternoon's experience was any indicator, it was a privilege she gladly forwent.

With Mr. Swindon making the final adjustments to her clothing in the sewing room, attention was now being paid to her hair and face. Thus, Madame Hortense's presence.

Also suited to Eleanor's financial situation, she didn't have a lady's maid. She dressed herself and did her own hair. Madame Hortense was in the process of tugging on and pinning up Eleanor's long hair, and none too gently. It was a wonder how the actors submitted themselves to this process every night. Not without sustaining external and internal injuries.

Concerned that she'd insulted Madame Hortense, Eleanor exchanged worried glances with Maggie, who was perched on a nearby stool. For all her rough methodology, Madame Hortense did have a dab hand with makeup and hair dressing. Her work for the stage was amongst the most admirable in London.

Since the woman was doing her a tremendous favor, Eleanor oughtn't be churlish about it.

"I *am* sorry, madame," Eleanor said, reaching out and taking the older woman's hand. "As you can see, I'm an unrefined sort of female, and unused to such attentions. The only time I can sit still is when I'm writing."

"That's very true," seconded Maggie. "When she's not at her desk, she dances around like a child denied a trip to the privy."

Madame Hortense huffed and tugged her hand from Eleanor's. She edged backward. Clearly, she needed further assuaging.

"When I learned that I would need to disguise myself as a man," Eleanor continued, "I came straight to the Imperial. Not simply because I knew Maggie but because I knew that, of all the cosmetic artists in the whole of this city, no one could possibly match you in skill. The work you did in creating that demon for Maggie's *Curse of the Midnight Prince* stole my breath. I was convinced that an actual demon trod upon the boards, not an actor. Half the women in the audience wanted to flee in terror."

Madame Hortense pressed her lips together, but a flush of gratification spread across her cheeks.

"And," Eleanor went on, "your ability in transforming women into men for breeches parts . . ." She shook her head. "Had I not looked in the program and seen the actresses' names, I would have demanded physical proof that they were indeed female."

For a moment, Madame Hortense did not move or speak. But then she slowly nodded. "It's true. I am the best."

"Then please, I beg of you, forgive me and continue on with your excellent work."

The woman sniffed. Then she moved back to where Eleanor sat in front of a lighted mirror and proceeded to tug her hair into ruthless submission. Madame Hortense shoved more and more pins into her hair—she'd look like a shedding hedgehog later when the pins were removed—and Maggie sent Eleanor a tiny glance of approval.

As Eleanor submitted to more of the makeup artist's attentions, Maggie suddenly asked, "Why?"

"Why what?"

"Why would Lord Ashford approach you and offer to have you accompany him on his nightly escapades, for the strict purpose of you writing about him? There are some aristos who seem to enjoy the attention, but Ashford doesn't strike me as one of them."

"Nor me," Eleanor answered. "I've been going over and over it, and I still haven't come up with a logical answer." She winced as Madame Hortense jabbed another pin into her scalp. "I cannot figure what the benefit is to him. He's got an agenda—I'd bet my printing press on it."

"Is it wise, then, to accept his proposal?"

"No," Eleanor answered bluntly. "But opportunities like this don't simply stride into my office in their polished Hessians every day. Nothing's stopping him from going to *The Well-Informed Londoner* or *Pauley's Miscellany*." Her two biggest competitors would relish the chance to write an in-depth series about one of the country's most eligible and notorious bachelors. "If I pass up the chance, I may as well bid a fond farewell to my paper and take up some truly degrading work, like writing burlettas."

Smiling, Maggie made a rude noise, accompanied by an equally crude hand gesture. Still, concern edged her voice as she pressed, "You *will* be careful, won't you? I know his type. They're as trustworthy as adders."

"I will be at all times on my guard." Eleanor fought to keep still as Madame Hortense stretched some kind of very fine net over her hair, containing the whole of it.

"And don't fall victim to his seductions, either," Maggie added.

Eleanor laughed. The idea was ludicrous.

From working on her own paper, Eleanor had been provided ample evidence that associations between noblemen and commoner women seldom—if ever—did well. Numerous females had been left with babes in their bellies and no means of supporting themselves when the attentions of their seducers had turned elsewhere. Usually those men found themselves upper-class wives, got on with the business of being aristocrats, and forgot about the lower-class women whose lives they had torn asunder.

Besides . . . "We're speaking of Lord Ashford. The nobleman who could have his pick of any woman he wants. The most desirable. The most beautiful. The last woman who'd attract that interest from him would be me, a lowly and unglamorous *journalist.*"

"Ah, don't go trolling for compliments," Maggie chided. "Besides which, there's no better way of manipulating someone than through sex." Cold cynicism glinted in Maggie's eyes, and, beneath that, a deeper hurt Eleanor knew her friend would never acknowledge.

"I will keep my eyes open and my legs closed," Eleanor vowed.

Though she was no virgin, she was at all times careful when it came to matters of scx. She'd learned long ago how to keep from conceiving, and marriage held no appeal,

not when she was master of herself and answered to no
man. Independence was the gem she clutched close. If her
past lovers had been disappointed by her unwillingness to
shackle herself to them, then it was a disappointment they'd
had to suffer.

She had her work, and control over her body and her purse
strings. Not many other women—aside from Maggie—
could claim the same.

"And now," Madame Hortense declared, "it's time for the
wig—the *perruque*," she corrected herself, as if remembering her pretense of being French.

The woman removed a wig from a wooden, head-shaped
block. The hair had been styled into a fashionable, tousled
crop of light brown curls, exactly the style popular with the
younger set of men.

Eleanor held still as Madame Hortense settled the wig
over her head, then adjusted it before pinning it into place.

"Her hair's shorter," Maggie conceded, "but she doesn't
look much like a man. More like one of those ladies who
wore their hair *à la victime*," she added, referring to the
women of the last century who had cut their hair short to
emulate the guillotine's unfortunate prey.

"But I am not finished!" Madame Hortense snapped her
fingers in Eleanor's face. "Close your eyes until I say to open
them. Same for you, Maggie. Then you will both see the
wonder of my skill."

Eleanor shared a smile with Maggie. Theatrical people
never were at a shortage for self-esteem. But she obeyed
Madame Hortense's command and shut her eyes.

It was a full half hour she waited. In the interim, the cosmetic artist applied all varieties of rather itchy items to Eleanor's face and rubbed countless pungent-smelling things,
which had to be paint, onto her skin. Something even went
onto her top lip. It wasn't a comfortable process. Rather ar-
duous, in fact, made even more so by the fact that her journalist's curiosity burned to know just what, exactly, Madame
Hortense was doing.

As the process went on, Eleanor distracted herself by describing everything in her mind. She'd certainly include this procedure in her article. Readers might be intrigued by what it took to change a female into a male.

Women might complain of the excessive amounts of time and effort it takes to attend to their appearance—applications of creams, unguents, blemish reducers, freckle-lighteners, perfumes, and a cornucopia of other nostrums and humbug all pressed upon the fairer sex, the object being the attainment of unattainable physical perfection. This, of course, also includes corsets, bust improvers, bust-reduction binding, curling papers and irons, and the heavens know what else, all done in the name of representing our "best" self to the world at large, should our own natural appearance fail us—which it inevitably does.

And while the natural-born male might have a decidedly less labor-intensive toilette, I would caution any of this paper's female readers from attempting to exchange their gender for another, for their activity is nearly as tedious and uncomfortable as our own feminine preparations.

"Now lift the curtain and look," Madame Hortense announced.

Eleanor opened her eyes and gasped. So did Maggie.

"That can't be me," Eleanor said, yet her voice came out of the face reflected back at her. She reached up to touch her face.

Madame Hortense swatted her hand away. "Don't undo all my hard work!"

The transformation was startling. All from the application of a bit of paint and false hair. Rather than a woman of thirty-two, a young man in his early twenties stared at her in the glass. Through artful shading, her nose looked broader, her jaw and chin more square. Madame Hortense had given her fashionable side-whiskers that matched the color of her wig. Eleanor even sported a shading on her top lip that suggested a morning shave starting to lose its battle as a mustache started to grow in.

"My God, Eleanor," Maggie breathed. "You're a damn pretty boy, but a boy just the same. I'll have to keep most of the women at the theater—and some of the men—away from you."

Eleanor turned her face from side to side. So this is what she would have looked like if her father had gotten his wish and she'd been born male. Too bad the poor sot was deep beneath the earth now, or else she'd show him what he'd missed out on.

What would Lord Ashford say when he saw her? Or would he even recognize her? The idea that he might actually mistake her for a man was a delicious anticipation. She'd love to catch him off guard, knock a little of his polish off.

The door to the dressing room banged open and Mr. Swindon bustled in, his arms full of clothing. The moment he saw Eleanor, he let out a little shriek and nearly dropped the garments.

"Oh, but this is marvelous!" He hustled forward, his eyes never leaving her. "Just exquisite. Well done, Miss Hawke. And hosannas to you, madame," he added when Madame Hortense cleared her throat loudly. "Forsooth, we have a genuine artist dwelling beneath the roof of this humble theater."

"He means himself," Maggie whispered, leaning close, and Eleanor had to stifle her laugh.

"Now for the second part of your metamorphosis." The costumer held out his arms, covered with clothes.

"I'll need some guidance," Eleanor said. She'd undressed men before, and watched them don their garments, but the process of getting dressed in masculine attire eluded her.

So Mr. Swindon helped her step into a man's combination. He strapped pads on her calves to help bulk up those muscles, then gave her a pair of white stockings that climbed up past her knees. She stepped into a pair of buff-colored knee breeches. This was followed by a long-tailed linen shirt and a cream-on-white embroidered waistcoat. Mr. Swindon hid her lack of Adam's apple with a very tall collar and neck-cloth, which threatened to cut off Eleanor's supply of air.

After she stepped into a pair of sleek low men's pumps, Eleanor let the costumer help her into a dark blue coat. Its shoulders were heavily padded, the width of the skirts a little wider to conceal her hips. She was given a pocket watch and a pair of gloves, along with a top hat perfect for an evening out.

"And *voilà*," Mr. Swindon said, his French accent far more convincing than Madame Hortense's.

Again, Eleanor looked into the mirror. She stood, agog, at her change. She'd entered the Imperial Theater as a woman, but now she was a young man of means and fashion. For several moments, all she could do was stare at herself.

Who *was* she? She felt oddly lost within this masculine persona, as if Eleanor had disappeared and a strange man had taken her place. Except the strange man was *her*.

"Oh, Eleanor," Maggie said on an exhale, her face aglow, "just think of the trouble you could get into."

"That's right," Eleanor said after a moment. "I'm a man now. I can do . . . anything."

The power was intoxicating. No wonder men walked around looking so smug. The world belonged to them.

And now she was about to enter that world. With Lord Ashford beside her. Eleanor smiled. Oh, it was going to be quite a night.

Bare-chested, Daniel stood before his mirror and dabbed shaving lather onto his face with a boar bristle brush. Once he'd sufficiently covered his cheeks and jaw, he ran his straight razor along the planes of his face, scraping off any whiskers that had emerged since this morning. Each stroke of the blade made a soft, rasping sound, and the aroma of sandalwood wafted up from the lather. He wiped the razor on a towel and continued the process, revealing more and more of his skin. A familiar, comforting routine.

He ignored Strathmore's sigh. His valet never approved of the fact that Daniel insisted on shaving himself—even though Strathmore had been in his service for over ten years and not once had Daniel permitted the valet to attend to his shave. Daniel's father, the old earl, hadn't approved of Daniel's practice, either. But, for God's sake, Daniel was a functioning adult, capable of looking after the state of his own facial hair. At least he relented and permitted Strathmore to pick out his clothes. But he put the clothes on himself. None of this being buttoned into his breeches nonsense.

As achievements went, it was ridiculously minor, but that was the odd hallmark of a title and wealth. Theoretically, he was one of the more powerful men in the country, yet when it came to matters such as one's toilette, a nobleman reverted to infancy. As if the responsibilities of his rank were too onerous to bear up under the weight of tying his own cravat.

Behind him, Strathmore laid out his ensemble for the evening, selecting everything with the care the valet always displayed. It was almost a shame for Daniel to take credit for wearing his clothing, when it was all Strathmore's expert eye.

In keeping with the valet's understanding of occasion and fashion, Strathmore had selected a burnished-bronze silk waistcoat and a deep-forest-green coat. Elegant, but not overly so, since Daniel wasn't attending any sanctioned Season event tonight. Just the right amount of restraint and flash for a gaming hell.

Finished with his shave, Daniel rinsed his face, patted on some tonic, and slipped on a fine white shirt, tucking the tails into his knee breeches.

Miss Hawke would likely be doing the exact same thing right about now. Dressing herself in men's clothing in readiness for the evening. Was she afraid of entering an exclusively male realm? Excited?

The latter, most likely. Miss Hawke didn't seem the type of woman who feared much. She'd seemed out-and-out thrilled by the idea of posing as a man and visiting a gaming hell. Bizarre woman. Yet he couldn't remember any of the ladies at any of the assemblies or picnics or other gatherings displaying half her enthusiasm. Either the young, husband-hunting girls had an air of frantic, desperate merriment, or the older women could barely contain their ennui at yet another Season.

It felt strange—unreal—to dress as he did every night, knowing that Jonathan was somewhere out in London, likely not dressing for an evening of elegant, yet wild, entertainment. But Daniel suppressed his guilt, the way he had to before each night's revelry. He needed to keep up the pretense while looking for Jonathan.

When Daniel had been out searching for his old friend, Jonathan's young sister Catherine had occasionally accompanied him. Jonathan wouldn't respond to Daniel alone. Catherine was the baby of the family, a late addition that Jonathan had doted over. She was all that mattered to him, even in his descent.

It was wildly inappropriate for a single man and a young girl not yet out to be in each other's company, especially in public, but Catherine had insisted. They'd visited docks, staked out brothels, gaming hells—all the places Jonathan had been rumored to be seen. And all to no avail.

If only Lord and Lady Holcombe, Jonathan's parents, weren't all but useless. Even when their heir, Oliver, died, leaving Jonathan the next in line, they'd been unable to do anything besides wring their hands and whine about the hurt to their own reputation.

Yet Daniel would have far preferred searching for Jonathan with Lord Holcombe to potentially hurting Catherine's reputation, but there had been no choice, especially after she'd come to him, begging for help.

Catherine wasn't even out yet. He hadn't seen her at a public assembly or ball—and certainly not at a gaming hell.

As he now fastened the row of silk-covered buttons on his waistcoat, a tap sounded at his door.

"Enter."

The apologetic face of Edinger appeared. "Forgive me, my lord, but the Marquess of Allam is below and requests a moment of your time."

Daniel frowned. Why would his godfather visit him at this hour, far past the time most paid calls? However, Allam was of the older generation, and now claimed the privilege of age by ignoring social custom.

"Send him up," Daniel instructed. He usually didn't have company when dressing for the night, but he hadn't seen Allam in weeks and didn't want to keep him waiting.

"Very good, my lord." The butler bowed and disappeared.

In a few moments, the tap of a cane in the hallway outside announced his godfather's approach.

"Lord Allam, my lord," Edinger announced, and bowed the older man in.

The cane and white hair were Allam's only concession to the advance of years. Otherwise, he was as tall and lean as he'd been since Daniel had stood only as high as his knee. Same hawkish features, same upright posture, same sharp gaze. Very much like his son Marwood, one of Daniel's closest friends—besides Jonathan.

"Allam," Daniel said, coming forward to shake the other man's hand. "This is an unexpected surprise."

"If it was expected, it wouldn't be much of a surprise," Allam answered, returning the handshake.

"One thing that hasn't changed—you still enjoy taking me to task." Daniel waved toward a nearby chair. "I can ring for some tea or brandy."

Allam lowered himself into the chair, his movements precise and controlled. "None of that. Helena expects me home for dinner within the hour. After thirty-one years of marriage, I've never disappointed her."

"At least where mealtimes are concerned."

His godfather sent him an icy glance before the cold veneer fell away and a grudging smile creased his face. "She is the center of my Ptolemaic universe," he conceded fondly.

As Daniel tied his cravat, emptiness spread through his chest. He'd known Allam and his wife his whole life, and had never met a couple whose esteem and affection rivaled theirs. Not even his own parents had shared as strong a bond. Once, as a young, romantic boy, he'd believed he'd one day meet a girl he could love the same way Allam and Helena loved each other. But those dreams had soon turned as brittle as autumn leaves, ground beneath the boot heel of reality into a fine powder.

He'd learned at a young age that earls didn't marry for love.

"But that is precisely why I am here," Allam said. "Your father's been dead for five years, and since none of those halfwits you call friends have the capacity to advise you properly—"

"I might point out that your own son is one of my friends."

Allam waved his hand dismissively. "Cameron has his own obstacles to overcome."

"Perhaps he could benefit from your counsel better than I can."

A shadow passed over Allam's face. "Once, he might have listened to me. Now . . ." He shook his head. "Don't distract me from the topic, lad. I've risked being late to dinner and my wife's wrath to speak to you."

Daniel continued to work on the knot of his cravat as an anxious Strathmore hovered nearby, ready to swoop in lest Daniel's neckcloth-tying skills proved anything less than impeccable.

"The suspense has me riddled with terrified anticipation," Daniel said.

Allam rapped his cane on the floor. "None of that fashionable irony! It's as if your entire generation has been infected with the disease of disaffection."

"Maybe because we find so little to engender true interest."

"Bloody rot," Allam returned hotly. "The world hasn't altered so much that one can't still feel a sense of wonder. Hasn't there been anything that piqued your curiosity beyond the superficial?"

A smart retort died on Daniel's lips as he recalled Miss Hawke at her desk, and her pacing the length of her office, a whirl of motion and thought. She had pierced the fog that had chronically enveloped him. But for all their closeness, he couldn't tell Allam about her.

Can't, or won't? Part of him wanted to keep her private, his own secret to enjoy alone.

The secret he bore regarding Jonathan held no enjoyment for him at all. And the two were soon to be inexorably linked.

"It's another Season," Daniel said instead. "There's no end to the amusements available."

"I'm not talking of amusement," Allam replied. "I'm talking of something bigger, something more consequential. Like marriage."

Daniel crossed his arms over his chest and leaned against a dresser. "Ah, here it is." He should have guessed his godfather's purpose in coming here tonight. Every few months, Allam dropped hints, and Daniel subsequently ignored them. But it seemed as though the time of hints was over, and a more direct approach was being undertaken.

"Shortly before your father went to his Maker," Allam said, gripping his cane, "he made me promise that I would see to the perpetuation of his title. And I made that promise."

"I know my duty."

"Do you? I see your name in the scandal sheets. All this gallivanting around, but to what end? How many Seasons have come and gone, and you haven't once declared your intention toward any girl."

"I might not care for any of the girls," Daniel answered.

"You don't have to *care* for them, only esteem them enough to give them your name. And in exchange, the girl will give you the heirs you need."

"What a romantic prospect."

Allam rolled his eyes. "You aren't a novel-reading chit, for God's sake. Helena and I were lucky, it's true, but you have more at stake than something as inconsequential as romance."

Daniel rubbed the spot between his eyebrows, where a headache brewed. This had been a deeply disturbing issue for him since before Jonathan had gone missing. "I understand that the young women on the marriage market are just looking after their own security. I cannot fault them for that. But . . ."

Allam leaned forward. "Yes?"

Spreading his hands, Daniel said, "Didn't it trouble you? Before you met Helena and were just another young buck attending assemblies. As soon as you enter a room, you're seen as the heir, or the title, but never . . ." He struggled to find the words. There were few people with whom he could speak as candidly as he could with his godfather. "Never as *yourself.*"

"I *am* the Marquess of Allam," his godfather answered. "It *is* who I am."

"You're much more than that. A contributor to the Royal Society who funds expeditions to expand knowledge of other cultures. A man with a love for breeding hunting hounds but who hates to hunt."

"Never seemed quite fair to the foxes," muttered the older man.

Daniel flung away from the dresser and paced his room. "My point precisely! You may be the Marquess of Allam, yet you have passions, needs. Is it wrong to want to be perceived as more than my estates?"

"You run those estates well. They also deserve a mistress, and heirs to inherit those properties."

Daniel fought frustration at Allam's avoidance of his question. "What will I leave them, my future offspring? Land, money, but what else? What purpose have I fulfilled? Nothing."

Allam's lips pressed tight. "You're still angry about it. That you couldn't join the army."

"I knew I never could." Daniel stared out the window, watching the sun dip beneath the skyline. He'd envied Jonathan's status as a younger son, which had permitted him the luxury of having a commission bought for him and going to fight Bonaparte.

That envy had changed to something else, something more complex, when he'd seen the toll war had taken on his friend. But Daniel had pretended *not* to see Jonathan's invisible wounds; he'd chalked them up to readjusting to civilian life, and soon Jonathan would be back to his old self. It would only take a little time. A little space.

How wrong Daniel had been.

"That doesn't mean you aren't still upset about it."

Outside, the city continued on in its timeless movements, always busy, ever moving. "I wanted to do my part, too."

"And you did. By keeping the backbone of British society in place."

Turning away from the window, Daniel raked his hands through his hair—causing Strathmore to exhale in exasperation. As usual, Daniel ignored his valet.

He dropped his hands. "I'm grateful—I truly am—for all that I've been given. But sometimes . . ." Again he struggled to find the right words, when he himself didn't know what he was trying to express. "Sometimes I wish for something more. Some greater purpose other than keeping the backbone of British society in place."

He couldn't tell Allam about Jonathan. While he wasn't happy for the circumstances, looking for his friend did give him a goal. Of course, Daniel would rather have Jonathan's situation secure, thereby depriving himself of an objective, but as long as his help was needed, he was determined to give every ounce of effort.

Allam sighed and shook his head. "I understand, lad. Why do you think I fund those expeditions? Gives me a sense of meaning. But we're bound by duty to honor our obligations. In your case, that includes taking a wife and begetting children. Soon, while you're young and healthy."

"So my future bride is a broodmare and I'm the stud."

"Save your crudeness for your toadies and actresses. I came here to offer my counsel, and now I've given it." Allam rose, his grip still tight on his cane, and walked stiffly toward the door.

Daniel intercepted him and placed his hands on the older man's shoulders. "Forgive my churlishness, Godfather. I've been . . . out of sorts for some time."

"I know," Allam said with surprising mildness. "The scandal sheets talk of nothing else but your attempts to distract yourself."

His godfather's words hit him like a punch to the chest. Is that what he'd been doing, with all his late-night revelry and wildness? Distracting himself from the absence at the center of his life? So it had been before Jonathan had vanished.

"I wish I could promise that you won't be reading about me again," he answered. "But I'm afraid it's going to get worse before it gets better. And lest you give me that censorious look again, trust me when I say it's all for a higher purpose."

"That's what every rake says," his godfather replied. "No one believes them, though." He clasped one of Daniel's hands and gave it a brief squeeze. "My own son won't heed my advice, but I pray you do. Take care of yourself, Daniel."

A hard knot unexpectedly formed in Daniel's throat. "I'll try."

"That is all I ask." Allam stepped back. "I'll see myself out. Enjoy the rest of your night. But not too much."

As the older man left, Daniel felt a mantle of smothering melancholy settle about his shoulders. It wasn't relieved by contemplating the search for Jonathan. Yet when he thought of his planned evening with Miss Hawke, the despondency that had enveloped him quickly burned away like dissipating smoke, leaving him strangely eager for the night's adventure.

Chapter 3

Much has been made in publications far superior to this unassuming periodical of the differences between men and women, and the struggles that arise when the two sexes attempt to interact with each other. It would be the grossest understatement to assert that two species could not be more oppositional. Perhaps this lamentable state of affairs could be remedied were men and women to mutually realize that what we believe we know about the other is entirely rubbish, and the only way to achieve understanding is to toss into the ash bin every assumption. Nay, this author humbly offers the suggestion that, in order to attain true understanding, men and women ought to trade places, if even for a single day . . .

The Hawk's Eye, May 4, 1816

Eleanor wasn't certain what made her more nervous—spending the evening in one of the hearts of masculine privilege, or the fact that for the entire night, she'd be fastened to Lord Ashford's side. Watching him. Listening to that rough, velvet voice of his. Observing him at play and being wicked.

In her disguise, she waited for the appearance of Lord Ashford's carriage outside the side entrance of the Imperial Theater. Though Maggie had offered to wait with her, Eleanor had declined, needing several moments alone to prepare herself for what was to come.

She tapped the walking stick Mr. Swindon had loaned her on the slick cobblestones. Maggie's warning echoed in time with each tap. Be cautious around the earl. A known seducer. With a hidden agenda. *Noblemen are as trustworthy as adders.*

Eleanor would simply have to avoid being bitten.

The thought of Lord Ashford *biting* her sent a pulse of electricity through her. That was precisely the thought she needed to avoid. He was her subject for her articles—nothing more. At some point, the articles would end, and she and the earl would part ways, each having gotten what they needed from the other.

She wouldn't be another used and discarded commoner. Didn't Maggie's own experience teach Eleanor firsthand the cold truth of what happened when the classes intermingled?

Though she ran a scandal sheet, she tried to cling to some shred of journalistic integrity. Otherwise, she might as well publish outright lies. Some other scandal sheets made up stories from whole cloth, like *Pauley's Miscellany* and that story about a Russian prince with a famed opera dancer. But her newspaper didn't do that sort of thing.

A couple passed by, and Eleanor stiffened. Would they know? Could they peer beneath the surface of her masquerade? She tried to affect a manly stance—legs apart, shoulders back. But the couple was too engrossed in each other to pay her any attention, and they moved on.

She deflated a little. She'd hoped for either a "Good evening, fine young sir," or else shocked whispers and pointed fingers. Instead, she got neither. Well, perhaps that was a fortunate omen. She'd passed men on the street countless times and given them no heed. Now she was one of their anonymous numbers.

More of Maggie's words resonated. As a man, Eleanor could get into any variety of trouble. She could go literally anywhere without fear. No one would question her presence or catcall her. She was free. Free of the burden of woman-hood, where every shadow contained a threat and numerous doors were closed to her. Not tonight. Tonight, she could do whatever she wanted.

Her head spun with the possibility.

Giddy with these thoughts, she almost didn't hear the sound of a well-sprung carriage clattering over the pavement until it was almost on her. She stepped back just in time to keep from being run down.

"Out of the way, lad," the driver snapped.

A bubble of excitement rose in her chest. The coachman had called her "lad"! Of course, he'd almost killed her, but that was a small matter compared to the fact that her dis-guise had worked.

Pressing back against the wall of the theater, she took a moment to admire the vehicle as it came to a stop. She'd seen the carriages of the wealthy, but usually at a distance, or whizzing past her. But this was her first opportunity to see one up close, and by God, was it a marvel. All dark lacquer, sleek lines, and an actual crest upon the door. The horses were beautifully matched, just as wondrous as the carriage, as they stamped and snorted, shaking their tack.

A liveried footman hopped down from the back of the carriage and opened the door. With the sun already low in the sky, the interior of the vehicle was swathed in shadows, so she could only hear an amused voice from inside. A voice she'd recognize if she stood in utter darkness.

"Miss Hawke?"

She nodded stiffly. How was she to answer? In a man's voice, or a woman's?

A broad, gloved hand appeared from within the carriage, then suddenly retreated. "Can't help you in," Lord Ash-ford said, almost laughing. "Very un-manly, and I'd hate to impugn your honor this early."

She stepped inside on her own, feeling how strange it was to move without skirts impeding her. Stranger still was, as she'd seen earlier, the carriage's being wonderfully sprung, so unlike the rough vehicles she was more accustomed to. It barely moved beneath her as she took her seat on the lushly upholstered squabs opposite the earl. The footman closed the door, and suddenly she was in a very small—though luxurious—space, with a man she hardly knew except through reputation as one of London's most notorious rakes.

Though it was dim within the carriage, her eyes adjusted quickly, and she finally saw Lord Ashford dressed in his evening finery. If he'd been stylishly appointed when he'd appeared in her office yesterday, now . . . now he was a revelation.

It hardly seemed sporting that a man could look both elegant and powerfully masculine at the same time. And yet Lord Ashford did. More than his beautifully cut and expensive clothes, though, was the ease and confidence with which he inhabited them—and his lean, muscled body. The carriage interior nearly radiated with the strength of his presence, yet he barely moved or spoke.

His eyes never leaving her face, he rapped on the roof of the carriage. It started forward. She gripped the strap to keep from flying into his lap. Managing to settle herself, she stared back at him. His features were slightly too rough to be considered classically handsome, but she couldn't look away from their lines and contours. His clean, straight jaw. The unfair brilliance of his cerulean eyes. Eyes that possessed far too much knowledge of the world and its sensuous pursuits.

Silence filled the inside of the vehicle for several moments.

"You're sitting wrong," he finally said.

She glanced down. Her legs were crossed—demurely, she thought, recalling instruction from her childhood. A lady always—

Oh. She wasn't a lady anymore.

"A man sits like that," he continued, "and he'll crush his bollocks to pulp. And another thing," he added as she adjusted her stance, "don't make that face when a man says something like *bollocks*. You risk looking like a milksop prig."

"Maybe I just have good manners," she retorted.

"Or you're a milksop prig. We're going to have to do something about your voice. It's like your bollocks haven't dropped."

"You enjoy saying *bollocks,* don't you?" But when she spoke, she lowered her voice to what she thought was a reasonable imitation of a man's timbre.

He shook his head. "Better not speak much at all."

"That's rather convenient for you."

His grin came as an unexpected flash of white, and it made her belly knot. "Everyone benefits."

"Horrible man."

"More like, *You rotten bastard*—when ladies aren't present. If they are, call me a bounder or cur."

"Do men really alter their conversation so much when in the company of women?"

His lids lowered slightly, but his eyes glittered bright blue. "You'll find out tonight just how much."

She couldn't stop her grin. "The prospect is both terrifying and thrilling."

"Don't smile, either."

"What! I've seen men smile."

"But you've got a woman's smile, through and through. And it brings out the tiniest dimple . . . here . . ." He reached toward her cheek, and she reared back.

"Men have dimples," she protested on a rasp.

"Not like yours. Small and soft and tempting."

It would be impossible for her to lower her voice to the depths Lord Ashford's had just taken. But his words not only caught her off guard; they seemed to catch him by surprise as well. He frowned and straightened.

"Not exactly used to complimenting the dimples on another man," he said darkly.

"But I'm not another man," she noted.

"And thank God for that," he muttered, "or else I could be tried for unnatural acts."

"Presuming I allow those unnatural acts to happen."

"There would be no *allowing* but a mutual participation."

She forced out a laugh as her face heated. "Are you trying to teach me how to flirt?"

His frown deepened. "That lesson is for later. For now, we should get our story in order. Who you are, how I know you."

"Fill in the details." She tapped her chin in thought. "Perhaps I'm a young gentleman of means who has just come into his inheritance, and you're introducing me to the Town."

"You're my distant cousin. A lad from the country," he added. "It's the only way to explain that waistcoat."

She scowled. "Out of fashion, perhaps, but not out of fortune. I've got a country estate in Lincolnshire, and this is my first visit to London."

"You're too young to be officially introduced into Society—"

"Back to those undescended bollocks," she said.

"—so you aren't on the bride hunt, and I won't be taking you to any official Season events."

"But gaming hells are appropriate for an impressionable lad?"

"With me as your guide and guardian," he said, a corner of his mouth turning up, "everything is appropriate."

She crossed her arms over her flattened chest. "I get the feeling that the opposite is true."

"And your name shall be—"

"Maximus Sinclair," she said.

"Ned Fribble," he declared.

Her lips pursed. "I will *not* be Mr. Fribble."

The earl gave a sigh of forbearance. "As you like. Ned Sinclair. From Lincolnshire. A young man of uncommon shyness. But try to make the family proud."

"I can't bring any more disgrace on them than you already have."

That seemed to startle a laugh out of him, and his expression turned puzzled. "I have the oddest feeling that I'm going to enjoy tonight."

"Me, too, my lord," she confessed.

"You'll have to address me as 'Ashford' for the duration of the evening. It'd seem suspicious if my relative addressed me as 'my lord.'"

"I could call you by a nickname," she suggested. "Ashy."

He scowled. "Nobody ever called or calls me 'Ashy.' Everyone knows me as 'Ashford.'"

"Even your closest family? An aunt, perhaps?"

He glanced around, as though someone might be listening in. "When we're alone, my godmother calls me . . . 'Danny.' But only her," he added hastily.

Danny. How ridiculously, utterly adorable. Especially given that the man seated opposite her seemed the very opposite of that childlike name. She tucked the knowledge away, hoarding it like ammunition. Or something even more precious.

"Are we headed toward the gaming hell, Dan—Ashford?"

He didn't rise to her attempt to bait him. "It's too early. Donnegan's doesn't even open its doors until ten, and even then, the crowds will be thin until midnight."

She checked her pocket watch, enjoying the novelty of pulling the timepiece from her waistcoat. Ten o'clock was three hours away.

"I already have our evening's agenda planned," he continued. "First, we'll take a stroll on Bond Street. You'll get a chance to practice being a man before heading into the lion's den of iniquity."

"But it will be just as likely that my true sex would be discovered on Bond Street than at the gaming hell."

He adjusted his cuffs, his movements sleek and controlled. "Foppish behavior is generally more expected where shopping is concerned."

"Foppish!" Too late she realized that her voice had come out on a very feminine sound of outrage.

He smirked, his point having been proven. "After a few turns up and down the street, we'll take our supper at the Eagle, my favorite chophouse." Realizing his mistake too late, he sent her a piercing look. "The Eagle's a haven for me—even more than White's. If, after our arrangement is over, I see one reporter there, spying on me, I'll go to *The Well-Informed Londoner* and have them print a retraction and complete disavowal of the article series. Wouldn't be so difficult for me to blackball your paper."

She didn't doubt that. And while she had to admire the lengths to which he'd go to protect his privacy, it chilled her how easily, how readily he wielded his power over her and people of her station. In the face of a nobleman's strength, there wasn't anything one of the middle or lower classes could do.

"The Eagle will be forbidden territory," she added, just to be sure he trusted her, "and I won't mention it by name when I write the article about tonight."

He exhaled, seemingly mollified by her concession.

"Once we've dined," he went on, "then we're on to Donnegan's for some gambling until the doors close for the morning."

"My," she murmured, "you truly do have the whole of tonight—and tomorrow—planned."

He actually looked abashed. "I like plans," he muttered.

"Clearly." But this was still a revelation. Who would have suspected that the rakehell earl was a man who enjoyed order and structure? She would have thought he'd chafe against such restrictions. Was he more responsible, more serious than she'd thought? Definitely not *too* serious, the way he took pains to quiz her.

The Imperial Theater was several miles from Bond Street, which left her and the earl with a goodly amount of time to ride in silence. After several moments, however, she couldn't keep quiet.

"You haven't mentioned my disguise," she burst out.

His eyebrows raised. "Oh, are you wearing a disguise?"

Scowling, she clenched her walking stick tighter, though it was a struggle not to brain him with it.

"In truth," he said, holding up placating hands, "it's remarkable work. I almost didn't recognize you on the street except for your . . ." He glanced away.

"My what?" Her eyes? No, he wouldn't be able to see them at a distance and in the dim light of dusk. Her hair color? She wore a wig, though it matched her hair's natural hue.

"Your arse," he finally said.

She started, then tried to twist and glance back at the anatomical part in question. "My coat hides it. And besides, we only met yesterday. It's impossible for you to have memorized the shape of my . . . my arse."

"Never underestimate a man's capacity for ogling."

"If I embroidered, I'd include that in my next sampler," she said drily. But in the midst of her exasperation, she became aware of two things: one, that he was aware of her physically; and two, that to one man, at least, she was recognizable as a woman. "Does that mean that anyone can tell my gender?"

"Doubtful," he answered. The sun had descended even more, and streaks of gold from streetlights and shop windows traced the clean lines of his face. "I think I'm more . . . attuned . . . to you than most would be."

She wasn't certain that provided comfort.

"The costumer and cosmetic artist at the Imperial did a very fine job," he said, as though eager to change the subject. Though she considered herself a worldly and generally hard-to-shock person, she couldn't stop her eyes from widening when he stared directly at the apex of her thighs. Admittedly, wearing trousers was a novel, and snug, experience, but *this* kind of inspection wasn't expected.

"They didn't miss any detail, did they?" he murmured. "Gave you a sausage and potatoes."

"It'd look awfully strange if I didn't have anything down there, wouldn't it?" She resisted the urge to give her faux genitalia a poke. "I have no idea how you men walk around with these ridiculous articles hanging between your legs."

"It's even worse when they're made of flesh and blood," he said solemnly. "They try to stage a coup against men's brains every day."

"But higher reason triumphs," she pointed out.

"Occasionally. It's a tenuous balance of power."

Thank God she'd grown up around very colorful, outrageous characters, and spent considerable time with Maggie and her wild theatrical colleagues, or else this conversation about men's genitals might have sent her into a state of waking unconsciousness.

"The costumer did a good job with that, too." He waved in the direction of her compressed breasts.

"With what?" she asked disingenuously.

"Your . . . chest," he said through his teeth.

"Come now, Ashford," she chided. "Don't try to fool me into thinking you have delicate sensibilities. You're the same man who couldn't resist saying the word *bollocks* to me over and over again. I think you must be talking about my breasts. Or would you prefer I use the word *bubbies*? Maybe *tits* would suit your sensitive nature. Or—"

"Your breasts," he gritted. "They concealed your breasts well."

"I suppose you got a decent ogling of them yesterday," she said. Though she was used to speaking with her normal circle in such blunt terms, it felt odd and . . . exciting . . . to talk with the earl so openly.

His silence confirmed that he'd done just that, despite the fact that she'd been wearing one of her most modest dresses.

"I should stare at your thighs just to even the score," she said. "Perhaps you should take your coat off that I might leer at you in your shirtsleeves."

"Later," he replied. "I believe right now we were discussing your breasts."

She fought the blush that threatened to heat her face. "I might not be wearing a corset, but the bindings they put on me make me feel like a trussed roast."

"A roast can be delicious," he said, velvet in his tone.

Maggie's warning, and the countless examples from Eleanor's own newspaper, flared to life. Aristocrats couldn't be trusted, and *this* aristocrat was a known profligate with a hidden agenda. Resisting his lures was imperative—but she couldn't hold him too much at bay, lest he weary of her and take his story elsewhere.

"Or stringy and tough," she pointed out.

"Best way to find out is through taste."

"We're dining in just a few hours. I'm sure your appetite can hold."

"I might have a taste for something else."

"Clearly not flirtation." She laughed. "Because we're practically drowning in it." She shook her head. "I bet you aren't even aware that you're doing it. Flirting comes as second nature to a rake like you."

He scowled at the word *rake*. "It's just a common form of currency. I flirt with my seventy-year-old housekeeper. It doesn't mean anything."

"Of course," she answered. But a strange sting accompanied his words. She shook her head at herself. Which was it she wanted? To keep herself at a safe and aloof distance, or to attract his interest? It couldn't very well be both. Besides, her own feelings were immaterial. All that mattered was getting the story. She'd simply have to remind herself of that.

The evening had barely begun, and already Daniel had acquired a novel experience. He'd never flirted with a man before. Miss Hawke wasn't a man, but she wore a very convincing disguise. Was he entering a new stage of his life, or was it something else that compelled him to coquette with "Ned"? He rather hoped it was the latter, as complicated as that would be.

As they continued on to Bond Street, it dawned on him that he hadn't had such an enjoyable conversation with anyone, male or female, in a goodly while. Each sentence was like practicing fencing—a strike, a parry, the excitement of wondering how and when his worthy opponent would strike next.

Though normally he enjoyed conversing with Catherine, all their conversations lately had been about what had happened to Jonathan.

Yet was this what he missed by only associating with women of his class—and actresses? Perhaps most females of Miss Hawke's station had her same intelligence and wit.

Doubtful. It was a rare enough quality in anyone. Logic alone would dictate that she was an uncommon creature, and a strange warmth threaded through him at the thought. Almost as if it was . . . a privilege . . . to be in her company.

And she was in no manner awed by his title. She treated him with refreshing candor and equality. Few dared the same.

She's a means to an end. For all her charm, don't let that slip your memory.

She was using him. Just as he used her. They'd reached a kind of equilibrium on the foundation of mutual manipulation and mistrust.

There was no creature on this earth more devious than a journalist. Writers, on the whole, were a slippery lot. Cunning-eyed creatures, sly observers who made the whole world fodder for their quills. Human emotion was something they lived to exploit. He'd best remember that.

At last, the carriage turned onto Bond Street.

"Bring us to an alley entrance," Daniel called up to the driver.

The coachman obeyed, and in a moment, the carriage stopped in front of a narrow but decently lit passageway between shops.

The footman opened the door, and Daniel alit from the vehicle. He had to stop himself from helping Miss Hawke step down. She saw to it herself.

The woman in question frowned as she glanced down the alleyway. "Are you planning on robbing me in there? I assure you, my lo—Ashford, your pockets are more richly lined than mine."

"I doubt that," he answered, "as I travel with very little cash."

Her snort was decidedly unladylike. "Should have figured. So if it's coin you're after, I can give you one pound sixpence."

He waved off her money. "Before we take a turn down Bond Street, there's one thing we need to practice." Gesturing toward the alley, he said, "Walk for me."

Her frown deepened. "I won't give you another opportunity to ogle my arse."

"This isn't about ogling anyone's arse." Though that wasn't entirely true, since it was nigh impossible for him not to watch the way she moved, or the shape of her body, even beneath her disguise. "It's about the nuances of being a man."

"And here I thought there were no nuances when it came to being a man."

"Just walk."

She shrugged, then did as he'd suggested. She strolled down the alley and then back.

When she returned to him, he sighed and shook his head. "It's as I feared. You move like a woman." She had a natural roll to her hips, a sway that indeed drew his eye to her arse. Yes, she was dressed in convincing masculine attire, but it was only a shell hiding the female beneath.

He'd also seen actresses in breeches parts before. And courtesans dressed in the sheerest gowns. But seeing Miss Hawke's legs encased in breeches, revealing their length and active energy, shot heat right to his groin.

"An odd correlation, given that I am a woman." But her mouth twisted. "What do I need to do, to move like a man?"

"Watch me." He strode up and down the alley, all the while conscious of her eyes on him. For the first few steps, he felt oddly awkward, knowing she watched. He was used to being observed—it came with being an heir and then a nobleman—yet something was different, knowing that *her* gaze was on him, assessing, judging. Did she like what she saw? He'd never had complaints from other women before. In truth, he fielded more than his share of compliments. Observation had taught him that he wasn't a plain man, not the way women and some men responded to him. But it didn't matter. He'd no control over his looks, his height. He might as well take credit for the tides.

Yet he wanted Miss Hawke to like what she saw when she looked at him. Why the hell should it matter to him what she thought?

Get out of your damn head and just bloody walk.

So he did.

"What did you see?" he asked when he returned to her, waiting at the entrance to the alley.

Her brow furrowed in thought. "I'm not much of an expert on refined female behavior, but even when I was a little girl, I was told not to run, not to swing my arms or make my stride too big. That"—she gestured to the alley, indicating Daniel's performance from a moment ago—"it's the diametric opposite to the way women are taught to walk. We're told to take up as little space as possible. Not attract attention to ourselves. Not claim anything as our own."

He started. None of this had ever occurred to him. He'd always suspected that women walked differently from men because of biology, but never from truly learned behavior, lessons that included how females were perceived or thought of themselves in the world.

"But you," she continued. "It's like everything is yours. You can claim it all, and no one will gainsay you. The way you hold your shoulders back." She tapped him on one shoulder. "Like you're afraid of nothing. You don't need to fade away or slide between spaces. Same with the way your legs eat up the ground. There's no fear. Not to mention," she added with a sly smile, "the presence of those bollocks you're so enamored of. That changes the mechanics of your walk. But they're your passport, aren't they? Your privilege simply hanging between your legs."

His laugh was short, and strained. Here he'd taken her into this alley to give her some simple instruction on the way to walk like a man, and suddenly he'd been given an entirely new insight into what it meant to *be* a man. What it meant to be a woman.

He'd thought he'd be the one in power here, but with only a few sentences, she'd stripped him entirely of that power. He felt oddly defenseless, even though she was right. Outside of this alley, he was always in control, given the benefit of his gender, his class.

It wasn't entirely a comfortable sensation, to be seen with such incisiveness. As though he had nothing to hide behind. Not his name, his wealth. He was only himself.

"That's a considerable amount to keep in mind when one is simply perambulating," he said instead of voicing these thoughts.

She grinned. "I could be entirely wrong. It wouldn't be the first time I fabricated motivations."

"Such a ringing endorsement for the credibility of your paper."

Her smile widened. Definitely not a man's smile. Too much prettiness. Too much . . . allure. "Never there, of course."

He waved toward the passageway. "Try again. If you think you can manage to put one foot in front of the other whilst plotting supremacy of the globe."

"I'll endeavor to do my best." She walked to one end of the alley and back again. "Well?"

"You move like your bollocks weigh two stone. They don't swing like a leaden pendulum."

"Show me again," she said, "and this time I'll pay particular attention to your genitals."

He narrowed his eyes. They'd spent too long in the narrow confines of the alley, too near each other. And the prospect of dangerous possibilities. "Lesson's over. Time to test your skills in the world."

Chapter 4

The ancient term "The Battle of the Sexes" has existed for millennia for good reason. For what else can we term the constant skirmishes, sorties, and clashes that transpire on a daily basis between men and women? Indeed, with such continual strife, it's a wonder that the population continues to grow . . .

The Hawk's Eye, May 4, 1816

Bond Street at dusk blazed with beautiful things and lamplight, throwing gold onto the streets and the passersby. The pedestrians walking along the pavement were as gorgeous and unattainable as the elegant objects in the stores. They lived and breathed a kind of life people like Eleanor could only dream—or write—about.

The people collected here, like the lovely articles in the shop windows, were all her favorite subjects of scandal.

She could barely keep the excitement to herself. She murmured to Ashford, "There's Lady D—. A known tippler at social gatherings. My sources say when she gets too much negus into her, she talks of her most outrageous secrets."

"Met her once at a picnic. Looks sober and sedate now," Ashford answered.

And so the woman in question did, walking with her son and daughter and stopping now and then to admire a hat on display.

"Yes, *now,*" conceded Eleanor. "Who knows what tonight's misadventures for the duchess might bring? More wine and tales of youthful indiscretions?"

"You sound positively gleeful at the prospect." But there wasn't much censure in his voice.

Eleanor shrugged, and tried to make the gesture as masculine as possible. But she overcorrected and looked like a longshoreman hefting a sack of flour. "How much and in what fashion the duchess handles her spirits is in her power."

"And it's your job to report it to the abstemious masses," he said drily.

"Perhaps through her example, others might walk a more temperate path."

He snorted a laugh. "What a sterling example you set for the city and the nation."

"As they say, it's supply and demand. Plus, I've got a business to run." She couldn't feel shame at what she did. She employed nearly a dozen writers, typesetters, and printers, plus the delivery men, and the shopkeepers and street-corner hawkers that sold her paper.

A corner of his mouth turned up. "That's more than most of my set can say. We let our men of business and land stewards handle the heavy lifting. Meanwhile, the gents down at White's bet how long it'll take old Lord Lawndale to finish a leg of mutton."

"What's the current record?"

"Two minutes, five seconds," he answered at once, which led her to believe he was not only one of the bettors but also the winner of that wager.

As she and Ashford continued their slow perambulation down the street, she concentrated on her walk, her posture, trying to remember all the things the earl had taught her. Difficult not to get distracted by the bolt of emerald silk velvet or a pair of aubergine kidskin gloves in the windows. Not when she had to pretend that she was a young *man* of means, with a man's privilege and interests. The only baubles that should concern her were the artificial ones that hung between her legs.

It was challenging, too, to remain focused, when part of her simply wanted to watch Ashford in his natural habitat. In the dusk, with the contours of his face cut sharply in golden light, masculinity radiating from him like a fire, she struggled to keep her gaze either ahead of her or on the shop windows.

She wasn't the only one affected by him. As they strolled, more than a few women's gazes lingered on the earl. Some coy—usually the younger girls accompanied by their mamas or maids. Some bold—the older women who were either married or widowed.

"You're a popular attraction," she murmured lowly.

"Reputation and title are magnets," he answered, dismissive. "And you shouldn't swing your walking stick so much. You aren't clearing a path through the jungle."

Trying to match his easy, long-legged stride, she followed as he moved on. A prickle of annoyance jabbed in her shoulders as she noticed that while Ashford drew many appreciative gazes, not a single passing woman gave her a second glance. Clearly, she wasn't nearly as eligible a prospect as the earl.

How irritating.

"None of the women are looking at me," she groused.

"You're not telling them to," he replied.

"Forgive me," she snapped, though she was careful to pitch her voice to a lower timbre. "I didn't realize I needed to wear a sign that read, 'Marvel at my manliness, ladies.'"

He shook his head. "Too literal. You tell them to look at you without words. By the length of your stride and the set of your shoulders. It doesn't come from here." He tapped his head. "It comes from there." He gave a discreet glance toward the front of his breeches.

She didn't particularly want to follow his gaze, but she couldn't help herself. It wasn't her normal policy to leer at a man's recreational regions, but she wasn't able to stop herself with Ashford. Heat rushed into her cheeks.

"You seem awfully enamored and interested in your . . ." She searched for an appropriate term to use when out in public. " . . . your *manhood*."

His laugh was unexpected, and rich. "It may surprise you that I don't think about my *manhood* constantly—though it is a favorite subject of mine. Every man is preoccupied by the state of his meat and veg."

"What a limiting existence," she said darkly.

"It can be. But the point I was trying to make—"

"Finally."

He shot her a glance. "Is that women know when a man is confident in himself. They can sense his self-assurance. And that confidence starts below the waist. Don't do that," he added when she attempted to channel that notion in her movements. "Never lead crotch-first. Looks like you're over-compensating."

"I just don't understand," she said, exasperated.

"It's attitude, not action. Walking like you know you could give a woman the best night of her life."

"A substantial boast."

His mouth crooked again with sensual arrogance. "Not a boast, but a truth."

Another pulse of heat moved through her. She'd definitely need to guard herself against him, even if he wasn't actively trying to seduce her. With as much confidence as he possessed, he could achieve his seductions without much effort at all. And wasn't that just a little embarrassing?

Yet she put her vanity and thoughts of him aside and unobtrusively observed him. Sure enough, he did move with supreme self-assurance, a masculine carnality that inhabited his whole being. She didn't doubt he could give a woman a night she'd never forget, and he knew it, too. But there was nothing licentious or lecherous in him. It was a general aura of male self-possession that radiated from him like a kind of invisible sunlight. Light in which any woman would like to bathe.

What if she could channel that self-possession into herself? She'd never lacked for her own confidence. *The Hawk's*

Eye couldn't exist if she didn't believe in herself. But this was something different.

Maggie had told her the secret of some of the more acclaimed actors at the Imperial. Instead of simply articulating their lines as histrionically as possible, they actually thought about what it must be like to *be* the character they played. To have their history. Their experiences. To become more than a pasteboard cutout of a role, they needed to truly *inhabit* that person.

So she could do the same with her role as Ned Sinclair. Imagine herself as a less-experienced version of Ashford. A man of wealth, privilege, experience—sensual knowledge.

The feelings moved through her in powerful reverberations. She stopped thinking and simply *was*.

And damn her if she didn't actually catch a woman's eye. Granted, the woman in question was a lady's maid, but she'd take whatever she could get.

"Much better," Ashford murmured. "I'd almost feel the sting of your competition."

"Almost?"

"You haven't got the means to carry through on your promises," he said with a tiny smile. "I do."

To distract herself from thinking of exactly how he'd make good on his silent vows, she said, "This is all highly educational, but it's hardly scandalous—sedately walking down Bond Street. I doubt my readers would consider any of this behavior truly rakish."

"I'd hate to disappoint your readers." A tinge of sarcasm edged his voice. "This should give them something to titter over their morning tea." He walked toward three people, moving with stately pace down the street.

The trio consisted of a middle-aged man, a handsome ash-blonde woman slightly younger than him, and a girl who looked as though she'd come out into Society within the past year. All of them were, of course, dressed quite finely. A wealthy family out for an evening's stroll before supper and the night's respectable entertainments.

"Sir Frank and Lady Phillips," Ashford said smoothly, bowing. "Miss Phillips," he added, addressing the young lady.

"Lord Ashford!" Phillips seemed shocked and pleased that the earl acknowledged him and his family. He was only a baronet, after all.

Ashford turned to Eleanor. "May I present my cousin, Ned Sinclair. He's in Town from Lincolnshire for a few days."

Eleanor had to remind herself to bow rather than curtsy when she and the Phillipses exchanged greetings. She also remembered to murmur, very lowly, "A pleasure," rather than launch into her usual harangue of reporter's questions. Why was the Phillips family on Bond Street tonight? Were they shopping for anything in particular? And what exactly were their plans for the rest of the evening?

All these queries she kept firmly tucked away. Tonight she was Ned Sinclair, young gentleman of leisure, not Eleanor Hawke, owner and editor of a newspaper.

She didn't miss the way Lady Phillips's gaze lingered on her for a moment—but not in a salacious manner. No, it was clear from the mercenary gleam in the lady's eyes that Eleanor—or, rather, *Ned*—was being sized up as a potential suitor for the young Miss Phillips, who now glanced shyly at the hem of her skirt.

"We don't ordinarily see you at this hour on Bond Street," Sir Frank exclaimed to Ashford.

"Ordinarily, no," the earl drawled. "But young Ned here is stranger to the sophisticated pleasures of this wicked city, and I thought to introduce them to him."

"And what do you think of our bustling metropolis?" Sir Frank pressed. "Rather a sight, eh?"

Before Eleanor could speak, Ashford cut her off. "Forgive Ned, Sir Frank. He's uncommonly shy and rarely says more than a word or two in a given day."

Eleanor managed to control her glare, and instead gave her best impression of an extremely bashful young man, pretending mortified fascination with the pavement.

"Ah, youth," sighed Lady Phillips. "How quickly it passes."

"But not with you, surely," Ashford said smoothly. "Have you command of the seasons? Surely they pass more slowly for you, and you've seen only eighteen summers."

"Oh, Lord Ashford," the older woman trilled. She was indeed a fine-looking female, hardly touched by time—a marked contrast to her husband, whose waistcoat struggled to contain his belly. His hair was marching slowly away from his forehead.

Struggling not to stare at Ashford, Eleanor marveled at the man's cheek. He was flirting with Lady Phillips as the woman's husband stood right there! It oughtn't surprise her, given what she knew of Ashford's wild tendencies, but it was one thing to hear and write about his rakishness, and something else entirely to witness it with her own eyes.

Yet, to her further surprise, he turned to Sir Frank. "I've heard that the grouse at your country estate are coming along remarkably."

"Indeed, yes!" The baronet lit up brighter than the shop windows. "I received a letter from my gameskeeper the other day. Just a moment. I have it somewhere." As he patted down the pockets of his coat, distracted, Eleanor watched as Ashford returned his own gaze back to Lady Phillips. It was a subtle glance, but one full of both humor and heat.

The lady at once returned the look.

Meanwhile, Sir Frank produced the letter in question and read aloud from it. Oblivious to the fact that no one seemed to care about the number of eggs found in one bird's nest, or the conditions of the hedgerows, he nattered on as if the subject was the most enthralling in the whole of human existence.

And as this happened, Ashford and Lady Phillips continued their silent flirtation, their gazes practically setting the air aflame.

The bold bugger! Eleanor had wanted a display of rakish behavior, and here she watched it with the same fascination one might reserve for a master painter creating a portrait fit for the Royal Academy. Granted, he hadn't swept Lady Phillips into his arms and kissed her, but the seduction was there just the same. The baronet's wife soaked up his attention eagerly. Her husband had to be a very inattentive lover—if his engrossment with the state of his grouse was any indicator.

Ashford flicked his gaze toward Eleanor, and then to Miss Phillips. Eleanor understood. The earl wanted her to practice her own flirtation skills on the young lady.

Eleanor shook her head slightly. She simply couldn't! Surely she'd make an utter ass of herself, especially in comparison to Ashford's masterful skill of the art.

But the earl wouldn't be gainsaid. He made it clear from his look that he wanted—nay, insisted—that she attempt some flirting.

She could outright refuse. Yet where was the fun of that? How would that look to her readers if she missed an opportunity to not only watch a rake at work but also attempt being a man of free morals, herself?

Besides, there could be no real harm in it. Ashford had made it clear that "Ned Sinclair" was only in Town for a few days, so he wasn't much of a prospect for young Miss Phillips.

It wouldn't be a very fruitful marriage, either.

Eleanor took a deep breath. Then attempted to catch Miss Phillips's eye. The young woman at first seemed resolute in avoiding "Ned's" glance. A blush stained her cheeks, and she twisted the strings of her reticule.

But, at last, Eleanor managed to ensnare the girl's gaze. Yet, now that she had Miss Phillips's attention, Eleanor wasn't certain what to do. How to look at her. Flirtation had never been Eleanor's strongest skill—with her past lovers, they hadn't wasted time on the complex dance of coquetry. Both parties had known what they'd wanted and gotten it with directness. It hadn't been especially romantic, but then, there'd never been much room for romance in Eleanor's life. It was more a struggle of survival. Female newspaper editors didn't have time for flowery declarations or avowals of undying love. She had physical needs to meet and a paper to run. Once one had been taken care of, the other took precedence.

Now, however, she needed to try her hand at what it meant to woo. How might she do it?

She glanced at Ashford, who was alternating between making interested sounds at Sir Frank's ongoing oration, and continuing his wordless seduction of Lady Phillips. Oh, but damn him, he was a handsome specimen, his features sharp yet sensuous, his dark brown hair fashionably tousled, and his blue eyes gleaming with wicked wit. And he did indeed seem to shine with that masculine confidence that was like chocolate to women. Irresistible.

If she could look at him without the protective veneer of their professional association, without the barriers she had erected to shield herself from his charm, how would she do that? What would such a gaze be like? What might it promise?

Bearing all this in mind, Eleanor turned her attentions back to Miss Phillips, imagining that she wasn't looking at the young woman but at Ashford.

Miss Phillips blushed a deeper pink. But instead of turning away or gazing at Eleanor with disinterest, the girl actually batted her eyelashes.

It worked!

Eleanor couldn't take the look too far. After all, "Ned" was a lad of not much experience, and he couldn't make vows he wouldn't be able to keep. So Eleanor had to temper her expression somewhat. Yet she let Miss Phillips know, through subtle locking of gazes, occasionally dropping away and then returning, that Eleanor was most assuredly interested in pursuing a more intimate association.

The girl was like clay in Eleanor's hands. For a moment, Eleanor felt a little sorry for Miss Phillips, who seemed to lack confidence where her allure was concerned. Her mother's beauty shone brighter. And the girl's fortune was decent, but not substantial. She'd face strong competition from the other debutantes that Season.

Abruptly, the game didn't feel quite as fun. Ashford

might feel easy toying with women's emotions, but Eleanor *was* a woman, and hadn't the same laissez-faire attitude.

She gave Miss Phillips an apologetic smile, then kept her gaze fixed again on the toes of her borrowed boots. It might sting the girl to be cut, but better to do it now than prolong the charade.

Ashford must have sensed her sudden change of mood, because he said abruptly, "Perhaps you can tell me more about the grouse situation at your estate another time, Sir Frank. Right now, I need to feed young Ned. You know how these lads are all bottomless stomach at this age."

"Of course, of course!" The baronet stuffed the letter back into his coat. "I do hope to see you again."

"Yes," Lady Phillips said with a small smile. "It would be a pleasure, Lord Ashford."

Eleanor supposed that if a man could be bold in his intentions, then a woman had every prerogative to exercise the same right. Which Lady Phillips clearly was.

They all took their leave of one another, and Eleanor was careful not to let her attention linger too long on Miss Phillips. The girl might be disappointed, but hopefully it wouldn't last too long.

"An impressive performance," Ashford murmured as he and Eleanor continued on their stroll.

"I was going to say the same to you," she replied lowly. "Here I'd been convinced that only Mr. Mesmer possessed such skills, but clearly I was wrong. You took a perfectly happy married woman and turned her into a slavering tiger ready for steak."

Ashford's stride didn't lessen. "In this case, the tiger has had many other steaks before. As had Sir Tiger." When Eleanor shot him a confused frown, he went on. "I make a point of never seducing or taking to bed married women— not unless I know for certain that their husbands are unfaithful."

Though this surprised her, she said wryly, "Honor among the elite."

"We don't get many opportunities to be honorable," Ashford noted.

Something in his tone caught her attention. "And that bothers you."

He affected a shrug. "I won't bore you with complaints about being too rich or too privileged. It's like saying, 'They've given me far too much delicious cake.'" He eyed her. "And it would be too harmful if you published what transpired just now."

"What am I to write, then?" she protested. "You promised me scandal, and there it was in all its crimson glory."

"The girl is barely into her come-out. You'll affect her chances on the marriage market."

Eleanor sighed. It was far easier to report on misdeeds and impropriety when she didn't meet the people involved.

"Be more selective next time," she said at last. "If there's something you don't want me to write about, then don't do it."

"I won't," he answered.

She didn't press him further on the subject of honor, yet she could still sense a degree of dissatisfaction in him. A kind of restlessness and impatience. It made her wonder. Here she'd believed that men like Ashford had everything they wanted. Could do whatever they desired with impunity, but at the same time, there were certain limitations that she hadn't considered. He could never work. Never truly set his mind to something and earn an honest coin in compensation for his efforts.

"Did you enjoy that?" she asked, nodding back in the direction of where they'd left Sir Frank and the others.

Again, another shrug. "Not much challenge in it. Lady Phillips has been compensating for her husband's long-term mistress for over a decade. She'd probably take a baboon in tight breeches to her bed if she thought it might get back at him in some way."

"I think you're better looking than a primate in trousers," Eleanor said. "Slightly," she added.

"You are all flattery, madam, I mean—sir."

"So you enjoy a challenge?"

"I do," he admitted after a long pause. "But there aren't many of them. There hadn't been," he added darkly, under his breath.

What did that mean? Yet she sensed that if she pressed him on the subject, he wouldn't say more. He had his secrets, this earl. And while she'd love to ferret them out, she feared that if she did, or tried to, he'd call a stop to their whole arrangement, leaving her with nothing but the prospect of what might have been.

They proceeded with the rest of their walk, greeting a few people and occasionally stopping to look at the shop windows. But Eleanor was preoccupied. Who would have thought that Lord A—d had more going on in his brain than the constant pursuit of pleasure?

Easier to paint him simply as an empty libertine, use him for the benefits he could bring to *The Hawk's Eye,* and then go about her business without a by-your-leave. But it seemed he was more than what he appeared.

More dimensional. More human. A man rather than a collection of scandalous behaviors.

It wasn't entirely a pleasant discovery.

Chapter 5

*What does a rake eat? How might he sustain himself?
Dearest reader, it might shock you to discover that
even the most wicked of men feeds not upon the
tender souls of trembling virgins but beefsteak (and
occasionally lamb or mutton). After all, the pursuit
of pleasure requires nourishment of the most primal
kind, and what could feed a man of dissipation better
than hot, sizzling flesh?*

The Hawk's Eye, May 4, 1816

Daniel stood just inside the doorway of the Eagle chophouse.
Miss Hawke had positioned herself just slightly behind him,
letting him lead the way. This was his world, after all. Though
she was a journalist in pursuit of scandal, she also seemed
to possess a considerable degree of sagacity, allowing him to
serve as guide. She could have simply plowed ahead, pushed
by enthusiasm and eagerness, blundering along and creating
snares and muddles. But no, she was wise enough to know the
value of discretion. An admirable trait in women *and* men—
and one he seldom encountered.

They'd left the commercial and visual pleasures of Bond
Street to get some supper before the night's diversions. He'd
been concerned about taking her to the Eagle. It was one of
his few refuges. A place he could let all artifice fall away as
he simply enjoyed the pleasures of a good beefsteak and pint

of ale. Even when Jonathan had been present, the Eagle had been for Daniel alone.

The chophouse wasn't the most elegant, even though its clientele tended toward the elite. The beams were dark with smoke, and the framed pictures on the painted walls could use a dusting.

Mr. Bell, the proprietor, hurried forward. "Ah, my lord, a pleasure to see you this evening!" The older man glanced at Miss Hawke. "And who is this young gentleman?"

"His cousin," she answered in that strange "masculine" voice she'd affected. Daniel wouldn't have been fooled by it, but everyone else seemed to be. Perhaps he was simply too aware of Miss Hawke's femininity—despite her profession and her current disguise.

"From Lincolnshire," he added, as if that explained everything.

Bell nodded sagely. "I'll show you to a special table."

"What's wrong with my usual place?" Daniel demanded, glancing toward the settle near the fire.

"Well, uh . . ." Bell coughed into his hand. "It only seats one."

"Then fetch a chair, man."

"Of course! If you'll indulge me and wait just a moment, I'll . . . yes . . ." The proprietor hastened away in search of a chair.

"Do you not dine with friends?" Miss Hawke asked after they were left alone.

"Not here I don't." There had been times that he'd taken meals with Marwood or Jonathan, but he seemed to prefer his own company when it came to dining, especially lately.

"Why?"

He smothered a curse. It was likely a hazard of spending time with someone in her line of work that he'd be peppered frequently with questions. But perhaps there was something slightly refreshing about keeping company with a person who was genuinely curious about the world, rather than simply accepting things as facts or remaining steadfastly superficial.

And he'd opened himself up to this when he'd invited her along on his nightly activities.

"Before the noise and bustle of the evening," he said, holding tight to the head of his walking stick, "I enjoy . . . being alone." Not entirely the truth, though there was a grain of veracity in it. For all the time he and Jonathan had spent together, Daniel also liked his own company, when he could be isolated within the sanctum of his thoughts.

She continued to stare at him. Clearly, his response wasn't enough to satisfy her scribbler's curiosity.

So he continued. "There are always so many voices around me. So many distractions. But they can get very . . . loud. Here, I can be by myself."

"You could be by yourself at home, too," she pointed out.

And lonely, he thought. Something about eating by himself in that cavernous dining room that could seat two dozen guests felt as hollow as the chamber itself. He would occasionally eat in his chambers, but he'd grow too restless, too aware of his isolation.

"I like this better," he said.

Fortunately, he was saved from the need for further explanation by the timely return of Bell. "Many apologies for the delay, my lord. All is in readiness."

They followed the proprietor through the maze of filled tables. As Daniel and Miss Hawke progressed, he'd give an occasional nod to acquaintances, ignoring their curious glances at his companion. He supposed that Bell wasn't the only one who'd noticed his preference for isolation, and here he was, breaking from his usual mold.

It felt . . . good.

Daniel wanted to offer Miss Hawke the settle, while he took the chair. But between him and "Ned Sinclair," he was the one with greater status, so the ruse had to take precedence over politeness. Miss Hawke sat down with an unconsciously feminine little flourish, which made him wince, but at least she remembered not to cross her legs.

"The usual to drink, my lord?" Bell asked once they'd been seated.

"Yes, ale for me," Daniel answered.

The proprietor turned expectantly toward Miss Hawke. She looked momentarily flustered.

"Ah . . . lemonade," she stammered. "No, I'm sorry. I'll have an ale, too, thank you."

"Very good, sir." With that, Bell rushed off, perpetually the busy host.

Alone again with Miss Hawke, Daniel said lowly, "Don't apologize. Not for changing your mind. And you don't thank a servant for doing his job."

She frowned. "I just don't want to put him out."

"It's your prerogative to do as you please. As a man. And a man of status, too." He shook his head. "Women apologize too much. Always begging someone's forgiveness for the smallest trifles. You catch a cold and apologize for being ill. Take a breath, and it's, 'I'm so sorry for using your air.'"

"Because we're taught to," she replied. "Men just take and take. Like they're the world's rude houseguests. *You're not going to eat that, are you? I'll just spread my legs and arms out in the omnibus and take up every last inch of space.* And we're harridans and harpies if we point it out. I suppose no one has ever said the word *no* to you."

"Untrue." He hadn't been able to join the army when the war had broken out. Of course, nobody had directly said no, since it was tacit that the heir couldn't go to battle, and he'd never asked. But he'd felt the restriction, just the same.

Yet she raised a valid point. That word was alien to his ears. Even Allam, outspoken as he was, refrained from outright denying Daniel.

How bloody irritating. As if he couldn't possibly have the fortitude to not get exactly what he wanted. He needed to practice more self-discipline.

Of course, he was learning more and more about that word *no* when it came to finding Jonathan. That's all he'd been hearing as of late when it came to that objective. But things had to change. It was imperative that they did. The man's life hung in the balance.

"Just once," Miss Hawke said, "someone will say no to you. And I'd like to be there when it happens."

"If you're looking for more fodder for your scandal rag," he rejoined, "that's a closed line of enquiry."

Yet she only smirked. "I can be very persistent, Ashford."

"As can I, *Ned*."

The barmaid, a tall, bosomy brunette, appeared beside the table. She smiled enticingly at Daniel. "The usual, my lord?"

That seemed to be the night's refrain. Much as he hated being called a rake, he made a piss-poor one if all his actions could be predicted. "Lamb chops tonight, Victoria."

Her eyes widened at his divergent order. My God, he was a hell of a dull bloke if switching from beef to lamb caused so much astonishment. He should wear his boots on his hands and see what kind of amazement that caused.

"Yes, my lord. And you, sir?"

"Lamb, too," Miss Hawke answered. "No—what's the house special?"

"Beefsteak, sir."

"I'll have that."

"Yes, sir."

The barmaid hurried away to place their order. As she did, Miss Hawke sent Daniel a triumphant little look. No apologizing, and no thanking the server, either.

He gave her a small nod. She was learning.

But there was more for her to learn.

"You could've given her arse a pinch," he advised.

"That's a masculine delight I'll gladly forgo," she answered. At that very moment, the barmaid's squeal could be heard across the room as some other gent decided to do the very thing Miss Hawke had declined.

"It's a wonder castration isn't more common," Miss Hawke muttered.

"The perpetuation of the human race is grateful that it isn't."

"But not the arses of barmaids. I might not get much respect as a female writer, but at least my bottom is free of bruises. My pride, however, takes a regular drubbing."

"Then why do it?" he asked.

"Because I love it," she replied simply, her gaze holding his.

What would that be like? To have something he cared about so deeply that he didn't care what kind of abuse he took, what sort of physical or psychological walloping he'd endure, all for love of that one thing? And to test himself to the limits of his endurance, in service to his great passion.

A filament of something hot and tight wound through him. *Envy.* He actually envied Miss Hawke her determination, her drive to accomplishment.

Perhaps when he'd finally succeeded in locating his friend, he ought to turn his attention toward finding a wife and raising a family to ensure a happy, healthy continuation of the Ashford name. He'd never been a disinterested master of his estates, but maybe he could apply himself more. Fund some of those technological innovations he'd been reading about. He could leave behind his gallivanting, and have purpose, like Miss Hawke did.

Good God. Just a few hours in her company, and he was thinking of turning his life completely on its head.

The woman was dangerous.

"Why here?" she asked, breaking his thoughts. She glanced around at the somewhat shabby chophouse, her gaze lingering on the faded paintings, the table stained with rings from countless pint glasses. "Surely there are more elegant establishments for a man of your rank."

"The Eagle serves the best steak in London," he answered. He nodded as Victoria delivered their drinks and left.

"Surely better steaks exist in London so that one doesn't have to put up with this." Miss Hawke glanced down at her feet, where the soles of her boots stuck to the tacky floorboards.

"It *is* a good steak. But I like that it's not the most soignée chophouse. It's not . . ." He picked through the thoughts in his head, trying to make sense of them. "It's not some rarefied palace of isolation and hierarchy. Over there," he nodded toward one table, where two men sawed happily at their beef, "those men are both industrialists. That man in the corner, the one with the green cravat. He's a baron, and his wife is the half-black daughter of a Caribbean merchant. Some places in the city wouldn't serve them. But here, they're treated just like anybody else."

Miss Hawke gently, thoughtfully rubbed at her chin. "I thought you toffs didn't like rubbing elbows with the *hoi polloi*. Wanted to keep the parvenus and plebes on the other side of the gate."

He leaned forward, bracing his forearms on the table. "Here's a scandal for you: not all of us toffs are the same. Some of us don't give a damn where someone's money comes from, or who they choose to marry."

"That *is* a scandal." But a corner of her mouth turned up as she spoke, poking fun at herself as much as him.

Bugger.

"But I have some scandal for you, too," she continued. "That table, with the six gents around it? My sources say they'll be visiting a brothel tonight, in honor of the youngest bloke's engagement to an iron mine heiress."

He nearly choked at how easily she said the word *brothel*. No decent female of his acquaintance would be so bold, or worldly. But then, Miss Hawke had made it quite clear she wasn't a *decent female*.

Daniel glanced over to the table in question. He knew two of the six gentlemen to be regular visitors of the bawdy house—which was reputed for having its girls wear gauzy dresses and fairy wings—but the others often trumpeted their virtue in public. And the young lad, a viscount's son, looked much more enthusiastic about going to the bagnio than he did about his upcoming nuptials, despite his parents' loud proclamations of the happiness of the union.

Very interesting, indeed.

"You've got an extensive network of information," he murmured.

She smiled mysteriously. "Information is my business."

"Does your information tell you that there's a nobleman here tonight who likes to wear women's clothing?" he asked. "I won't say who."

"I know about the man in question," she said in riposte, "and his modiste says that he prefers ruffles to lace on his drawers."

He folded his arms across his chest. "No shocking you, is there?"

"It takes quite a lot. But," she added with a smile, "I'm hopeful for this evening."

Watching Ashford eat wasn't shocking. He wasn't raised by bears, after all, and actually used a knife and fork when cutting into his lamb and potatoes. Nor did he smear gravy all over his face. But she almost wished that he did, so that her fascination with him could lessen.

Sadly, he had beautiful table manners. Not overly fussy, nor excessively crude. As she bent over her—admittedly excellent—steak, she watched him discreetly. He held his knife comfortably, using it to cut large but precise bites of meat, which he smoothly ferried to his mouth. Instead of plowing through his food, he took his time to chew and savor. Nor did he talk with his mouth full. In truth, he hardly spoke as they dined, but the silence didn't feel uncomfortable.

She must be used to dining with starving writers and actors, to find a man simply eating lamb chops to be a sensual act. Yet watching him dine was a pleasure, so much so that he eventually glanced up and said, "Your meat's getting cold."

So much for being discreet. Well, she could throw him, too. "My meat's perfectly hot."

He raised a brow.

"Juicy, too," she added, and popped a bite into her mouth. The earl coughed.

"Something caught in your throat?" she asked sweetly.

He glowered at her as he took a long drink of ale. "I thought it was my job to shock you."

"Then you'd better get to it," she answered. "The score is decidedly in my favor."

He set aside his cutlery. "I wasn't aware we were keeping score."

"We are now. Unless you're concerned about being beaten by a woman," she added.

"But you aren't a woman," he countered. "At least, not tonight."

"Have you forgotten my true gender already?"

"Unlikely," he said with surprising vehemence. "Not the way you eat."

She rolled her eyes. "There's something inherently feminine in my eating habits, too?"

"It's not your fault you're a woman through and through."

"Thank you for your tolerance," she said drily.

He gave a small bow. "I am all consideration, madam, I mean—young Ned."

They resumed their meal. She tried to eat in a more manly fashion, but without resembling a prized boar, which was her first impulse. "Being a man is a tiring business." She sighed.

"Truer words," he muttered, and took another bite.

She tried to concentrate on her meal, but his very presence distracted her. She needed to remember exactly what she intended to reap from this venture with the earl, and why she was engaging in this escapade in the first place.

He had the most incredible hands she'd ever beheld—broad, long-fingered, exquisitely masculine.

Always fall back on the journalistic line of inquiry. It never failed to protect her from feeling too much. "You inherited your title at an early age."

He lifted his brow again, the model of an imperious gentleman. Perhaps he used that as *his* protection. "Is this for the article?"

"Would you answer my questions if it was?"

"Are you in the habit of answering questions with questions?"

"Are you?" she countered.

He leaned back. "Do you think anyone asks me many questions?"

"Don't legions of servants wait on earls?" *Ha!*

"How much experience do you have with earls?"

She scowled. He was better at this game than she had anticipated. "Isn't it possible for me to extrapolate?"

He grinned. "Based on what evidence?"

She fought a growl. Letting him win would be unthinkable. "How much would I need to make an accurate assessment?"

"Isn't that what this whole venture is about?"

She banged her fist on the table. "Point to you, Ashford."

Damn him if he didn't look handsome, even when gloating. "You make a worthy opponent, Ned."

And damn her if that little bit of praise didn't feel like a shot of warm brandy swirling through her belly. "Yet you didn't answer my initial question."

He fixed her with an intense, piercing gaze. "Anything I tell you about me or my family would have to be left out of the articles. Again, if I see one word appear in the paper that I don't sanction, I'll denounce you in as many periodicals as exist in the whole of Britain."

She leaned back, slightly stunned by his fierceness. "You cannot have it both ways, Ashford."

"As you're so fond of reminding me," he replied coolly, "I'm an earl. I can have it as many ways as I desire."

That, she didn't doubt. She herself had little recourse, as a business owner and as a woman. When it came to power, the deck was stacked in his favor. Maggie's words of warning drifted through her mind again. Eleanor would have to be on her guard around Ashford. For many reasons.

She could let the matter drop. If what he said couldn't be included in the article, did it matter? All she needed to do was accompany him on his rakish activities, not learn who he was beneath the libertine's veneer.

Yet she did care. She wanted to know. To know him. Even if only for her own understanding.

"As you wish," she said at last, yet she couldn't help but add for emphasis, "my lord."

He gave a clipped nod. Instead of looking at her, his gaze roamed around the chophouse before finally settling on his knife lying beside his plate. Distractedly, he ran one of his long, square-tipped fingers up and down the handle of the blade.

"My mother died in childbed," he said after a long pause. "She and her newborn daughter are buried in the family plot at the church in Somerset." His voice was stark, almost cold, yet resonant with old pain.

"I'm sorry," she said. Nothing else seemed to be appropriate.

His gaze flicked up to her, and past hurt continued to reverberate there. "I was only three at the time, so I don't have many memories of her. Just the smell of lilacs and the feel of her coral beads in my fingers." He looked down at his fingers, as if recalling the sensation. Then his hand curled into a fist. "I didn't have any other siblings, and my father didn't remarry."

She sensed he didn't want to dwell overlong on the painful aspects of his past. "Risky, if you were the only heir."

"I have cousins," he said. "Decent enough blokes who would've been perfectly acceptable as heirs."

"That's quite a ringing endorsement."

He shrugged. "I'm sure they'd say the same about me. Perhaps even worse, given that I am a reprobate *rake,* after all."

"*Reprobate* is your word, not mine," she noted.

"True. I'll just have to prove how much of one I am. Flirting with a married woman doesn't seem to have convinced you of my less savory qualities."

"Pfft. Haven't you read my paper? Dalliances are far more common than passionate, faithful marriages."

"Except in the case of my father," Ashford noted bitterly. "Poor sod. Oh, he took a mistress after my mother died, but he refused to marry again. Still, there are romantics of the older generation that said when he died, it was of a broken heart." He made those words sound as impossible as magic spells.

She asked, "Are you a romantic of the older generation?"

"I believe too much port and mutton caused my father's death, not a broken heart." He gazed at her cynically. "Come now, you cannot write what you write and believe in such tripe."

She sighed. "I wish I could say that I cling to the legends of true love, but if I ever did, experience has taught me otherwise."

Setting his hands on the table, he asked, "Experience that you write about, or your own?"

She forced out a laugh. "I thought I was the prying journalist, not you."

"More evasions." He shook his head.

"We're experts at that art." She pushed her plate away, no longer interested in her food.

Spreading one of his hands on his chest, he affected a shocked expression. "I am the very soul of disclosure. Haven't I just spun the woeful tale of my own family?"

"That you did, and every word of it shall remain carefully locked away in here." She tapped her forehead. Intriguing, how he played the role of the cynic, especially when it came to his history, but he hadn't been able to fully disguise the loss he felt at his parents' passing, especially his mother.

If this was something that he normally kept hidden, what other secrets were buried in the earl's heart? And what would she give to learn them?

It shocked her to realize that she truly did crave knowing more of him. His secrets. His truths. The man, himself. And not just for *The Hawk's Eye*. But for herself alone. And therein lay the greater peril.

Chapter 6

Oh, gentle readers! The sights I witnessed! All that I might report back to you on the wickedness that dwells beneath the surface of our seemingly pious Town. It must come as a stunning surprise, as it did for this unassuming author, that behind the porticos of some of this city's most esteemed neighborhoods exist temples erected to the pursuit of that most elusive and fickle of women, Lady Fortune. And she keeps company with our nation's honored gentlemen, though after last night, I hesitate to use the term "gentlemen" . . .

The Hawk's Eye, May 4, 1816

"The infamous Donnegan's," Daniel said as his carriage pulled up outside the gaming hell.

"It can't be very infamous if I haven't heard of it," countered Miss Hawke. She peered through the carriage window to get a better view of the place.

He tried to see it through her keen writer's eyes. The building itself looked like any house in this part of Mayfair—large and austere, with tall columns and potted plants adorning its white façade. Hardly the sort of place a notorious rake might disport himself.

"There are more scandals in heaven and earth than are dreamt of in your philosophy," he paraphrased. As the footman jumped down from the back of the carriage and opened the door, Daniel added, "Sometimes, a scandal truly does want to be hidden."

He stepped down from the vehicle and waited for her to join him. She alit, her movements in the unfamiliar male clothing seeming to grow easier with each passing moment. It was a convincing disguise, but he couldn't forget that the breeches she wore covered *her* legs, and though her calves were padded, he still kept looking at them in their stockings. What might she look like in such an ensemble without all the padding and cosmetics?

Too appealing, he decided.

"Then why take me here?" she asked, standing beside him. "Haven't you any loyalty to your fellow profligates?"

"None at all. Nor they to me. We'd all push each other in front of the omnibus if it meant our own benefit."

"There's that honor among aristos," she said drily. Still, he could hear excitement in her voice—likely at the prospect of being in an all-male enclave. Well, it wasn't entirely devoid of female company, but she'd learn that soon enough. A pulse of his own excitement worked through him—the thrill of experiencing Miss Hawke's discovery.

How long had he felt much exhilaration about anything? Searching for Jonathan didn't fill him with pleasure, only the need to see it accomplished. But this—taking part in his world through a new set of eyes, and not just any eyes, but Miss Hawke's—was a new gratification.

He ascended the steps, with her accompanying him. A liveried footman bowed and opened the inconspicuous door. Once inside, another servant took their hats and canes, then ushered them down a hallway.

The corridor opened up into a huge, cacophonous room. Daniel had seen the interior of Donnegan's hundreds of times, but he kept his gaze on Miss Hawke, watching her reaction.

"If you're overwhelmed," he murmured, "just pretend you're a boy down from the country."

She nodded but hardly paid him any mind. Instead, she gazed with wide eyes at the enormous room crowded with tables, where every sort of game of chance was played. Card games, dicing, and roulette, imported from France. The games themselves didn't seem to interest her so much as the men thronged around the tables. This wasn't a sedate parlor. Some men had shucked their jackets, their neckcloths undone, their waistcoats partially buttoned. They shouted and waved fistfuls of cash, jostling one another, spilling glasses of wine down their once immaculate shirtfronts and onto the floor.

England's leading lights clustered around the tables and acted like wild beasts. Daniel counted cabinet ministers, leading public figures, noblemen.

"It's *Debrett's* gone feral," she muttered.

"Please keep an eye on your hands," he said lowly. "In case someone tries to bite them off."

"They look particularly carnivorous." She nodded toward the women weaving between the tables. Dressed in semitransparent gowns that revealed nearly everything, the females in question draped themselves over the gamesters, plying them with wine and murmuring into their ears. They sat in the laps of men in chairs, toying with their hair and the buttons of their clothing.

"It's not meat they feed on," Daniel noted. "Observe the fat gentleman in the corner with the redhead." The woman's fingers danced all over the man, who chortled and threw money down on the hazard table.

"She's robbing him blind," Miss Hawke breathed.

Indeed, as they spoke, the fat man's pocket watch vanished, as did the glittering brilliants adorning the front of his waistcoat.

"Someone has to notice and complain," Miss Hawke said.

Daniel shrugged. "No one cares. Everyone in this chamber has enough timepieces and diamonds to make the losses negligible. They consider it money well spent." As he spoke, the fat man gave the redhead a squeeze, and she laughed.

"Why not just go to a brothel?" asked Miss Hawke.

"Oh, there are rooms upstairs." He nodded toward one chap who ambled up some stairs, his arms around a set of matching blondes.

"And you make use of those rooms?"

He shook his head. "Some men prefer red wine to white. I prefer my women of the less commercial variety."

"My heart soars at the poetry of it all."

Shrugging, he said, "What's sex but another form of commerce?"

"And what's a rake without his cynical detachment?" she countered.

"A vulnerable fool," he said.

"Oh," she said with a smile, "that's very good. I'll have to remember that for the article."

Thankfully, she didn't pull out a notebook and start scribbling. Which meant that she had a prodigious memory. Something he both relied on and needed to guard himself against. At the least he had ensured she would never write about his family or Jonathan. Threatening her gave him no pleasure, but she was as yet an untested quantity, and a journalist, to boot. He couldn't trust her.

Nor could she trust him. There was some comfort in that.

"Come," he said, waving toward the gaming area. "Time to join in on the fun."

Eleanor hadn't taken half a dozen steps beside Ashford when suddenly four men appeared in their path. She recognized all of them from their frequent appearance in *The Hawk's Eye*—especially the man who seemed to be the leader of the group. Cameron Chalton, the Viscount Marwood. The eldest son and heir to the Marquess of Allam—Ashford's godfather. A singularly small world, this realm of the elite.

Marwood wore his black hair longer than most, and even

sported dark stubble on his lean cheeks. Hard to imagine a man with a more outrageous reputation than Ashford, but Marwood seemed to excel at decadence.

"Ashford," Marwood said with a mocking half bow. "You rotten son of a bitch."

"Marwood," the earl answered easily. "You filthy whoremonger." With less affection, he addressed the three men accompanying Marwood. "Offham, Ticehurst, Welfort."

The other gentlemen tripped over themselves, bowing and offering servile greetings. She recalled their names from sundry articles in *The Hawk's Eye,* usually in connection with carryings-on at the theater, or any of the countless pleasure gardens that sprang up like gaudy weeds all over London. Some of this intelligence she'd gained through her information network, and some she'd learned firsthand in her investigations through the city.

"My father came to visit you earlier," Marwood noted.

He did? thought Eleanor. The Marquess of Allam was a powerful man, even more so than Ashford, with a reputation for plain talk and straightforward dealing. Allam never made it into the pages of her paper because he maintained such scrupulously honorable behavior. It resulted in an exemplary life but dull reading. Wasn't that always the case?

"Enjoining me to think of marriage," Ashford said. "The fate of the title, my responsibilities as earl, et cetera."

A flicker of emotion crossed Marwood's face, something more than the disinterest he affected. "I'm glad he's giving his usual august, boring speeches to you rather than me."

"We're both lost causes, you and I," Ashford replied.

"He hasn't given up on you, though," his friend answered. Again, that darkness crossed his face. A conversation was being held beneath the surface of this one. When she returned to the office, she'd have to look through old issues of the paper for references to Lord M—d, piece together his mystery.

Then Marwood's gaze flicked over to Eleanor, and she felt the intensity of his dark eyes all the way to her shoes. "Who's the duckling?"

"My cousin from Lincolnshire," Ashford said.

Eleanor pitched her voice down low. She stuck out her hand. "Ned Sinclair."

Marwood stared at her. Then burst out laughing. His toadies joined him in his laughter. For a moment, panic iced down Eleanor's neck, and she glanced at Ashford. Did Marwood and his friends see through her disguise?

"Good God, lad." Marwood wiped at his eyes. "Have your bollocks dropped yet?"

What is it with these toffs and their obsession with testes?

"Of course they have," she answered gruffly.

Ashford slung his arm around her shoulder, and she fought the urge to stiffen at being pressed so close to him. "Don't quiz the boy," he said. "Just this morning, he proudly showed me his three chest hairs."

"There were five, not three," Eleanor grumbled.

Her comment set off another round of guffaws, including Ashford's. Damn the bastard, he seemed to enjoy making her the butt of his friends' jests. "Ned's" pride felt the sting, and she struggled with the desire to elbow him in the ribs. Hard.

Marwood turned to one of the women sashaying by. "Jenny."

Thankfully, Eleanor was used to visiting Maggie at the theater and seeing strange women parade around the dressing room in states of almost complete nudity. But she oughtn't act too accustomed to the sight, since "Ned" probably hadn't much experience with partially clad females. She widened her eyes and tried her best to call up a blush.

"My lord," Jenny said with a provocative smile. She dipped into a curtsy so low that Eleanor swore she could see straight down the front of Jenny's dress, all the way to her navel.

It was an inward-facing navel.

Marwood took Jenny's hand and gently pulled her toward Eleanor. "Young Ned here is as green as cabbage."

Jenny swayed toward Eleanor. She ran one smooth hand

down Eleanor's cheek. "Barely has a whisker on his face, poor lamb."

"He needs experience, don't you think, love?" Marwood drawled. "Take him upstairs and break him in a little. My treat," he added, winking at Eleanor.

"Uh . . ." True panic gripped her. What was she supposed to do? There would be some very awkward explaining—and some bribes to pay—if Jenny discovered that Eleanor's manly goods were as false as Jenny's hair color.

Ashford reached out and plucked Jenny's hand from Eleanor's face. "Very generous of you, Marwood. But my aunt would never forgive me if I returned her son with a case of the French pox."

"Here now," Jenny exclaimed. "I'm clean, I am." She murmured under her breath, "I think."

A sovereign appeared between Ashford's fingers, which he held up in front of Jenny. "Thank you for your time, Miss Jenny. But kindly step away from my cousin. Perhaps hie yourself to someplace on the other side of the chamber, if you'd be so courteous."

The coin disappeared somewhere into the folds of Jenny's translucent dress—though where it went, Eleanor had no idea. There seemed to be no hiding anything in that gown.

"Good luck at the tables, my lord," Jenny cooed before dissolving into the crowd.

Marwood and his friends all booed at Ashford and Eleanor in disappointment. "Why must you spoil our fun?" demanded Marwood.

"Maybe I'm becoming dull in my old age," Ashford said.

Rolling his eyes, Marwood said, "This from the man who challenged me to a race climbing the rotunda at Vauxhall."

"It was a tie, as I recall."

"Only just," Marwood countered. "I would've beaten you if champagne hadn't made my boots slippery."

Eleanor gleefully filed all of this away in the archives of her mind. These articles were going to be marvelous—so ripe with scandal that they wouldn't be able to keep any issues of the paper in newsagents' hands. Perhaps she ought to increase her print run ahead of time, just in case. Or maybe she'd sell more papers in the future by making current issues scarce.

It was all too delicious to contemplate.

"Though I promised Ned's mother that I'd return him to Lincolnshire without the pox," Ashford said, "I also vowed to Ned that I'd give him the full London treatment, and bankrupt him at the tables."

"Excellent plan," Marwood agreed. "We'll come with you."

"One corrupting influence is enough," Ashford said with a smile.

Instead of taking offense, Marwood nodded sagely. "Wise. There's only so much degeneracy a young lad can take in a single evening."

"I'm game," Eleanor objected. She could get twice the mileage from her story if not one but two rakes accompanied her this night. But Ashford sent her a quelling look, and Marwood laughed.

"Good thing the boy has you to look out for his best interests," Marwood said. "Else you'd have to ship him back to Lincolnshire in manacles and leg irons."

"Your approbation means the sun and moon to me," drawled Ashford.

In response, Marwood gave them both a short, mocking bow. After wishing them a good evening, he wove his way through the crowd, followed by his fawning entourage.

"He could've stayed," Eleanor grumbled once Marwood had gone.

Ashford shook his head and guided them toward one of the card tables. "Don't need to tell you the reputation Marwood's got. He's one of my closest friends, and even I think he's poisonous."

"I can handle myself with dangerous men," she countered. "Look how well I'm managing you."

A corner of his mouth turned up. "I wasn't aware I was being *managed*."

"Because I'm so deft at it."

"Even so," Ashford continued, "I know your secret and Marwood doesn't. He could manipulate you in a very unpleasant way if he learned the truth."

"He's as bad as that? I thought Lord Allam is his father. Shouldn't that count for some degree of virtue?"

"That apple," Ashford said, "didn't fall close to the tree. In fact, it threw itself off the tree's branches, rolled down a hill, and straight into the nearest theater box, where it surrounded itself with a variety of strawberries of dubious repute."

Eleanor fought to keep her laugh to a deeper, masculine chuckle. "Oh, for God's sake, never become a writer. You just murdered a poor metaphor in the most brutal way."

"The metaphor had it coming."

Something tugged on the corner of her thoughts, and she placed her hand on Ashford's sleeve, stopping them both in their progress through the gaming hell. Bodies swirled around them, like a river of iniquity.

"You didn't have to do that," she murmured.

He looked impatient. "I told you, Marwood's—"

"Not him. I meant the way you behaved toward Jenny." She glanced around, then lowered her voice. "She's hired female company, but . . . you gave her courtesy. The same courtesy you'd give a lady. Not many men would do that."

"Surely they would," he protested.

"I've seen it. They'd treat her as if she didn't have any feelings. As if she wasn't human."

His cheeks darkened. "Of course she's human."

"Few men see women like her that way."

"Trying to ascribe some kind of altruism to me?" He made a dismissive gesture. "That's a fool's errand."

She smiled up at him. "You haven't forgotten that I'm a journalist by trade. I make my living—"

"Through fabrication."

"Embellishment, not fabrication," she corrected. "But that's based on observation. And I see far more than you'd like me to. Including the fact that you think of courtesans as people deserving of respect."

"What a poor example of a rake I am."

"But a rather sterling man."

He snorted. "I'm not working hard enough at my dissolution." He waved toward the card table nearby. "Time to put my rakish reputation to the test."

"I wonder, though," she murmured, glancing around the room. "It seems that every titled nobleman is here—except Jonathan Lawson, the Duke of Holcombe's heir." She peered at Ashford. "You two are awfully close—or were, if I remember properly. Went to Eton and Cambridge together. You were inseparable until he shipped overseas."

"How do you know all that?" he said stiffly.

"I'm a journalist, if you recall. It's my business to know."

"It's not your business to know everything." His voice had gone tight, hard.

"But I'd think that the young man would be here, of all places. Celebrating his new role as heir to a dukedom."

"If you persist in these impertinent observations," the earl said through his teeth, "the night will be over in mere seconds."

She blinked at him. His violent, angry response mystified her. As did his friend's absence. But she didn't doubt that Ashford would carry through on his promise, and likely have her bodily thrown out of the gaming hell.

"Very well," she said as mildly as she could. "Consider the matter as exiled as Bonaparte."

He nodded, but still looked taut and guarded.

Eleanor followed as he walked to the game table, but she placed all this new information in her mental cabinet, to be reviewed later. Lord Ashford was certainly not what he appeared, or the figure he presented himself to be. Maybe he wasn't even aware of it, but beneath his handsome, wicked exterior, there beat the heart of a genuinely decent man— and perhaps there was the true story.

But could she write about it? Could she write about him, coming to know him as she did?

And what of his friend—Jonathan Lawson? Was there something to his absence tonight?

The earl was using her for some unknown purpose. This she understood. She used him, too. A simple exchange. Yet it didn't seem simple anymore.

Damn and hell—suddenly she'd developed an ethos. And at such an inconvenient time, too. It was like a sickness. One without a cure.

Chapter 7

Dame Fortune is indeed capricious, for why else would she dangle before us prospects that could either lead to our greatest pleasure or most calamitous ruin?

The Hawk's Eye, May 4, 1816

As his anger cooled, Daniel debated. Should he take Miss Hawke to the sedate table, where older gentlemen played piquet? Or would she and her writing be better served by the more complex, and unrestrained, games of baccarat, hazard, or *vingt-et-un*? Glancing over at her as she surveyed the room beside him, a gleam of excitement in her eyes, he knew his choice—definitely the wilder option.

He was still thrown by her observation that Jonathan was missing from the gaming hell. Naturally she'd notice something like that. Daniel himself had been searching for his friend every time he set foot in Donnegan's, hoping against reason that Jonathan would show up. But tonight, as it was each time, he was disappointed.

He shouldn't have gotten so upset with Miss Hawke. She'd surely latch on to that suspicious behavior and search out the answer. If she pressed him, he could always claim that he and Jonathan were feuding for some reason, and the mere mention of his "former" friend's name angered him. That would suffice.

"Have you much experience with games of chance?" he asked.

"A little." A small, wary smile curved her mouth.

He couldn't let himself be distracted by that smile. It wouldn't serve him well if he was caught staring at his "cousin's" lips.

"Let's avoid hazard for now," he said. The rules were complicated, and though she claimed "a little" knowledge of gaming, he didn't want to tax her overmuch on her first night in a gambling hell. If she got too lost, it wouldn't translate well in her article. "Same with baccarat. *Vingt-et-un* should do us very well."

He struggled with the impulse to put his hand on her back and guide her toward the baize-covered table. Instead, he led the way, the crowd parting for him as he walked. He had to trust that she followed.

The card table was thronged with men, and though the game required concentration, these young bucks were more interested in shouting their enthusiasm with each turn of the cards. Women draped themselves on the players, cheering on their night's benefactors, or else commiserating with their losses. A dealer stood at the head of the table, his implacable expression a contrast to the exuberance of the players.

"We ought to watch a few hands before we play," Daniel murmured to Miss Hawke.

She threw him a grin. "Too safe. No scandal in that."

He raised his brows. If it was scandal she wanted, then he'd give it to her.

"I'm staking this young gentleman a hundred pounds," he said to the dealer.

The grin faded slightly from Miss Hawke's face. It wasn't the highest amount he'd ever played, but for a woman of her class, a hundred pounds was enough to sustain someone comfortably for a goodly while.

"Yes, my lord," the dealer answered. "And for you?"

"A thousand pounds."

Even above the din, he heard Miss Hawke's soft inhalation.

But the other players didn't look shocked. If anything, it was standard procedure for a man of his stature to start off with a stake of a thousand pounds.

"That's just the beginning," he said lowly into Miss Hawke's ear.

She shook her head. "You aristos are mad as circus elephants."

"I thought circus elephants were well trained."

"Until they decide they've had enough, and then they trample everything in their path." She glanced down at his shoes. "Maybe I'd better check for a smashed mahout under those big feet of yours."

He scowled, the size of his feet and hands always subject for self-consciousness. Earls weren't built like laborers, but he'd always been too oversized for his role in life, as though he'd been intended for the fields and not a ballroom.

"Careful," he growled, "or one impertinent journalist might feel the wrath of my appendages."

"You wouldn't kick a lady," she insisted.

"I don't see one standing here."

She flashed him a gesture so obscene, so unexpected, that he couldn't help but laugh.

Stacks of chips appeared before them on the table as they took their seats, with her to his right.

"The rules of the game are relatively simple," he said as they watched the dealer distribute cards. "Shouldn't tax you overmuch."

"What a relief." She sighed. "This usage of my brain is *exhausting*."

Of course, he'd been an ass in saying that—to her especially. From their brief interaction, he already knew she was one of the most intelligent people he'd ever encountered.

"I'm assuming that the number twenty-one comes into play," she said, "given the game's name."

Cards flew from the dealer's hands, and both Daniel and Miss Hawke watched him carefully.

"The aim is to wind up with a hand of cards totaling more

than what the dealer holds," he explained. "But," he added, "it's got to be equal to or lower than twenty-one points. Each card has a point value based on the face number, except for aces and face cards. Knaves, queens, and kings are worth ten points. Aces are either one or eleven, depending."

She gazed up at him with round eyes. "You mean there's mathematics involved? I may fall into a swoon of despair."

"I won't catch you," he answered.

"Very unmanly," she agreed. "Just throw a glass of wine in my face to rouse me. I'm sure, after everything I've written about you, you long for the opportunity to toss a drink at me."

"Be lying if I said the thought hadn't occurred to me. But that's when I thought *E. Hawke* was a man."

"Tonight, he is."

Yet despite her convincing disguise, he never lost his awareness of her as a woman.

Reminding himself that they were still in the thick of a male haven, he quickly explained the rest of the rules to her. All the players were given one card facedown, same as the dealer.

"Now, look at your card," he instructed her, "and make your wager based on that card."

She did so, carefully peering under the card and shifting it just slightly so that he could see what she'd been dealt.

An ace. Could be high, could be low. He'd gotten the eight of diamonds.

"I'd—"

But she waved off his suggestion. "I'll continue," she announced to the dealer.

"I'm in for another, as well," he said.

A second round of cards was dealt, facedown again. Daniel had gotten the seven of spades.

Miss Hawke wouldn't show him her card.

"I bet seventy-five," Daniel said to the dealer. Fifteen wasn't especially strong, but he'd won on worse. Besides, what did the money matter to him? To any of them?

The other players also joined in. Daniel glanced at Miss Hawke. She'd go out, most likely, otherwise the night's games would be over for her before they'd even begun.

"I'm in, too," she said. "Seventy-five, also."

He stared at her. "I won't stake you more than that hundred," he said lowly. He could afford it, but it seemed fundamentally wrong to throw money at her, as if it might somehow impugn her journalistic integrity.

"Good," she answered, "because I'd hate to have to owe you."

"Another card?" the dealer asked Daniel.

"I'll stand," he answered.

Gamblers either took a third card, or else they stood. And when the dealer turned to Miss Hawke, she said, "I'll stand, as well."

After the last round of cards was distributed, the dealer finally revealed his hand. An eight and a knave.

Daniel had lost. As had most of the men who'd remained in the game. They groaned and cursed as their hands were too low to beat the dealer's.

Then Miss Hawke turned over her cards. She had her ace, of course. And a nine of hearts.

She smiled enigmatically as the dealer called out that she was the winner. Daniel stared at her. It had to be luck.

So he believed, until . . .

She won the next hand.

The next, too.

And when she did lose, it was only a minor amount.

Her stack of chips was growing far faster than anybody else's. Everyone at the table, including the dealer, gaped at her. Some of the men congratulated her for her luck and skill. A few others grumbled, but she met their disgruntlement with good cheer. She was also neatly, carefully, extracting stories from the other players, getting them to reveal their greatest losses and wins at the tables. More fodder, no doubt, for her stories.

She was playing the whole night effortlessly.

"You rooked me," he said lowly.

"Not a bit," she answered, barely containing her smug smile.

"You said you had 'a little' experience playing."

"'A little' is such a relative term," she answered. "To us, a lion is a fierce, giant creature, but to an elephant, it's a little cat."

"What is it with you and elephants?" he muttered.

"I like elephants. They seem like wise, gentle creatures. Except when they rampage, of course."

Daniel pulled her away from the *vingt-et-un* table before the dealer decided to garrote them. People eddied as they moved from table to table.

Finding a sheltered spot in the corner of the room, Daniel asked, "What other games do you have 'a little' experience with?"

"Hm." She tapped her chin thoughtfully. "Loo, piquet, faro, hazard, baccarat."

"Is that all?"

"Oh, and whist. And Pope Joan. And speculation. And—"

"Clearly, you keep very reputable company."

"I'm with you, aren't I?" She smiled angelically at him.

He guided her toward the hazard table. "Let's try again. And this time, I suggest you lose *big* every now and again to keep the management from throwing us out on our arses."

She accompanied him as they headed to where a loud throng of men played at the dicing game. "I can't help it if I'm naturally lucky."

"Somehow, where you're concerned, I doubt pure luck is involved."

She gave him a shocked look. "Are you disputing my honor? Surely that's an offense that warrants a challenge to a duel."

"Keep your damned voice down," he growled as men nearby glanced at them. "Or else you'll secure us a spot at the park with pistols at dawn."

"I was only jesting," she protested as he dragged her toward the hazard table.

"A dangerous jest," he threw over his shoulder, "especially in a place like this."

"Have you seen men challenge each other to a duel here?" She peered closer. "I know that you've been challenged."

They took their positions, readying to play. Miss Hawke, continuing to inhabit her male persona excellently, seemed to follow his directions, because she didn't win more than two rounds in a row, and when she did lose, she was careful that the amount was substantial. Despite his words of caution, grudging admiration for her knocked around in his chest. She was a born gamester, and clearly the possessor of some bloody sharp wits.

He'd grown weary of gaming hells, especially searching them fruitlessly for Jonathan, but having her beside him made the experience fresh again.

The play continued on for hours, the wild atmosphere swirling around them as players wagered outrageous sums of money, jewelry, properties. The air was thick with the smell of sweat, wine, and perfume. Half-dressed women continued to hang on the players, some of them performing outrageous acts in front of the whole company. Their fingers disappeared into clothing, and more flesh was bared.

Miss Hawke didn't seem to bother to hide her shock. Young Ned Sinclair would likely be just as stunned as she might be at the carrying-on. While playing the different games didn't seem to faze her, the activity around the games did indeed give her plenty of fodder for her newspaper.

As they tried their hands at sundry activities, Miss Hawke kept up a continuous running commentary for his ears alone. Observations about the players, or other witticisms that had him chuckling.

At one point in the night, Daniel excused himself to use the men's retiring room—he wasn't fond of relieving himself behind a screen, as the other players seemed comfortable doing. On his return, he ran into Marwood.

"Must be a clever lad, that cousin of yours," his friend noted.

"Why do you say that?" Perhaps Marwood noticed Miss Hawke's skill at the tables.

"Because you've been laughing at his little asides all night."

Had he? "Wit runs in the family."

"If so," Marwood answered, "it skipped your branch entirely."

"Did you know that every male in my family took top pugilism honors at university?" Daniel asked.

"We fought each other at Cambridge, and, if I recall, it was a draw."

Daniel gave a slight tap of his knuckles to Marwood's stomach. "Perhaps time hasn't been kind to your skills in the ring."

"One way to test that," Marwood noted.

"Name the day and time," Daniel said good-naturedly. "Been a while since I've had a decent opponent."

"Why are you always threatening to hit things, cousin?" asked Miss Hawke, appearing beside him. She shook her head and gave a baleful glance toward Marwood. "A blight on the family honor, he is."

"Makes me look almost saintly by comparison," Marwood agreed.

Daniel raised his hands. "Let's not succumb to hyperbole, lads."

"Why not?" Miss Hawke replied. "You told me it's the only way to get women into bed."

Before Marwood could speak, Daniel pulled Miss Hawke away to another corner. Marwood drifted away with a laugh.

"I do believe you're trying to besmirch my rakish reputation," Daniel muttered.

"I wasn't aware you wanted to protect it," she answered innocently.

"Only from the calumny of journalists." He stopped to grab two goblets of wine from a passing server. After he took a drink, he said, "I'm still in debate as to whether or not having you accompany me is a mistake."

She smiled at him over the rim of her glass. "The best things in life often start out as mistakes."

"Have you made many of them?"

"No," she replied.

"Then how do you know whether or not good things come from mistakes?"

"I don't." She shrugged. "But it *sounded* good, didn't it?"

He chuckled, then realized he was doing it again. God, when was the last time he'd laughed so much? Certainly not at all, since Jonathan's vanishing.

"How did you learn to play so many games of chance?" he asked after taking another drink.

"I came up with writers, actors, artists. All of them loved to gamble. By the time I was eight, I could beat a veteran gamester. My mother, too, knew her way around a card table." Her expression darkened slightly.

He'd believed he was the one with secrets, but it turned out that Miss Hawke had plenty of her own. And he wanted to learn more about them.

"What—" he began.

"I thought I was the reporter," she said, cutting him off. "And here you're asking me all the questions. Let's get back to the action." She drained her glass and set it on a nearby table. Daniel had no choice but to follow suit.

They played at more games, with her energy never flagging. It had to be exhausting, pretending to be a different gender—yet she kept up the ruse, retaining all the lessons he'd taught her earlier. She jested with the other players, or else accepted their jibes with jocund grace.

There were no windows inside the main gaming hall, but given the number of blokes nodding off or passed out in the corners, it had to be morning. Daniel checked his pocket watch. Nearly six thirty. Where had the time gone? He had barely been aware of the hours passing.

It was Miss Hawke. She'd kept him consistently entertained and engaged throughout the night. Even when accompanying Marwood, he'd never enjoyed an evening at Donnegan's as much.

Was he so used to the endless nights of debauchery that his evenings had grown dull, or was she so extraordinary? He suspected the latter.

"Closing time, gentlemen," announced one of the dealers. Burly blokes began herding the crowd toward the door.

Ahead of this exodus, Daniel led Miss Hawke down the front hallway. They stepped out into the morning, both of them squinting in the light. Her borrowed suit was rumpled, and her thin mustache drooped as its adhesive loosened. Best to get her into the carriage before anyone took too close a look at her and realized the truth.

His coach pulled up moments before the rest of the crowd tumbled out of the gaming hell. Miss Hawke and her curved arse climbed into the carriage, and Daniel threw a wary glance over his shoulder. Hopefully, he was the only man who noticed her heart-shaped posterior beneath her trousers. Fortunate that most of the men exiting the club were either nearly asleep, drunk, or both.

Daniel clambered in, and the footman closed the door behind him.

"I'll have my coachman drop you at your lodgings," he said.

Yawning, she shook her head. "Can't have a 'man' entering my rooms. I'll need to return to the theater and change from Mr. Sinclair to Miss Hawke."

He, for one, would be glad to see her in a dress again. "The Imperial Theater," he called up to his driver.

In an instant, they were off, trundling down the streets as London began its morning routine.

"The day's just starting for them," Miss Hawke murmured, glancing out the window at the passing vendors, housemaids, and shopkeepers, all on their way to their labors. "Off to work." She shot him a sly look. "Suppose that's something you haven't much experience with."

Though she only teased, it stung. "I consult with my man of business, write letters to my estate managers. And yes, I do sit in parliamentary sessions. I might not be a navvy, digging trenches, but I do what I can." Even he could hear the defensiveness in his tone.

"You're right," she conceded. "We've each different roles to play in this world. I can't take you to task for doing exactly what you're supposed to." She pressed a hand to her chest and looked pious. "For example, I am tasked with providing moral guidance to my readers."

He smiled at her self-deprecation. "And did you get enough examples tonight of depravity to serve as object lesson to those readers?"

She cast her eyes heavenward. "Such depravity. It fair made my heart shrivel and my soul blanch to behold it."

"Was it as bad as that?" He stretched out his legs, and the side of his knee brushed against her lower thigh. A flash of heat traveled up his limbs. Whatever tiredness he might have been feeling vanished in an instant.

"Quite, quite bad," she said, grinning. "A bloke next to me lost a prized racehorse on one turn of the cards. Doubt his father will be much pleased with him."

Daniel shook his head. "The lad was an idiot, staking such an excellent beast on a hand that was clearly rotten. But then, brains aren't always guaranteed with a title."

"Does that include you, Ashford?" she quizzed.

"Well, it was me that approached you for these articles," he noted, "so clearly I don't possess much for a mental gearbox."

"Or maybe that was the smartest thing you've ever done."

It certainly was dangerous, especially if she ever learned his true motive. But he couldn't regret his choice. Not yet, at any rate. Though he'd have to tread lightly with her, for many reasons.

"That decision has yet to be tested," he said.

She smirked. "Guess you'll have to read tomorrow's edition."

"So soon?"

"Of course. Can't sit on this story for too long. Though," she added after yawning again, "I might need to drink a few cups of strong tea before I attempt to tackle such an epic yarn." She stretched, and he found himself hoping for a glimpse of her curves beneath her coat and waistcoat—despite the fact that she was bound tightly.

"How does a rake spend his morning after a night at a gaming hell?" she asked.

He rubbed at his jaw, feeling the stubble of his incipient beard. It always took a matter of hours before his whiskers defeated his shave. There had to have been some Viking blood in the Ashford line to explain his hairiness.

"Sometimes I have a light collation," he said. "A roll and some fruit. Sometimes I'll take a nightcap of whiskey in my study. I never have enough of a head to read the papers. So I'll watch the fire until I feel myself start to doze. Then my valet collects me, and I tumble into bed."

"Sounds . . . lovely," she said without a trace of irony. "A bit of quiet time just for yourself. I wouldn't mind something like that."

"I'm sure it could be arranged."

Yet she chuckled lowly. "Oh, my lord, when one runs a business, there's no room for dozing by the fire. Every hour of every day has to be in pursuit of the almighty pound. We work every day of the week. Only Sundays are days of rest."

"Exhausting," he said.

"But exhilarating, too." Her expression brightened. "I'm responsible to no one but myself. And it's my hard work that ensures that my employees get paid, that my paper gets read. Better that than be some husband's drudge, or worse—a decorative object." She shuddered.

He couldn't fault her reasoning. He wouldn't want either role for himself. Something else brewed within him at her words. She had such purpose, such determination. Things he lacked. What must it be like, to be so driven? He could feel the energy and resoluteness emanating from her like heat from a fire. A fire whose warmth he craved.

They neared the theater, and suddenly he was reluctant for the night to come to a close. What if he invited her to a coffee house? Or maybe . . . she'd be willing to have that drink of whiskey with him in his study. No. His home was his private sanctum. As for a coffee house, well, her disguise wasn't holding up very well after hours and hours. Better to just end the evening and stay protected.

Yet when the carriage neared the theater, disappointment shot through him, heavy like iron in his belly.

A curious thing happened when the coach stopped. Miss Hawke didn't immediately climb out. Instead, she sat there, her gaze shifting around, occasionally alighting on him. A delicate tension threaded through the compartment, thin but electric. He sensed it like a bright web covering his skin.

She started when he leaned forward.

He watched his hand reach out and peel off her mustache, then stroke the soft skin just above her top lip.

"I prefer you as a woman," he murmured.

"I prefer me as a woman, too," she said, her voice low.

This close, he saw the widening of her pupils, her slightly parted lips. She smelled of old wine and cheroot smoke, but the aroma combined with the scent of her skin. What might she taste like? Damn him if he didn't hunger to find out.

Half a second before he lost his mind, he regained his senses. The hell was he doing? She was a sodding *journalist*. They had a professional relationship, or rather, he was using her to further his own objectives. Getting involved with her in any capacity beyond these articles was utter madness.

He pulled back. She seemed to recollect herself at the same time, pressing into the squabs as if to put as much distance between them as possible.

"I'll . . ." His voice was gravel, and he cleared his throat. "I'll send word about the next night's activity."

"That sounds acceptable," she answered distractedly, her own tone suspiciously breathless. Jesus, did she *want* him to kiss her? Even worse. "I should . . . I'm going to . . ." Her hand hovered over the handle. "It's been . . ."

"Yes," he said.

They both jumped when the door to the carriage opened. The footman stood there, impassively waiting. Daniel couldn't tell if he was grateful for the servant's presence, or resentful.

"Good night," he finally said.

"Good morning," she answered. Then got down from the carriage. He watched her go, waiting to see if she looked back at him. But she didn't. When he finally got home, he let out one long exhale, but whether it was from relief or dissatisfaction at her absence, he didn't know.

Chapter 8

*One of the greatest pleasures in life, that cultivates
the greatest quality of mind, refinement, and
delicacy, is the nurturing of a written correspondence
with an individual of sensibility and taste.*

The Hawk's Eye, May 6, 1816

Quill in hand, Eleanor stared at the blank page in front of
her. Yet the words stubbornly refused to appear. She looked
at the nib of her writing implement, as if some kind of block-
age there prevented words from flowing out. But, no, it was
sharpened, clean, and ready. The impediment to writing was
her.

She sighed, set down her quill, and stretched her neck.
That ought to get her to focus. Yet when she picked up her
pen and dipped it in ink, the nib simply hovered over the
page, unmoving. A drop of ink dripped onto the page.

Growling to herself in exasperation, she blotted the paper.
Much as she'd like to crumple it and throw it to the floor,
paper was expensive, and she couldn't afford any waste.

She rubbed at her forehead. This article about several
young women of quality fainting at a zoology lecture wasn't
going to write itself. Yet every time she tried to put down
words, something kept blocking her.

Rather, some*one*. Ashford's face appeared again in her
mind—not his immaculate appearance at the beginning of

their evening together but his raffish, almost scruffy looks by the time the night drew to a close. Her hand had itched to test the feel of his dark stubble against her palm. Still did.

His voice, his laugh, echoed silently. The scent of soap and fine wool and tobacco curled in her memory. She couldn't forget the way his gaze had darkened when he'd finally removed her mustache and touched her top lip. His hand had been gloved, but she'd still felt his touch, her own fingers now brushing back and forth over her lip as if she could recapture the sensation.

There had been a moment in the carriage—a brief, charged moment—when she'd thought he'd kiss her. And she had wanted him to.

Groaning, Eleanor dug the heels of her palms into her closed eyes. She leaned back in her chair.

This was unacceptable. It had been three days since their night at Donnegan's. Three days, during which she'd written and published the first article. Despite the fact that sales of *The Hawk's Eye* were up and she ought to be strategically planning her next move to take advantage of the surge, she'd been preoccupied, restless. Unfocused.

Because of him. That damned rakish earl.

She would've thought writing the article about their misadventures might serve as catharsis, cleansing memories of him like an exorcism. Granted, the possession was by a particularly handsome, physically fit, and witty demon, but she didn't want him possessing her. She belonged to herself. Certainly not to one of her writing subjects. Definitely not to the blasted Earl of Ashford.

But she couldn't stop thinking about him. He was like . . . like an infestation. Yes, that's how she'd consider him. As if he were an annoying, but persistent, infestation of mealworms in her mental pantry. He wouldn't seem nearly as alluring if she thought of him spoiling her flour and wriggling around in her sugar.

Wriggling in my sugar.

Good God—that was a phrase that didn't help.

She shoved to her feet. Writing was simply impossible right now. She'd have to distract herself some other way. Leaving her private office, she walked out into the main room. Writers were bent over their desks, furiously scribbling. A flare of irritation welled. Clearly, none of her staff were haunted by the specter of the earl. *They* didn't wonder what he was doing at that very moment. If he dined with friends or was alone again at the Eagle. If he'd enjoyed her article.

In fact, there had been no communication between them in three days. Another wave of annoyance swelled. Would it have killed him to send her a little note? A *Thank you for our night*? Or, *Jolly good work on the piece*? Perhaps even, *You owe me a hundred pounds*?

Though, technically, he'd staked her, and if Donnegan's had sent payment, they'd likely delivered it to Ashford's residence. Even so, he might have had the graciousness to needle her about it, or her gambling skills. Or *something*.

"Anything you need, Miss Hawke?" asked Delia Everhart, one of *The Hawk's Eye* writers.

Eleanor realized she'd been standing in the middle of the writers' room, simply staring off into nothing as her mind churned.

How ruddy galling.

"How is the article about the noblewoman and the Chinese acrobat coming?" she improvised.

"Oh, you know," Delia said with a smile, "tumbling along."

Shaking her head, Eleanor moved on down the row of desks and inquired with each staff member on the progress of their work. Unlike her, everyone at the paper was alert and productive. By the time she spoke with her printers on the status of the latest issue, thirty minutes had passed, but inspiration still hadn't struck. She was going to have to drag herself back to her desk, chain herself there, and make herself work.

If only writing about ladies reacting to a discussion of monkeys' mating habits was half as inspiring as writing about the earl.

" 'Scuse me?" a voice said behind her.

She turned and faced a man in livery. Livery she recognized.

"Yes?" she asked.

The bewigged servant bowed and held out an envelope. Her name was scrawled across the outside, and, when she turned it over, she knew the insignia pressed into the wax. The Earl of Ashford's crest of a hawk holding a sword in its talons.

She took the letter from the footman and handed him a coin. The servant bowed again but didn't leave.

"Are you to wait on a reply?" she asked him.

"Yes, ma'am."

"Give me a moment," she said and strode to her office. Seating herself at her desk, she cut open the letter and began to read.

Meet me in the stables of my home in two days hence, at midnight. Mr. Sinclair's presence will not be required, but you in the clothing of a woman of questionable reputation is.

Yrs, &c.

—A.

The unmitigated cheek of that man! Not a single *please* or *if you'd be so kind* anywhere to be found in his laconic, imperious, dreadful little note. A note that nevertheless made her smile.

She was going to see him again—and her heart beat double time at the prospect. Ah, damn. She oughtn't be so excited by the idea of being near him once more. The article had helped sales considerably, and she needed to build on *that*.

Professional, Hawke, she reminded herself. *Stay on your side of the desk.*

Except she couldn't. Not when she planned on spending

another evening with him doing . . . well . . . she had no idea
what she'd be doing, but whatever it was, it required particular garments. How very intriguing.

Yet she said none of this in her reply. Pulling out a sheet
of foolscap, she wrote:

*Mr. Sinclair is grateful his presence isn't required.
Define "questionable reputation."*

—E.H.

Sanding then folding her response, she marched it out
to the waiting footman. He took her note, gave her yet one
more bow, then left.

She returned to her office to labor over her article. It was
not unlike trudging through frozen treacle in nothing but her
stockings, carrying a hippopotamus on her back. This agony
went on for an hour before she was interrupted by a knock
at her door.

Glancing up, she beheld the footman standing there. He
strode forward and handed her a scrap of paper. There again
was the earl's crest on the back.

She opened the letter.

*Questionable reputation: of dubious character, disso-
lute, louche. Really, E.H., for a writer, you display a
shocking lack of vocabulary.*

—A.

Her response:

For a toff, you display a shocking lack of manners.

—E.H.

Half an hour went by before another letter appeared, the
footman looking slightly more aggrieved than last time.

Dress like a tart. How's that for manners?

                    —A.

Precisely what I'd expect from you.

                    —E.H.

I live to gratify you.

                    —A.

Excellent.

    —E.H.

*P.S. This communication must cease unless you want
your footman and coachman to mutiny.*

She was disappointed when there were no further letters
from him, even though he'd heeded her advice. Carefully,
she tucked his correspondence into a compartment in her
desk and locked it.

So, in two days she was to dress like a tart and meet him
at his stables. Obviously, he intended her to obey his sum-
mons. She could make a point of not going, but that was
simply obstinacy for its own sake. The whole point of her
association with him was to come with him on his nightly
romps and grow the circulation of her newspaper.

She smiled to herself. He wanted her to dress like a tart,
hm? Well, that might be his command, but she'd obey it on
her terms.

Sitting in his favorite chair at White's, Daniel read again
Miss Hawke's account of their night's escapades. He pressed

his lips together tightly to keep from laughing aloud at her description of donning her masculine costume, then he sobered as she reflected on the differences between men and women's societal roles.

He skimmed over the parts that discussed him. He was a subject of which he was heartily tired, and even Miss Hawke's talented quill couldn't make him interesting to himself. But this was the fourth time he'd read the article again—not out of a fascination with himself but with her. Her ability. The quality of her writing. The quality of her incisive mind, which shone like a beacon through her work.

The first time he'd read the article, he'd done so with a healthy dose of wariness. What, exactly, would she say about him? And how might she say it? He had perused *The Hawk's Eye* before, but not knowing which writing was hers. Now he had a sample, and damn him if he wasn't impressed.

To begin with, she didn't portray him as a complete and utter human disaster, a walking cautionary tale of too much power, too much money, and too much time. Though she hadn't pulled her punches, either.

> *Lord Rakewell's wit cannot be disputed, nor his intelligence. Though this humble writer has to wonder what he might accomplish should he apply his considerable mind to concerns more weighty than the turn of an actress's ankle, or the next card in the deal. Indeed, were he to harness his not insignificant mental ability to a higher purpose, we might all benefit. For now, however, the only benefactor of his brain is himself, and even then, his fields lie mostly fallow.*

It surprised him how much her words had stung, though they weren't as sharply skewering as he imagined she might be able to write. She also wrote them knowing that he would inevitably read the article, which might explain why she wasn't as cruel to him as she might have been. Not to spare his feelings but to ensure that he'd continue to allow her to come with him at night. A cunning creature, this Miss Hawke. Perhaps she ought to have been named Miss Fox.

But what kept him reading was the actual caliber of the work and her often perceptive observations, which awakened him to new insight about the human condition and Society in general. He almost regretted that *The Hawk's Eye* didn't strive to be more than a scandal sheet. Surely she could write for a truly distinguished newspaper, like the *Times*?

Maybe the *Times* wasn't especially open-minded when it came to the gender of their writers. Perhaps Miss Hawke had turned to her scandal sheet because that was the only forum she had available to her. If so, it was a ruddy shame. The *Times* doubtless had a wider circulation than *The Hawk's Eye,* which meant fewer people read Miss Hawke's work.

But maybe not. Glancing over the top of his paper, he saw several members of the club reading *The Hawk's Eye* and chuckling to themselves. None of them suspected he was Lord Rakewell, which suited him fine.

If only Jonathan were here. He'd laugh at the article about Daniel, and be soberly contemplative when it came to Miss Hawke's thoughts about the differences between the sexes. An introspective man, Jonathan could be. If only he'd decided to pursue the life of a Cambridge don instead of the military—everything would be different.

Daniel returned to the newspaper he held. His exchange of letters with Miss Hawke earlier today was the first time since that night that they'd had any communication. And that had been by his decision. He'd needed distance from the woman, especially after he'd come so damned close to kissing her.

But many times over the past few days, he'd found himself thinking of things she might find particularly interesting or amusing, and wanting to tell her about them. Either by letter or, preferably, in person. And all of those impulses needed to be extinguished. He had to remember what purpose she served to him, and the dangers of getting too close to her. She saw too much already.

Yet that didn't stop him from recalling the shape of her legs beneath her trousers or the husky timbre of her voice when she laughed. That didn't stop him from dreaming of her, where her masculine attire magically dissolved, revealing the woman's body beneath.

A voice spoke close by, startling him from his reverie. "Rather nice bit of exposition, don't you think? I particularly enjoyed how she described Lord Broodington as 'one of the wildest men in the whole of the city. Lord preserve any virtue that stands between him and his desires.'"

Marwood stood beside Daniel's chair. Unsurprisingly, he, too, carried the issue of Miss Hawke's paper.

"Interesting article," he continued. "I wonder if anyone knows that you're Lord Rakewell."

"Keep your voice to a dull roar, if you please," Daniel snapped.

"And there is no Cousin Ned," Marwood said.

Daniel glanced around to ensure no one was listening. "If there is, it would be a great shock to my aunt and uncle."

"Why?"

"Because their sons are named Jasper, Edmund, and William," answered Daniel.

Marwood shook his head. "Why would you allow a journalist into your life?" he pressed.

It was impossible for Daniel to tell even Marwood the truth, though they were friends. "Maybe our continual round of debauchery has led to ennui," he said instead. "Maybe it seemed entertaining."

But Marwood frowned. "I suspect an ulterior motive."

"You've known me almost my whole life, Marwood," Daniel said. "Have you ever observed me engaged in anything that doesn't give me some gratification or profit? Even just a momentary amusement."

"It's precisely because I know you that I'm wary." He pointed a finger at Daniel. "You're up to something, and if you won't tell me what, I might just have to seek out the answer myself."

Panic iced along the back of Daniel's neck. As much as Marwood was a dissolute rake, like Daniel himself, his marks at university had been excellent, and he possessed a keen and discerning intellect, for all his mad carousing. Though distracting Miss Hawke was Daniel's main intent, if Marwood also looked too deeply into Daniel's true activities, it could be disastrous. The man could not hold a secret for long. He'd tell someone, and that someone would tell someone, and soon Society would be like a pack of vultures pulling apart the sprawled body of Jonathan's family's reputation.

"As you like." He waved his hand in bored disinterest. "Chase after dust motes, if it amuses you."

Marwood stared at him for a moment before shaking his head. "Shall I see you at the theater tonight? There's a new play by the mysterious Mrs. Delamere, and she's often quite diverting."

"Perhaps I'll see the first few acts," Daniel answered, "but I've other entertainments scheduled for later tonight."

"Something with your female scribbler, perhaps?" His friend lifted a brow.

Daniel picked up his paper. "Have a dreadful afternoon, Marwood."

"Have an excruciating day, Ashford." With that, the other man strode off, whistling a tune from the latest theatrical sensation. A devotee of the theater, was Marwood. He hadn't missed a single burletta by the enigmatic Mrs. Delamere since first her subversive work began appearing on the stage.

Once Marwood was gone, Daniel laid the paper on his lap and gazed abstractedly into space. He ought to have considered that someone in his social circle would deduce he was Lord Rakewell, and thus question why he'd permit the liberty of a journalist acting as his shadow. But most of them would be satisfied with the same explanation he'd given Marwood. It was just his damn bad luck that Marwood could puzzle things out so well.

He'd have to worry about Marwood later. Right now, he had an appointment to keep.

A footman had his carriage ready and waiting as he strode from the club. He called up the direction to the driver, and they were off. He needed to get his mind focused. Stop his thoughts of Miss Hawke. Block out his concern over Marwood's suspicion. But both were difficult as the coach drove on toward Mayfair.

It stopped outside a town house on Dorset Square. He alit and mounted the stairs leading to the front door. Before he could even knock, the door opened, and a somber butler greeted him.

"Miss Lawson awaits you in the Green Salon, my lord," the butler intoned.

After handing over his hat and walking stick, Daniel went down the hallway. No one needed to show him the way, and he was as good as a member of the family, anyhow. Though the home was furnished in the latest style, and everything was scrupulously clean, tension and heaviness lay over the enameled clocks and Gainsboroughs, as if the family's worry and despair had its own barometric pressure, weighing down everything within the house. He pushed through it as he walked, and felt it trying to drag down his own shoulders. The responsibility had fallen to him, and he was the only way to get this home—and its inhabitants—to its former condition. He was the key.

He stopped outside the doors to the Green Salon, and, after knocking and receiving permission to enter, went inside.

A young blonde girl in mourning black sat upon the striped sofa, her hands knotted in her lap. Catherine Lawson was pale in the afternoon light, but then, these past weeks had slowly leeched the color from her cheeks, as if loss and fear had bled the life out of her. Now she looked ashen, and far older than a girl of seventeen ought to appear.

She didn't speak when he entered, only nodded when he bowed.

They always had their meeting in the Green Salon, since it was at the back of the house, and sheltered from the other rooms. As if what they discussed couldn't be heard or borne anywhere else.

She waved him toward the chair opposite the sofa, and he sat. Silently, she offered him a cup of tea from the tray set up on the small table, but he held up a hand, declining the beverage.

Finally, she spoke. "Any sign of him?"

Regretfully, he shook his head. "He wasn't at Donnegan's."

Her fingers unknotted, and she rubbed wearily at her eyes. "That's one of the most infamous gaming hells of London. Surely he had to be there."

"What can I say? I looked for Jonathan, but he wasn't anywhere to be found."

"Perhaps . . ." She gulped. "Perhaps he was upstairs with . . . with one of those women."

"I was there all night, my dear." He tried to make his voice as gentle as possible. "There wasn't a sign of your brother."

Abruptly, she stood and walked to a demilune table. A newspaper lay folded across the top of the table, and he had a sudden feeling he knew exactly which paper it was.

"You might have been too busy to notice," she said tartly, picking up the newspaper, "keeping company with that female journalist."

Ah, he expected this would be coming. "I'm capable of doing several tasks at once. Believe me, I might have been using Miss Hawke as a diversionary tactic, but that didn't stop me in my search."

Her shoulders sagged. "Forgive me, Ashford."

He resisted the impulse to go to her and pull her into a fraternal embrace. Catherine might be young, and alone, but she was proud, too. She'd only push him away. It was already difficult enough for her to reach out to him for assistance.

Instead, he poured a cup of tea and walked it to her. She took it, but her hands shook as she sipped at her beverage. She set the cup aside, stood, and looked up at him, her blue eyes so very much like Jonathan's it was eerie. And now her eyes bore the same shadows that her brother's held, but for very different reasons.

"I read an article in the scandal sheet," she said. "About a certain Lord Rakewell. I couldn't help thinking of the similarities between him and you."

"You were always a clever girl," he said.

"But why would you invite such scrutiny?"

"Because of you and Jonathan," he answered. "To throw the scent off our search for him. I assumed that with the attention on me and my supposedly rakish ways, the journalist wouldn't have a chance to learn what you and I were doing."

Catherine bowed her head. "Thank you. Whenever I think your kindness must reach a limit, you prove me wrong and are kinder still."

"You deserve kindness," he answered softly. "You and Jonathan, both."

Her mouth twisted. "The world hasn't been so benevolent toward him."

He carefully set a hand on her shoulder, and it was a measure of her worry and weariness that she didn't shake it off. "It's been my sad experience that those who deserve mercy the most are the ones who are often denied it."

"Whoever is in charge of making the rules is sorely in need of instruction," she said bitterly. "I thought that men who served their country in war would return home to glory and peace. But that hasn't been the circumstance with my poor brother."

"No, I'm afraid it hasn't."

"So dashed unfair," she said, tears choking her voice.

Unfair was a terrible understatement. At school, Jonathan always took the less popular boys under his wing and kept them from being tormented by bullies. But, unlike Daniel, Jonathan was a younger son, and had to make his way in the world. The commission in the army had been purchased for him. Jonathan had been proud of his bright, gleaming uniform, and he'd made an excellent peacetime commander, beloved by his men. But war had broken out, and Jonathan had gone abroad to fight.

Thankfully, he'd survived. And with all his limbs intact, unlike other veterans. But his scars were invisible. Daniel had thought he and Jonathan would resume their friendship where it had left off. In that, Daniel had been proven very wrong. Jonathan had been inattentive, his concentration and memory limited, and his sentences would trail off, unfinished. He'd lose his temper easily, too. At first, he'd just snap an angry retort, but then things had gotten worse. Throwing things. Punching walls. And then laughing wildly as blood had run down his hand.

No one had known what to do. Least of all Jonathan's elder brother and parents. They'd insisted he was fine, just needed a little time to get back into the pattern of civilian life. Even Daniel had believed that what Jonathan needed was time. But the same kind, amicable man was gone, replaced by a mercurial, angry stranger.

A stranger that began to prefer a rougher, seedier crowd.

Jonathan stopped attending assemblies. He didn't go to any of the Season's sanctioned events. He didn't come to White's or any other club, never went to the theater or the races. He took up with a band of miscreants, men who weren't just disreputable but downright criminal. As the second son to a ducal title, such actions were beyond scandalous and bordered on the disgraceful.

And then, he disappeared.

A wave of self-recrimination flooded Daniel as he stared at the top of Catherine's head. He should have done something sooner. Tried harder to reach out to Jonathan. But it had been so unpleasant being in his company, so frightening, that when Jonathan had stopped talking to him, he'd let his old friend go, missing their friendship but telling himself that Jonathan was a grown man who could make his own decisions. But that had been simple indolence on Daniel's part. The hard truth was that Jonathan had needed help, and Daniel hadn't given it.

No one had. Except Catherine. But she was just a girl, and couldn't hold back the flood of her brother's demons.

It was a bitter measure of Daniel's self-absorption that he hadn't realized Jonathan had vanished until the news had come down that the heir to the Duke of Holcombe had died of fever.

Daniel had attended the funeral. And Jonathan had been absent from the ceremony. That in itself had caused a small tempest of scandal. Perhaps, Daniel had reasoned, Jonathan had been traveling and was at that moment making his way to join his family in their hour of grief. And accept his new role as heir.

Yet the night of the funeral, Catherine had appeared on his doorstep in the small hours of the morning, her face soaked in tears. She'd pleaded with him for assistance. She'd had nowhere to turn.

He'd given her a brandy, sat her down by the fire. It had taken some time, but eventually he'd learned the truth. And it wasn't a pretty truth. Because it revealed just how much he'd failed his friend.

"It's been nearly a month," Catherine said now, turning away. "And not once has my brother written me. I caught a glimpse of him once, outside Drury Lane, and he was so changed, I almost thought I was looking at a stranger."

"You're certain it was Jonathan?" Daniel pressed.

She twisted her hands together and nodded. "You understand how close we are. *Were*," she corrected herself. "I know him. I doubt anyone else would, though."

He stared bleakly out the window at the garden in the back. The spring had been a cold one, and summer seemed even more shy in making an appearance. The normally bountiful plant life that Catherine spent so much time cultivating was all but bare twigs and brown grass now. Hard not to see that as a reflection of the fruitlessness of Daniel's current search.

"Damn," he cursed softly to himself. He hated this feeling of powerlessness. He'd failed Jonathan before, and now he had to *do* something to make everything right.

Going public or to the authorities regarding Jonathan's disappearance was impossible. The disgrace could ruin the entire family, especially Jonathan and Catherine.

Daniel had been combing the city, with and without her, in search of Jonathan. Everything until now had been fruitless, but it was only when he began to read about himself in *The Hawk's Eye* that he realized how precarious the situation truly was. If someone like Miss Hawke caught wind of what fate had befallen Jonathan—Daniel shuddered to think of the consequences. Catherine would be completely unmarriageable, her life over before it had begun. And Jonathan . . . Jonathan would be lost entirely. Even his title couldn't shelter him from that kind of scandal.

But Daniel's rakish reputation had its uses. No one questioned his presence in the less respectable parts of town, making him the perfect vehicle for the hunt. He didn't care if it hurt his own reputation. Like Miss Hawke, he had none to speak of, and even so, his gender and title sheltered him from the worst of the harm.

"And now you're consorting with *reporters*." She shuddered. "I thought the company we encountered along the docks was low."

"Miss Hawke isn't as bad as that," he heard himself say, then cursed his incautious tongue.

Catherine's expression sharpened. " 'Miss Hawke,' is it?" She stepped closer, some of the darkness sifting away as the eternal pleasure of gossip lured her. "Tell me about this woman. The one who wore male clothing and was so very, very bold."

"Nothing to tell," he demurred. "I needed to divert the attention of the press, and she was eager for a story. *Finis*."

He wouldn't say how his thoughts kept drifting back to Miss Hawke, how he eagerly anticipated their next encounter, the way a growing fascination with her threaded through him. If Catherine searched his jacket right now, she'd find Miss Hawke's notes tucked into the inside pocket. Over where his heart beat.

"Can you trust her?" Catherine asked.

"No. But I don't plan on trusting her."

Dealing with Miss Hawke was dangerous.

And she was dangerous to Daniel, too. He was becoming far too interested in her—and after just two encounters. If he spent more time in her presence, he might truly be in trouble.

But approaching her had been his idea in the first place. All he needed to do was keep his wits.

"Have a caution with this Miss Hawke, Ashford," Catherine said, as if reading his thoughts. "From her writing, she seems very perceptive."

"She is," he said, "but I can play the game, Catherine. Even better than you," he added with a teasing smile. "After all, I've been at this much longer than you. I'm an old, old man." Fifteen years older than her, in fact.

"Even old men make mistakes," she countered. "Think of poor King Lear."

"I can always count on you to speak the truth, like Fool or Cordelia." He checked the clock on the mantel. "The hour grows apace, and I've a few leads to track down."

"I'll fetch my cloak." She started for the door.

But he stopped her with a gentle hand on her arm. "These places are too perilous for you, even in my company. If I hear or see anything, I'll report back before approaching him." The likelihood was that Jonathan would bolt if Daniel attempted to reach out to him without Catherine's presence.

"Be careful," she urged him again.

He gave her what he hoped was a reassuring grin. "Always."

Leaning up on her toes, she pressed a kiss to his cheek. "It's really too bad you are so old." She sighed. "I could easily see myself falling in love with you."

If their age difference prevented her from forming a romantic attachment, then he was grateful for it. A sweet, gentle girl like Catherine wasn't for him. But what sort of woman *did* suit him, he'd no idea.

As Daniel collected his hat and walking stick from the butler, he remembered Miss Hawke's laugh, her sly hazel eyes. An entirely unsuitable woman. Yet one he couldn't stop thinking about.

His destinations tonight were dangerous, but perhaps none of them held the peril Miss Hawke did.

He'd see her in two days. He couldn't wait. And that, more than anything, alarmed him.

Chapter 9

London after dark presents its own unique sets of dangers—yet the enticements of the city at night are often too alluring to resist.

The Hawk's Eye, May 8, 1816

Pulling her hood up and her cloak tightly around her, Eleanor hurried through the darkened streets of Mayfair. As she passed St. George's, the tolling bell gave her fifteen minutes until midnight. Though Ashford's home was less than a quarter of a mile away, the distance easily manageable, she didn't want to be late. Then she chided herself for her extreme punctuality. It wasn't as though the earl would simply leave without her to . . . wherever it was he was going. He needed her to come with him. That was the whole point of this enterprise: writing articles about his nightly escapades.

And that's all, she reminded herself. It was all about the newspaper. And whatever motive compelled Ashford to have made the proposition in the first place.

She still hadn't deduced what that might be, and while she burned to know more, pushing too hard might cause him to pull back. Given how well *The Hawk's Eye* was selling now on the strength of the first *To Ride with a Rake* piece, she'd be a dunderhead to lose this opportunity.

But the articles weren't all that compelled her to walk

a little faster, her heart to pound a little harder. Certainly not him. Or his damned notes, which she foolishly read and reread over the course of the last two days. Until she'd memorized them.

As she hurried on, she avoided streetlights, clinging to the shadows that fronted the palatial homes of Mayfair and Marylebone. A woman on her own at this hour was obviously commercial, and as she'd rather not use the knife in her boot on anyone making unwanted advances, it was best to simply prevent being accosted in the first place.

But her strategy didn't quite work.

"Where you going, pretty thing?" a sauced gentleman tottering home slurred.

She knew better than to answer, so she kept silent.

"Oi, proud little tart. Too good for me?" He grabbed her as she passed.

With one neat move, she took hold of his wrist and held him tight as her knee made a forceful acquaintance with his groin. She dropped his wrist as he crumpled to the pavement, groaning. Without looking back, she walked on.

It shook her a little bit to be accosted. Yet she'd protected herself. Fear was something that could be conquered.

What a flaw of nature's design, that men should walk around with their greatest weakness just dangling between their legs. Those bollocks Ashford and his compatriots were so obsessed by were simply bothersome. She'd have to allude to that flaw in her next article.

Thinking of writing calmed her somewhat, and she continued on.

She reached Manchester Square and stopped, agog. Her lingering distress gave way to amazement. Ashford's home was here, in the heart of wealth and privilege. Finding the specific address, she stared up at the column-lined front, towering three stories high. Good Lord, he was just one man, with no close living relatives, and yet he had this . . . mansion . . . all to himself. Her own room would fit inside his dining chamber, she'd wager. Looking up at the edifice, it struck her again how vast the difference was between them, in almost every way.

Yet, despite the huge chasm of gender and class that divided them, she couldn't wait another moment to spend time in his company.

So, swallowing uncharacteristic nerves, she made her way around to the mews, then hastened along them until she reached the stable yard. No shared coach for him. The stables housed half a dozen sleek horses with better pedigrees than most people of Eleanor's acquaintance.

"Right this way, miss."

Eleanor jumped as a young stable lad appeared beside her, waving her forward. Trying to regain her composure, she gave him a slight nod, and walked on toward the stables. So, she was expected. She wondered what Ashford told the staff. *I'll be expecting a woman dressed like a trollop at midnight. Show her to the horses.*

Therein lay the privilege of rank. One could make commands like that without anyone questioning the why and wherefore of the demand.

She went into the structure—a grand brick building with arched doorways that led out the yard. Torches burned on the walls. And while the stables themselves were architectural wonders, what truly caught her attention and caused her to gasp out loud was Ashford, and the vehicle he stood beside.

"Good God," she breathed. "I've never seen one like it."

"I should hope not," he said. "Had it custom made."

Of course he had. Only an earl, and a rake, would have such a vehicle. The high-perch phaeton was a work of art, so tall, open, and beautifully constructed that it nearly brought tears to her eyes. The wood of its carriage was polished to a satiny sheen, and the slim brass fittings seemed to glow in the torchlight. Its seat rose up high, most likely giving the driver and lone passenger the feeling of flying. Compared to this phaeton, all other wheeled conveyances might as well be lumbering, awkward behemoths that trundled down the street with all the grace of a drunken whale.

Two stunning matched bays snorted and stamped impatiently in their tack, eager for movement. In his black coat, wine-colored waistcoat, snowy white breeches, and tall, gleaming boots, Ashford looked as gorgeous and sleek as the animals.

Her heart set up a knocking rhythm at the sight of him. Combined with the phaeton he stood beside, she'd never seen a more lethal combination.

He eyed her cloak critically. It hid her entire body, and with her hood up, she was completely covered except for her face. She knew what he was thinking. He'd asked her to dress like a trollop, and here she looked like an escapee from a convent.

Well, she was only a writer, but she wasn't above a little bit of theater. She flipped the sides of her cloak over her shoulders and tossed her head so the hood fell back. Revealing herself.

Oh, but the look on his face was something she'd treasure until her dying day. If she accomplished nothing else in her life, making the Earl of Ashford goggle like a schoolboy was worth engraving on her tombstone. *Here lies Eleanor Anne Hawke. She made a Rake of the first water gape.*

"That dress . . ." he managed to rasp.

"Courtesy of the Imperial Theater again," she said, "though I requested they make a few modifications. Mr. Swindon, the costume designer, was very accommodating."

Ashford's directions to her might have been to attire herself like a woman of impure virtue, but there were many ways a woman could ensnare a man's interest. The obvious choice would have been to wear a low-cut gown of lightweight, sheer fabric. But that would have been unoriginal. Instead, Eleanor wore a dress that could be considered severely plain, its neckline high and sleeves long. Rather like a day dress for visiting relatives.

Except Eleanor's gown was made of crimson silk. Shiny, tight satin. With the torchlight playing across the fabric, she knew that while the cut of the dress was modest, it showed off her every curve. Each time she shifted, the satin clung and blatantly hinted at her figure.

It was also the sort of gown one couldn't wear bulky undergarments beneath. Making anyone wonder whether she wore any underthings at all.

Not the sort of thing a virtuous woman might wear. Even if said woman was a journalist. If anyone from *The Hawk's Eye* saw her in this ensemble, they might expire of shock.

She was glad she wasn't going to cross paths with any of her employees tonight.

Just in case, and to further disguise herself, she wore a black wig, styled by Madame Hortense into sensuous, tumbledown curls that suggested rising shortly from bed. The good makeup artist had also powdered Eleanor's face, rouged her cheeks and lips, and applied a beauty spot just to the left side of Eleanor's mouth.

"You look like the world's most expensive tart," Maggie had said, looking at her in the dressing room mirror. "Mind, you look worth the cost."

"Thank you," Eleanor had answered.

And she gave thanks again, seeing the expression on Ashford's face now. She'd been worried that, after their last adventure, he'd think of her more as "Ned" or some kind of epicene cross between man and woman. But there was no risk of that anymore. Especially the way Ashford's gaze kept lingering on her hips and breasts.

"This will suffice?" she asked, knowing full well that it did.

Still staring at her body, Ashford could only nod mutely.

"I haven't much eye for style," she continued, "but I felt that it would be trite to wear something scanty. It seems better to suggest rather than reveal, don't you agree?"

"Right," he said dazedly, seemingly fascinated by her chest.

"The funny thing about a woman's eyes," she went on cheerfully, "is they're located not on her bosom but on her face. Though most men might think otherwise. Good thing you aren't an anatomist."

At last, he tore his gaze away from her breasts and up to her. "The hell did you expect?" he demanded. "You show up in a dress like that and suppose I'll stare deeply into your eyes?"

"Ah, so it's *my* responsibility to control your response?" She *tsk*ed. "How very sad, that you're so weak of will, you require someone else to regulate your actions."

"Don't sound so smug," he grumbled. "It's a damn provocative dress and you know it."

"Maybe so," she relented. "But why are you so angry about it? I did follow your instructions, didn't I?"

"You did," he grudgingly allowed. But as to the source of his anger, he didn't say.

Eleanor didn't question it. She simply enjoyed having a little of the power in her hands, for a change.

"So, I'm dressed like a tart," she said, "and you've got the world's fastest vehicle. Dare I guess at what our evening's plans are to be?"

His ill humor faded slightly, and he gave her a secretive smile. "Get in, and find out. I only hope that wig of yours is pinned on securely."

With that enigmatic comment, he climbed into the driver's seat, giving her a chance to do some ogling of her own. White breeches made for excellent informers, and they told her that the earl had a most excellent, tight backside. A sportsman, this bloke. With all the right muscles to prove it.

If he could mount a phaeton with such strapping grace, what else might he be able to mount?

She didn't need rouge to tint her cheeks red. The images that floated through her mind did so all on their own.

He reached down to help her up. The image of temptation itself.

"Why do I feel like Persephone being offered a lift by Hades?" she wondered.

"You're dressed more like Aphrodite." His gloved hand engulfed hers, and he easily lifted her up. "I suppose that makes me Adonis."

"Modest." She laughed, settling in beside him. There

wasn't much room on the seat, so their legs pressed close. Warmth from his body seeped into hers. She resisted pulling her cloak shut to serve as a protective barrier. That would reveal how much he affected her, and she couldn't allow that. "Perhaps you're ugly old Hephaestus."

"But ugly old Hephaestus knew how to use his hammer." He picked up the ribbons and gave them a snap.

He kept the bays tightly reined. The horses maintained a sedate pace as they trotted out into the stable yard and then through the mews, until they were finally on the street.

Though the animals moved at a tame speed, riding in the tall, beautifully sprung phaeton did indeed feel like flying. Eleanor soared above the street. She'd never been so high up before. And while part of her wanted to cling to the sides of the carriage in terror of falling off, she mostly reveled in the sensation, as though her many dreams of flight had finally come true.

They drove in silence through the darkened city. Occasional pedestrians stopped and stared at the phaeton as it rolled by, and she couldn't blame them. It was like seeing a mythical creature prancing down Oxford Street, trailing rainbows and magic in its path.

"What an expensive toy," she murmured, stroking the leather of the seat.

"What's the point of a toy," he answered, "if it isn't costly?"

"A stick and a hoop don't cost much."

"Sticks and hoops are for boys," he said. "I'm a man."

As though she needed reminding. There was something very primal and intoxicating about seeing a man drive a carriage, and drive it well. As though he had perfect mastery of everything. And while she didn't care for domineering men, Ashford drove easily, skillfully, without an ounce of braggadocio or pretension—and it set off a curl of heat low in her belly. One could extrapolate such skill into other arenas. Blast her for thinking so metaphorically. A hazard of her profession.

"Where are we going?" she asked. "Another gambling hell?"

He shook his head. "Wouldn't be very interesting for your readers if we repeated something."

"Vauxhall?"

He feigned a yawn. "That place is dull as a sermon."

She didn't think so, with all its music, lights, dancing, pavilions, and plenty of darkened pathways to shelter dalliances—but a rake might have wearied of such pleasures.

"The theater?"

"The last performance tonight ended half an hour ago."

What kind of place was he taking her? Somewhere that required her scandalous ensemble. Somewhere he'd want one of the most expensive, status-worthy vehicles available—so people would be looking at them.

"An orgy?"

He gave a choked laugh. "There's getting up close and personal in your articles, and then there's *too* personal. I've no desire to have your readers follow my *every* move. Unless," he glanced at her, one eyebrow raised, "you *want* to go to an orgy."

"Of course not," she said immediately.

"Prudish, Miss Hawke?"

"I'm not a virgin," she heard herself answer. "I know what goes on between men and women. I've experienced it myself."

"And you found it unpleasant."

She couldn't believe she was having this conversation, and with *him,* of all people. Her sexual history wasn't precisely a topic she felt utterly free to discuss without restraint. Though she'd grown up in an unconventional way, people of her acquaintance didn't exchange stories of their sexual peccadillos like recommendations for pie shops—her especially. She'd much rather listen than reveal things about herself.

But something about him pushed her, challenged her. To be a little more bold, a touch more daring. Maybe she was taking in his rakish ways through osmosis. Or maybe there was something about *this* man that urged her to greater and greater daring, as though testing the limits of her own strength.

"If we're being candid," she said primly, "my encounters of the amorous variety have been quite . . . pleasant." He didn't need to know about what a complete and utter disaster her first time was, but that's what she got for sleeping with another virgin—a young writer fresh from the country who spent considerable time asking, "Am I doing this right?" With the answer being a resounding, "No."

But that had been her first time. Since then, Eleanor had had a grand total of three other men to her bed. An actor, another writer, and a very charming naval lieutenant. The fact that she'd no intention of getting married had spurred her on in pursuit of lovers. Why should she deny herself this essential component of life simply because she didn't want a husband? Naturally, though, she'd taken precautions. Maggie knew a wide variety of techniques for preventing things like babies and disease—one of the benefits of working in the theater, Eleanor supposed.

"Pleasant isn't enough," Ashford said. "You should aim higher. Try for transcendence, magnificence. Life-altering."

She slanted a skeptical gaze toward him. "Rather tall boasts."

"There's no point in boasting," he answered. "I only speak in truths."

She shook her head. The man was dreadfully delusional. Or . . . going to bed with him really would be as exceptional as he claimed.

Given the way he drove this phaeton, he was either compensating, or he was a truly gifted lover.

Another wave of heat washed through her.

"Regardless," she said, trying to turn the topic away from a naked Ashford, "while I have no qualms about the sexual act itself, it always seemed to me that an orgy would be awfully . . . sticky."

"They are," he replied. "And they have a peculiar smell. They're seldom as entertaining as one might hope."

Oh, dear. So he'd been to an orgy or two in his time. Naturally, her paper had reported back on some of the wilder Society gatherings, though nothing quite as outrageous and dissipated as an orgy.

Was there no experience he hadn't had? And why did she have such a damn good imagination that she could picture him clearly in a tangle of limbs, doing things she'd only seen in wicked illustrations sold in the back rooms of print shops?

"So, no orgy then," she said.

"No orgy."

She'd never used or heard the word *orgy* so much in her life. "Then where?"

"Here," he said, pulling the phaeton to a stop at the eastern edge of Hyde Park. Gathered on the grass were about half a dozen other high-flyers, all driven by young bucks. Some of them had women of doubtful morality beside them. A few were on their own. But as the vehicles were parked on the lawn, more people milled around—young men and fast-living women, all of them drinking champagne, admiring the vehicles, and . . . waving around stacks of money. As though they were placing bets. But on what?

"Welcome," he said, "to your first-ever phaeton race."

Chapter 10

This modern era has a fascination with speed. We want our ships to sail faster. Our goods to arrive from the country with greater rapidity. There is talk of using steam engines to power vehicles from one end of our nation to the other. Always faster, faster, faster. One can only speculate where this obsession with haste will lead. Adventure? Or headlong into crashing disaster?

The Hawk's Eye, May 8, 1816

Eleanor had been to Ascot, Newmarket, even the Derby at Epsom. She'd seen steeplechases, harness races, and flat racing with just a jockey and a horse on a level track. There had been formalized races for predetermined prizes, and impromptu contests run on side streets and in parks. It was nigh impossible to live in England without witnessing a horse race at some point in one's life. The British were mad for their horseflesh, mad for gambling, mad for racing.

But she'd never witnessed a sight like this one. Phaetons almost as expensive and beautiful as Ashford's were collected together, the drivers all sizing each other up. A few grooms held torches, casting flickering light and shadows as the elite of Society gathered in preparation for their own spontaneous competition.

"A race to where?" she asked Ashford as they slowly

made their way through the crowd. Murmuring amongst themselves, the spectators parted as the phaeton rolled past. Excitement and anticipation were like a looming thunderstorm on the verge of breaking. Eleanor's own pulse had begun to hammer. She had no idea what to expect.

"Primrose Hill and back," he said.

A distance of approximately four miles. If the driver of a carriage such as this went flat out, at this time of night, with minimal traffic . . . well, she had no idea how long it might take, only that it would be fast, reckless, and wild.

"It's going to be dangerous," he continued, confirming her suspicions. "I'll leave you here and then return."

"And miss the race itself?" She shook her head. "Absolutely not." Part of her was terrified at the prospect of hurtling along in the dead of night in such a high, swift carriage. But the other part of her relished the notion. It was one thing to write about someone else's adventures. Quite another to have adventures herself. Frightening, yes, but thrilling, too.

"Ashford," a man in another light carriage called out. "Decided to join us after all."

"Grew weary of listening to you prate on at White's, Daventry," he called back. "What are the stakes tonight?"

"Two thousand to enter."

"Done," Ashford replied, as Eleanor inwardly gaped at the astronomical sum.

"Who's the sweetmeat?" Daventry asked, eyeing Eleanor. She recognized the name, but not the man. A typical buck who attended the Cyprians' Ball at the Argyle Rooms and lived on the largesse of his forthcoming barony. Lord D—y, as he was known in *The Hawk's Eye,* had a regular mistress installed in St. John's Wood, but that didn't keep him from dallying with dancers, actresses, and demimondaines. He was occasionally mocked in the pages of Eleanor's paper for his intemperance in drink and his tailor's bills.

She fought the urge to cover herself with her cloak. A strumpet would display her wares, after all. It was just good business practice.

"Ruby," she answered before the earl could speak.

"Tell you what, Ashford," Daventry said with a leer. "Let's make things a little more lively. If I win, I get not only your two thousand but your Ruby, as well."

Eleanor sat up straight. Lord, what should she do? A real soiled dove wouldn't protest, but there was only so far her commitment to this role, and the newspaper, would go. And it wasn't into Daventry's bed.

"Like hell," the earl growled.

"Oh, come on, Ashford," chided another man Eleanor recognized as a knight with a habit of trailing after the Prince Regent's retinue. "You never used to be so stingy with your ladies."

He wasn't?

"Where's your sporting spirit?" yet one more bloke reproved. Eleanor didn't recognize him, but he seemed of a type with all the other rich, reckless young men.

"There something special about your little gem?" Daventry waggled his eyebrows. "A special skill she's got that you're not willing to share?"

"The lady's not for the taking." Ashford sounded truly angry now.

Though the other men seemed to blanch a little at his tone, they were too far gone in their taunts to leave it alone. Their voices rang out in a chorus, demanding that "Ruby" be part of the stakes of the race. Just when Eleanor thought Ashford would get down from his seat and personally thrash each man with a horsewhip, she placed her hand on his tense forearm.

"Go ahead and wager me," she murmured. "They'll get suspicious otherwise."

"Let them," he snarled.

"If you don't," she said lowly, "they might eventually make the connection between 'Ned,' 'Ruby,' and the articles. They'll wonder who I am. They might guess—and then no one will allow you to join them in their nightly revels. We'll have to stop the newspaper series."

He cursed under his breath. The prospect seemed to alarm him. More than she would have suspected. Was he so attached to his libertine way of life that the idea of not documenting it caused so much concern?

What a strange notion. One she'd have to consider later.

Right now, I have to convince him to wager me. God above, I can't believe I just thought that.

"Think of it this way," she pressed. "I have so much faith in your abilities as a driver that I'm willing to take the chance."

"You haven't seen me truly drive," he noted.

She attempted a smile. "That's faith for you. It exists in the face of a total absence of evidence."

"Have you considered a career in the church?" he asked. "I've never heard more inspiring words."

"I'll do all my moralizing in the pages of my paper, thank you."

Meanwhile, the chorus of demands that "Ruby" be added to the stakes grew louder and louder. Ashford's jaw clenched, and he looked to be in debate with himself.

"Are you certain?" he finally rumbled.

"Quite." She wasn't at all. But what choice did she have?

He drew a breath. Then turned to the assembled crowd. "All right, you pack of jackals! Ruby goes into the pot."

The men, and even some of the women, cheered. It seemed the most peculiar thing to rejoice over, but that was the wealthy and idle for you. A bunch of bedlamites if ever she saw.

"Let's get this race underway," Daventry announced. "Drivers, line up."

As Ashford flicked the reins and guided his phaeton into position beside five other vehicles, Eleanor leaned in. "You'd better win," she hissed.

"I never lose," he answered in an undertone.

"There's always a first time. And it could be tonight."

A woman in a low-cut gown stepped forward, her arm upraised, her hand holding a kerchief. She seemed to be waiting for something. Silence descended, broken only by the horses snorting and stamping their eagerness to run.

The tension mounted even higher. Eleanor's heart decided it liked it better in her throat than her chest, and took up lodgings there.

Suddenly, the woman dropped her kerchief.

Ashford snapped the reins. The phaeton leapt forward. The race had begun.

Daniel had raced before. Numerous times. But never with a passenger. Not only did it change the balance of the carriage but it also changed his own internal balance.

Concerns about Miss Hawke's safety were paramount. But he also had to win this bloody race. Or else she'd wind up in Daventry's bed—and that, Daniel couldn't allow.

He drove the phaeton at breakneck speed from the park, trying to concentrate only on the road ahead of him. If he focused on his competitors, or on Miss Hawke in that damned red satin dress, he couldn't do his job. Either he and the journalist would crash, or one of the other carriages would pull ahead. Neither were options he wanted to entertain.

A film of sweat slicked his back as he carefully regulated the horses' pace, not wanting them to exhaust themselves too soon, but still keeping enough of a lead so that he didn't have to overcome a deficit.

Buildings and streetlights streaked past as the phaeton surged forward. Daniel's heart beat in time with the horses' hooves. What the hell had he been thinking, taking her along on this bloody escapade? He should've anticipated that she would want to ride with him, dangerous as the race was. But there was no way he could have known that, in addition to the money, Miss Hawke herself was part of the stakes.

They sped up to make the sharp turn from Bayswater to Edgware Road. Checking over his shoulder, Daniel saw Daventry and then Paulson close at his heels. Both men were hunched over their ribbons, pushing their horses as hard as they could.

Daniel gritted his teeth as he drove faster. The world whipped past in a night-dark blur. Thank God he saw well in the darkness. Perils such as lampposts, trees, and the occasional pedestrian all lurked in the shadows, appearing suddenly.

Some sodding fool had left a cart out in the middle of Old Marylebone Road, and Daniel pulled tight, guiding his carriage around the obstacle. Behind him, several horses whinnied in shock, and men cursed as they either pulled up short and stopped, or else struggled to get around the cart.

Normally, he'd be grinning like a fool at this point, intoxicated by the race, by the speed. A rare opportunity to feel true excitement. But he couldn't feel that same thrill, knowing he was imperiling Miss Hawke.

He glanced over at her, expecting to see her eyes wide with terror, her face ashen.

She was smiling. Widely. Her eyes were alight with exhilaration. She caught his eye and laughed.

"Faster!" she called above the clatter and rush of the wind.

His own fear faded, replaced by pleasure and excitement. God, she was as mad as he was—and nothing could have pleased him more.

A few cab drivers cursed as Daniel and Miss Hawke sped by at a blistering pace.

Finally, they entered Regent's Park, and then the horses began to tire. Daniel ignored the paths, driving over the grass, and the phaeton bounced like an India rubber ball. Just ahead was Primrose Hill, but as Daniel and Miss Hawke neared, they were overtaken by Daventry.

Daniel swore. For all Daventry was a preening coxcomb, he was also one of the best hands at racing. The results of a life of dissipation—a skill that no one truly needed, in service to an expensive game. But Daniel wouldn't let himself be beaten. He didn't care about the money. But however committed to her role as a tart Miss Hawke might be, he'd sooner run Daventry into a wall than allow her to go to the blighter's bed.

Up ahead was the oak they used as the turning point for the race. Daventry made his turn around the tree.

"Looking forward to knowing you better, Ruby," Daventry called as he passed, heading back toward the city.

"Sod off, jackanapes," Miss Hawke muttered.

Daniel's thoughts exactly. He snapped the ribbons, pushing the horses harder. They careened around the oak, nearly balancing on two wheels to take the turn. The phaeton jounced as it made the curve. Daniel feared he'd lose control of the animals and the carriage, and they'd go tumbling over to smash into the ground and thickets.

He breathed in. Getting in command of the vehicle, and himself.

Somehow, he managed both. The phaeton balanced itself and raced onward, with Daniel in control.

Miss Hawke laughed again. "Bravo!"

"No celebrations yet," he growled. They still had half the distance to go, and Daventry was in the lead.

He promised he'd reward his horses later, but for now, he needed them to give their utmost. So he snapped the reins again and called out to them in his most commanding voice. "Phantom! Swain! Time to move!"

Bless the creatures, they seemed to hear, and obey. Their legs stretched out as they took the road, necks straining as they hurtled onward.

Miss Hawke gripped the front of the seat, leaning forward as if she could somehow get the carriage to move even faster. Daniel himself bent low, his gaze all the while fixed on Daventry's phaeton ten yards ahead of them. The rest of the competition had fallen back, unable to keep up.

The second half of the race flew by. He knew only the straining of the reins in his hands, the beat of the horses' hooves, the rocking of the vehicle, and the rush of his blood in his ears. He was a knife's edge, sharp and swift.

"Yes! Faster!" Miss Hawke shouted above the rush.

"Are you this demanding in everything?" he called, winking.

"Only where speed is important." She winked back. "There are moments where it's important to take one's time. And others where a hard, fast drive is best."

Heat flooded him.

At last, Hyde Park loomed up ahead. And the gathered crowd, cheering as the racers made their approach. But Daventry still led. Daniel didn't give a tinker's damn about his reputation or his money if he lost. All that mattered was keeping Miss Hawke away from the others.

"Damn it, move!" he roared to his horses.

The distance between his phaeton and Daventry's shortened. Yard by yard. Foot by foot. Until they were beside each other, running in tandem.

The finish line beckoned. Triumph or failure.

Daniel wouldn't accept failure.

With one last crack of the ribbons, he urged the horses. And, heroic animals that they were, they made a final surge. Until they crossed the finish line. It took them some distance to slow after the pace they'd set. The animals needed to cool down.

"Did we win?" Miss Hawke asked breathlessly.

"Don't know." He slowed the carriage, then brought it around to the assembled spectators, where Daventry also walked his horses to cool them.

Several moments passed as people debated amongst themselves, differing opinions clattering like horses' hooves.

Lord Carew, who often served as judge for these events, finally stepped forward. He hooked his thumbs into the pockets of his waistcoat and glanced back and forth between Daniel and Daventry. Everyone fell silent. Waiting the final decision. And Carew, blast him, seemed to enjoy the attention—and tension—for he waited an ungodly amount of time before speaking.

"The winner is . . ."

Not a single breath was drawn, including Daniel's. He felt Miss Hawke next to him, vibrating like a plucked bowstring.

Carew finally spoke. "Ashford."

The crowd burst into wild cheers and applause, while Daventry cursed. Daniel nearly leapt in relief, but then he felt Miss Hawke's arms around him, embracing him.

"You did it!"

She was silky and warm and deliciously curved. And his blood was high. His body primed.

He couldn't have held himself back if he'd wanted to. But it was unstoppable, inevitable.

He pulled her tight and close. And kissed her.

Chapter 11

Reckless behavior is not the sole province of the young. At least they have the excuse of their paltry number of years to justify their foolish behavior. But when the rash, nay, imprudent action is undertaken by those of more mature years, there is no convenient pretext, and one is left only with the taste of regret, and the desire to do it all over again . . .

The Hawk's Eye, May 8, 1816

Stunned, Eleanor was completely incapable of movement. Everything still whirled around her: the race, the close call at losing, the speed that continued to resonate in her body, Ashford's mastery of the phaeton. She was all sensation, barely capable of thought. There had been those agonizing minutes when she'd thought she'd really have to serve as Daventry's prize—and then she and Ashford had won. Exhilaration had surged through her.

And then . . . the earl kissed her.

For a moment, shocked inertia locked her in its vise. His mouth pressed to hers. His arms and torso were solid around and against her. Her own grip surrounding his shoulders loosened slightly. But her body understood what her mind could not.

Ashford was kissing her. And like hell would she waste this opportunity.

Her fingers dug into the strong muscles of his shoulders. She felt the firm, silken texture of his lips, the slight rasp of his incipient beard. She basked in the sensations and urged his lips apart with her own. He opened readily to her as the kiss deepened, grew hotter. More consuming. His tongue swept against hers. She tasted tobacco, expensive spirits. His own unique flavor.

Delicious. And devious. A woman could grow intoxicated by his taste, addicted to the feel of him. No wonder he had the reputation he did. His kiss would make any woman demand more, and more. This, she realized, was what she'd been waiting for, since the day he first strode into her office.

Energy vibrated through them both. Fiery and alive. Neither dominated; each traded strength and power, him leading, and other moments she was in command. They were balanced yet vital, communicating in a primal language that all their words had danced around. *I want you.*

His hands slid down, spanning her waist as he pulled her closer. She pressed her chest to his, relishing her softness to his muscular solidity. Threaded her fingers in his hair to bring him closer still.

Loud hooting and catcalls were buckets of ice-cold sound thrown over her. She pulled back. Her hazy vision focused. As it did, mortification took the place of desire.

They were surrounded by a crowd of gawkers. All of them staring at her and Ashford kissing. Many of the throng were calling out suggestions, especially to Ashford, as to what he should do next, and with what degree of vigorousness.

She wasn't prudish, but she'd been in the middle of the most passionate kiss of her life. That wasn't something she intended to share with an audience.

Though she wanted to either call back an insulting suggestion or shrink into herself, she did neither. Instead, she slowly slid her fingers out of Ashford's hair, turned, and gave the crowd a brazen smile and sardonic curtsy. The kind a seasoned woman of minimal reputation might give.

Ashford himself seemed to be in something of a daze. He blinked for a moment, as though recalling where he was, then glared fiercely at the pack of onlookers. Yet he didn't release his hold on her. If anything, he seemed to shield her body with his own, as though protecting her from the invasive gazes and comments of the crowd.

"I can see why you wanted to hold on to her, Ashford," Daventry called above the sounds of the throng.

"Two thousand pounds," the earl growled back. "And not another damn word from you."

The other competitors finally arrived, many of them looking the worse for their efforts. Several of the other carriages now sported deep gouges along their sides, and one looked as though its left rear wheel was on the verge of popping off its axle. Everyone—including Ashford and, no doubt, herself—appeared windblown and slightly dazed. Though her own state of confusion had more to do with the kiss than the race.

Promissory notes were handed over, since no one had two thousand pounds on their person. Good-natured ribbing was also exchanged as the losers complained about their faulty vehicles, Ashford's extraordinary luck, the alignment of cobblestones and stars. Ashford, however, kept largely silent, and she might think him almost angry as he accepted his accolades and congratulations, as well as his money.

Finally, the group started to break up as people dissolved back into the night. In pursuit of other thrills, perhaps. Or home to lick their wounds.

Ashford drove sedately from the park, saying nothing. The horses most likely needed their rest. She hoped the animals would be amply rewarded back at the stables. But first they needed to return to Ashford's home.

She and the earl rode together through the streets gone even more quiet. A bell somewhere chimed two o'clock in the morning. No one of any honorable intent walked the city at this hour. Certainly she and Ashford hadn't been up to anything one might consider reputable.

Though the phaeton was open on top, tension weighed heavily, as though a dense, low-lying fog clung to her and Ashford. She didn't know how to feel about what had just happened. Emotions crashed against each other like ships colliding in a bay. Her body still buzzed with energy—a combination of so many thrilling moments that had just transpired—delighting in the pleasure they'd created together. But damn if this wasn't a complication that neither of them needed. He was the subject of her articles. A means to an end. He had his own agenda, too. They were both untrustworthy. Adding a physical component to their arrangement made things too knotty.

He broke the silence. "Look, I—"

She spoke at the same time. "It's probably not—"

They stumbled over each other, fumbling their way toward conversation. "Go ahead." "No, you first." "Honestly, I—"

"For God's sake," he growled, "just speak."

She smoothed her hands over her skirt. Cleared her throat. What was wrong with her? She'd been accused more than once of being too candid, too direct. But she had to be in order to succeed as a woman in a man's world. Why should she quail now? And with him, of all people. He understood the kind of woman she was.

"That was enjoyable," she said, staring straight ahead. "More than enjoyable." Why not tell the full truth? "The best kiss I've ever had."

"Likewise," he rumbled, still sounding furious. With her, or himself, she couldn't tell.

"But it can't happen again."

"No," he said with an irritating lack of hesitancy, "it can't."

"You don't think I have ethics," she continued, "but I do. And the conflict of interest would be too great if we were to take this thing between us to its logical conclusion."

He stared at her. "You think me so much a rake that a kiss cannot be merely an end unto itself?"

"Yes, some kisses lead to nothing more. But not *that* kiss."

Slowly, he nodded.

"And we oughtn't pursue it any further," she continued.

"Agreed," he said.

She fought the urge to glare at him. Did he have to be so amenable about this? Couldn't he fight just a little for following their attraction?

But she couldn't have it both ways. He respected her decision, concurred with it. That ought to please her. Yet somehow, it didn't.

"Fine," she snapped.

"Fine." His voice was also edged as he took them farther from the park.

If they were in concordance, why did they both sound so bloody angry? For herself, she was irritated that she'd fallen prey to a rake's notorious charms, despite all the warnings she'd received and given herself. Though she wrote a scandal sheet, she meant what she said about having some degree of integrity. She couldn't maintain that if she went any further with the earl—much as her body wanted to. Besides, she had no way of knowing whether the kiss they'd shared was part of his greater scheme. He could be planning on manipulating her to his advantage, and to her detriment. She couldn't permit that.

It wasn't as though she didn't know handsome, charming men. The Imperial Theater was thick with them, and they often made it clear to her that they'd like to pursue an amorous relationship. She'd managed to refuse them all, knowing what a disaster it would be to take an actor as a lover. And there were the other attractive, beguiling men of her circle of acquaintanceship.

She resisted them easily. They were like good-looking dandelion puffs blowing past her on the breeze. She couldn't take any of them seriously.

But the earl. . . . He resonated within her. Drew her.

Yet she had to withstand his allure. Predominantly out

of self-protection. Commoners and noblemen made a bad combination.

She also had a sense that it would never be a simple physical attraction between them, and the sooner she cut off that burgeoning attachment, the better.

It didn't make her happy, though.

"Where am I taking you?" he asked.

She almost laughed. She wondered that, herself.

"To the Imperial," she said. "My landlady sleeps lightly. She'll hear your carriage outside and see 'Ruby' climbing the stairs to my rooms."

"How will you get home from the theater?" he pressed. "It's not safe for you to be out alone at this hour."

Damn him, did he have to be so protective, so courteous?

"I can sleep there," she said. "There are couches in the dressing rooms. I'll go home in the morning. My landlady is used to me sleeping sometimes at the office, so she won't be suspicious if I don't come home tonight."

"Can't be very comfortable," he muttered.

Neither is this, she thought.

"Oh, the sofas are stuffed with moldering straw," she answered breezily. "But I've slept on worse." Especially during those lean years in her childhood.

He didn't seem to like the idea, but his silence as he continued to drive seemed to indicate that he was as accepting of it as he'd ever be.

It was a longer journey to the Imperial than she would have liked. Especially now that she was deeply, palpably aware of him beside her. Now she knew what his body felt like against her own. His lean muscles. His long hands on her waist. His soft, commanding lips pressed to hers.

She felt a little like Pandora, letting out all the demons, only to be left with the pathetic specter of hope rattling around an empty box. No way to undo her knowledge or take back what she'd been compelled to do. The kiss had been entirely mutual, and now she paid the price, since it was a single occurring phenomenon.

At last, they reached the darkened theater. He drove around to the side entrance, which was barely lit by a single, flickering lamp.

"Do you have a key?" he asked, eying the locked door.

"Kingston, the stage manager, is always here. He'll let me in."

Ashford gave a clipped nod. He continued to hold the ribbons, looking between the horses' ears, but not at her.

How did one end a night like this? Where she'd dressed like a lightskirt and raced through London to Primrose Hill at speeds she'd never dreamed possible? When she'd passionately kissed the most dangerously seductive man she'd ever met? What did one say?

Good night seemed terrifically paltry and anemic. But nothing else came to mind.

So she said nothing. Yet before she could climb down from the high seat of the phaeton, he'd already gotten out and was reaching up for her.

She let her hand slide into his. Warmth from his skin sank into her, threading through her body. An idle thought drifted into her mind, and once she stood upon the pavement, she impulsively tugged off his glove. The leather was slightly split along the palm's seam. Odd—quality like that wouldn't tear apart easily.

Eleanor tried not to notice how large his glove was as she tucked it into a pocket sewn into her cloak. Instead, she focused on his palm. She brought it close to her face, trying to see it in the semidarkness.

"Your hands are hurt," she murmured. Dark red stripes from his tight grip on the reins marked his flesh. Her fingers hovered over the wounds.

He shrugged. "It's a trifle."

"They'll want some salve and bandaging."

"A drink of whiskey and it won't matter."

She shook her head at him. "Such a man." She lowered her voice. " 'Nothing can hurt me. I'm made of gunpowder and bronze.' "

"Iron," he said. "Bronze bends too easily."

She huffed out a disbelieving laugh. The audacity of him.

"Come inside," she said, "and I'll wrap your hands."

He raised a brow. "Didn't know doctoring was part of your substantial skills."

"It's not," she admitted. Other women seemed to have the gift of healing, yet she never did. "But I've read novels."

It was his turn to laugh—a low, rueful chuckle. "I'll let my valet attend to it. He's patched me up more than a few times."

Naturally. A rake would need mending after all his wild exploits.

She frowned over the injuries. "I don't see similar scars. But this isn't the first phaeton race you've entered."

He was silent for a moment. "Gripped the reins a little tighter this time," he finally said. Grudgingly.

Which meant he hadn't been quite as calm or in control as she'd thought. And though he'd run the race before, there was one factor that hadn't been in place in those earlier contests.

Her.

He'd been concerned about her. Worried. And that had changed how he'd raced.

Oh, but she wanted to punch him. And kiss him again, too. She didn't think she could feel both desires for one person at the same time. But then, he was teaching her all manner of things about herself.

It slowly dawned on her that she still held his hand. It formed a solid, warm weight, cradled in her palms. And it was a beautifully masculine hand, made even more so by the injuries he'd sustained. She had the absurd impulse to kiss those angry red marks, as if she could heal them.

The bastard.

Yet she didn't let go of him. Glancing up, she saw him staring down at their hands, too. His nostrils flared. His jaw tightened. And she knew, absolutely, that he wanted to kiss her again.

Just as she knew that she wanted him to.

She dropped his hand. Took a step back.

"Get that looked at," she said.

"I said I would."

"Good."

They stared at each other a moment longer, the air thick with possibility and the fight for noble impulses to win out over the baser ones.

Finally, she turned and pounded her fist on the stage door. Silence reigned as she and Ashford waited. From within the theater, footsteps grew louder. Until they stopped on the other side of the door.

"We're sodding closed!" a Caribbean-accented voice shouted inside.

"It's Eleanor Hawke, Mr. Kingston," she answered. "I need to spend the night."

Dead bolts were slid back and locks clicked, then the door opened. Kingston's dark brown face appeared in the gap. He looked at her with concern, then the concern gave way to suspicion when he gazed at the earl.

"Everything all right, Miss Hawke?"

"Just working on a story."

The stage manager nodded sagely, as if that explained everything. Which it did, in truth. He held the door open wider for her and shot Ashford another glare.

"My thanks, Mr. Kingston," she said.

"Anything for a friend of Maggie's," he answered.

Eleanor took a step toward the theater, then glanced back at the earl. He stood beside the phaeton, looking opaque. But his hands were curled into fists at his sides, despite his wounds.

"Well . . . good night," she managed, and winced at the banality.

"Night," he answered.

She hovered, uncertain. But what else was there to say or do? After giving him a nod, she strode into the theater. Kingston closed the door behind her, fastening all the locks.

For which she was grateful. Because without that barrier between her and the earl, she had a terrible suspicion she might go running after him, demanding they finish what they started.

It was going to be a long, uncomfortable night on the dressing room sofa.

"This is a first for you, my lord." Strathmore daubed ointment onto the welts lining Daniel's palms. The stuff stunk of sulfur and burned like retribution—as if Cook's special remedy was made of Hell itself.

But as Daniel sat in a chair by the fire in his bedchamber, he held himself still and made no noise of complaint as his valet doctored his injuries. He deserved the pain, after all, being so incredibly stupid as to take Miss Hawke on the phaeton with him during the race. What if he'd made a mistake? What if the carriage had tipped or crashed into another vehicle? Not only might he have broken his thick skull but she could've been hurt, or worse.

"Weren't you wearing gloves?" Strathmore pressed.

"Not thick enough ones, I suppose," he answered. He reached for the glass of whiskey on a nearby table. The bandage on his left hand made it somewhat difficult to grasp the tumbler, but he was determined, and finally brought the rim of the glass to his lips. There. The alcohol scalded its way down his throat and served as its own balm to injuries that couldn't be treated—except with spirits.

Strathmore glanced over at the lone leather glove thrown across Daniel's dressing table. Its mate had gone missing somehow. But the one that remained bore tears across the palm, evidence of just how hard Daniel had pulled and held the reins.

"I'll write a letter of complaint to the glover," the valet sniffed. "It's a disgrace that his work cannot take a small amount of stress."

Daniel bit back a laugh. *Stress* was such a short, simple word, that couldn't barely contain the whole of the evening. God, yes, he'd been terrified that something might happen to Miss Hawke. But also . . . damn it . . . also . . .

It had been one of the best nights of his life. He'd never had a thrill as he'd had tonight. Sharing the excitement of the race with her—and she *had* been excited. During the race itself. And after.

He took another swallow of whiskey, then tipped his head back and stared at the flickering shadows on the ceiling. Jesus, that kiss. He'd ask himself what he'd been thinking, but he already knew the answer.

Daniel hadn't been thinking at all. He'd simply wanted. And taken. And maybe he was a bloody bastard, but he couldn't make himself regret it, not when that kiss had been so explosive, so rich with heat and possibility. If he'd ever wondered if Miss Hawke's tongue could do more than trade banter, he had his proof now.

Her kiss had been alive and responsive, carnal, aware. Demanding. She knew what she wanted and how to get it. No shrinking flower, this Miss Hawke. She was a woman grown, and he gave thanks for her experience—while cursing it at the same time.

Because he wanted to kiss her again. Wanted more than just a kiss.

He could blame that damn red dress. He could blame the exhilaration of the race. But neither gave the full truth. Since their first meeting, everything had been building toward this. Every barb they traded, every sly look or witty retort they exchanged—it all led to that kiss.

"What's that, my lord?" Strathmore asked, wrapping strips of linen around Daniel's other hand.

"I said nothing."

"You . . . growled."

"Not an uncommon sound for me to make." Daniel examined his valet's handiwork. "Nicely done. Now get yourself some sleep," he added, not unkindly.

Strathmore bowed, collected his physicking supplies, and retreated from the bedchamber. Leaving Daniel alone with his wounds, his whiskey, and his thoughts.

Though it was nearly three in the morning, Daniel felt no compulsion to sleep. Restlessness pushed at him. He stood, taking his empty glass with him, and walked to another cabinet that held his particularly private store of alcohol. After getting a refill, he stalked to the fire and stared into its flames, contemplating the patterns made from heat and light.

What a chaos his life had become. Between his search for Jonathan, his arrangement with Miss Hawke, and the damned inconvenient attraction between him and the journalist, never had things been in such upheaval.

His blood surged when he was with her. As though . . . as though he was truly alive. For the first time in . . . He couldn't remember when. It was like waking from a long hibernation to discover a green and thriving land, when before all had been gray and lifeless. Even thinking of her now set his pulse to kicking, his body stirring. For all his reputation, he wasn't so much a cad that he'd drive back to the theater and demand that he and Miss Hawke continue where they'd left off. But damn if he didn't want to.

They couldn't. And there could be no repeat of the kiss. He wanted Miss Hawke, but he owed it to Jonathan to keep his head and keep his trousers buttoned. He couldn't allow anything with the scandalmonger to get too complicated. As if they hadn't already.

Restlessness continued to beat in his blood, despite his resolution. He could go out again, but the thought of gambling, or drinking, or carousing all felt shallow and shrill. Solitude suited him better now.

He paced over to his bedside table and pulled a book from a drawer. *The Duchess's Secret*, by "A Lady of Dubious Quality." The latest sensational erotic novel by the anonymous female author. The books had been making the covert rounds, traded in clubs and card rooms, thin volumes slipped easily from pocket to pocket. But Daniel had the sneaking suspicion that more than a few women were also reading the salacious books.

Erudite, it wasn't. Yet he wasn't in the mood for some intellectual opus on philosophy or science. He wanted distraction, and what better way to distract himself than with some quality filth?

He strode back to the fire, threw himself into the chair, and opened to a page at random. It wasn't as though the plot mattered.

"I gasped in delight as the stablehand's lips closed around my—"

He snapped the book shut. Only one line in, and he could go no further. Because when he pictured the stablehand, he imagined himself. And the face of the naughty duchess belonged to none other than Miss Hawke.

This was going to be an interminable night.

Chapter 12

*Fear is a peculiar engine. It can either trap us
in its web, rendering us unable to move as we
await our grim fate, or it can spur us into action.
There are dangers to both responses, of course.
Quiescence leads to torpidity which ultimately leads
to stagnation. But a reckless flight headlong into
the arms of that which frightens us can result in
unforeseen circumstances. Circumstances which can
be most dire . . .*

The Hawk's Eye, May 11, 1816

A dockside tavern at night was no place to take a lady, especially a lady who was no more than a girl of seventeen. The Double Anchor boasted—if that was the right term—one weak lantern outside, though it would have been for the best if no one had been able to see the grimy, ramshackle façade, its shutters hanging in awkward angles, the glass within the windows warped and grimy, the bricks lining the front stained with God only knew what. Daniel had no desire to investigate the black streaks running down the face of the tavern.

He and Catherine sat inside his least impressive carriage, staring at the front of The Double Anchor. Had Daniel been alone, he would have approached on foot, lest the carriage attract too much attention. But, damn it, Catherine's presence was a necessary evil, one he regretted every time. But as Jonathan's beloved baby sister, she was the only one her brother might respond to.

No doubt if Jonathan took one look at Daniel's face, he'd bolt, and disappear deeper into the underbelly of London. Deep enough that Daniel's already slim chances of finding him would vanish entirely.

But that didn't mean he had to like bringing an innocent like Catherine to a dung heap like The Double Anchor. He bloody hated it.

"Ready?" he asked.

She took a deep breath and nodded, pulling her drab cloak tighter around her. Per Daniel's instructions, they both wore their dullest, cheapest clothing. But one couldn't completely hide years of breeding. They'd still stand out amongst the riffraff, no matter what he and Catherine wore. A hazard of being part of the aristocracy. There weren't many, but that was one of them.

Also because of Daniel's instructions, tonight they traveled without a footman on the back of the carriage. Another way they'd attract attention. So he opened the door himself, and climbed down. He helped Catherine out, and a strange thought flashed through his mind. Her hand felt much smaller, more fragile, in his than Miss Hawke's did. For all Catherine's immense strength and courage, she was still so slight, so delicate, especially compared to Miss Hawke.

He shook his head, dislodging the idea. Now wasn't the time to think of the journalist, or how she'd haunted his every waking—and dreaming—moment since the phaeton race three days ago. Now he needed to focus on finding Jonathan and keeping Catherine safe as they searched.

But he wouldn't have been able to go looking for his old friend if it hadn't been for *The Hawk's Eye* reporting on his theoretically more scandalous activities. The brighter spotlight on his other deeds threw the shadows deeper to hide activities such as this. It took Miss Hawke's attention away from his search, and for that, he was grateful.

The cries of gulls intermingled outside with the screech of a fiddle inside. A man's prone form splayed on the dirty pavement, cradling a bottle of gin. The drunkard partially blocked the doorway, so Daniel used his boot to shove the man aside. Too far gone into his stupor, the tippler didn't notice or make a sound of protest. He did let out one single snore, before settling down again.

Daniel placed his hand on the doorknob. He had a pistol tucked into his coat and a knife in his boot. Beyond those weapons, he had his fists. Bloody foolish to walk into a place like this—especially with Catherine beside him—unarmed.

This wasn't the first time he and the girl had found themselves in such a location. Though every time, he hoped it would be the last. Would tonight prove different?

He pushed open the door. The fiddle play didn't stop, precisely, but there was a small judder in the bow across the strings when he and Catherine crossed the threshold. A dozen heads bent over their pints turned in their direction. So much for staying discreet. Nothing to be done about that.

Slowly, he and Catherine threaded their way through the battered assortment of tables and the men huddled around them. The tavern was like any of dozens Daniel had seen since first he'd begun his search for Jonathan. Filthy, cramped, hot, with smoke-stained timbered beams crossing the low ceiling. The structure hadn't been *built* so much as *grown,* like a fungus. Tonight, the fungus was populated by a collection of drunkards, reprobates, dockworkers, and sailors. A game of dice was being played in the corner. A prostitute sat on a sailor's lap, halfheartedly toying with his hair.

Daniel kept his attention split between reaching the bar and keeping an eye on Catherine. Brave girl kept her chin tipped up. She didn't shrink into herself, but wisely, she didn't try to meet anyone's gaze, either. Men like these would read that as an invitation.

Finally, he and Catherine reached the bar, where a scrawny, balding man eyed them dubiously.

"What you want?" the tapster demanded.

"Information," Daniel answered. "And discretion."

"None of them things is cheap."

"They never are." Daniel slid a coin across the chipped bar top. "Looking for someone."

"Lots of someones here." The barkeeper smirked as he tucked the coin away.

That was debatable. The tavern seemed filled with many no ones.

Catherine pulled a miniature of her brother from the folds of her cloak and showed it to the barkeeper. "Him."

The man squinted at the small portrait. It had been painted years ago, before Jonathan had gone to war, and showed him with heartbreaking excitement about the life he was to lead, little knowing what his future would actually entail.

"He'd look different now," Daniel added. "Thinner, most likely. Showing signs of hard living."

After a moment, the tavern keeper shook his head. "Naw. Even when they're slumming, gentry folk don't come here. They didn't," he added, eyeing Daniel and Catherine, "until now."

Though this trail was far from a sure thing, disappointment was lead in Daniel's stomach. He kept hoping, time and again, that each filthy rattrap he visited would be the last, and that he'd finally locate his old friend. But tonight was just as much of a waste as any other.

Still, he had to cling to hope, for Catherine's sake.

He slid another coin across the bar. "That's for keeping your mouth shut about our questions."

The money disappeared instantly. "'Course, gov."

Whether or not the tavern keeper would keep silent was debatable. Gossip was a common currency. Everyone traded in it. But Daniel had to do his due diligence and try to hide their tracks. If Jonathan got word that people were looking for him, he'd burrow deeper into the shadows, and then he'd truly be impossible to find. But if Catherine could reach out to him, appeal to him, then maybe, just maybe, they might be able to bring him home.

"Might want to try the Lady Anne five blocks over, if you're looking for a toff who likes rattling around these kind of places," the barkeep suggested, then looked expectantly at Daniel.

He gave the man another coin. Moving away from the bar, Daniel placed one arm around Catherine's now sagging shoulders and guided her toward the door.

She gave a small yelp. Daniel pivoted and saw that one of the patrons had a thick paw wrapped around Catherine's wrist. She fought to tug herself from his grip.

"How much?" the man demanded. "I never had me a taste of quality before."

"For you," Daniel answered, "nothing." His fist shot out and plowed straight into the man's face.

Instantly, the sot released his grip and toppled to the ground. Out cold.

"The rest of you will get the same if anyone so much as *contemplates* her," Daniel said flatly.

Everyone instantly became fascinated with their drinks. The path to the door was remarkably clear thereafter. In a few moments, Daniel and Catherine were back in his carriage, heading toward the majestically titled Lady Anne. Though he expected the place didn't live up to the grandeur of the name.

"I keep hoping," Catherine said quietly. "But it's like dying a little every time they say no."

Daniel reached across the carriage and took her hand in his. "We'll find him. I swear to you—"

She gave a laugh that was far too mature and embittered for a girl her age. "Please do not make promises you cannot keep."

"Then I'll try to find him until breath leaves my body."

She nodded slightly, squeezing his hand. "Thank you. That's more than I could ever ask for."

"Jonathan deserves it. *You* deserve it."

"I've been reading about you," she said with a little smile. "I mean, I've been reading about Lord Rakewell. The phaeton race."

He gently released her hand and leaned back. "Ah, yes, my rakish exploits."

Daniel had also read the article. Now that the piece was out, some of the people at the race might have determined the identity of Lord Rakewell, and that Ruby was the journalist.

Hopefully, they were too deep in pursuits of pleasure to truly notice, or care.

Despite the fact that he'd actually lived the experience, he'd found Miss Hawke's account of it to be compelling, exciting reading. While perusing the piece, he'd actually doubted for a few moments the outcome of the race. She knew her business as a writer, that Miss Hawke.

Though he wondered if he could call her "Miss Hawke" now that he'd kissed her. It seemed cold and distant compared to her Christian name. Eleanor. He had to think of her that way, considering the fact that his dreams of her had been getting progressively impolite. Decidedly carnal. Her peeling off that red dress . . . him tasting that ripe mouth of hers . . . tasting more than her mouth . . .

He shook his head. He couldn't have such erotic thoughts when Catherine sat nearby.

Something Eleanor did *not* write about was the kiss. It did and did not surprise him that she left that detail out. A more sensationalist writer would gleefully exploit the event. But either she was exceptionally private, or she didn't want her own reputation called into question.

Either way, he was grateful she'd omitted the kiss. It kept it strictly between them. Almost as though it was private and . . . special. Yes, there'd been many raucous spectators, but despite their presence, the kiss still belonged to him and Eleanor alone.

"Jonathan loved phaeton racing," Catherine murmured, interrupting his thoughts. "I wasn't supposed to know about it, but I could always tell when he'd been out, speeding around in that high-flyer of his." A smile touched her voice.

"He always boasted he could beat me," Daniel said.

"Did he ever win against you?"

"No. But just before he went abroad to fight, he said he'd return and trounce me." Melancholy settled heavily in Daniel's chest. That rematch had never happened. Perhaps it never might.

"And he said he'd teach me how to drive," Catherine added, sadness dimming her voice.

Daniel almost offered to teach her himself. But until he had proof that Jonathan was no longer alive, showing Catherine how to handle a carriage was his friend's prerogative.

"He still might," he felt compelled to say.

"He might," she agreed. Though doubt tinged her words. Like Daniel, Catherine was losing hope. And damn it if that fading hope didn't break his heart.

He'd even looked for Jonathan at the race, as one of the spectators. But if he'd been there, he must have been too transformed for Daniel to recognize him.

She seemed to rally herself, forcing another smile. "A gaming hell. A phaeton race. Where will you take your journalist next on your profligate adventures?"

"That's to be decided." There were any number of dissolute places he could bring Eleanor. Yet a question gnawed at him: where did he *want* to take her? And how would it make her think of him? A distressing thought: he actually desired her good opinion. It mattered to him.

When had that changed? Since the kiss? No—before. Somewhere along the way, he began to respect her, and need her respect in return. Things that never mattered to him before, not with anyone.

Before he could pursue that alarming thought any further, the carriage stopped. He peered out the window at the Lady Anne tavern. It looked much as The Double Anchor did—a miserable edifice holding a miserable collection of miserable souls.

He fought a sigh. Jonathan might be in there. Or, worse, he might not. No way to know but to go inside and start this grim process all over again.

His one consolation was the thought of seeing Eleanor again. It might not make up for the bleak search for his friend, but she remained one ray of light in a world draped in shadows.

Eleanor made her way back from the pie shop down the street, carrying her luncheon. As she did so, she spotted a familiar carriage parked outside her office. Immediately, her heart began its version of a military tattoo, and the paper-wrapped pie in her hands nearly slipped to the pavement. Logically, she knew she'd see the earl again. He'd even sent a note the day before stating that they'd meet soon. But that didn't quite prepare her for the visceral thrill of seeing his carriage and knowing he was nearby.

Nervousness and excitement warred against each other. She stopped in the street, ignoring the curses of those whose paths she blocked.

It was just a kiss. People kiss all the time and the world doesn't go spinning off its axis.

Yet her world had. If she'd been distracted after her evening with Ashford at the gaming hell, these last few days had seen her fit for a long stay in an asylum. She'd caught herself staring off into space, her fingers on her lips, remembering the feel of his. She'd been unable to grasp her thoughts. They'd been like ships disappearing off maps. Eating had been all but impossible. The mutton pie she now held was a token gesture toward feeding herself when she had no appetite to speak of, her stomach constantly somersaulting.

It was bloody disconcerting, especially because she prided herself on her level head. That equanimity had packed up its belongings and set off on a journey, giving no indication where it was going or when it would return. If only she could follow it and drag it back into place. Right now, she could truly use as much self-possession as she could muster.

A small, cowardly part of her wanted to turn and walk in the other direction. Hide until the earl gave up and went home. She had a strange fear of what she might see in his gaze when he looked at her. Would he think less of her for kissing him back? The idea was rubbish, of course. If a man kissed a woman and didn't expect her to participate in said kiss, then he was an idiotic boor who only wanted to force his attention on unwilling victims.

Ashford was not an idiotic boor.

"Oi, out of the way, missus!"

She jumped to one side as a man pulling a cart full of fish went barreling past her. And while she didn't appreciate the sound, or smell, it did snap her out of her paralysis.

The Hawk's Eye didn't achieve its success because she took the easy way out. When fears, doubts, or other obstacles presented themselves, she'd always tackled them, and to hell with her uncertainty. Nothing was ever accomplished by sitting still.

She knew what she *ought* to do. Tell him that it couldn't happen again. Especially if the series of articles was to continue. And she did want it to continue. Sales had gone up yet again in the wake of the phaeton race piece.

But if he *did* attempt another kiss, she wasn't entirely certain she could resist the temptation. Wasn't even certain she wanted to resist.

All this was speculation unless she gathered up her courage and marched over and confronted him. So, after handing the pie to a nearby beggar, she did just that.

As she neared the carriage, the coachman called down to her. "He's inside, miss." He pointed toward the building that housed *The Hawk's Eye*.

She nodded her thanks, then went in. Stepping inside, she had a long view between desks, where her writers were busy scribbling out their stories, even on a Saturday. But all of them kept glancing over at her private office, where the door was closed. She'd left the door open when she'd gone out to pick up her luncheon.

Her pulse gave another kick.

The writers silently tracked her movement as she approached her office. She felt their gazes on her, as if she walked to the gallows or a promised reward.

Outside the door to her private chamber, she hesitated. Should she knock? It was *her* office.

After taking a deep breath, she opened the door.

"You're sitting in my chair," she said.

Ashford was, in fact, seated at her desk. He appeared as though he'd been in the middle of looking over the latest proofs spread out on her desk's surface. His fingers were folded together, and he balanced his chin on his interlaced hands as he read. He looked the model of intellectual contemplation.

He also looked, she realized with dismay, appallingly good-looking. Cleanly sculpted and handsome as a falcon. Dressed impeccably, of course. She vaguely noticed his hat and walking stick balanced on a side table in the corner of the room. Dark hair just slightly damp and curling, as if he'd bathed within the hour.

Ashford looked up when she entered, and she resisted the impulse to smooth her skirts and her hair. Doubtless she appeared as frazzled as she felt. Compared to him, she probably looked like some kind of frowzy burrowing creature emerging from beneath a hedgerow to blink at the sun. He dazzled her that much.

Her gaze went immediately to his mouth. She forced her eyes back to meet his.

"There wasn't anywhere else to sit," he said.

"I don't normally entertain guests," she answered. "This is a place of business, not a parlor for receiving visitors."

"Clearly, given you and your staff's sterling sense of hospitality." He rose from the desk, seeming to fill the space with his lean height. "Nobody offered me a single cup of tea. Including you."

"As I said, this is a place of business. If you wanted tea or a gracious reception, I can recommend any number of fine establishments within a half mile. I'm sure they'd be happy to have your patronage."

"But I prefer to be patronizing here," he said.

"And you're doing a marvelous job of it."

So they weren't going to speak of the kiss. She wasn't going to tell him that he'd been occupying her every thought for days. Or that she'd wanted his mouth on hers with the same desperate craving with which a sweet lover needed bonbons. No, they weren't going to talk of any of this.

She took another step into her office, deliberately leaving the door open. "What are you doing here?"

"Ah, more of that famed graciousness," he said.

"Well, you're no stranger to where I work." She crossed her arms over her chest. "You did storm in here several weeks ago, after all."

"I didn't *storm*," he countered. "I *ambled*."

"You don't *amble* anywhere. You *stride* or *stalk*."

"I hadn't realized you spent so much time thinking of synonyms for how I walk."

Her face heated. She'd been contemplating many, many synonyms for him. Most of them flattering. If only she didn't possess such an extensive vocabulary.

"I'm a writer," she answered. "Words of all varieties are my currency. I'm far richer in words than I am in coin."

He moved around her desk, then sat on the edge, crossing one leg over the other. "Truly, if words were money, you could buy me a hundred times over."

"If I bought you," she couldn't resist saying, "what should I do with you?"

His gaze darkened, his body tensed, and she wondered if she'd just made a critical mistake. They weren't to go down this path, yet she couldn't seem to stop herself.

Seeking a distraction, she noticed a large box set to one side on her desk. It was so substantial that it was a wonder she'd missed it before. But then, he had a tendency to muddle her thinking, so that all she saw was him.

"What's in there?" she asked.

"The reason for my being here."

"You could have had it delivered rather than bring it yourself," she pointed out. "I imagine an earl doesn't play errand boy very often."

The most ridiculously charming flush spread over his cheeks. "Yes, well." He cleared his throat. "My footmen can be clumsy, and I didn't want them damaging it."

If anything, the servants Ashford employed were overly fastidious and careful, proud of their responsibilities. Earls didn't employ ungainly footmen.

"Who's it for?" she asked.

He frowned. "You, of course."

Her brows lifted. "A present?"

"Part of our arrangement," he said. "Operating expenses, et cetera."

"I'd like to see this 'operating expense.'" She reached for the box, but he edged it from her grasp.

"The 'operating expense' has a small price," he said.

She planted her hands on her hips. "I'm half afraid to ask."

"The price is this: I want a tour of *The Hawk's Eye*. You see, my dear Miss Eleanor Hawke, you seem to know everything about me." His smile did alarming things to her bones, turning them to aspic. "Now it's my turn to uncover your secrets."

Chapter 13

Behind every printed sheet of paper is a story that extends far beyond the margins. Consider, dear reader, that the very item you hold in your hands now and read for amusement has undergone a journey that rivals any traveler for effort, peril, and hope. Let no scrap of writing go unacknowledged, for therein lie the dreams of many.

The Hawk's Eye, May 11, 1816

Eleanor wasn't certain about revealing her secrets, but when it came to the running of a newspaper, in that she was fully conversant. Easier to speak of her work here than to delve into other, more personal topics.

Still, Ashford's interest in the paper seemed odd.

"I didn't know the operations of a newspaper were at all interesting to earls," she said bluntly.

"Earl Stanhope invented a printing press over a decade ago," he pointed out.

The fact that he knew this set her back for a moment. But she managed to recover. "That, he did. In truth, our own presses are Stanhopes."

"I'd like to see them."

She frowned at him. "Again, I wonder why."

"Idle curiosity, call it," he answered at once, lightly. "The whims of the wealthy."

She had a sense this wasn't quite the truth—his words came too readily, too blithely. As though disguising some other motive. But what might that other motive be? He certainly couldn't be interested in starting his own paper. Then, what?

There wasn't much reason to refuse his request. After all, she'd nothing to hide or be ashamed of when it came to the running of *The Hawk's Eye*. It was her proudest accomplishment. Why not show it to him? Show him what she'd built herself.

She wanted him to see that. See what she'd done.

As if . . . his opinion mattered.

The fact that it did—it mattered quite a lot—shook her. She'd gone most of her life forging a path for herself, ignoring the voices of dissent inside and around her. It was either that, or let herself fade into obscurity, be swallowed whole by the cold, unfeeling machine of life. But she'd fought back, keeping her head held high, her ears covered whenever someone told her, "You cannot do that. What an absurd idea—a woman running a newspaper."

She'd gone ahead and done it, despite every obstacle.

What if Ashford dismissed what she'd worked so hard to achieve? How would she bear it?

Because she always did. And she had a hint of suspicion that he, of all people, wouldn't dismiss or demean her. Somehow he'd know what it all meant to her.

"This way, then." She waved him toward the door to her office. But he was too polite, and gestured for her to precede him.

She stepped out into the large room outside her office, and he followed. The writers continued to work, but she could sense their attention.

"We do all the writing in here," she said, gesturing to the bigger chamber, crammed full of desks, people, and paper. "I keep a staff of ten full-time writers, plus day jobbers who fill in any gaps we might have."

"Where are your editors?" he asked, glancing around.

"You're standing next to her."

He gazed at her, a look of both gratifying and annoying surprise on his face. "All you?"

She shrugged. "It's all we can afford," she said. "And I don't trust anyone else to review the articles."

"How very . . ."

She waited for the expected words. *Controlling. Mannish.*

" . . . unusual," he said.

"The Hawk's Eye is my enterprise. I try to take care of her the way a mother might tend to her colicky infant. Changing nappies is just one of my many responsibilities."

"When you say that the paper is your enterprise," he said, "you mean you inherited it, correct?"

"I mean nothing of the sort." She planted her hands on her hips. "I purchased a struggling little rag five years ago and turned it into *The Hawk's Eye.* And before you ask, the funds were entirely my own—and loans given to me by friends. I paid them all back, with interest, within two years."

"Friends? Not family?"

"I've no father, no brothers. Never been married. Everything in my bank account was placed there by me alone. Years of saving and deprivation to achieve my goal."

"Saving?" He spoke the word as if he didn't know what it meant. A corner of his mouth tilted in a self-mocking smile.

She shook her head at him. "It's what us plebeians must do if there's something we want to purchase."

"I simply cannot understand that." Yet she saw a gleam of what looked suspiciously like respect in his eyes.

"You'll have to stretch the limits of your imagination, Ashford."

"Oh, I try." He sighed. Despite his indolent artifice, he stared at the busy writers' room, his gaze far sharper than a man affecting languid disinterest. "And . . . you built this all yourself."

"I did."

He said nothing in response, though he frowned slightly,

as if grasping the enormity of the task she had set out for herself. She waited. Would he say something trivializing? Mock her ambition, especially as a woman? Others had done so.

A cold fear clutched her stomach. She'd survive if he did say something disparaging—but it would be a rocky road to traverse.

"I see" was all he said.

It wasn't praise—but she almost didn't want it. Better to have this unadorned acceptance than effusive approbation. As if her work was worth more than pretty baubles of words.

"No chastisement for behaving in an unfeminine manner?" she pressed. "No mockery?"

"Not from me."

"Why?" she demanded.

"Consider it part of a wealthy man's eccentricity," he said with a shrug. "I can afford to think in more abnormal ways, because no one will gainsay me. I've too much power."

She began to walk down the row of desks, and he kept pace beside her. "Like Caligula making his horse a consul."

"Caligula thought he was a god."

"Don't you?" she wondered.

He rewarded her with a grin. "Most men think of themselves that way."

"That explains quite a lot about your sex's tendency toward delusion."

"For a woman who's never been married," he said, "you have quite a few opinions about men."

"I'm very observant," she replied. "Besides, just because I haven't had a husband doesn't mean I don't know the male sex intimately."

"How intimately?" he asked, one brow raised.

"I cannot reveal my sources," she answered. They'd reached the end of the room and now stood in front of a thick wooden door. She placed her hand on the knob. "But I can show you part of what makes *The Hawk's Eye* so successful."

"By all means."

She turned the knob and opened the door. Instantly, sound assailed them. Metal clanking, and the pound of a mallet. They entered a second chamber, twice the size of the writers' room. Rows of printing presses lined up, and men in aprons busily fed sheets of paper into them. Overhead, sheets of printed papers dried, like exotic plants hanging from tree branches.

"This," she said, opening her arms wide to encompass the chamber. "Unlike other smaller newspapers, who contract out their printing, We save costs and increase our distribution by doing all our printing in house."

"A noisy house," the earl said above the din.

"The price we pay, and gladly. In the first days, we farmed out, but then I reviewed the numbers and realized we could make much bigger strides if we invested in our own presses." She nodded toward the large cast-iron machines. Two workers manned each press, churning out page after page. "These are Stanhopes, though you already know that." She led Ashford forward, and they watched the two printers laboring quickly to produce sheet after sheet of the next issue.

"I've read of the man's work," he said above the clang of the machine, "but never saw it with my own eyes. Looks dangerous."

"It can be, if operated by a novice. But I don't employ novices."

He asked, "How many sheets can you print in an hour?"

The fact that that even interested him astonished her. "Four hundred and eighty. That's twice the rate from the old wooden and metal machines. And the effort to operate a Stanhope press is considerably less than the old machines, as well."

Ashford watched the printers with a slightly detached, bemused expression, his hands clasped behind his back. She thought he might be bored by the process. Even though the inventor of the press she used was an earl, most noblemen—especially those with reputations as rakes—generally didn't find the wonders of this new industrial age particularly compelling.

Despite his aloof attitude, he asked the printers questions about how everything worked, and what it took to become a master printer. Though he drawled his questions, as if he couldn't quite be bothered to hear the answer, let alone ask the question itself, the things he asked were insightful. Surprisingly deferential.

Instead of watching the presses, as she normally liked to do, her attention was solely fixed on Ashford and the keen, perceptive sharpness in his gaze, regardless of his languid attitude. She even caught hints of respect in his expression as he talked to the workers. There was no dismissiveness, no aristocratic sneering at the labor involved.

The printers cared about the work. And it appeared that some part of Ashford cared, as well. Almost in spite of himself.

It crept into her. On soft cat's feet. A feeling that went beyond attraction—for of a certain, the earl was an attractive man, and he drew her on a primal level. Yet there was something more to him. Something else that pulled her toward him, knotting around her, making her heart jump and her blood speed whenever she heard him speak. When he stood close, or when he aimed that smile at her, as he did now. That smile that was more than a little self-deprecating, and full of awareness and intelligence.

Goddamn him. Why the hell did he have to be so bloody *likeable*? Why couldn't he conform to what she believed dissolute noblemen to be? His charm, she expected. But not this. Not his intellectual curiosity, his esteem for work and people who had to earn their bread.

Once he'd exhausted his questions, she led him away from the row of presses. "I'm saving to buy a steam-powered Koening press," she explained. "The *Times* has them, and it'll make the whole process even faster."

"Won't that put men like those" Ashford nodded toward the printers—"out of work?"

Damn bastard, showing concern for her employees.

"They'll all be trained on the new equipment," she said. "The process will go faster, but we won't lose any men to it."

"Ah." He actually seemed relieved by her answer, then caught himself showing too much interest. "Not that it matters to me, of course."

"Of course," she said with limited conviction.

"What's all that activity there? It fair makes my head ache with its industriousness." He nodded toward one end of the room, where more apron-clad men gathered around large trays.

"Those are the compositors—typesetters," she clarified. "They take the written pages and turn them into proofs for printing."

The typesetters took metal letters from large cases and arranged them in composing sticks, which were then transferred to the type galleys. "Once the galleys are filled," she explained, "everything is tied together into one unit."

"So it can be moved without falling apart," he speculated.

"Exactly. We make a proof, and then it goes to a proofreader, who makes sure there aren't any errors."

He made a show of looking amazed. "You actually allow someone else to review the proofs?"

In response, she sent him a rude hand gesture. Then admitted, "At the beginning, the proofreader was indeed me. But then my responsibilities became too great, and I had to hire somebody."

"What a devastating blow that must have been."

"I barely recovered." She waved toward another of her workers. "That gentleman is the stoneman. He's converting the tied bundles of type into forms, which is what gets placed on the press."

They both watched as the stoneman arranged the pages of type onto a flat imposition stone.

"It requires a discerning eye to get the job done right," she continued. "Taking into account the page size, and the paper used, many pages can be printed at the same time on a single sheet—which saves us money, of course. This part of the process also makes certain that the pages are facing the correct direction, and are in the proper order."

Much of the noise came from one man wielding a mallet to tap in pieces of metal, filling in the blank sections of the pages. He leveled the type, too, making certain that the surface was flat.

"Here's the final step before printing," she said, gesturing toward the men taking away the cords holding the type in place. They used keys to lock everything—type, metal blocks, additional pieces, and the frame—into place. "That's the *form*. That's what goes to the printing press. And once it's printed, we dry the sheets"—she waved overhead to the inked pages—"then put them in our folding machine. Finished papers are bundled up and sent out to newsagents."

She planted her hands on her hips. "And now you know, very loosely, how a newspaper is run."

He made a small, elegant bow. "It's been most . . . educational. Much to my chagrin," he added.

"What an imposition on your lackadaisical existence," she said drily.

"Is there somewhere a little more quiet?" he said above the din.

"Why? I've answered your questions."

"While this has been, to my vexation, an eye-opening experience," he answered, "I haven't learned everything."

"What else is there?"

He leaned close, filling her senses with his nearness, and spoke lowly. "Your secrets."

It didn't surprise Daniel that she immediately strode from the printing room and hastened to her office. After all, no one wanted to confess their secrets in a noisy room full of one's employees.

What had brought him here in the first place? Yes, he'd

wanted to give her his gift, but another desire had driven him. As if he couldn't stop himself from wanting to know more of her. A growing need that had been building ever since . . . ever since he'd met her, he realized. He'd simply planned on dropping off the box, seeing her reaction to opening it, and then leaving. Yet once he'd set foot inside her offices, a greater demand built. A demand for knowledge. Of her.

But he'd had to protect himself. Cloak himself in layers of nonchalance. As if he could fool both of them into thinking he didn't care as much as he did.

Perhaps she didn't know—but she was too astute to let anything slip by her. His own understanding came with a goodly amount of fear. With the exception of Jonathan and Marwood, he didn't get close to people. It was easier, safer that way.

When it came to her, however, he couldn't seem to stop himself. She pulled upon him with a magnetic force that could no more be denied than the laws of physics themselves.

Still, he strove for control.

He now stayed close at her heels. As soon as he entered her office, she shut the door behind them, though she did not draw the blinds. The box still sat on her desk, and she looked at it with alarm before seating herself. There was no other chair in the small room, so Daniel had to remain standing. He did so comfortably, his hands folded behind his back.

"I have no secrets," she said.

"Everyone has them," he replied. "You, of all people, should know that."

"Not everything is worth printing in my paper."

"I'm not interested in what gets printed in your paper. But the editor and owner of the paper holds a certain interest for me."

"I cannot see why," she snapped.

"Call it more of my aristocrat's idiosyncrasy." He was reluctant to divulge something that he wasn't comfortable revealing to himself.

She narrowed her eyes. "I don't believe that. There was more than idle curiosity when you were talking to my workers. Stands to reason there's more going on here than you're telling me."

He paused. Should he? It was a hell of a risk. But worth it, he realized. "A truth for a truth, then."

"All right."

"Because," he said candidly, "I've never had a kiss like the one we had after the phaeton race. And I want to learn everything I can about the woman who can kiss like that."

His bluntness seemed to catch her off guard. "I don't make it a habit of kissing strange men, you know," she muttered.

"I rather hope not," he answered, "because if you did, you'd have no time for writing, editing, proofreading, or anything else. There would be a line of men around the block, queuing up for the chance to kiss you."

"Then I'd send them home disappointed."

"But consider how disruptive that would be, getting up every five minutes to shoo away herds of young bucks all vying for your attentions. And you're stalling," he added.

She folded her arms across her chest. "I don't owe you any answers," she said sullenly.

"I gave you my truth. Now you owe me yours."

"And if I refuse?"

Straightening, he brushed a fleck of paper from his sleeve. "Then *To Ride with a Rake* will be only two articles, and no more."

Her lips tightened into a line. "I might've suspected you would descend to blackmail."

"Leverage," he corrected. "*Blackmail* is such a brutal word."

"It's my job to pick words very precisely," she said. "And I stand by my original choice."

"Very well." He exhaled. "I see you are determined to extract some tiny measure of honor from me. You don't have to speak of anything you don't want to."

"Thank you," she said tartly.

"But if you want to know what's in here," he said, setting his palm on the large box, "then you might favor me with the merest hint about yourself."

"You'd really withhold that to get what you want?" she demanded.

"Of course," he answered easily. "Haven't you noticed, Miss Hawke? Ethics and morals are in short supply where I'm concerned."

"I have noticed," she grumbled. "Too bad they don't sell them with the haddock at Billingsgate market."

"Ethics smell worse than fish," he countered.

"And are just as perishable." She glowered at him.

For half a moment, he thought she might refuse him. But he banked on her writer's curiosity.

His gamble won out, because after a minute, she said, "What do you want to know?"

Everything. Touring the premises of *The Hawk's Eye,* seeing the running of a scandal rag through her excited, passionate eyes, kindled a need to learn all that he could about her. To delve into her innermost self. What drove such a woman as her? He envied her that drive, that determination. Envied, and admired.

He'd tried, as much as he could, to smother that sentiment, but the more he saw of what pushed her, what she cared about, feelings shoved against the bulwark of his inner defenses. Defenses that had, for so many years, kept him sheltered behind walls of disinterest and the weary pursuit of distracting pleasure. And here she was, full of energy and vitality, and those fortifications began to fracture.

"One moment." He abruptly left the room and walked out into the main chamber where the other writers were gathered. Spotting an empty chair, he grabbed it and, to the wondering eyes of the people around him, carried it back to Eleanor's office.

He set it down in front of her desk, then closed the door behind him. Taking a seat, he said, "That's more accommodating."

"I've never been very accommodating," she replied.

"Today's your first day. Now, you asked me what I'd like to know."

"You rather forced my hand to ask you," she said defiantly.

"I get what I want," he said. "Nobleman's prerogative, and all that."

"I think they might have the right idea in America. No aristocrats."

"Plutocrats, however," he pointed out. "And even without my title, I'd have a sodding lot of money."

She threw him a sour look. "Gauche of you to keep reminding me of that."

"Perhaps all this rubbing elbows with the laborers of London has made me so."

"I've kept to the rules, *my lord*," she said acidly. "Took you on a tour of my paper in exchange for looking in this box. And now you've gone and changed the rules."

He smiled. "Rules shift and change all the time."

"Then they aren't *rules* but *suggestions*."

"Such is the nature of government."

"And in this regime," she said tartly, "you are in command. As always."

"Really," he objected, enjoying himself considerably, "you act as though I'm as bad as a Borgia."

"Poisoners, those Borgias." She tapped a finger on her chin. "Maybe they had the right idea."

"Now you're making it far more difficult than it needs to be. Just answer a simple question, and then you can see what I've brought you." He patted the box in enticement.

She sighed, looking up at the ceiling. "What do you want to know?"

It was a bittersweet victory, winning out over her. He could have bantered back and forth with her all day, but his own curiosity was too strong to withhold from her any longer. Yet what he was about to ask would reveal not just her secrets but his own. His secret that he found her deeply fascinating and wanted to learn whatever he could of her history, of herself.

"Why did you become a writer?" he asked.

For a moment, she said nothing. Would she guard herself too much to reveal this about herself? But this seemed the key to her, and he wanted that key.

At last, however, she said, "Because of my father."

"He encouraged your efforts? A rare thing for a father to do for his daughter."

"He was a drunkard," she said flatly. "A Grub Street hack who, more often than not, was too far in his cups to finish his writing assignments. I learned early that if I wanted to eat, I had to finish the work for him."

Daniel stared at her. "You . . . wrote his articles?"

She turned her gaze from the ceiling to the top of her desk, running her fingers over the blotter, circling splatters of ink. "From the time I was fifteen. He was so drunk or bleary from his dipsomaniacal rampages that he actually believed he'd written the pieces himself. He learned the truth one day when he woke up on the floor and found me writing what was supposed to be his review of a novel. After that, he let me take over completely. It gave him more time to drink."

Daniel thought he'd been astonished before at learning that she'd bought the newspaper herself, rather than inheriting it. But he felt utterly staggered, pinned in his chair. "And your mother?"

A small, fond smile toyed at the corners of Eleanor's mouth. "Kind. Warm. Taught me everything I knew about gambling. But . . . she wasn't particularly inclined toward motherhood. She left when I was nine. I had to leave school to take in mending, though the schoolteacher lent me books. It was just me and Father, after that."

"The scribbling sot." It stunned him, the sudden wave of anger on her behalf.

Her smile turned wry. "Father did the best he could, given his fondness for gin. It was almost like a sickness with him. As if he couldn't help himself."

Still, the fury went unabated. Someone had needed to look after young Eleanor, and no one had. And where had

Daniel been during this time? On his Grand Tour. Carousing. Caring only for the next pleasure. He couldn't have known about Eleanor, of course, but a blade of self-blame pushed itself between his ribs.

"He had a young daughter to raise," Daniel heard himself growl, as if he couldn't stop himself from speaking. "He bloody well should have helped himself."

Unexpected, the depths of his rage. He couldn't stop himself from picturing a young Eleanor, forced to take care of herself and her drunkard of a father. Other children worked. It was a cruel truth of this world. He always gave flower girls and crossing sweeps extra coins. Who'd seen to Eleanor's needs when she had been a girl? Who had looked after her? She had.

"Is he still in his cups now?" he demanded. If so, Daniel would seek the man out and . . . well, he didn't know precisely what he'd do, but someone had to make Mr. Hawke pay for what the inebriate had done to Eleanor.

"He sleeps in Cross Bones," she said.

The paupers' cemetery.

"He's been there for over a decade," she continued. "A shame, really. If he'd waited a few more years, I could have afforded a decent burial."

The flatness of her tone belied the pain in her eyes. Daniel's hands itched to reach across her desk and weave his fingers with hers. But he sensed such a gesture wouldn't be appreciated. Not at that moment, anyway. Yet he could sense beneath her armor an aching vulnerability. One he wanted to shield and care for.

Care for? Aside from Catherine's and Jonathan's, and occasionally Marwood's, when had he cared for anyone's welfare beside his own?

And yet he felt an ache in his chest when thinking of Eleanor, young and alone, fighting for survival when everyone around her had abandoned her. Her brazen, bold persona had been formed in the blistering forge of experience. She hadn't collapsed. She'd endured, survived. Thrived, if *The Hawk's Eye* was any indication.

"Took me a while, though," she went on, a little more brightly. Rallying herself. "I did more hack work under my own name. Seemed there were newspapermen out there who didn't much care about the gender of their writers, so long as the work got done. And I did it. Worked my way up the ladder as a writer and editor. Became the assistant to a man who ran another rag."

"So industrious." But his attempt at insouciance sounded hollow even to him.

"I couldn't work for anyone anymore," she said. "I wanted life on my terms. So I saved. Bought this place—with the help of my friends, like I said. It used to be one of those dreadful women's etiquette journals. I changed all that," she added with pride.

He couldn't fault Eleanor her self-satisfaction. If he'd accomplished half of what she'd done, he'd be feeling smug, himself. And she'd done it all with the handicap of her sex in a world that didn't favor women advancing themselves.

"Ever consider writing something more than just a scandal sheet?" he asked.

Her smug look vanished, replaced by a scowl. "This isn't *just* a scandal sheet," she said bitingly. "It's years of hard work and sacrifice."

"Of course it is." He peered at her. "But I've read your work. You could do so much better than scribbling about the likes of Lord A—d. Your work here is very good. You deserve more than this. This paper could be truly important, instead of just a trifle."

Now her frown was thunderous. "What a bloody dismissive, demeaning thing to say. After everything I've told you about myself. All the sweat I've poured into *The Hawk's Eye*. And I can 'do better'?"

"Perhaps I didn't pick my words correctly," he allowed.

"Perhaps you damned well didn't," she snapped. "I am exactly where I want to be, doing precisely what I want. I give people entertainment. With a dash of education. But if I can give them a taste of relief from their everyday lives, then I consider my efforts well spent." She stood. "Better this than writing deportment manuals or moralistic novels where the heroine always dies at the end."

Her rage was a palpable thing, hot and edged.

He, too, stood. "There's clearly no reasoning with you when you've willfully taken umbrage at what wasn't intended to give offense."

"Yes," she said acidly. "Clearly the fault is mine for being offended. How very hysterical and unreasonable I'm being."

"You are," he said tightly. "I'm offering you a compliment."

She pointed to the door. "I will unreasonably tell you to leave now."

"Eleanor."

Her eyes blazed. "I may have kissed you, but I didn't give you leave to call me by my Christian name." She drew a breath. "Good-bye, Lord Ashford." Her heat had cooled into pure ice.

He often spent time practicing his pugilism skills. He knew the benefit of a strategic retreat. Now would be such a time. So he grabbed his walking stick, donned his hat, and gave her a clipped bow before leaving.

It was only later, as he sat in his carriage, wondering how everything had gone so horribly awry, that he realized she hadn't opened the box. And he'd so wanted to see the look on her face when she saw what he'd brought her.

He wondered now if he ever would.

Chapter 14

Is there any surer way to ensnare a woman than through the judicious usage of silk?

The Hawk's Eye, May 11, 1816

Damn. *Damn.*

Eleanor wanted to throw something. Anything. But all she had in her office were stacks of paper, and those weren't particularly satisfying to hurl against a wall. She mulled kicking her desk, but her boots weren't very sturdy, and she'd probably hurt herself.

So she closed the door to her office and allowed herself the release of swearing. Considerably. At great volume.

Why was she so bloody angry? It wasn't as though Ashford hadn't expressed opinions she had never heard before. People called her work, and *The Hawk's Eye*, trash. Or they damned it, and her, with faint praise. *You're too talented to waste yourself on ephemera. Why don't you try writing something* real? *Something with actual substance?*

She'd spoken the truth to the earl. She took great pride in her work. In what her newspaper did. There was nothing wrong with providing an hour's entertainment, especially when the reality of most people's lives was often grim and unrelenting. If she could give a harried mother a moment's respite, or relieve the tedium of a banking clerk's day, then what was wrong with that?

These were all arguments she'd made in the past, and with countless people, male and female. She didn't expect most to understand the why and wherefore of what she did.

Yet she'd hoped, somehow, that Ashford would be different. He hadn't appeared so. Not at first. But it had seemed that his opinion of her work, of *her,* had changed. And she'd been glad of it. Someone who understood her. What pushed and drove her ambition, her love.

It had felt so good.

But she'd been wrong about him. He was just like the others. Trivializing what she toiled over. Thinking her somehow "better" than the thing she adored. As though she couldn't judge for herself what deserved her focus and energy.

Disappointment curled in her acidly. She cursed herself for thinking that he was different. Because, in spite of himself, he'd shown some interest in the running of the paper. As no other man had ever shown. Because he'd been angry on her behalf for her youthful struggles. Only Maggie had shown her as much sympathy, but Maggie was the only other person Eleanor had allowed to know of her past. Certainly, Eleanor hadn't ever revealed her early history to any man. She could tell herself that Ashford had forced her disclosure, but she knew differently. It had been her choice to bare herself to him in that way. And she'd wanted to.

She'd wanted him to be special. His opinion mattered to her. That had been her mistake.

Her gaze fell on the large paperboard box, still sitting on her desk. She'd given up the story of her childhood in exchange for learning the contents of that box. And now she didn't even want to look inside.

No, that wasn't true. She still burned with curiosity to know what was in it. But another part of her wanted to return it unopened.

Her fingers twitched.

"Hell," she muttered. She opened the box.

Eleanor unfolded the tissue paper surrounding the contents. And inhaled sharply.

It was a gown. The most incredible gown she'd ever seen. Deep sapphire silk that gleamed like the depths of the ocean. Pearls and sparkling beads adorned the deep neckline, as well as the edges of the short sleeves. Gently, she lifted the gown from the box. A gauzy cape hung from its shoulders, embroidered with silver thread. The wearer would appear to float as she walked, the cape swirling behind her like a magical mist.

Experimentally, she held it up to herself. Hell and damnation, it would fit her. Perfectly.

How did Ashford know? He must've gone to the Imperial and gotten her measurements that way. The bastard.

Her breath caught again when she saw something else in the box. Gently setting the gown aside, she reached into the box and picked up the object within.

A mask.

Made of white silk, the half mask was also adorned with seed pearls and silver embroidery. Silver and blue ribbons would fasten the mask to the wearer's face, concealing her identity while also highlighting her eyes.

Eleanor would look incredible in such a thing. She wasn't vain—perhaps a little vain—but she knew this with a deep certainty. With her blonde hair and hazel eyes, the sapphire silk would complement her beautifully.

She closed her eyes. Emotions and desires warred within her like ancient foes on the battleground.

She desperately wanted the gown.

She couldn't possibly accept it.

Even if she and Ashford hadn't argued moments earlier, she would not be able to keep the dress. He had to have known that. Yet he'd given it to her, anyway.

What the hell had he been thinking?

Quickly, before she could change her mind, she sat down and scribbled out a note. Sealed it. She put the gown and mask back into the box. Then she opened her door and called in Peter, the newspaper's errand boy.

"Take this"—she held up the note—"and that"—she

nodded toward the box—"to the Earl of Ashford, at Manchester Square. If he asks for you to wait for a reply, don't."

"Say 'no' to an earl?" Peter looked dubious.

"Just drop it off and go. Leave it on the front step for all I care." She paced back to her desk, sat, and picked up an article that needed editing. When Peter didn't move, she snapped, "Go on!"

The boy gulped, but he gathered the box and hurried out of her office. As soon as he left, she set down the article and rested her head in her hands. She wasn't entirely certain, but there was a good degree of likelihood that her *To Ride with a Rake* series had just ended. Angry melancholy swamped her. It had been a profitable series for *The Hawk's Eye,* and she'd be sorry to lose what momentum the paper had gained by discontinuing the series.

Even worse, though, was the fact that she and Ashford had parted so bitterly. And over things that should never have happened in the first place.

She probably wouldn't see him again. Another wave of sadness threatened to inundate her.

Forcing it back, she lifted her head and picked up the article again. Whatever her personal feelings might or might not be, she had a business to run. Sentimentality was for those with ample coffers.

A half hour later, Peter appeared in her door, short of breath. "I left it, just like you said. Ran away before anyone could stop me."

She unlocked the top drawer of her desk and pulled out a small pouch. From the pouch she extracted a coin and handed it to Peter. "Thank you."

He tugged on his forelock and trotted away, ready for the next errand. Though she doubted anything else he did today would be as unusual as throwing a stunning gown and mask at an earl.

There. It was done. *They* were done. It had been . . . amusing, and profitable, while it had lasted.

And she wouldn't miss him. The way his eyes twinkled

when he made a particularly witty riposte. The admiration in his expression when he looked at her. His long, strapping body, or sinful mouth. No, she wouldn't miss any of that at all.

A footman in a familiar livery entered the writers' room and made the long walk to her office. Beneath his arm was the box.

That son of a bitch.

"I won't read it," she said when the footman approached and held out an envelope.

"I'm told not to leave until you do," the servant answered.

"Then you won't be returning to your place of employment, because I am not going to read that letter."

"Yes, madam." The footman positioned himself in one corner of her office. And stood. Still holding the box and the note.

She decided to ignore him. She also ignored the curious glances from her employees as they went in and out of her office all day, noting the footman in the corner. Most newspaper offices didn't have liveried servants. *The Hawk's Eye* was no exception. But she supposed that, until he eventually gave up, the footman was staying for now.

He stood, barely moving, for hours. Simply stared ahead, into that unseeable distance that all servants seemed to regard when standing in attendance. Credit was due. The young man, whatever his name was, made an excellent footman. He also drew the notice of some of the female writers on staff. Eleanor couldn't blame them. He was a handsome, tall lad who filled out his uniform very nicely. Good calves, too.

But she didn't care if he looked like a hero straight from the *Thousand and One Nights*. He was a nuisance who represented an even greater irritant—and regret.

She worked for the whole of the day, refusing to acknowledge the footman. Half a dozen articles were edited, and she penned her own piece decrying false modesty. Lamps were lit against the setting sun. Still, he waited.

It was nearly eight o'clock. Time for her to go home.

She rose, donning her coat. "Are you going to stay here all night?"

"Yes, madam. I was told if I left for even a moment, I'd have no job waiting for me upon my return to the earl's house."

More unkind names for the earl filled her head. He knew, he *knew* that she'd discover this, and he counted on her sympathy for the footman.

What choice did she have but to read the damned letter? She snatched it from the servant's hand and tore it open.

You don't have to accept the bloody dress. Consider it a temporary ensemble. But you'll need it and the mask for our next rakish excursion in three days hence.

—A.

He still wanted to continue their association? After she threw him out of her office?

Either he was a lunatic, or he truly needed her to write these articles for some still opaque reason.

Or maybe, maybe, he wanted to see her again.

Most likely he needed the articles. She doubted he craved her company, especially after today.

"I'm to wait for an answer, too, madam," the footman said.

"Of course you are."

She sat herself down behind her desk, pulled out a sheet of paper, and inked her quill.

What was she supposed to write? *Go bugger yourself* seemed like a nice option. *Don't order me around like a lackey* was another. Also, *Find someone else to write your sodding articles. Your thoughtless dismissal of my hard work broke my heart.*

Instead, she wrote, *Name the time. We'll meet at the Imperial. —E.H.*

She had a paper to run, after all. It had nothing to do with wanting to see him again. Not one bit.

Daniel couldn't recognize the sensations that danced over the surface of his skin. They were tight, uncomfortable. As he sat in his carriage, heading toward the Imperial, it took him some moments to realize that what he felt were nerves. Raw, edgy nerves. Even when gambling for the highest stakes, he was never anxious. But going to meet Eleanor tonight, he understood with disconcerting clarity that this feeling was apprehension.

He wanted to see her, yes, but there was an unknown element, too. They hadn't parted well, and their subsequent correspondence hadn't precisely been warm, either. What mood would he find her in tonight? Her fury was a hot and powerful thing. And she'd been angry with him. Very, very angry.

Gripping the head of his walking stick, he stared out at the passing city, deceptively quiet in the night. But beneath the sleeping façade lay a place full of seething life. And tonight, he and Eleanor would plunge back into that cauldron.

Why the devil should it matter what she thought of him? Why should he care that she was furious with him?

Because it did matter. A great deal.

That realization was sobering enough, without his already tense mood tightening even more the closer he got to the theater.

It surprised him that she'd even agreed to accompany him tonight. He'd thought for certain that she'd end their association—especially after his misstep with the gown. But her business sense appeared to have won out over her personal ethics. To a point. The dress would have to go back after this evening. The modiste, Madame Clothilde, seldom had her exclusive creations returned. She would no doubt be shocked and perhaps even insulted by the reappearance of the gown—though substantial financial recompense might smooth over any of the dressmaker's hurt feelings.

But damn, did he want to see Eleanor in that gown. He'd thought of her coloring specifically when selecting the fabric and describing the embellishments. His own ensemble was a complement to hers in color and material—an old-fashioned courtier's rig, with a full frock coat, waistcoat, and knee breeches. He even carried a tricorn hat, though he drew the line at wearing a wig. It might have spoiled the effect somewhat, but he had his pride. Wigs were for his grandfather's generation.

He adjusted his silk half mask. The item was supposed to give its wearer some anonymity, but he couldn't lose himself fully in his disguise. Not with his taut anticipation at seeing Eleanor thrumming through his veins. He couldn't remember who he was anymore. He thought he'd known himself as well as one knew a familiar piece of scenery. A cliff here. A gnarled tree there. But now the landscape was shifting, readjusting itself, and he found himself . . . lost. In himself. Craggy mountains where before there had been only a smooth plain. New rivers rushing through what was once a dry field. His mask only enforced that sense of otherness.

At last, the carriage pulled up outside the theater. But Eleanor wasn't there. Instead, a dark-haired woman waited outside the performers' entrance. A stern expression marked her handsome face. Before the footman could leap down from his perch to open the door, the woman approached and leaned in the window to the carriage.

"You're playing a dangerous game, my lord," she said tightly.

He fell back on his armor of politeness. "Have we been introduced, madam?"

"I know you, Lord Ashford," she answered, "though I doubt you know me."

She wasn't an actress—he knew most of the female performers here at the Imperial, and he'd never seen her on the stage. The costumer? No. Ink stained the woman's fingers. A writer. Which had to mean . . .

"You're the playwright, Mrs. Delamere," he realized.

Her brows lifted. "I'm not a public figure."

"No, but your works are. I've a friend who never misses your new burlettas."

She looked as though she fought the urge to preen. Instead, she made herself look stern again. "Eleanor doesn't know I'm talking with you, but I'm here to give you a warning. If any harm befalls her at your hands, I'll make Tourneur's *The Revenger's Tragedy* look like a springtime gala."

Now it was his turn to raise his brow. "Do you threaten me, madam?"

Her grin was small and vicious. "It might seem inconceivable to you that a commoner might offer bodily harm to a peer. Indeed, I might be thrown into gaol for such an offense. But Eleanor is my dearest friend, and you'll find me quite creative and single-minded when it comes to protecting those I care about."

"An admirable quality," he answered, liking this plainspoken playwright. "And I can assure you that hurting or harming Eleanor ranks at the very bottom of things I intend to do."

"Ah, but intention and deed can often be very different things," she replied, leaning on the window frame. "You've some ulterior motive in inviting her to come with you on your escapades. That much is clear to both Eleanor and myself." Something appeared to trouble her, and she bit her lip as if to keep from speaking of it aloud.

Had Eleanor told Mrs. Delamere about their kiss? If they were indeed "dearest friends," chances were good that she had.

In his most lofty tone, he said, "No disrespect was intended—"

"Again, it's not a matter of intention, but the end result. You're a nobleman. The most untrustworthy lot," she muttered to herself.

"What transpires between Eleanor and me concerns only us," he said. He had more biting words to use, but he had to respect her gender, even if she didn't respect his rank.

"But it doesn't, my lord. She's alone in this world, as am I—which means we've had to make our own families. Eleanor and I have the advantage of sisterhood without the complications of blood ties. So I will say one final time that should anything happen to her—anything she doesn't wish for, or results in her pain—I will seek you out and make you extremely repentant."

"Your point is quite clear, madam," he said coolly. The insolence of this woman! It was almost commendable.

Mrs. Delamere glanced over her shoulder. "Keep your mouth fastened about our conversation. She can be rather . . . foul-tempered . . . when she feels her authority is undercut."

Before he could answer, the stage door opened and Eleanor emerged, carrying her cloak on her arm.

All thoughts of what he was or was not going to say fled like a receding tide, leaving him like a fish gasping on the shore.

He hadn't been wrong. The colors and cut of the gown flattered her. In the most excruciating manner. The silk embraced her curves lovingly. All images of her as "Ned" vanished entirely. She didn't even look like the tart Ruby. No, she was far more elegant, regal and sensual at the same time. With each step, the gauzy cape attached to her shoulders flowed out in sapphire ripples. Instead of another wig, her hair was uncovered, pinned up in intricate curls with pearls winking among the blonde waves. The half mask brought her eyes to vivid light. She wore long white gloves, but combined with the crescents of bare flesh between the gloves and her sleeves, and the low neckline of the gown, he had ample evidence that her skin was satiny and smooth. He ached to touch her.

Yet he held himself still as she neared the carriage. She held herself stiffly, her back straight, her chin tipped up.

She hadn't forgiven him.

Mrs. Delamere stepped back as the footman opened the door to the vehicle. The servant held out a hand to help Eleanor in, but she didn't take it. Instead, she stayed where she was, eying Daniel from the pavement.

"What were you two discussing?" she asked warily.

"The earl's plans for tonight," Mrs. Delamere answered.

"A masquerade," he filled in. "At a certain nobleman's house. Secret invitation only."

"Sounds like the kind of night you toffs enjoy," the playwright said under her breath.

"What's the point of being a toff," he answered, "if we can't have secret invitation masquerades where we revel in the perquisites of being nobly born?" He turned back to Eleanor. "I trust my plan for the evening meets with your approval."

"My readers will enjoy an account of such an entertainment," she said. Which wasn't precisely the kind of enthusiasm he'd been hoping for, but it would have to do for now.

"Shall I wait up for you, Cinder Maid?" Mrs. Delamere asked.

"Not tonight, Fairy Godmother." Eleanor clasped her friend's hand, sharing with her a look of wry humor. "Tonight, I'm in charge of my fate."

With that, she allowed the footman to help her into the carriage. She settled opposite Daniel in a rustle of silk, smelling of soap and spice. Good God, but she was dangerous. Beautiful, alluring. Enticing. Claws out, ready to shred him.

She was as intricate as one of those puzzles from China, interlocking pieces that would take time, patience, and wisdom to unlock. Usually, he avoided such complexities, especially in his choice of female companion. Now, he was pulled toward her inexorably, fascinated by all the knotty and obscure parts of her.

He now understood himself even less than he understood her.

The footman closed the door and climbed back onto his perch. Meanwhile, Mrs. Delamere shot Daniel a look fraught with meaning. He looked back coolly but still couldn't help respecting the playwright's protectiveness of her friend.

"Good night, my children," Mrs. Delamere said, waving her hand like a monarch.

"Good night, Maggie," Eleanor answered with a small laugh.

But her laugh faded as the carriage pulled away. Now she and Daniel were alone, and they had no one and nothing to protect them from each other.

Chapter 15

Anonymity is a dangerous, powerful thing. It can provoke in the most sedate, rational human the urge to behave as inappropriately as one likes, with nary a consequence to one's actions, believing one to be sheltered from the laws of common propriety. Oh, reader, it a most perilous illusion.

The Hawk's Eye, May 15, 1816

The silence that reigned in the carriage was amongst the most uncomfortable Daniel had ever endured, and that included the silence that had fallen when, after a night of indulging in physical pleasure with Lady Jane Reynolds, he'd called her Joan. He'd taken a slap to the face for that—rightly so—and Lady *Jane* had treated him to a long period of purposeful muteness whenever they'd crossed paths.

He'd felt a little foolish then, but he hadn't experienced this tight pain, this awkward, strained sense of realizing that he'd made a grave error but didn't know how to repair it. And *wanting* to repair it.

Eleanor stared fixedly out the window, her hands folded in her lap. She'd donned her cloak, and it cocooned her protectively in silk. Later, she would emerge from that cocoon, butterfly-like, to dazzle everyone at Marwood's masquerade. But for now, she held herself apart, distant. She was so cool to him that it was a wonder his breath didn't mist in the chilled air.

"You haven't said anything about my costume." It wasn't

much of an opening volley, but he needed something to break this silence.

Her gaze flicked from the window to him, then back again, all without showing the slightest change in expression. "Old-fashioned. Like its wearer."

"Suppose I deserve that," he said.

"And worse," she added. "But unlike others, I can keep my unkind opinions to myself."

"Eleanor—"

"I didn't say you could call me that." Fire snapped in her eyes as she glared at him.

"Seeing as how we kissed each other," he answered, "falling back on 'Miss Hawke' seems regressive. And, despite what you believe, we're nothing if not progressive."

"Hardly seems fair to grant you that intimacy when I don't have the same."

He spread his hands. "You call me by the name all my friends know me by."

"I want more." She tipped up her chin. "If you're to use my Christian name, then I demand the same honor."

"What—call me Daniel? Nobody uses that name."

"Then I'll be the only one. My privilege."

He frowned. It was merely a name. And yet it did hold a particular intimacy, something reserved only for those closest to him. It wasn't a coincidence that no one referred to him as Daniel. As Eleanor said, she would be the only person who did. A secret bond, linking them together, as though they held hands beneath a table.

He liked it.

"Very well," he grumbled. "Daniel, then. But only in private. It would be suspect otherwise."

"Daniel," she repeated, and he discovered a new pleasure at that moment. Hearing her say his name. He took gratification in the shape it made on her lips, and the slight huskiness in her voice as she sounded the consonants.

"Eleanor," he answered. Though it was shadowed in the carriage and though she wore a mask, he thought he detected a slight flush in her cheeks as he said her name.

If he thought that this exchange resolved the tension between them, however, he was mistaken. Another strained silence fell, like a mostly dead mouse dropped at one's feet by a cat.

She would not be as forgiving as Lady Jane Reynolds, who had eventually invited him back to her bed after several weeks of punitive wordlessness. In that case, too, the prize had been less valuable. He could always find another lover. But losing Eleanor's good opinion stung. No, it did more than sting. It *hurt*.

My God. He was going to do it. Apologize. Perhaps for the first time in all of his adult life. Though he had begged forgiveness from Catherine for failing Jonathan so miserably.

Still, that had been a unique—and awful—experience.

"What I said earlier," he began, his voice a rusty growl. "At your office."

"I remember," she said tightly. "It's etched into my memory. Like acid. That I could 'do so much better than scribbling about the likes of Lord A—d,' and that the paper was 'just a trifle.'"

He winced. Did he actually say those things? Clearly, he must have, because she had an excellent memory and wouldn't invent such insults.

"You've every right to hate me," he said.

"Oh, do I?" she asked brightly. "Thank you for giving me permission. I'd been concerned that I despised you without good cause, but now I see that I do."

He grimaced. "There's no possibility that you are going to make this easy on me, is there?"

"Everyone else does," she replied. "But I'm not like other people."

"No, you assuredly aren't. You're better than they are."

She merely stared at him, her mouth forming a thin line. Facile compliments wouldn't work with her, which he should have known.

"Am I?" She tilted her head. "Even though I write '*just* a scandal sheet'?"

He rubbed at his jaw, as though he'd taken a punch. "Poorly chosen words, I admit."

"It's not the words I object to," she retorted, "but the sentiment behind them."

"I regret that, too."

"Do you?" She peered closer at him. "You could simply mouth platitudes at me in order to benefit your own agenda, and keep me writing about you. Yes," she answered before he could make a denial, "I know that there's some secret reason why you approached me in the first place. But I'm more concerned about raising my subscription numbers than I am about your rationale for using me."

"That reason has to remain my own," he said darkly.

"As you like," she said airily. "But you'll understand my reticence in accepting your . . . well, actually, I don't know. Is this an apology?"

He gritted his teeth. Admitting he was wrong was an unpleasant, and novel, experience. Privilege had always been his, which meant very few people ever denied him or took umbrage at his actions—or words. He had enough power so that he needn't care what others thought. Whether or not they approved of him. If he should feel any sense of shame for what he did.

And yet, with her—especially with her—it was very different.

"It is," he finally growled.

"Then say it," she answered.

"I . . ." He took a steadying breath. Crossing into a new frontier. For Eleanor. "I apologize."

She didn't immediately throw wide her arms in acceptance, but she didn't dismiss him, either. That was something. He'd hurt her, though. And badly.

He continued, "I demeaned something that clearly means a great deal to you. Your life's work, in truth. I suppose . . ." He fought to find the words. "Why do you think I run around doing ridiculous things like wagering fortunes at gaming hells, or racing phaetons, or going to masquerades?"

"Because you're rich and bored," she answered.

Her response cut him, for its speed as well as its accuracy. "There are other noblemen with passions. With ambition. They're involved with politics, or they fund scientific advancement. Or they concern themselves with any number of other interests. But I . . ." He glanced down at the fists his hands made. " . . . I've never found that. No cause. No purpose. I hungered, but could never find anything to sate that appetite."

He laughed mirthlessly. "Fine problem to have, I suppose. Too much money. Not enough responsibility. You think me a hollow man."

"I think," she said with surprising gentleness, "that you're still in search of yourself. That doesn't make you hollow. It means you're a strong vessel, waiting to find the right passion to fill you. I'd be more concerned if your aimlessness didn't bother you."

He waved his hand impatiently. "This isn't to ask your pity. I don't want it, nor do I deserve it. But it's merely to explain that, when it comes to caring deeply about something, I've little experience. And I learned that I can be a ham-fisted boor when it comes to the dreams and aspirations of others. But that wasn't my intention. Especially not with you."

"Because you need my newspaper."

"Because of *you*, damn it," he rumbled. The words themselves unsettled him, as if a great crack in the earth had suddenly opened, eager to swallow him. Yet he didn't tumble forward and disappear into darkness. Nor did she push him into the chasm. Instead, she watched him, wary, uncertain, and . . . intrigued.

More words tumbled from him. He was unable to stop them from rushing out. As if he needed them to be said. To continue the transformation of himself that had begun weeks ago when he'd walked into her office for that first time.

"I sodding *envy* you," he heard himself say. "I bloody

respect you. And there are damn few people I can say that about. But I see what you have, what you've built, and it makes me . . ."

Made him what? He could barely articulate the feelings to himself, yet they wanted to be spoken aloud, made real.

" . . . makes me esteem you. And . . . it makes me . . ." He exhaled roughly. Unable to believe that he was about to give voice to these secret emotions. Yet he had to. For her. And himself.

"Ashamed of myself," he said, almost angry. "For wasting the privileges I've been given. So, yes, I apologize. I put myself on a fragile pedestal because you make me feel . . ." He clenched his jaw as if to keep the words in.

"What?" she whispered softly into the silence. "Make you feel what?"

He spoke through clenched teeth. "Small."

She sat back. Raw and wounded, the word hung in the air. He couldn't believe he'd said everything aloud. Couldn't comprehend the depths of his admission. He—one of the wealthiest and most powerful men in England—walked around with a broken, empty core. He could buy whatever he wanted. He could make anyone do anything. He was physically very strong. And yet, and yet . . .

Because of his inner weakness, he'd resorted to demeaning one of the few people he truly admired. And that shamed him.

He'd watched her, though, through his confession. And seen how, little by little, her fury had ebbed. Her expression softened, and understanding shone in her eyes—framed by the mask.

She looked at him as though . . . she'd been given a very precious gift. Which she had. He threw baubles and trinkets at women with careless abandon, but never had he presented any of them with something as rare or fragile as his broken self.

And she cradled it carefully. He saw that in the gentleness in her gaze, the small, tender smile that curved her lips.

"There's nothing small about you," she said quietly. "You're the most outsized person I know."

"Bluster," he said.

She shook her head. "There's truth in it. You give yourself too little credit."

"For the first time," he answered, "I'm being fully honest with myself. And I was a bully to you. I'm sorry," he said again. "I said cruel, inconsiderate things. Things I regret. Not because of my agenda but because I was wrong."

He waited for her to mock him. Or make some biting comment to set him in his place. She was not a soft woman, and he'd hurt her. Which meant that his opinion of Eleanor mattered to her. And that was a grave responsibility he wouldn't neglect.

She was proud, too. It would not surprise Daniel if she cut him down.

"Forgiven," she said quietly.

He lifted a brow. "Because you want my good favor for the articles?"

"Because you made a mistake and admitted it," she replied. "Because I believe your sincerity. And, as much as I do want these Rakewell pieces for *The Hawk's Eye,* if I thought you truly unrepentant, I'd put an end to them. I value myself and my work too much to stay in the company of someone who doesn't regard me with the same value."

"Wise," he said.

"Not always." She smiled. "And," she added quietly, almost reluctantly, "I might have . . . overreacted."

He lifted a brow. "Indeed? The flawless Eleanor Hawke admits a fault?"

"I never said I was flawless," she snapped. "I'm as fallible as anyone else. And I do make mistakes. Including being somewhat sensitive when it comes to the topic of my work and subject matter." She made an angry, impatient sound. "We're slow-moving targets, us writers of entertainment. They call us hacks, panderers, scribblers. You name an insult, I've heard it: our readers are fools; the writers themselves are imbeciles; we have no talent. And God forbid a *woman* should attempt to write something that isn't moralistic tripe. Then the insults are tripled."

She took a shaking breath. "Forgive my lecture. But it's something of a sore point for me."

"Understandable," he said. "Never thought of what it must be like to be on the receiving end of so much contempt. Although," he added with a wry twist of his mouth, "I've been on the other end of your paper's scrutiny. Yet I'm not affected by it."

"I won't give up my work," she said. "Even if Prinny himself denounces me."

"No one wants his good opinion."

"You know the Prince?" Her eyes went round.

"I avoid the Carlton House set. Even I have my standards."

"Very well." She laughed. "Then I wouldn't stop even if Shakespeare, Dr. Johnson, and Miss Austen all criticize me. No one else might think my work has value, but I do. And I have over a thousand readers who feel the same way."

She fell silent for a long while. As did he. They both seemed uncertain as to what to do next.

Then she reached across the carriage. She took one of his hands in hers.

"Thank you," she said softly. "For . . . all of it."

She seemed to know he wouldn't want more than that, with the revelations too fresh and primal to accept anything beyond the simplest of balms.

He could only nod and squeeze her hand, some unnamed emotion hot and tight in his throat.

The carriage pulled to a stop. Daniel glanced out the window. They'd reached their destination.

"Are your readers ready to learn what goes on at masquerade?" he asked.

"Even if they aren't," she said with a grin, "I am."

The footman opened the door and waited.

Daniel offered Eleanor his arm. "Then let us venture

forth into what promises to be a most educational evening."

When she clasped his forearm, he realized that he was looking forward to the next few hours with unseemly enthusiasm. He'd never before entered into an inferno like this with a woman like her—a woman he truly cared about.

As Eleanor stepped from the carriage, her hand on Daniel's arm, excitement poured through her in an effervescent cascade. A small part of her was still bruised from his earlier words, and it would take more time and show of good faith from him for that injury to heal. And she felt the impact of his revelations, too. How open and exposed he'd left her. The intimate confession of the truths of his heart. It stunned her that a man of such importance could feel even the slightest amount of uncertainty. Yet he did. And he'd revealed that to *her*.

She knew with certainty that he'd never spoken of such things to anyone else. She'd been given a privilege.

He was more than subject matter to her. Far more. And, it seemed, she was more to him than the means to an end. They'd become . . . *friends* didn't quite encapsulate everything that they were to each other, and it didn't quite delineate the uncertainty that still existed between them. Yet it was as close to anything that could define what they had become.

Nor could she deny the thrill that came from the promise of a night with him in the heart of wickedness. She'd written and heard about parties like these masquerades, but she'd never been to one herself. And now she was about to.

With him. It wouldn't be half as stimulating without having Daniel beside her.

Daniel. She couldn't believe he'd granted her the honor of his Christian name, and yet now that he had, it seemed precisely right. Together, they could be Eleanor and Daniel, not Miss Hawke and Lord Ashford. Something for them alone.

But she couldn't forget the reason for their intimate association. She was here tonight to see the world of the wealthy at play and report back to her readers. So she made herself observe everything with close attention.

The house they stood in front of belonged to none other than Lord Marwood. It was a grand, imposing structure on Mount Street, as immense and stately as Daniel's home. Carriages stood outside, with masked figures in elaborate fancy dress descending from their vehicles and queuing up to go inside. The tall windows fronting the mansion had been opened, and laughter and music bubbled out like sparkling wine to splash onto the street, offering the promise of pleasure.

Waiting their turn to go inside, Eleanor spotted all manner of costumes on the masked guests in the queue. These attendees also laughed and were already deep in the process of flirtation, offering each other outrageous compliments and making theatrical gestures.

Speaking lowly so no one but Daniel could hear her, she said, "I see three Cleopatras, two Caesars, four medieval knights, Queen Elizabeth, Aphrodite, and Bacchus. And something that appears to be a cross between a cat and a courtier. You toffs do enjoy pretending to be someone else."

Daniel gave a wry smile. "With the world's eyes on our every movement, can you blame us?"

"I suppose everyone needs the chance to escape from themselves," she murmured.

He shook his head. "Don't think too much about it. This is a chance to liberate yourself. Take the opportunity for what it is."

He'd liberated himself in the carriage, telling her things about himself she knew he'd spoken of to no one else.

"What is it?" she whispered.

"Freedom," he murmured back. "A mask gives us the chance to be anyone at all."

"Assuming you're already someone to begin with," she pointed out. "Some of us aren't so noteworthy."

"Ah, but you don't believe that about yourself," he chided gently. "I've seen you at work. I *know*."

He did   and that almost frightened her.

"Tonight," he continued, "you needn't be responsible for the livelihood of dozens of people. You don't need to concern yourself with page proofs, or the content of an article. Or even who you are as a writer. There's no room for thought this evening. It's pure existence."

She wondered if he was telling himself this as much as her. Because of what he'd said in the carriage, and all it signified. He'd exposed his deepest self to her, and now was the time for sensation and experience.

"It does sound appealing," she admitted.

Could she free herself? Every moment of her life was tightly controlled. Of necessity. She had a business to run, people relying on her. And while she did have a duty tonight to record everything that she saw, perhaps she could seize the chance, as Daniel said, to cut the moorings that lashed her to the pier of responsibility. Be whoever she desired. Take what she wanted, and let the consequences be damned.

Another wave of exhilaration crashed over her. There was so much possibility tonight. She could sail into the teeth of the storm and laugh into the wind and rain. With him beside her.

She cast a surreptitious glance toward Daniel. He'd asked for her opinion of his costume, and while she'd made a cutting remark, in truth he was devastating in it. Anyone who might have questioned the masculinity of the previous century's fashions for gentlemen had only to look at him to realize how virile a man could look in tight silk. The breeches emphasized long, lean thighs, and his calves were a wonder in their stockings. His frock coat hugged his wide shoulders and the full skirt accented his narrow waist, while the embroidered waistcoat revealed the muscularity of his torso. He'd opted not to shave, so dark, piratical stubble shaded the clean contours of his face. The mask he wore drew attention to his roguish blue eyes and wicked mouth.

A mouth she'd tasted, and longed to taste again.

Really, it wasn't sportsmanlike for a man to be so anni-hilating to a woman's self-control. He ought to be regulated, like a weapon.

As if reading her thoughts, he leaned close and said softly, "I've never seen anyone or anything as stunning as you in that gown."

"A rake's idle flattery," she said at once.

"A man speaking the truth," he answered.

Her breath squeezed out of her lungs, as if someone had closed a fist around her. Heat washed through every corner of her body.

Devastating, this man.

Before she could formulate a response, they reached the front door, where a servant took the invitation from Daniel, then waved them inside. Another servant took their cloaks and ushered them upstairs.

Climbing the stairs toward what had to be a ballroom, Eleanor was assailed by a thousand details. The house itself was astonishing—huge, filled with priceless objects, art, and furniture. Silver candelabras cast flickering shad-ows as servants with trays bearing drinks and sweetmeats passed by.

Finally, they reached the ballroom. They paused at the entrance to the chamber to take in the scene. Half the can-dles in the giant chandeliers were unlit, keeping everything from being too bright, too revealing. But she could make out other details. A few tiny lanterns dangled from potted trees, giving the impression of a fairy land. Huge bolts of shim-mering white silk hung in swags from the ceiling, adding to the atmosphere of enchantment. In one corner of the massive room, a group of masked musicians played within an indoor lacquered Oriental pavilion.

A riot of color filled the ballroom as the guests swirled and danced. Jewels shone. Silk gleamed. Women's bell-like laughter combined with men's deep chuckles in harmonies of silver and bronze. Champagne flutes chimed against each other. Servants with trays circulated, offering oysters, savory bites, sugared cakes.

"I feel like if I eat something," she said to Daniel, "I'll be trapped in an otherworldly kingdom forever."

"But what a place to be trapped." He took an oyster from one of the trays. His eyes never leaving hers, he tilted his head back. Gulped the oyster down.

Her limbs felt liquid. Her heart thundered.

Licking his lips, he said, "There's nothing quite like an oyster. Well, there is, but you can't go around offering it on trays."

Her cheeks heated. She could survive in this strange new world. Not only survive but thrive. "Imagine if they walked around with platters of sausages."

"I believe a full-scale orgy might break out."

"We're halfway there already." She nodded toward the shadowy corners of the ballroom.

Couples were locked in passionate embraces, kissing in plain view of the other guests. Eleanor fought to keep from staring. Unlike the kisses and caresses she saw at the gaming hell, these were between members of the gentry, not courtesans and clients. Clearly, the restrictions of propriety were entirely forgotten once the threshold of the ballroom was crossed.

Heat pulsed through her. Especially when she saw one Roman soldier's hand disappear up a Chinese princess's skirts. They could be the highest-ranking and most respected members of Society, but at this gathering, they were free to indulge in their most basic needs.

"Are there any rules here?" she whispered to Daniel.

"Only one," he answered lowly. His breath was warm and tobacco-scented against her cheek. " 'Obey no rules.' "

"Easier to speak of slipping the tether than doing it."

"The only hand on the reins now is yours."

Part of her wanted to know the identities of the guests. It would make for even more scintillating reading. But another part of her wanted to give the attendees their freedom. She'd describe what they were doing, of course, but refrain from speculating as to who they might be.

She *did* know who the man dressed in all black was, however. Their host—Lord Marwood. His height and coloring were unmistakable. He led a wild country dance in the middle of the ballroom. Instead of the usual sedate movements of a quadrille, there was far more touching in this dance, with men picking up their partners and swinging them around so their skirts lifted. The women wrapped their legs around their partners' waists as they spun.

"Never seen that dance before," she murmured.

"It's called the King's Courtesan," Daniel replied. "And I believe our host invented it."

"A talented man, Mar—I mean, our host."

"Shall we join the dancers?"

A bold invitation from him. Almost shocking—though he *was* a rake. Yet never quite so bold with her. Did he want more than just kisses? And did she?

She watched the dance, imagining herself and Daniel out there. Her legs wrapped around him. The thought both excited and terrified her. Terrified her because she wanted it so badly. But she couldn't lose herself too much, and certainly not this early in the evening.

"Let us survey the land a little more," she said.

"As my lady wishes." He pressed a long hand to his chest and gave an old-fashioned bow.

Several corridors led away from the ballroom, and Daniel guided her down one. A chamber door stood open, and they looked inside. Men and women gathered around a table, where rows and rows of tankards lined up. Several servants with pitchers of ale hovered and refilled mugs as they were drained. Onlookers shouted their encouragement.

"Drinking contest?" she whispered.

"A hundred pounds per cup," he said.

"Looks like Catherine de Medici is winning."

Indeed, the woman in question was throwing back tankards and demanding refills twice as fast as any of her competitors.

One Henry VIII staggered away from the table and collapsed to the ground, groaning. Several other drinkers looked bleary and struggled to finish their mugs. But not Catherine de Medici. She kept going until, at last, the remainder of her competition slid to the floor or ran for the retiring rooms.

More shouts and laughter. Money changed hands. The Medici princess accepted handshakes and pats on the back, her eyes remarkably clear for someone who'd just ingested enough ale to stun a whale.

Eleanor applauded the woman's efforts before she and Daniel moved on.

With one arm, he pressed her back against a wall protectively. She didn't know why until the sound of wood striking wood filled the corridor. Then she saw the source of the odd sound. The goddess Diana and a sultan were fencing. With pool cues.

The duelists scurried back and forth, trading strikes, laughing and calling each other the most outrageous names. Until they disappeared around a corner, taking their battle with them.

Yet Daniel didn't release her right away. He kept his body pressed against hers. The first time she'd ever felt the entire length of him snug to hers. They fit together with aching faultlessness. He was long and hard and lean, tight against her softness.

He stared down at her, his hands braced on either side of her head. Though he wore a mask, desire was written plainly in his face. The darkening of his eyes. His flared nostrils.

"Didn't want you to get caught in the crossfire," he murmured, words like velvet.

"It looked like Diana had the upper hand." Eleanor sounded as though she'd run up several flights of stairs, though she remained perfectly still.

"Don't count the sultan out. His form was good."

And Daniel's form was exquisite. His gaze flicked down to her mouth. She wanted to raise herself up on her toes, put her mouth to his. Yet something within her craved drawing the moment out longer. Waiting for the release.

Instead, she said, "Won't the host mind if his pool cues are destroyed?"

He finally stepped back, and she instantly missed the sensation of his body against hers.

They continued walking through the maze of hallways. "He encourages it at these gatherings," Daniel answered. "He believes no act of creation can come without some destruction."

"He must read William Blake."

"Blake, Byron, and, of course, the Lady of Dubious Quality."

Ah yes, the infamous Lady, penning her anonymous erotic tales. Her identity was entirely secret to everyone but her publisher, and he wasn't about to kill his golden goose by revealing who she was. But it remained one of England's biggest mysteries. Eleanor had to admire the Lady for her audacity and bravery. And, it had to be stated, the unknown woman had a way with a pornographic scene.

They found the gaming room, where guests wagered sums just as outrageous as those at Donnegan's. Eleanor and Daniel sat in for a few hands of *vingt-et-un*. As they played, she allowed herself another kind of play. Touching him on his arm, or running her fingers along his jaw to congratulate him on a particularly good hand of cards. He, in turn, cradled her palm against his, or toyed with her curls. Each small touch, every brush of flesh against flesh, her excitement built higher and higher.

Yet she wanted more than this.

After winning several rounds, they moved on from the gambling. In a great hall with vaulted ceilings, two gentlemen were climbing priceless tapestries, with people cheering them on.

Truly, she'd never witnessed such wild behavior.

"Give someone a mask," she said under her breath, watching the scene.

"It's time for you to stop watching," he said, drawing her away and back toward the ballroom, "and start doing."

Everything that had happened in the past few weeks, and that very night, coiled within her. The two of them seemed capable of anything now. "What did you have in mind?" She all but panted her words.

He stepped back into the ballroom. The unmistakable sounds of a waltz were starting up, and couples were taking their places on the dance floor. Though the dance itself had lost some of its forbidden flavor—they danced it at Almack's, after all—the couples here were standing even closer than propriety dictated, allowing their bodies to actually touch, rather than keeping a respectable distance between them.

His fingers threaded with hers, sending electricity spiraling through her. With an enigmatic smile, his hand in hers, Daniel gently pulled her onto the dance floor. As if leading her to bed.

"Can you waltz?" he asked with heat and intimacy, as though asking if she was a virgin.

"I can," she answered. A candid admission of her own carnal wisdom. His jaw tightened.

They took their positions. His hand at her waist, hers on his shoulder, their other hands clasped. His body snug against hers. As they'd been in the hallway. Only this time, they were in full view of dozens of other people.

A new thrill pulsed through her. Experienced, she might be, but not in *this* way. They were making bold and overt statements to themselves, and to everyone, about what they wanted from each other.

The music began, and they started to move.

He leaned down and whispered in her ear, "You're now part of the story."

Chapter 16

There is no more metaphorical activity than dancing.

The Hawk's Eye, May 15, 1816

She ought to have known. Should have expected it. Logically, a man who could control the reins of a racing phaeton and who moved with Daniel's fluid, masculine grace would also be a marvelous dancer. He'd likely had a dancing master, too, as men of his rank usually did. As he'd taken her hand and led her onto the floor, she'd readied herself, knowing that what she was about to experience would be enjoyable. She'd waltzed a few times with other men before—enjoyed the teasing rhythm, the giddy spin, the press of a man's hand at her waist—and nearly all of those times had been rather pleasant.

But as the first notes twirled around the ballroom, and Daniel began to move her in the steps of the waltz, *rather pleasant* seemed a terrific understatement.

There were no other words for it: he was seducing her. Each turn, each sway, and she felt the resonance of their bodies together. His hand at her waist was an exquisite burn, despite the fabric between them, and his fingers enfolding hers were long, eloquent. Beguiling. How else might he touch her, and where? She ached to know.

Eleanor risked a glance up at him. His gaze smoldered as he watched her, as if she were the only creature in existence.

The only thing worth seeing. Though she felt more than a mere *thing* to him. She was, at that moment, *everything*.

"You oughtn't look at me like that," she murmured as they danced, the room spinning around them.

"Like what?" His voice was silken.

"Like you're imagining me in just my underclothes."

"I'm imagining you in far less."

Heat spread through her, centering in her breasts and between her legs. She'd never been this aroused in a public place before. It was shocking. Thrilling.

"You have a good imagination," he continued, turning her in the dance. "I'm sure you've pictured me without my clothing. I hope you *have* thought of me naked."

The word *naked* sent another bolt of electricity through her. It was such a, well, *bare* word, free of pretense.

"Rather conceited of you to assume that," she managed to sniff.

"I live and breathe conceit," he said with a half smile. "As I'm sure you've noticed, with me being a toff, et cetera."

"There's a goodly amount in that '*et cetera*,' " she said.

"We've become more than our social ranking to each other," he said, more serious. His hand tightened at the curve of her waist.

"You're not so much *that lofty earl* to me anymore," she confessed.

"And it's been a very long time since I've thought of you as *that female writer*. You're Eleanor."

She nearly stumbled to hear him murmur her name as if it was the first word of a seduction.

"And you're Daniel," she returned, allowing herself the boldness and intimacy of his name, here, in the middle of this masked dance. She alone knew him, who he really was.

"Confess then—you have thought of me naked," he pressed as he continued to move her expertly across the floor. It wasn't a question.

She couldn't deny it. Many an hour had been lost in contemplation of what sunlight must look like on the muscles of his shoulders, or tracing the contours of his abdomen. Would he have a bit of a belly, as men often did, or would his stomach be flat and hard? She could feel him now through her dress. No belly. Not a bit of fat on him at all. He was all lean muscularity. Everywhere.

And it was impossible to picture his abdomen without her mental gaze trailing lower . . . picturing that particular part of him. The part she felt against her now, cradled against her stomach. Thick and curved and very interested in her.

"I'm a writer," she replied, trying to concentrate on keeping her footing. "I can't help where my thoughts take me." She needed some balance, so she said casually, "I might wonder what any number of people might look like naked."

"But it's *me* you picture, just as I picture you."

She couldn't tear her gaze from his. Her heart beat thickly, and her mouth dried.

They continued to turn and turn, but the lightness in her head didn't arise from the dance steps. He managed to pull her closer, their bodies locked tightly as they continued to sway.

"I . . ." Echoes of Maggie's warnings resounded. *He's dangerous. His kind are never good for women like me. Be careful.*

Yet she couldn't. Stopping this now was as impossible as keeping a boat from plunging over a waterfall. There would be a fall, a glorious, freeing drop. But what lay at the bottom? Clear water, or rocks upon which she'd be dashed.

If she continued this dance, let it move on to its logical progression, what would become of her? She could all too easily see herself becoming utterly beguiled by him, consumed by him. Losing herself entirely. Because she knew, she *knew,* that they would be magnificent together, and her body would crave him desperately once she had a taste.

"I need a moment." She broke away from him and hurried from the dance floor, searching out the retiring room. All she wanted was a minute apart from him, some time to collect herself. Things were moving too quickly, slipping from her control, and she sought some fragment of sanity.

Eleanor moved down a dimly lit corridor. She'd seen other women passing in this direction, so surely the retiring room had to be set up somewhere around here. The music quieted as she moved away from the ballroom, passing a few women returning there.

Masculine footsteps sounded behind her. Daniel. Following her.

"A few minutes alone," she threw over her shoulder.

The voice that spoke wasn't Daniel's. "But then you might get away."

She spun around as a hand closed around her forearm. A tall man dressed as an Indian prince loomed over her.

"Remove your hand," she said icily.

"Again, I fear you'll slip away," the stranger answered. His grin must have been intended to be flirtatious, but it only seemed lascivious.

"And I repeat myself." Anger roared through her as she spoke between her teeth. "Your attention is unwanted. Let go of me. Now."

The stranger tugged her closer, the scent of wine strong on his breath and in his clothes. "Come now, pretty blue star. I saw you dancing with that courtier. Don't play at being shy."

"Does this strike you as shy?" She kicked him. She missed his groin but landed a solid blow on his upper thigh.

He staggered in pain, releasing her abruptly. She stumbled back, then straightened when a dark, menacing shape appeared behind her would-be assailant. Someone grabbed her aggressor by the throat, clutching him so tightly the man made desperate choking sounds.

"What the lady started," the newcomer said, his voice hard with fury, "I'll finish."

Daniel.

Her assailant gasped, "She was asking for—"

"They never do," Daniel growled. He cocked back his fist, then threw it into the man's face.

The stranger went limp in Daniel's grasp. Daniel released him, and the man slumped to the floor.

For a moment, the only sounds that could be heard in the corridor were faint notes of music, and Daniel and Eleanor's heavy breathing. They both stared down at the prone form of her erstwhile attacker.

"What'll we do with him?" she asked.

Daniel glanced around, then nodded toward a closed door. "Stash him in there. Grab his feet."

After opening the door, revealing a small drawing room, Eleanor picked up the stranger's feet while Daniel held him beneath his arms. Together, they hefted the unconscious man and carried him into the unused chamber.

Instead of carefully setting the man on the settee, in silent agreement she and Daniel simply dropped him to the ground. He made a satisfying thud as he landed. It didn't stop the shaking in her hands, however.

"Too bad the room is fully carpeted," she muttered, glaring at him. "What are you doing?"

Daniel searched through the drawers of a desk, until he produced a quill and an ink pot. He walked them over to where the man sprawled. "Hold this." He put the pot of ink into Eleanor's hand.

She watched, baffled at first, and then with growing satisfaction, as Daniel dipped the quill's nib into the ink and began to write on her assailant's forehead.

I attack helpless women, Daniel wrote.

Anger and fear continued to reverberate through her in hot echoes. Struggling against giving her assailant that power over her, she turned to flippancy as a shield against him. "I object to the term *helpless.*"

Daniel glanced up at her, as if assessing her mood. He matched her lightness with his own, though there was still a hard edge to his voice. "Give me some artistic license."

They both stepped back and looked at her attacker. It would take some time for the ink to wash off the stranger's skin. She knew very well the permanence of ink stains on flesh. While she might wish more harm on the bastard, her assailant would feel the repercussions of his actions for quite a while.

She turned to Daniel. He'd come to her—defended her. How many other men had done the same? Exactly none. She was a modern woman, independent and self-sufficient. She didn't want to be captivated by displays of old-fashioned gallantry. And yet she couldn't stop herself. He'd protected her.

"Do you still need some time alone?" he asked her, his voice gentle with concern. "I can take you somewhere else. Somewhere safe."

"Air, please," she said.

Daniel offered her his arm, which she took. He was steady and solid beneath her, settling her frayed nerves.

As they departed the chamber, they left the door open so anyone might find the insensate man in his humiliating position.

They skirted around the edges of the ballroom, dodging more couples in more heated embraces. Finally, they reached tall French doors that opened onto a long, wide balcony. The terrace overlooked a shadow-strewn garden, which doubtless concealed more couples.

The balcony itself was almost entirely unoccupied, save for one man and one woman, standing close to one another and murmuring in the universal language of flirtation.

Daniel guided Eleanor away from the light, toward the darker recesses of the terrace. Reaching the farthest edge of the balcony, they stopped, and she released her hold on him. She braced her hands on the stone railing and inhaled the night air deeply. Though it was May, the evening was a cool one, but the chill felt good, soothing in its way, as her anger and horror at her close call slowly ebbed away.

Closing her eyes as she tilted up her head, she recalled the fury on Daniel's face as he efficiently dispatched her assailant. It was a thoroughly uncivilized thing for him to have done, especially as she'd already freed herself from the stranger's clutches, but blast her if Daniel punching that blighter didn't give her a primitive thrill.

His solid warmth engulfed her as he stood behind her, his arms stretched out as his hands rested beside hers.

"I wanted to kill him." The rumble of his words vibrated through her.

"Me, too, but he's not worth hanging for." She opened her eyes and stared out at the dark shapes of the hedges and trees. Someone out in the shadows giggled.

"But you're worth killing for," he said.

She continued to stare out into the night, but his words reverberated through her stronger than a cannon's boom. What could she say to this? If no one had ever protected her before, of a certain no one had ever said they would kill for her.

My God. How can I resist him?

Here, in the darkness, with danger having passed just moments ago, she was incapable of pretending. Layers and walls fell away, a lifetime of self-protection drifting off into the night like mist. She could only speak the truth of herself now.

"You set me adrift," she confessed.

"And you anchor me," he answered.

"I'm . . ." She struggled against giving voice to secrets she dared not admit even to herself. " . . . I'm afraid."

"Of me?" He sounded incredulous.

"Of myself. Of us."

For a long while, he was silent. Had she repulsed him with her honesty?

Then—"It's an unknown territory for both of us. Neither has the advantage."

"And now?"

"Now . . ." He leaned closer, close but not threatening. "Now we explore it together."

"What if I don't want to?" she felt compelled to ask.

He stepped away instantly, and her body cried out in complaint. As did the rest of her. "Then we stop. It's your decision."

She drew in a breath. Let it out slowly. Here was the

turning point. She could walk away before any real damage was done.

But she couldn't. Every part of her hungered for him.

"My decision . . ." She took another breath. The world was changing, and she was the agent of that metamorphosis. "Is *yes*."

There was half a moment when everything was still, silent. Then he stepped close again, his body bracketing hers, pressed all along her back. Something within her shattered into bright pieces.

His lips trailed down her neck.

Fire coursed through her. "This has always been a losing battle, hasn't it?"

"Losing means winning." His hands slid up her arms, tracing lacework of flame wherever he touched, until he reached her shoulders. He turned her around. Cupped her head with his broad hands. And brought his mouth down on to hers.

It seemed like forever since last they'd kissed. It seemed like moments ago. But time meant nothing when his lips caressed hers, silken and deliciously assertive. Almost at once, she opened for him, her tongue stroking against his. His rich flavor filled her. She pressed her hands to his chest, feeling the hard pound of his heart beneath her palms. Her fingers curled, clutching at him, as the kiss went deeper. The rail of the balcony pressed into her back, but she didn't care. She only reveled in the taste of him, the feel of him.

This kiss was filled with heat and intent. Blatantly carnal, the way his mouth took hers. And the press of his hips to her own revealed just how very aroused he was. His desire matched hers, and she rubbed against him, taking power and pleasure in their shared response. Deep in his chest, he growled. She responded with a low moan, her body aflame.

"I want you," he rumbled. "Now."

"Daniel—"

He groaned, but stilled. "Stop?"

"I was going to ask how long it would take to summon your carriage."

"Less than a minute."

"Fetch it."

He took a step away from her, and even with the minimal amount of light that reached them in the corner of the terrace, she saw the clear outline of his arousal in his breeches. Her heart thundered as the ache between her legs grew.

He shook his head, smiling wryly. "You're the only person to order me around like a servant."

"But you obey," she purred.

His eyelids lowered. "Willingly. Until it's my turn to give the orders."

She raised a brow. "I don't take well to being told what to do."

"Then we'll just have to fight it out." He reached out a hand. "Come. I'm not letting you go until you're naked in my bed."

Another wave of heat pounded through her at his words.

She laced her fingers with his. An echo of him leading her onto the dance floor. But that had all been a prelude to this moment. A steady, unstoppable building toward what they both desired.

"And *then* you'll let me go?" she asked.

"Absolutely not." He tugged her close and kissed her again with an animal hunger. The polished, urbane earl was gone. He was a man of primal intent now.

"Hurry," she whispered, pulling back. She didn't want to wait. Didn't want to think about the meaning of what she was about to do. All she wanted was this moment, and to hell with the consequences.

Daniel always took pains to pay his staff well. He'd assumed that the better compensated servants were, the more likely they would be to do their jobs with utmost efficiency.

He wasn't wrong, and thank God for it. His carriage pulled up outside Marwood's house with gratifying speed, and the footman opened the door, permitting Daniel and Eleanor to enter. In less than a minute, they were en route to his home. Eleanor sat on one side of the carriage, Daniel on the other. Some of the pins had escaped her hair, and curls trailed down her back and framed her masked face. His own costume felt tight, restrictive.

"You're too far away," Eleanor murmured, stroking the cushions of the seat beside her.

He curled his hands into fists. "Have to be." His voice had never sounded deeper.

"Don't you want to kiss me again?" She gave him a wicked little smile. She'd always been a bold woman, but this boldness was new and had the power to raze him to the ground.

"Can't remember my own damn name," he rasped, "I want to kiss you so badly. But if I start, I'm not going to be able to stop. Not until I make love to you. And I don't want our first time together to be in a carriage." His fingers reflexively uncurled and curled, as if he could distract himself from reaching for her. "I've waited for this."

"Have you?" Surprise was plain in her voice.

"You don't know the patience I've had to call upon." Each moment in her presence before now had only whetted his appetite, drawing him tighter and tighter upon the bow of desire. "I want to take my time. All night. There's not an inch of you I'm going to neglect."

Her smile faded and she looked wide-eyed. "Oh."

So they said nothing, not touching, for the duration of the journey back to his house. The air in the carriage seemed to glow with heat and expectation. By some incredible force of will, he managed to keep his hands to himself, but now he knew the feel of her even more, and his body had its demands.

They finally arrived, the coach pulling up outside the front steps.

"Not the mews this time?" she asked.

"No sneaking in," he answered. "We go in the front door. Together."

He stepped out of the carriage, then handed her down.

She stood beside him and stared at his house, a look of wariness replacing the flirtation.

Frowning a little at her sudden caution, he led her inside, the butler and footmen bowing to him and Eleanor. He disposed of his hat, cape, and mask, and did the same with her cloak. Strangely, her fingers seemed slightly unsteady as she untied the ribbons of her own mask and presented them to the waiting butler.

She glanced at Daniel, then looked away, as if the sight of him without his disguise—and the protection of hers—was too intimate.

"Wine in the study," Daniel directed the head servant.

"Yes, my lord." The butler discreetly faded away.

Daniel's gaze remained fixed on Eleanor as she turned a slow circle in the vaulted entryway of his house. "It's much bigger inside than I'd anticipated," she whispered.

He shrugged. "Half the rooms aren't used, since it's only me."

"I've never been in a nobleman's home before tonight. Marwood's and now yours. I've written about them, but never gone in. Strange to have the experience at last."

"The houses are often drafty and cold," he said. "Not very comfortable."

"But designed to impress."

"Are you impressed?" He asked this only half in jest.

She looked at him, finally. "The truth? You and me . . . we come from very different worlds. I always knew that. But seeing this"—she waved at the tall domed ceiling of the foyer, the marble floor, and the portrait of the second Earl of Ashford hanging over the enormous curved staircase—"makes it all so much more concrete."

"You know *me*." He took a step toward her. "We're not so different, truly."

"Perhaps not so different in some ways," she allowed, edging slightly back. "Yet in others . . ." She ran her hands down the front of her skirts, another protective gesture. "It frightens me a little."

"Don't fear me." He hated the thought of her being afraid of him.

"I don't. Not you."

Something loosened within him. "When you see all this . . ." He gestured toward the grand foyer soaring around them, the chair that had been in his family since the time of the Restoration, the enormous chandelier sparkling above. "I hope you feel more than fear."

"I'm . . ." She gave a self-conscious laugh. "You'll think me ridiculous."

"Impossible."

"It also . . . excites me." Her eyes flashed as she glanced at him, embers of her desire still glowing.

A delicate touch was needed. With his other bedpartners, he'd done his best to ensure their pleasure and willingness. Nothing was less enticing than a lover who didn't want to be there. But with those women, he hadn't felt the same near desperation that he felt with Eleanor. If those women had changed their minds and gone without sharing his bed, he would have suffered a little bodily, but he'd known he would endure. If Eleanor left, Daniel would mourn her loss the rest of his life.

Daniel bit back on his thwarted desire. Like hell would he force or cajole her into something she didn't want to do. But what he wanted, what he needed, was *her*.

To keep her by his side. To make her happy. To give her whatever she desired.

This night couldn't end. Not now. If they spent the whole of the hours before sunrise only talking, that would be enough. He simply couldn't part with her.

"I'll show you what a rake does during a night alone at home." He held an arm out, directing her toward the study at the back of the house.

She accompanied him as they made their way down a corridor lined with more ancestral portraits, Chippendale tables, and blue-and-white Yuan dynasty vases. He watched her taking in all the details of his home, seeing her perceptive gaze lighting here and there, assessing, analyzing, her mind never at rest. Was she even now measuring the social gulf that stretched between them, embodied in a century-old silver candelabra?

Yet she'd said that the difference between them also excited her. He could bathe her in luxury, indulge her every whim and want. As he longed to do. She'd had so little indulgence in her life. He hoped to be the one to give it to her.

They reached the study, finding a fire already lit. Two empty glasses and a decanter of wine awaited them on a table by the fireplace. A pair of wingback chairs also flanked the hearth, ready for them.

She stepped inside and stared at the rows and rows of books. A slow smile spread across her face.

"These must be inherited," she said, running her fingers over the spines of several books.

He straightened. "I've bought many of these myself."

Pulling one volume from the shelf, she consulted the title page. "Joseph Banks's *Endeavour* journals. And the publication date is last year." Her brows rose. "Is this what a rake does at home? Read?"

"Sometimes." He nodded toward a chessboard in the corner. "Play against myself occasionally."

She wandered over to the board and studied the pieces. "I've no head for chess. But give me a deck of playing cards . . ."

"I already know what happens there." He scowled without heat as he trailed after her. "I have no desire to be rooked tonight."

"What else does a rake do when ensconced in his den of iniquity?" she asked, moving away from the board. She eyed his desk, where several documents and letters were scattered, some half completed. A grin spread across her face. "Write poetry? I hear you can't call yourself a rake without penning some verses honoring a woman's breasts."

A sudden idea struck him, making him grin as well. "Think you could write a better poem than me?"

She placed her hand on her hip. "I *am* the writer, after all."

"Very well, my boasting lady." He folded his arms across his chest. "I propose a contest."

"A *poetry* contest?" She stared at him in disbelief.

"Better than poetry. A duel. Writing limericks. The dirtier the better."

"And what are the stakes?" she pressed.

"For each limerick one person comes up with, the other must . . ." Must what? "Perform a dare."

"Do something silly?" She shook her head. "I'm in no mood for silliness tonight. And we can't wager money, because you're Croesus and I'm poor Diogenes in his tub."

"Then what would you like to wager?"

She tapped her chin. Then her expression turned wicked. "I have it. The other person must remove an article of clothing."

He liked the sound of that. "But," he added, "the victor gets to remove the piece of clothing."

Her smile turned wicked as she took the paper and pen. "Prepare to get naked, my lord."

Chapter 17

While much is made of the coquettish language of fans, of gloves, of eyes and sidelong glances, few give proper recognition to the most potent language of flirtation—that of words themselves.

The Hawk's Eye, May 15, 1816

They sat themselves before the fire, Daniel in one chair, Eleanor in another. He poured them both glasses of wine and was pleased that his hands didn't shake to betray his eagerness to be with her. The firelight did wondrous things to her, casting her in gold and shadow as she took her glass and sipped. She wasn't the first woman to have sat with him beside the hearth, but he could barely recall those other females when she was here, now. He had a feeling that after tonight, no matter what transpired, he'd remember no other.

"How do we begin?" she asked.

"We try to come up with limericks," he said.

She rolled her eyes. "That much, we've determined."

"If you're asking me to formulate rules," he answered, "you're sorely out of luck. I break rules, not make them."

"I do the same," she replied, leaning back in her chair. "But between the two of us, I believe we can come up with something usable for this battle of wits." She glanced up at the ceiling, contemplative. Then she snapped her fingers. "Whoever devises the first limerick gets the choice of what article of clothing to remove from the other."

A very pleasurable prospect. "And so forth."

She smiled over the rim of her glass. She was relaxing, becoming more at ease. More herself. "You're very amenable to the rules. Unless you have done this before."

"Tonight is my first time."

Her laugh was low and husky. "Imagine that—I've finally found something *you* haven't done before."

"Seems that you bring a certain degree of originality into my life," he admitted, then took a drink as a result of his candor. She wasn't the only unsettled one. Eleanor lowered her lashes, and glanced up through them. "And you mine. But come, you're delaying. It's time for the contest."

They fell into silence, thinking. His brain churned as the fire crackled. Why had he thought of this competition in the first place? Well, he'd wanted a way to make her comfortable. He hadn't counted on the rule of stripping away garments. Though he had a certain facility with words, when faced with such high stakes—namely, undressing Eleanor—his mind went infuriatingly blank.

She broke the silence. Standing, she held up her glass and declaimed with the sobriety of a parson:

> *"The pretty young lady from Surrey*
> *Always got dressed in a hurry.*
> *Her drawers she forgot in haste,*
> *The wind blew her skirts to her waist,*
> *Revealing her bum, which was furry."*

A laugh broke from deep in his chest. "I can see my competition is going to be stiff." *Among other things.*

"Point to me, I believe," she said. She waved at him. "On your feet. It's time for me to claim my first prize."

It seemed the act of writing, even without a quill, unwound her. Made her more confident and unrestrained. Things he craved from her.

Daniel set aside his glass. "First?" He raised a brow as he stood. "That assumes there will be more."

She grinned impishly, a sight that went straight into the center of his chest. "Oh, doubt that not, my lord."

As he stood, she slowly walked in a circle around him. She stroked her chin in contemplation as she eyed him from the top of his head to the soles of his feet. His heart thundered as he endured her scrutiny. Yes, she certainly had grown more bold over the span of the night.

"What first?" she murmured.

"My shoes," he said.

She made a scoffing noise. "Too prosaic. And while at some point I wouldn't mind seeing your feet, that's not what interests me at the moment. No," she continued, stepping back and studying him, "the coat goes."

He did as she ordered—a part of him enjoying being under her command, when he was so used to being the one in control—and started to shuck off his silk frock coat by loosening the sleeves. He started when she stepped behind him. Ran her hands slowly up his arms.

His body reacted immediately, tensing and tightening beneath her touch.

She continued to stroke upward, until her hands settled on his shoulders, her fingers running over the muscles there. He caught fire everywhere she caressed him, but he fought to hold himself still. She stroked along his shoulders until she reached his coat collar, then her fingers hooked into the fabric and tugged.

"Never been like this with my valet," he rasped.

"I should hope not. Otherwise you ought to either sack him or give him a raise."

She pulled and he helped, and together they gradually peeled away his coat. It was only the first layer of his clothing, but he felt profoundly bare once the article had been removed and cast aside. He now stood in his shirtsleeves and waistcoat, body ablaze from this simple act.

Standing back once again, she stared at him, her own gaze hot as it lingered on his arms, shoulders, and torso. Undressing him further with her eyes alone.

"Quite a spicy game we've devised," she murmured.

"Always liked spice in my food," he answered. "Why should this game be any different?"

She shot him a saucy look. "It might get too hot for you. You could burn your tongue."

Goddamn, he wanted to taste her. But he marshaled his straining control. He wanted this to be only about her. Her comfort. Her pleasure.

"How long has it been?" he asked softly, dangerously. "Since you last sweated?"

"Too long," she answered after a moment.

A primitive, primal part of him growled with satisfaction. He knew she was no untried virgin—was glad of it, in truth—but that didn't mean he relished imagining her with other men. And he would make certain that, if he and Eleanor become lovers, she'd remember no one else but him. Words suddenly popped into his head, and he recited:

> *"A scribbling lady from Grub Street*
> *Who sold many a broadsheet,*
> *A good tupping she did need,*
> *So I wish Godspeed*
> *To the swain that attempts the great feat."*

His first reward was her honeyed laugh. Followed by her musing. "A good tupping, hm? Wherever could I find such a thing?"

"I have a few ideas," he answered. "But first, it's time to claim my prize. Hold still."

Narrowing the distance between them, he watched the rapid rise and fall of her breasts beneath the front of her bodice. He picked up one of her hands, allowing himself the pleasure of stroking up and down her arm, feeling the strength and silk of her.

Leisurely, he began to remove her glove. He tugged lightly on each finger, loosening the satin that clung to her. Then he reached for the top of her long glove, which skimmed above her elbow. Inch by inch, he eased the satin down, baring her flesh.

He watched her observing the spectacle, her breath coming faster and faster. Until at last, he stripped away the glove, completely uncovering her left arm. He gave her naked skin one stroke, from the curve of her elbow to her wrist. Traced a pattern on her palm. And then moved on to the other glove.

By the time the second glove joined its mate on the floor, both Daniel and Eleanor were nearly panting. His waistcoat and breeches did nothing to conceal his rampant erection—he'd never been harder, and all from the removal of a coat and some gloves.

He stepped closer, needing to kiss her, to feel her even more. But before he could move, she spoke breathlessly.

> *"A worldly, bad lad from the Lake*
> *Was England's most notorious rake.*
> *His lovers were many*
> *From London to Kilkenny,*
> *'Til his cock dried out like a cake."*

Daniel started. But of course she knew that his main estate was near Bassenthwaite Lake, in the Lake District. There wasn't one scrap of information about him or the aristocracy that she didn't seem to possess.

Then he laughed. "My cake won't dry out as long as it's well iced."

Her mouth curved. "Sugar is costly."

"All good things are," he replied.

"Speaking of cost," she said, "I have a prize to collect." She scrutinized him again, her gaze alighting on different articles of clothing. He might as well be naked already, the way she looked at him, and the desire pounding through his body.

Her hands slid up his torso. He groaned at her touch. Daniel was as taut and quivering as a stallion scenting a mare. He felt animalistic, all thoughts of civilization gone. Only need and hunger filled him.

She bypassed the buttons of his waistcoat, her hands continuing upward. Until they reached the folds of his old-fashioned neckcloth. With the same painstaking leisure with which she'd removed his coat, she undid the fabric around his neck, slowly, slowly untying it. Her fingers brushed the underside of his jaw, and then, finally, the bare skin of his neck.

The neckcloth drifted to the ground, adding to the growing pile of discarded clothing.

"I've always wanted to see this," she whispered, lightly touching the tip of a finger to the hollow of his throat.

Jesus, she was going to kill him.

Hoarsely, he said:

> *"A rake and a writer did duel*
> *Though neither of which was a fool.*
> *With words they did battle,*
> *Verbal sabers to rattle,*
> *Until they wound up in bed together."*

"That doesn't rhyme," she said.

"I don't care," he answered.

"Daniel—"

"My turn." He knelt. "Place your hands on my shoulders."

Without questioning him, she did as he directed. He reached beneath her skirts, the fabric rustling and shimmering around him, until he found the top of her stocking and the small band of silken flesh above it. He stroked her there on her thigh, feeling her warm skin, noting with triumph how she trembled. For him.

He caressed downward, bypassing her garters, but taking in the sensation of her stocking-clad legs beneath his hands. Thighs. Knees. Calves. Strong and supple. Lower still, to her ankles.

"Lean on me," he rumbled. When she did, he picked up one of her feet and undid the ribbons of her slippers. The slim shoe dropped to the floor, and he took a moment simply to hold her silk-covered foot in his hand. He'd never considered a woman's foot to be particularly erotic, but there was something so trusting, so open and honest about touching Eleanor this way, that it filled him with a roaring heat.

He performed the same service for her other slipper, removing it and putting it aside. Something very much like a moan escaped from the back of her throat. He remained kneeling, and, through the silk of her gown, nuzzled along her belly and just above the apex of her thighs. What had been a burgeoning moan turned into one of full voice. She threaded her fingers into his hair.

"Daniel," she breathed. "God. Kiss me."

He wasted no time, rising to his feet and pulling her close for a deep, openmouthed kiss. She clung to him, giving herself fully as she took from him, too. The passion of her. He was a powder keg ready to explode at the slightest touch of her spark.

"Over there," she gasped, breaking away and glancing at the sofa.

Much as he burned to make love to her at once, he shook his head. "I said I wanted you in my bed, and that's where I'll have you."

She looked disappointed. "Is it far?"

"I've got long legs."

He lifted her up in his arms and strode to the door. He shouldered it open, then paced down the corridor. Steadily, he climbed the stairs. Nothing would be rushed tonight. He'd give them both more pleasure than they could stand, and then he'd give them more.

Whatever she wanted, she would have. As he reached the landing and then paced quickly to his bedchamber, he made this vow to himself. Everything was hers—especially himself.

Logically, Eleanor knew everything would change. How could she pretend journalistic objectivity when all she wanted was to make love with the subject of her articles? And given what Daniel had said, what he'd done, he had precisely the same goal.

But as she entered his bedchamber in his arms—she still couldn't believe it—she couldn't bring herself to care that things would alter. She wanted him. He wanted her. Nothing else at that moment seemed to signify.

Was this really happening? She and Daniel were on the verge of becoming lovers. That handsome, proud earl who had marched into her office weeks ago. Yet he was so much more than that now. He was a strapping man of flesh and intent. And he wanted *her*. It seemed to be something so wondrous, so fantastical, that it had to be a product of her imagination. But no, it was real. The truth of it resonated through her.

She had a brief impression of his substantial bedroom, lit only by a fire. Heavy, dark furniture, Persian carpets, a landscape painting over the hearth. Then she found herself deposited carefully in the middle of an enormous canopied bed, and the details of the room faded away. All that mattered was him, standing at the foot of the bed and quickly starting to tear off the remainder of his clothing.

"Slow down," she said, propping herself up on her elbows. "You aren't the only one who's waited for this moment."

He stilled in his movements. "Not the only one," he murmured.

It was a bold confession of her own thoughts and desires. But this was a time and place apart, where truths could be spoken without fear of reprisal. He was the only man she trusted so much. Not only with her body, but herself. She held his gaze. He did as she requested, undoing his waistcoat button by button and tossing it to the carpet. The fire glowed behind him. She could clearly make out the shape of his body in his fine linen shirt. Unhurriedly, he plucked at the lacings of his shirt so that the neckline gaped open, revealing the contours of his upper chest. Dark hair scattered over his pectorals. Her mouth watered, thinking of that hair trailing even lower. Did it go all the way down?

She didn't have to wait long to find out. He grasped the

hem of his shirt and pulled it over his head. Muscles bunched and flexed with the movement. And then, ah sweet heaven, he was bare to the waist.

"You don't have a nobleman's softness," she said huskily.

He arched a brow as he planted his hands on his hips. "Do you have much experience with shirtless aristocrats?" That might have been a hint of jealousy in his voice, much to her gratification.

"None, but I can guess. Drinking and feasting and making merry cannot promote a certain physical robustness." It stunned her that she was capable of speech at this moment.

Pressing a hand to his flat abdomen—and, yes, the hair on his chest trailed down into a line that dipped beneath the waistband of his breeches—he said, "Gout plagued my ancestors, and I wanted to ensure it didn't bedevil me. I fence, box, ride, swim." His gaze darkened slightly. "Anything to keep moving."

As though he were outrunning something. Perhaps himself. Whatever the cause, his actions had worked their enchantment on his body. He was hewn and sculpted, finer than any statue she'd seen at the British Museum, and she was particularly beguiled by the lines of muscle running in lovely chevrons down his hips, also to vanish beneath his breeches. Pointing the way.

Without his shirt or waistcoat, the shape of his arousal formed a thick curve underneath his trousers. Her hands itched to touch him. But she willed herself patience.

"You may continue." She waved her hand airily, as if she could somehow make light of her need for him. It was a false hope, however.

He gave her another courtly bow, and it was a far different beast when the action was performed without a shirt. She watched the play of his muscles, feeling like a pagan queen accepting a tribute.

He toed off his shoes and then removed his stockings. All that was left were his breeches and smallclothes.

Her pulse soared off like a kite slipping free as his hands

went to the fastenings of his trousers. With an instinct for torment, he took his time, slipping each button free. He stepped from his breeches, revealing himself only in his thin drawers. He might as well have been nude. The fabric was nearly transparent, allowing her to see plainly the beautiful shape of his upright cock. Tugging the drawstring open, he peeled away his drawers.

And now he stood before her, truly naked.

Lord help her. He was beautiful. Lean and hard and carnal.

"If this is the result of a life of dissolution," she managed, "then I commend your every effort."

"Enough talking." He knelt on the edge of the bed and began to prowl toward her, like a wolf stalking his prey. "It's your turn."

But she could still play at seduction. She arched her back, rising up onto her elbows, her chest pressing upward so that the neckline of her gown dipped even lower. Then, slowly, she rolled onto her stomach, presenting him with her back. "This gown wants removing."

He didn't play fair. Instead of going straight for the closures of her dress, he skimmed his hands up her legs, stroked along the curve of her bottom, and lingered at the small of her back.

Pleasure shivered up her spine. No man had ever taken this much time with her, shaping pleasure from the simplest acts. Silk rustled all around her—her gown, the counterpane beneath her. She was awash in heat and sensation.

Finally, he began to undo the fastenings, one by one.

As he did, he eased open the back of her dress, revealing more of her skin. His breath caressed each inch of flesh, and she shivered when he pressed his lips down the length of her exposed spine.

"That should do it," he murmured.

She should say so. They had only just begun, and already she was pliable as melted wax.

She rolled onto her back, easing away from him, then

stood. With her gaze holding his, feeling like the incarnation of sensuality, she stripped away her gown.

She'd never done anything so bold. Yet it felt profoundly right with him. To liberate herself completely. Be the sensual creature that dwelt beneath the surface of her pragmatic, businesslike skin.

Kneeling at the side of the bed, Daniel helped with the removal of the gown, peeling it from her body. His hands lingered, stroking and caressing. Stoking her flame ever higher. And then the dress was off. He threw it aside without concern for the silk or pearls, as if it was just one bothersome obstacle between them, and not a phenomenally expensive work of art.

Now she was only in her undergarments.

She started to work at the lacings of her stays. He batted her hands away, and she held herself still as his long, dexterous fingers plucked at the laces.

In an astonishingly short amount of time, her stays were gone, flung aside like more detritus. She wore nothing but her chemise, drawers, stockings, and garters.

"I've never had stays removed so quickly," she said wryly. "Some men practice playing an instrument, or work on their fencing. But you've spent your time perfecting another art." She didn't quite keep the jealousy out of her tone, much to her irritation.

He only smiled enigmatically. "Consider it all rehearsal for this moment."

"You're a glib scoundrel."

"I don't know words half as well as you do," he answered, trailing a finger along the neckline of her chemise, scattering embers of sensation. "I know pleasure. And bodies."

"You possess far more knowledge than that," she gasped.

He leaned closer. His mouth brushing against hers, he murmured, "I know *you*."

Her eyes drifted shut as his finger went back and forth across the neck of her chemise. He did know her. More than anyone else. A thought both thrilling and a little frightening.

But then thoughts and fears scattered when his finger dipped lower, circling the tip of her breast.

Her breath caught at the pleasure and intimacy.

He kissed her, long and thorough. She leaned into him, reveling in the feel of their bodies pressed together with only the thin fabric of her undergarments between them.

Suddenly, cool air danced across her skin. Opening her eyes, she saw that her chemise was gone. Her drawers hastily followed suit. More of his rake's magic. She was clad in only her stockings and garters.

He stared at her for a long, anticipatory moment, taking in every part of her with his gaze. "Yes," he said thickly.

She let him look his fill, strength and arousal pouring through her in bright waves. At that moment, as he gazed at her with naked hunger, she felt the most desired woman in the world. The most powerful.

"Take them off," he growled, glancing at her stockings.

Feeling bold and free, she planted one foot on the mattress. Her gaze on his, she deliberately undid her garter and, little by little, peeled away her stocking. One leg bare. Then she did the same with her other leg. She was rewarded for her efforts with the twitch of his cock and the tightening of his jaw.

"You undo me," he rasped.

Good to know she wasn't the only one lost in this sea of need.

She beckoned to him. "Show me," she said.

Chapter 18

Poetry is no substitute for experience.

The Hawk's Eye, May 15, 1816

Eleanor allowed him to draw her up onto the bed. They stretched out together atop the silk counterpane, naked limbs entwining, hands everywhere. Learning each other. Discovering. He was in all ways thorough as he touched her, neglecting no part of her body.

One by one, he pulled the pins from her hair, until the mass of it tumbled in curls and whorls around her shoulders. He rubbed a lock of her hair between his fingers, then against his lips.

She felt drugged, adrift, both cast to sea and anchored only by Daniel. In the rasp of his palms against her skin. The whispered praise and promises he trailed over her, mouth hot and demanding. On her neck. Her collarbone. The inside of her wrist. Everywhere she was responsive. His stubble deliciously abraded her flesh.

Gripping his forearms, she marveled again at the lean strength of him, reveling in the contrast of their bodies, yet united by one purpose—to be as close to one another as possible. To shape pleasure together.

As they lay upon the bed, facing each other, his broad hand cupped her breast, once more stroking the tip. Lightly pinching it. She writhed. Then his touch moved down, between her breasts, along her midriff and abdomen. Until he found the place between her legs, where she was wet and aching for him.

His touch was light at first, tracing her, educating himself in what she liked best. His instinct was flawless. She almost believed him inside her mind, her body, for he stroked and caressed her to unbearable pleasure. He circled the sensitive nub with a light touch, then more strength as she responded to him. His fingers rubbed up and down her folds, tracing her opening. And when one of his fingers slid into her, she arched up from the bed with a gasp. All the while his mouth was on hers. He played her expertly, creating sensation everywhere. It built, in hot, bright waves.

And then the wave crashed over her. She bucked, crying out, as release clutched her. Yet he continued to stroke and touch her until another orgasm crested and broke. He pressed at the spot deep within her that was its own shining sun of pleasure.

At last, she fell back, limp and wrung out, sweat filming her.

"Oh," she somehow found the strength to gasp, "you clever, clever man."

He grinned wickedly. "Finally, you think I'm clever."

"In some things," she said with a teasing smile. "I'm still the better writer."

"There's no challenge to your quill. Not from me. But," he added with a sly, sensuous look, "I've got another challenge for you."

"Oh?" She raised a brow.

"How much more pleasure can you withstand?" he dared her.

Pulling him close, she kissed him. He tasted rich and luscious, like aged whiskey, with an edge that whetted her appetite for more and more.

He shifted, his body slick and lean. She loved the feel of him in motion. Especially when he moved so that he stretched above her, covering her. He braced himself on his forearms, the muscles of his shoulders in hard relief, and his face tight with hunger.

He nestled between her legs. It was here, at last. This moment. That seemed so impossible, and yet all she ever wanted. There was a profound intimacy as they stared into each other's eyes. She felt herself tumbling, falling, with no hope of ever stopping her free fall. She wasn't sure she wanted to stop.

The head of his cock circled her entrance. She was shaken anew by their intimacy. This language of lovers, which had more meaning and depth than she'd ever known. And it drove her need for him higher. More slickness gathered, a combination of them together. He cupped her head between his hands and held her gaze as he slid into her. He filled her completely as she gripped him.

"God," he growled.

She sank into sensation. "Yes."

They took a moment to simply feel one another. Him deep inside her. Her surrounding him. Them, together.

A surprise. An inevitability.

They were meant for this. Not merely sex, but this joining. So complete. So absolute.

She lost all means of thought as he started to move his hips. He stroked within her in long, deep thrusts. Each one perfect. Again. Again.

Their breath mingled together, gasping, and his back grew damp. He knew her—her body, her mind. There was no part of her that didn't feel him within her. She held on tightly, her legs wrapping around his waist, giving him as much of herself as she could.

"Daniel . . ." She moaned. "More. Everything."

"All of it." His thrusts grew stronger, more intense. He kept nothing back. And she took it all, spinning into a tempest of pleasure. Pleasure that she'd never known until then. Brighter and more potent than anything she had experienced.

What could make her feel this way? It had to be his skill

as a lover. He was a man who knew the needs of women and how to satisfy those needs.

Yet it was more than his body and hers. It was *themselves*. Their connection.

Her heart ached as her body burned. She understood it then, through the glowing haze of ecstasy. This wasn't just about physical sensation.

Foolish. Believing I could make love with him without feeling anything more than affection.

She knew better now.

Was she anything more to him than another conquest? They'd made no promises to one another. No avowals had been exchanged. She couldn't hold him to something neither had agreed to.

She should have been more careful. Protected her heart.

Too late. Too damn late. She brimmed with an emotion she feared naming. Yet avoiding its name didn't give it any less power over her. Didn't give *him* more power.

She wanted to pull away, but the pleasure was too wondrous. She was awash in it. Hopeless to fight her body's needs. Needs that he knew how to fulfill.

He angled his hips so that he rubbed against her most sensitive place. And in an instant, another climax had her.

Seconds later, he pulled back, freeing himself. His own release came a moment after, spilling hotly onto her belly. He was tight everywhere as he threw his head back and groaned a primal sound of deep pleasure and satiety.

They panted and shuddered in the aftermath, him still stretched out above her. Almost protectively covering her body with his. Finally, he rolled onto his back. Her eyes drifted shut. She felt a corner of the sheets on her stomach as he cleaned her.

He gathered her close, tucking her head against his neck, holding her as if she were something quite valuable but easily lost. Without him holding her, she very well might drift away, caught on tides of sensation.

"You're so beautiful," he rumbled. "So damn perfect."

She would've given up an eternity if it meant having this with him. The pleasure continued even after the physical act was over. Yet she couldn't speak. She only sank deeper into herself and the glow of what they had created. Sleep threaded up her limbs, looming close. But while lassitude crept closer, weighing her down, other sensations hovered at the periphery. Fear. Sadness. As she began to drift away, she realized nothing she could write would alter that fact that everything had changed.

For the first time in his life, Daniel was eager to wake. His body, however, was having none of it, his limbs relaxed, his eyelids heavy. His whole body, in fact, felt very well used from the kind of exertion that could only come from making love all night.

Eyes still closed, he smiled to himself. He and Eleanor had enjoyed themselves thoroughly, bestowing on each other a kind of pleasure he'd never known in the whole of his dissipated life. It was all the better because it had been with *her*. It was more than just two bodies coming together, it had been two minds, two hearts.

They'd made love twice more after the first time, waking at different times to tease and rouse the other into full awareness. He wanted to seize every moment of this experience with her. Hold it closely, jealously, like a dragon guarding its treasure.

He'd known that taking Eleanor to bed would be extraordinary. What he hadn't counted on was that the pleasure of it had reached past the physical into something else. Something much deeper and more profound. Eleanor had wit, determination, bravery, and all he wanted to do was cherish them, cherish *her*.

This couldn't be . . . No. He refused to believe it. That was an emotion he wasn't capable of feeling. At least, he didn't believe so. He'd no experience with romantic feelings, and he regarded those sentiments with the kind of awed wariness an explorer might feel when observing a tiger for the first time.

His eyes flew open. Turning his head, he found the bed beside him cool and empty.

Eleanor was nowhere to be seen. Raising himself up on his elbows, he noted that her gown was missing. But a small scrap of paper lay upon the heap of his discarded clothing.

He sprang up from the bed and strode to the paper. A note, he discovered. In her handwriting.

> *Thank you for the use of the gown. I will clean and return it to you by end of day.*
>
> *—E.H.*

Disappointment plunged through him like a landslide. Yes, of course he wanted to enjoy her body again, but he sought more than that. He'd been looking forward to waking beside her, hearing her jest with him, seeing the morning light upon her skin. He wanted to know her fully in the day—the puffiness of her eyes upon waking, her tangled hair, the beautiful reality of her apart from their nighttime adventures. The truth away from the fantasy.

Usually, his bedpartners had been interchangeable. She was different. He'd thought . . . well, damn it, he'd thought what they'd shared last night had been special in some way. Yet her note was aloof, distant. As if last night hadn't happened, and she was still stuck on that dress.

He thought he heard a step on the stairs. It couldn't have been one of his servants. They were too well trained and moved as silently as shades. It had to be Eleanor. She wasn't gone yet.

Throwing on a robe, he stalked from his chambers. She wasn't in the hallway. Or on the landing.

There. He spotted her halfway down the stairs, heading toward the foyer. And the front door. Her gown was rumpled, her hair down. She'd dressed in a hurry—and that fueled his ire even more.

Hearing his footsteps behind her, she whirled around on the step, her eyes wide. He stalked close to her, standing one step above her.

"The hell do you mean," he demanded, taking hold of her arm, "creeping out like a damn thief?"

She seemed taken aback by his anger, as if she didn't expect him to be upset.

Tipping up her chin, she said, "I—"

"Am I interrupting something?" said a young feminine voice below. Both Daniel and Eleanor whirled to look down into the foyer. Appearing in the Yellow Drawing Room's doorway stood Catherine.

He was caught upon the sharp blades of indecision. If he hastened upstairs and dressed, he risked having Eleanor slip away. But it was bloody scandalous, even for him, to talk with Catherine wearing nothing but a silk robe.

The hell with it. He'd rather risk the scandal than lose Eleanor.

Catherine glanced back and forth between Eleanor and Daniel with a look of shock, then growing understanding. She might just be a girl, but she was a girl who knew the ways of the world. Meanwhile, Eleanor was doing the same thing, looking back and forth between Catherine and Daniel, her own gaze incisive.

Damn and hell. Everything was spinning out of his control. The thorn of a headache hooked itself behind his eye.

He forced himself to calm, releasing Eleanor's arm. "Please." He waved her ahead of him, down the stairs and toward the Yellow Drawing Room.

She looked uncertainly at him, then down at the Yellow Drawing Room. Almost as though she expected him to drag her down there. But he remained all courtesy and waited. Finally, she headed down the stairs.

Once they were inside the chamber, he shut the door behind them. What was a little more scandal at this point?

He already knew the reason for Catherine's presence. Though he'd been spending his nights with Eleanor to draw attention away from his search for Jonathan, now there was no going back. Everything was out in the open. "It's a little early, I think. He won't be out until later."

She cast a slightly embarrassed look toward the floor. "I've . . . been paying some street urchins to look for him."

"I see." Under different circumstances, at any other moment, his pride might have stung a little bit that she didn't fully rely upon him to find Jonathan. But with Eleanor here, clearly wearing last night's gown, watching him and Catherine—everything was in the process of being shot to hell.

"Is this the writer?" Catherine asked.

Eleanor looked from him to Catherine, and back again. He watched the questions form in her eyes.

"I'm the writer," she answered. "And who are you?"

Before Daniel could speak, Catherine gave a polite nod. "Miss Catherine Lawson."

"The only daughter of the Duke of Holcombe," Eleanor said immediately.

Damn. Of course Eleanor, with her encyclopedic knowledge of high Society, would know who Catherine was. And that she wasn't related to Daniel, except by the connection of his friendship with her brother.

More questions filled Eleanor's gaze. Still, she curtsied. "Unless my understanding of etiquette is sorely behind the times, this isn't precisely a fashionable hour for visiting."

"Well . . . no," Catherine admitted.

"Undoubtedly, I don't consider myself particularly smart when it comes to how I dress," Eleanor continued. "Function, not style, is more important to me. Is that . . . gown . . . the latest innovation from Paris?" She eyed Catherine's decidedly threadbare ensemble.

Goddamn Eleanor and her continuing insight. It was one of the parts of her he admired, but right now, he wished she could be a little less perceptive.

Uncertainty brimmed in Catherine's eyes as she looked up at Daniel.

He muttered a curse under his breath. What could he do? Continue to hide his real mission from Eleanor? He'd already revealed it. And she might learn more on her own. It would be far better if she heard the facts from him rather than from another source.

Hell. This was no easy decision. Yet at the heart of it, sudden understanding struck him. He trusted Eleanor. Trusted her enough to grant her the truth.

Somberly, he contemplated the task before him. But it wasn't just his secret to keep.

"You'll have to tell her," Catherine said, as though reading his thoughts. "Or else there's no knowing what she'll publish in that paper of hers."

"She's standing right here," Eleanor interjected, planting her hands on her hips. "And, depending on whether you're honest or not, that will certainly affect what I decide to print."

Still, he continued to hesitate. He'd never made such a momentous decision before.

"Tell her, Ashford," Catherine said, weariness making her sound far older than seventeen. She dropped into one of the chairs. "I cannot keep the weight of secrets to myself any longer."

There seemed to be no other option. Catherine had given her permission. And, if he wanted to be honest with himself as well, he, too, felt the strain of carrying the burden. A heavy load that was always with him. At least speaking of it might release some of the pressure, like a valve.

So, taking a breath, Daniel revealed the grim details to Eleanor. Jonathan's return from the war. His decline and descent. His ultimate disappearance, and his family's inability to do anything about it, even after his elder brother passed away.

"Upstanding people," Eleanor said under her breath. "I knew about them, of course, but only the superficial elements. Never the . . . darker details."

Catherine reddened. "Undoubtedly, my family isn't of much use when faced with, ah, difficulties."

"A deeply troubled son isn't a difficulty," Eleanor said. "It's a call to duty."

Daniel said, "The Duke of Holcombe doesn't have an expansive imagination when it comes to duty. Not even when it comes to his son and heir."

He detailed his and Catherine's quest for her brother, unproductive though their searches had been. He even revealed the true reason why he'd approached Eleanor to write the articles in the first place—as a means of throwing her off the trail so that he might continue to track down his old friend without her eyes upon his other activities.

It felt like a purge. One of those old medieval cures. Or even a bleeding. An attempt to balance the humors. All the darkness and uncertainty of the past few months spilled out upon the plush carpeting.

When he was finished, he felt worn out, spent. Catherine, too, looked pale and drawn, as though hearing her brother's story again brought on fresh pain. He crossed the room, took her hand in his, and gave it a reassuring squeeze, though he felt anything but certain.

"And there it is," he said, his voice hoarse. "The whole of it. It would be worse than catastrophic should anyone find out about Jonathan's descent and disappearance. Even a dukedom has its limits to scandal. You remember what happened to the Duke of Sawfort's son last year when it was discovered he lived at a brothel and frequented opium dens? He and his family became pariahs. His sisters cannot find men willing to be their husbands, and the sons have fled to the Continent."

"I recall." Eleanor's glance toward him was opaque, but her gaze softened, turning sympathetic as she addressed Catherine. "I'm heartily sorry, Miss Lawson, for all that you and your family have endured." Sincerity marked her words and shone in her eyes.

"Thank you." Catherine produced a handkerchief and

dabbed at her eyes, though she seemed almost too weary for tears.

"There haven't been enough men in Parliament arguing for the welfare of veterans," Eleanor said darkly. "Former soldiers see and endure such horrors. That changes a man. Yet they're expected to return to civilian life as if waking from a dream, leaving all that behind them. An unfair demand."

"It is." Catherine sighed. "And I'm afraid that what my brother woke to was even more of a nightmare. I hope—we hope—that he can be brought back from those shadows. If it isn't too late."

"You'll find him," Eleanor said with conviction. She looked as though she was going to stride across the room to Catherine, but her gaze snagged on Daniel, and she stayed on the other side of the chamber. "And with your care, he'll be brought back to himself."

"Again, that is my hope," said Catherine.

"You're very young to be so courageous," Eleanor said, warmth in her voice.

"There wasn't much choice," the girl answered.

"There was indeed a choice," Eleanor returned stoutly. "Most girls, most *people,* would hide from or crumble beneath such a burden. But you've done admirably."

Though she still looked exhausted, Catherine smiled with appreciation at Eleanor's praise. Kindness and sympathy continued to radiate from Eleanor.

When she turned to Daniel, however, her expression was as impenetrable and unreadable as midnight.

"I have to go," she said. "It's late, and I need to get to work."

"And we need to go, as well," Catherine added. She released Daniel's hand. "One of my informants told me someone closely matching Jonathan's description was spotted in Wapping early this morning. He has a limp now, but the hair color matched."

Eleanor walked quickly from her side of the chamber to the drawing room door. He caught up with her.

His hand threaded with hers. In a low voice, he asked, "What will you do?"

He'd just entrusted her with his most guarded secret, but he had no idea what she would do with it. Had last night changed anything for her? And what about now? She'd finally learned the truth he'd kept concealed from her, and now knew why he'd approached her for the articles in *The Hawk's Eye*.

But they'd had no time to talk of last night. Or anything else.

Was she angry at his concealment? Could he rely upon her to keep the secret of Jonathan's disappearance? And what was this ache he felt when he beheld the distance in her gaze?

Damn, he'd never thought much about the feelings of his lovers. They would use each other for mutual enjoyment, and part ways as impersonally as business partners ending a corporation.

Yet he needed to know what Eleanor thought, what she felt. They'd only just begun to forge a bond between them—was that all gone now?

Everything was in bloody chaos.

"I don't know," she answered simply. Then slipped from his grasp. He would not grab for her again—if she stayed, it would be by her choice. And if she left . . . that was her decision, too, much as it sent a wrench of pain through him. She might never return.

He could only watch as she walked out of the drawing room. Then out into the foyer. She stepped across the threshold of his home. Morning sunlight swallowed her. She disappeared.

He turned back to Catherine, who now stood and paced the room. She stopped and took one look at his face. A new sorrow filled her gaze. "Love is terrible, isn't it?" she murmured.

Daniel started. "Who said anything about love? And what do you know of it?" he asked, his words edged with anger at the whole bloody situation. "You're only a child."

Her smile was rueful. "I lost my childhood when Jonathan returned from the war. And I know enough about love to realize that it mostly brings pain."

He rubbed at his forehead. Was this love? He had no experience with it.

He was raw and aching, uncertain in a way he'd never experienced before. He wanted nothing more than to retreat like an injured animal to lick his wounds. Wounds that had been caused by the most delightful, maddening knife.

But Jonathan might be out there. Whatever he might or might not be feeling for Eleanor, he had his duty to his friend, and to Catherine. He was torn, a new sensation for him. Whatever happened today, the echoes of this morning with Eleanor would continue to reverberate—for a long, long time.

Chapter 19

It is a common enough assertion that one demands honesty exclusively in one's dealings. After all, who does not desire to know the truth? Yet the desire for perfect transparency and the actual practice of it can be received with wildly differing responses.

The Hawk's Eye, May 18, 1816

Eleanor sat in one of the velvet-lined boxes at the Imperial, arms propped on the railing. She watched without seeing as the theatrical troupe rehearsed Maggie's latest play—something that involved many doors, and the opening and slamming of those doors. The actors stood with pages of the script in their hands, posing, always posing, as they called out their lines. Maggie herself hovered at the edge of the stage, though the manager, Mr. Courtland, seemed to have things well in hand as he maneuvered the actors like chess pieces. But Maggie always watched rehearsals. She'd confessed to Eleanor that she could never allow her work fully to be handed over to someone else. Eleanor understood that impulse very well.

Even now, Maggie stepped forward, gesticulating as she suggested a particular piece of stage business. Courtland shook his head. Maggie ignored him, moving one of the actresses into position. Courtland moved the actress back to where she'd been before. The poor performer looked mystified as the writer and the manager squabbled over her like a contested toy, tugging her back and forth. The orchestra held their instruments at the ready, in case anything should be resolved and they could actually perform their jobs.

The ghost of a smile touched Eleanor's lips. Yet her heart twisted with indecision and worry. She'd written her latest article about Daniel two days ago, and today would see the piece distributed in the latest issue of *The Hawk's Eye*. He'd read it. All of London would read it.

She'd given back the gown. In return, he'd sent her a plain but excellently made quill sharpening set.

For the first time in her life, she wondered if she'd made the right decision with an article.

That wasn't the only doubt tormenting her. It had buried like brambles beneath her skin, until she'd had to take refuge away from the paper, somewhere that might offer her a measure of distraction. So she'd come here, to the theater. Yet despite the dramas occurring on the stage, she thought of nothing but Daniel. Of them.

He'd bravely revealed much about himself that night, leaving himself open and exposed. An act of profound trust. He'd protected her. Then tried so very hard to make her comfortable in his home.

They'd finally made love. And it had surpassed her every experience. Not merely because the physical sensations had been sublime. But because it had been *him*. Because he knew her, and had striven to give her pleasure at any cost.

The line between writer and subject had been irrevocably crossed. It had some time ago, but that night was the sun setting on any prospect of objectivity.

Especially after he'd told her about his missing friend, Jonathan Lawson. A highly esteemed, powerful family's darkest secret. Entrusted to her.

She'd always known that he'd had an ulterior motive. No one would willingly offer themselves up to that kind of exposure and scrutiny without having some rationale. And his had been a strong one.

She couldn't muster any anger at being used. Had she been in Daniel's place, she would have done the same. At the beginning, especially, there had been no connection, no bond, between them. They'd been mutual exploiters.

All that had changed. They were so much more to each other now. Whenever she thought of him—which was constantly—her heart throbbed, and electricity danced through her body. She'd alternate between waves of inexplicable happiness and grayest melancholy.

What was it? How to explain these feelings?

The action onstage had degenerated into a full-fledged yelling match between Maggie and Courtland. Their voices bounced off the empty walls of the theater. Actors clustered in groups, watching the action, though they seemed quite familiar with these confrontations between the writer and the manager. An older actress even yawned into her script. Yet no one was foolish enough to step between Maggie and Courtland. The actors and orchestra seemed resigned to waiting.

Maggie had warned Eleanor about becoming involved with Daniel. And, imprudently, Eleanor had assured Maggie that nothing would happen. That she'd remain aloof and untouched by Daniel's charm. Had it merely been a matter of magnetism, glib compliments, and rakish charisma, Eleanor would have been safe. But, damn it, there had been so much more than that.

The revelation had come as an intriguing surprise.

He'd shown himself as he truly was. A man of strength. Honor. And uncertainty.

Though he'd hidden it behind a veneer of nonchalance, she knew he cared about her work. He hadn't been able to disguise his respect and admiration when she'd shown him the paper's operations. Even seemed to appreciate the mountain of work she'd put into the paper, that it was her creation alone. What other man—especially of his station—would ever feel that way about a woman's efforts?

And what was she supposed to do now? He'd read the

article soon, and know what she'd done. But what did it all mean?

She rested her forehead on the railing, closing her eyes.

Had she gone and fallen *in love* with him? Despite all precautions? And knowing that love between a man of his station and a woman of hers could only end in disaster?

As a journalist, she had to question everything. Investigate.

What did love feel like? That, she didn't know. Yet when she thought about Daniel, her heart leapt. Time apart from him made the world seem gray and wearisome. Her mind constantly strayed to him like a ship upon a current. And when she thought about her life without him, everything within her grew heavy and dull.

If this isn't love, I don't know what is.

Disaster. An unmitigated disaster. Even if, by some act of God, he returned her feelings, they couldn't do anything about it. An earl. A woman of no name, no blood. People who would, under most circumstances, have no truck with each other. Yet she and Daniel had come to know one another through the articles. They knew their innermost secrets and selves.

Perhaps they might enjoy each other as lovers for a time, but it could never be anything more. He was an earl. She was not just a commoner but a woman who worked. They had no future together. She'd read—and written—accounts of noblemen and women who'd dallied with those not of aristocratic blood. It never worked out well for the commoners. They were often disgraced, cast aside by their lovers as well as their friends and families. Left alone and humiliated.

At the thought, the animal of her heart snarled and slunk. It didn't like being denied. But what choice was there?

She thought again of his friend. Daniel risked everything to find the missing, fallen Jonathan Lawson. A man lost to himself after the horrors of war. Daniel could have turned away from Miss Lawson's plea, concerned about the scandal to himself if he went in search of the disappeared man, but he hadn't. And that made the ache in Eleanor's chest grow, like a dark star.

She knew one thing: sitting here at the theater, lost in her thoughts, would only generate more confusion and doubt. She needed to *do* something. To move. To act. How? She didn't know. This was virgin territory.

For years, she'd reported on the actions of others, observing the world but not being fully part of it. Then Daniel had come into her life, and all that had changed. She was in the world now. There was no hiding, no turning away.

And there was something she had to do.

Daniel had never respected the power of a newspaper before. They were only ink and paper, after all, and his social position was largely untouchable. The prerogative of the aristocracy. He hadn't cared—not very much, anyway—what the papers said about him. But it wasn't his own reputation he was concerned about when he picked up the latest issue of *The Hawk's Eye*.

It was Catherine and Jonathan's.

He'd revealed their deepest secret to Eleanor. True—it was at Catherine's urging, but the damage, whatever it might be, was done. The truth was out.

Sadly, the expedition he and Catherine had undertaken to Wapping had been unsuccessful. If Jonathan had been there, he'd vanished again by the time they'd arrived. They had combed through taverns and cheap lodging houses. To no avail. The whole of the day had been one exercise in frustration after another. His heart had been divided in two, thinking about both finding Jonathan and seeing Eleanor again. And Catherine had been too upset afterwards for Daniel to leave her on her own. By the time he'd seen her settled, it had been too late to go to Eleanor.

Sitting now beside the fire in his study, he had the most recent issue of *The Hawk's Eye* on his lap. Unread.

Could he truly, fully trust her, even after everything they'd had together? And what did it say about the nature of their . . . association . . . that he now questioned her?

Every moment of wakefulness had been spent in edgy contemplation of Eleanor. What she meant to him. And he to her. How they could navigate the rocky shoals of social position, duty, and honesty.

There was only one way to know for certain whether or not he'd made a mistake in trusting her.

So he picked up the newspaper. Began to read. The only sound in the room came from the patter of rain against the windows and the pop of the fire behind its grate. And the crinkling turn of pages as Daniel read the latest *To Ride with a Rake* article.

At great and detailed length, she reported on the masquerade, and he nearly smiled at her descriptions of the outrageous evening. It *had* been outrageous. Her sharp and observant eye had picked out details he'd forgotten about or hadn't noticed, down to the overabundance of Cleopatras, and the steps of the scandalous dances. The wild, unbridled atmosphere was captured with expressive language, though she named no names.

However, she described her near assault in cold, brittle words, not hiding her anger and contempt for the man who'd tried to hurt her. Daniel found the paper crumpling in his hands as he went over the account, his own rage boiling up again like a flame brought higher beneath a simmering pot. He'd let the bastard off too easily. If Daniel ever encountered him again, he'd be certain to beat him thoroughly, until breathing became an agony.

No one hurt Eleanor. And if they were fool enough to try, Daniel would make them regret it to the end of their days.

Had he hurt her with his own deception? If he had, he'd do everything in his power to make things right between them.

He kept reading. After the description of her assault, she wrote a little more about the masquerade.

The article came to a close. It said nothing about the kiss he and Eleanor had shared, which didn't surprise him. She'd only harm her own reputation by admitting it. And she certainly omitted them making love.

But . . . there was naught about Jonathan. Not a word about Catherine. Or the Duke of Holcombe. That whole sordid, sad tale was omitted.

Daniel pawed through the paper, searching other articles for mention of the family's secret. Nothing. It was as if Eleanor hadn't heard the most hidden, darkest confidence. As though the conversation, and what it revealed, had never happened.

Slowly, he lowered the paper. It drifted to the floor, released by numb fingers.

She'd kept her silence. Shown herself to be trustworthy, honorable. A stab of shame lanced him, that he might briefly doubt her. But there'd been no cause for his doubt.

That swell of emotion filled him again—the emotion that Catherine had been so quick to name, and he feared. But there it was. Making him feel both enormous and small. But mostly powerful. Potential thrummed through his veins.

God—was it true? Did he love her?

The word didn't terrify him this time. Instead, it felt profoundly right. The cornerpiece to a structure, making it stronger, more stable.

He loved her. The thought rocked through him, pinning him in place, as though stuck through with a knight's lance. But it was a good wound. An injury that healed more than it hurt.

A small whisper curled through the back of his head. *What if she doesn't want me?* He'd caught her trying to sneak out of his house, after all. And earlier this morning, her masquerade dress had been delivered to him without a note. He'd actually held it up to his face and inhaled, trying to catch her scent.

But was it all delusion? A one-sided madness? God—could he bear that?

He shot to his feet. He had to see her. Talk to her. Tell her . . . he wasn't certain. But the need to be with her burned him like the urge itself to live.

She hadn't responded to the quill sharpener he'd sent her. But she hadn't returned it, either. That itself was a good sign. He had to seize whatever possibilities he could.

After he pulled the bell, his butler appeared.

There must have been a look of urgency on Daniel's face, because the butler asked, "The carriage, my lord?"

"Have the grooms saddle Winter for me," he directed. "No, I'll take Dame. She's the fastest."

"Yes, my lord." The butler bowed and disappeared.

After hurrying upstairs, Daniel dressed for a fast, hard ride through the streets of London. He'd see Eleanor within the hour, but even that wasn't soon enough. *See her. Be near her.* These thoughts drummed through his blood.

What would he say? At the least, he'd thank her for her discretion. Apologize for ever doubting her. Tell her . . . God . . . he didn't know. Reveal his feelings? Yes. No.

Or he could show her. Shut the door to her office, pull the blinds, and hold her close.

Edinger arrived to announce that his horse was ready. In an instant, Daniel was outside, mounting up. The horse beneath him was eager to run. Almost as eager as him. It took just the touch of his heels to her flanks to get her into motion. But no matter how fast the horse sped through the streets of London, weaving between carriages, wagons, and other horses, it wasn't fast enough. Not when his heart pounded, and Eleanor awaited him.

Except that she didn't.

Daniel arrived at *The Hawk's Eye,* threw a coin to a nearby crossing sweep to watch his horse, then strode into the newspaper's office. He walked down the length of the desks toward Eleanor's closed office. Though he'd been to the newspaper several times before, his appearance was enough to generate more stares from the writers. He ignored them. Instead, pausing in front of Eleanor's door, he took a deep breath. She was there, on the other side of that door. And he had so many damned things to say to her.

He curled his hands into fists. Then uncurled them.

Before he'd met her, he'd hardly known a moment's uncertainty. Now his life was wracked with it. But he didn't hide, either.

He knocked.

Silence.

He knocked again. More silence followed.

"Elea—Miss Hawke," he said through the door. "It's me. Lord Ashford," he added for the benefit of the eavesdropping writers.

Still nothing. He frowned at the nearby writers, all watching him. Daniel's expression must have been fierce. No other way to explain the kind of wary amazement on the writers' faces. One young man—Daniel recognized him from the first time he came here—tried to speak, his mouth opening and closing, his throat working. But no sound emerged from the lad.

Daniel could wait no longer. Turning back to the door to Eleanor's office, he put his shaking hand on the doorknob. Then let himself in. Words jockeyed for position, struggling to come out all at once, as he entered.

Disappointment hit him like a punch. She wasn't at her desk. She wasn't anywhere in her office.

He returned to the writers' room. "Where is Miss Hawke?" he demanded of the young man. "With the printing presses?"

The boy finally found his voice, though it took several attempts. "She hasn't been here for an hour. My lord," he added hastily.

"Where is she?"

The writer paled and swallowed. "Out on a story."

"Which story?"

"Didn't say, my lord." The lad's forehead wrinkled. "Think she said something about needing a disguise, though."

He knew at once where she'd be. The place where she'd undergone all of her transformations, from "Ned" to "Ruby." Most likely, she'd also gone there to complete her metamorphosis to masked siren.

Striding from the newspaper, he retrieved his horse from the crossing sweep—giving the tiny boy another coin for his trouble—and set off for the Imperial Theater.

He reached the theater in a fever of impatience. Eleanor blazed in his mind, a beacon he had to follow.

Daniel knocked at the stage door. The man guarding it eyed him with some suspicion. So Daniel gave the bloke some money—always a way to get a door open.

After breaching the door, he raced up several flights of stairs and found himself in the wings of the theater. Anarchy immediately engulfed him. Dancers flounced back and forth—a few giving him speculative, inviting looks—and a baritone practiced beside a pianoforte. Workers in dusty clothing hammered at scenery, just as the actors onstage seemed equally engaged in destroying the scenery with their line readings, guided by a slightly portly fellow. Meanwhile, a dark-skinned man with a Caribbean accent and folio of papers shouted at anyone who would listen to him.

This was most assuredly not the peace and rarefied atmosphere of White's.

Daniel scanned the throngs, looking for a glimpse of Eleanor's blonde head. Nothing. Another stab of disappointment knifed him. He hadn't gone to war, but he'd never learned what it was to surrender.

He was an aristocrat. He knew his way around the backstage of theaters. There were warrens of rooms, some overflowing with actresses and dancers in various states of undress. Rooms that housed costumes and props. Any number of places where Eleanor could be.

He turned, intending to find her.

And found himself face-to-face—or rather her face to his chest, since she was not a woman of tall stature—with Mrs. Delamere.

The playwright didn't look at all awed or impressed by Daniel. In fact, she seemed on the verge of contempt. Her hands were planted on her hips, and she glared up at him.

"She's not here," Mrs. Delamere said without preamble. He noticed that she didn't add "my lord" at the end of her sentence.

"Where has she gone?" he asked, equally blunt.

"If she hasn't told you," she replied, "then I see no reason why I ought to."

"I mean only to speak with her."

"What you do or don't say isn't of concern to me." She flicked a scornful glance up and down him. "I know how your kind works. Honeyed promises that all turn to ash."

"You don't know anything about me," he said tightly.

"I know the look you put on my friend's face," she returned.

If he wasn't in a battle with this woman, he'd have more time to think on what this meant. That his feelings were shared.

But the playwright was mulish, glaring up at him. "As if you didn't know."

He gritted his teeth. "I don't—and I can't—unless I see her."

"Why should I betray her confidence?" Mrs. Delamere crossed her arms over her chest and tilted her chin up. She was a handsome woman indeed, with bold features and a considerable amount of black hair, but when she looked at him as though he was Satan himself in a beaver hat, her features turned hard, her dark eyes biting.

"Did she say not to tell me where she was?"

That biting glance slid away for a moment. "Not specifically."

"You do no harm in revealing her whereabouts."

"Except that I do," she fired back. "As I said, I know your sort, *my lord*. People like us—*women* like us—are disposable to aristos. Using Eleanor for your entertainment, throwing her away like an empty sweet wrapper once you've tired of her—I won't let it happen."

His voice went very soft. "Who says I'll tire of her?"

For a moment, her brazen façade fell away. She peered at him curiously, the same insight in her eyes that marked Eleanor's gaze. Something in his voice, his face, and posture, must have shaken her.

Actors and stagehands surged around them like eddies in a river, yet neither he nor the playwright seemed to notice as they faced each other.

"Your class always does," she finally answered. "Us plebes are nothing but toys to you."

"Whoever wronged you in the past," he said, "mark this—*I am not him.* And I have no intention of hurting Eleanor. Not now. Not in the future."

This, too, seemed to unnerve her. But she rallied once again, glowering at him across the few feet that separated them. "No intention. That doesn't mean you won't."

"I'll do everything in my power to keep her safe," he vowed. "And I have a considerable amount of power."

Yet the playwright vacillated, her lips compressed into a tight line as she internally debated.

"You want to see me brought low?" he demanded. He swept his hat off his head, spread his hands in supplication. "I am. I ask you, respectfully, humbly, to tell me where she is. Because I find that without her . . ." He fought to find the words. "I'm only a shell. A glossy, brittle shell. I've got to tell her this. Whatever the consequences, she has to know. Margaret," he added, letting her know that he could be familiar, too.

It was the most he'd ever said of his feelings for Eleanor. To anyone, including himself. And he shook, faintly, at the voicing of it. He'd endured boxing matches, fencing bouts, phaeton races, and duels. Nothing struck fear into him. But this did.

For a long, agonizing while, Mrs. Delamere said nothing. Only stared at him. Judging. Assessing. Taking his measure. As though he was a character in one of her plays, one she was still trying to figure out.

Finally, she said, "She went to the costumer and obtained some shabby clothing. Then she left. Said she was going to St. Giles."

One of the worst slums in London. "And you let her go?" he demanded angrily. "Alone?"

"You know Eleanor. She wouldn't be dissuaded. But she took my pistol."

Daniel rubbed at his forehead. Why the hell would Eleanor go to such a godforsaken place? The young writer at her offices had said she'd gone to research a story. But she'd always been more interested in high Society than the stories that could be found in a rough area like St. Giles. Even during the day, it was a neighborhood to be avoided if one could. Families lived there, yes, but it was notorious for its gin houses and low company.

Exactly the sort of place Jonathan might be found.

Understanding rocked him. Good God, Eleanor had gone looking for Jonathan. On her own.

Chapter 20

It is sadly noted that the keeping of a confidence appears to be a dwindling art, as many of us today would rather reap the temporary harvest of scandal—which feeds so many but for so short a time—than enjoy the enduring fruits of silence, which can nourish countless souls.

The Hawk's Eye, May 18, 1816

East London was not a part of the city Eleanor knew well. *The Hawk's Eye* covered the scandalous aristocratic personages of Mayfair and Marylebone, not the working poor of Whitechapel and Bethnal Green. Other newspapers reported on the salacious details of East London's crime-ridden streets. But Eleanor was never interested in reveling in the details of someone else's pain, so none of her writers— including herself—ever ventured farther east than the City.

The sun had just reached its zenith, and she moved away from it. The buildings became shabbier and shabbier, crowding close together, all but crumbling where they stood. Barefoot children and people in threadbare clothing drifted up and down the street. A sad, angry miasma clung to the winding lanes. It was a measure of Eleanor's disguise that no one bothered to beg her for spare coins. Yet she kept her hand resting lightly upon her pocket, where she'd tucked Maggie's pistol. Though it was broad daylight, a kind of semi-twilight hung over St. Giles, and Eleanor would take no chances with her safety.

Where to begin? The gin shops seemed the best prospect. She turned toward Seven Dials, then pushed deeper into the neighborhood. Filth coated the street, and people and dogs picked through rubbish, looking for anything of use. Eleanor's grip on her pistol tightened.

She had once seen a print of Jonathan Lawson, so she had a general idea of his appearance. He'd resemble his sister, too. Fair and genteel. She also imagined that, no matter how far he'd fallen, his demeanor and accent would make him stand out from the ragged crowd. She'd mentioned at the paper that she was writing a story. That could be her cover as she searched for him. There were tales that wealthy people liked to take tours of run-down neighborhoods to marvel at and mock the poverty. Much the way visitors once toured Bedlam. She could use this as her screen—saying she was writing about this new phenomenon.

And if she did find Jonathan Lawson—what then? Could she, an utter stranger, convince him to return to his family? The odds were slim, but she had to try. For the sake of him and his sister. And for Daniel.

Even though she walked through one of London's most infamous neighborhoods, the throb of her heart had nothing to do with the potential danger around her. It was *him*.

By now, he would have read the latest issue of the paper and seen what she'd done. A trembling excitement and doubt gripped her. She'd deliberately ignored a scandalous story. To protect him and his friends. It was as good as a public declaration of her feelings for him.

When she did see him again, what would she say? How might she explain herself, and how she felt? She wasn't certain that her feelings were reciprocated—though the quill sharpener was a gift he would know she'd appreciate. In fact, she'd sharpened nearly a dozen unneeded quills just to feel as though he were with her.

A sign was painted onto the side of a building, showing a

raven perched atop a plow, with a tankard gripped in its foot. *Gin, one penny* was written beneath the image. She couldn't see through the greasy windows, but she heard the harsh laughter emanating from inside, and had read enough accounts of gin houses to have a good idea of what awaited her.

She already had her questions in mind: Was it true that the toffs had been coming to St. Giles? What did they look like? Women, men? Young, old? From these details, she might be able to determine if Jonathan Lawson had been around.

She took a deep breath, and regretted it as foul air rushed into her lungs. One hand rested on her pistol, the other on her pad and pencil.

Was this the most foolish thing she'd ever done?

No. Falling in love with an earl ranked as her most unwise act.

Steadying herself, she prepared to enter.

The sound of horse hooves clattering on the cobblestones broke her concentration. Someone was racing through the streets at a breakneck speed. A reckless move, given the condition of the pavement and the number of people thronging the lanes. The crowd itself seemed surprised, murmuring with astonishment.

Eleanor turned away from the door to the gin house to watch the spectacle. And found herself unable to move, as though someone had driven rivets through her feet.

Daniel. Rising above the crowd. Galloping right toward her. Looking like a man journeying on a perilous but vital quest. He rode his horse expertly around the carts and people choking the street. His gaze darted from one side of the lane to the other, searching. And when his gaze lit on hers and held with a fierce intensity, she truly felt that no power on earth could make her move from this one spot.

He pulled his horse to a stop right in front of her. The animal pawed and chuffed. And the man breathed heavily, as though he'd traveled a long distance, and quickly, to find her. Which, she realized, he had. He must have gone to the

Imperial, where Maggie had revealed her whereabouts. Not a short distance to cover. Yet he was here now.

She stared up at him. He looked down at her as though she were an emerald at the bottom of a riverbed.

For several moments, neither spoke. Spectators gathered, drawn by the sight of a wealthy man on an exquisite horse, though none dared approach him.

He reached down to her, offering his gloved hand.

"Get on," he said, his voice deep.

"Jonathan—"

He continued to hold his hand out to her. "I've searched for him here and found no sign. We can look again another day."

She stared at his proffered hand, wide and long. A hand she'd felt explore and caress every part of her body. That had reached into the heart of her and held on tightly. It belonged to a man who had raced hellbound for her, a man who now burned her with the intensity of his gaze.

She'd wanted his touch these past days. Ached for it, thinking she'd never know it again. Finally, though, it could be hers once more. Yet for how long? And what would he want of her?

Slowly, she slid her hand into his. A gasp left her lips as he effortlessly pulled her up in front of him. She sat across the saddle, with him behind her, keeping her steady with his lean, solid body.

"Hold on," he commanded.

She grabbed fistfuls of the horse's mane—the animal didn't seem to mind—and they surged forward. St. Giles disappeared behind them as they rode west, back toward Mayfair, and questions unanswered.

"**T**hat was a bloody foolish thing to do," Daniel thundered. They hadn't spoken at all during the ride to his home. But she'd been aware of the tension radiating from him. Silent and severe.

Once they'd arrived, he'd ushered her immediately into his study. No sooner had he shut and locked the door behind them than he whirled on her, his expression dark as shadow.

"I had a pistol," she replied.

"And after you'd discharged your one shot," he said, "you'd have no means of protecting yourself."

"I have this," she said, tapping the side of her head.

He snorted. "You can't think yourself out of it when five brutes attack you."

"But they didn't," she pointed out.

"They might have."

They faced each other, only inches separating them. The door was just at his back—they had barely made it into the room at all before he'd had to unleash himself. He was all fury, barely contained.

She frowned at him. "This anger's unnecessary."

"You might've been killed, or worse—and for what?" he demanded.

Quietly, she said, "For your friends. For you." *There. I've said it.*

That stunned him into silence. His jaw tightened, and his stare seared into her.

Her pulse climbed into her throat. She'd never spoken words like that to anyone. Always, always, she'd carefully sheltered her heart, knowing full well that this was a world of jagged edges that tore into unguarded flesh. So she'd contented herself with ambition for the newspaper, and occasional physical gratification, and told herself it was enough.

It had been enough. Until he'd walked into her office, full of self-righteousness and outrageous schemes.

Daniel moved slowly, as though through water. He brought his hand up, and held it, hovering close. As though asking her permission to touch her.

Breath coming quickly, she gave a small nod.

Carefully, he cradled her head. His expression gentled, becoming softer, almost awed. Which shook her even more. He was a proud man. Yet, as an outsider looking in, trying to peer into his mind, she thought he seemed humbled by her, and her naked confession.

"You undo me," he said, his voice a rough rasp.

She grasped his wrists. His pulse hammered beneath her touch. "We undo each other," she said plainly. "This can't end well."

An earl and a commoner. They could never be more to each other than lovers. For a time. And then responsibility would finally claim him, and he'd have to take an aristo wife. Or at least one with a substantial fortune. Eleanor was neither noble nor rich, and she never would be.

He couldn't be hers forever, no matter their intentions. Only a few years ago, there had been a young baron— Fleming had been his name—who'd fallen in love with an opera dancer. The two had flouted Society by marrying. And while the baron might have been grudgingly admitted into a few homes, his wife had not been. Lord Fleming's family had refused to see her, as had most everyone else. The first year or two, both had bravely faced their status as pariahs. But eventually, their fall from social grace had torn them apart. The wife now lived at a country estate, and her husband stayed in Town—with a new mistress.

Lord Fleming and his opera dancer had had love at first, but it hadn't protected them. It would almost certainly be the same for Eleanor and Daniel if they attempted anything more than an affair.

An affair it would have to be, then. Better that than nothing.

A corner of her mouth tilted up, bittersweet. "But what a time we'll have of it while it lasts." For however long they might have.

They were silent together. She realized the impossibility yet inevitability of their situation. This was what they could share.

With a soft growl, he lowered his lips to hers. She met his kiss with her own hunger, opening to him, taking and giving. It had been days since last they'd kissed, and it felt like coming up for air after too long underwater. She gasped into his mouth, taking her first real breath since they'd parted. He pulled her close. She wrapped her arms around him, reveling in the strength of his body and the palpable need vibrating in him. A firestorm roared through her, demanding more.

Yet she couldn't give into it. Not yet.

She pulled back, just enough to whisper, "I want to help find him."

"It's not your burden," he said lowly.

"And it's been yours for too long. Let me assist you." She gave a small smile. "I may write about scandal, but I worked my way up the ladder by reporting every sort of story. I know a thing or two about investigations."

He exhaled roughly as his hands wrapped around her waist. "It's dangerous."

Her smile was wry. "I hadn't noticed, being in St. Giles with the gin houses and the cutthroats."

A small amount of tension eased from him. "A step up from the usual company you keep. Writers, theatricals."

"Rakish earls." She held him tightly. Goddamn this man, who worked his way into her heart more and more with each passing moment. Had she known what would happen between them, she might have marched him out of her office immediately that first day and never agreed to their arrangement.

But that would have deprived her of this, of him. And she'd rather suffer later than deprive herself of him now.

She said, "We'll do this *together,* you and I."

For a moment, he said nothing. Then: "For a journalist, you display remarkable ethics."

She laughed quietly. "Consider it an effect of your excellent example."

"I am in all things the epitome of righteous behavior."

"Especially when it comes to the seduction of virtuous writers," she noted.

He raised a brow. "It's not seduction when both parties are willing."

"So speaks the man with a notorious reputation."

"If anyone was beguiled," he added, "we beguiled each other."

She gave him an impudent smile, pressing herself against him snugly. "Oh, did I tempt you?"

"Wench, you know you did." His flash of a smile nearly undid her, so white and dissolute.

"We've degenerated into name-calling now." She shook her head. "The last refuge of those deprived of wit."

"Now who's calling names?" He grinned.

An ache of future sorrow throbbed through her. She could not imagine what her life would be like without him. Didn't want to. Though it was inevitable.

"We'll find Jonathan," she said with as much conviction as she could muster.

Yet he looked dubious. "I'm beginning to wonder if he's still alive. Catherine and I have been searching. Nothing. Hints here and there, but he's elusive as a ghost."

She broke from their embrace to pace—though she didn't want to let go of him, it was easier for her to think when in motion.

"Have you no other leads?" she asked. "No potential clues as to where he might be?"

He strode to the fireplace, then stared into the fire. "Every one we've tried has proven false."

Easier in a way to think of locating his friend than to consider the imminent heartbreak that awaited her. "What of his old habits? His prior haunts?"

"I've tried all those. His club. His former cronies." Daniel turned to face her. "He's cut himself off from everything and everyone he's ever cared about or once enjoyed."

Though for the majority of his life Jonathan Lawson had been a second son, he still had a reputation—for kindness. Even Eleanor knew about it, and how he was unusually dedicated to giving time and money to charities. It had been joked that he was *too* good, except he still loved what young men loved—spirited company, and women. Especially women. "Everything?" she pressed.

His brow lowered thoughtfully. "There's one possibility . . . remote, nigh impossible, but I'm holding out hope." He walked to a fine wooden box perched on one corner of his desk. Opening the lid, he pulled out an object and held it up for her.

It was not what she expected.

"Cheroots," she noted. Walking over, he handed it to her, and she gave the cheroot an appreciative sniff. Rich notes of earth and spice drifted up—but she had known that fragrance many times on his clothing, and in the flavor of his kiss. Heat washed through her at the memory.

"This is my particular blend of tobacco," he explained. "I get it from a shop on Church Street. The tobacconist's specialty is making custom cigars and cheroots to suit the individual tastes of his patrons. His is the most exclusive tobacco shop in London. Jonathan's father always purchases his cheroots there."

"Does Jonathan also buy his tobacco from the Church Street shop?"

"He smokes the same blend as his father—or he started to when he came back from the war," Daniel said. "Catherine told me her brother developed a kind of mania for it before he disappeared. When they'd run out, he'd become wild, angry. Break things. Until someone hurried over to the tobacconist and purchased several dozen cheroots."

Eleanor tapped her lips, contemplative. "He smoked a different kind of cheroot before he left for the war?"

"Yes. Acquired at a shop on King's Street. But that changed when he returned from battle. Why?"

She held up the cheroot Daniel had given her. "I've only to take one sniff of this, and I instantly think of you. You flood my senses." Her cheeks heated, despite the intimacies they had shared. It still felt so new to reveal herself to anyone—though she knew she could trust him beyond all the instinctive wariness of her heart. "If I were to take this with me, all I'd need to do was smell it, or better yet, light it, and I'm with you again."

He didn't throw her admission back in her face. Instead, he looked pleased. "Then, by all means, keep the cheroot."

"I will," she answered. "But the fact that Jonathan changed from his own blend of tobacco to his father's—it seems significant. He likely grew up with his father smoking the same kind of cheroot. It was a scent of home, of comfort and security. A time in his life when he wasn't wracked with memories of horror. When he was a carefree boy."

"So he switched when he returned," Daniel concluded, "in an attempt to recapture that lost time. That lost self."

She nodded. "No wonder he'd fly into a rage when he ran out. It was a kind of tether to who he once was."

Daniel rubbed at his forehead. "Damn it—I knew he'd fallen far and hard, but I never knew how much he tried to cling to what he'd lost." He glanced out the window, where pale sunlight sifted through the curtains and spilled upon the Persian carpet. "If he's alive, he *must* be found. That's why I've instructed the tobacconist to let me know whenever anyone purchases those cheroots."

"Any luck so far?"

"None yet." He paced to the window, which looked out into the gardens. She noticed that the plants hadn't fully bloomed due to the unusually cold weather.

He continued, "I thought of it some time ago, but it didn't yield any information, so I changed my tactic. Still, there may be a chance. Yet I'm afraid that chance grows smaller by the day, by the hour."

She crossed the room to stand beside him. Eleanor stroked her hand along his back, offering comfort how she could. "You haven't failed him, Daniel."

His smile was full of self-reproach. "I saw him before he vanished. I knew something was wrong. His eyes . . . they'd changed. They looked hollow. Barren. When there were signs of life in him, he was a feral thing. Desperate. And I . . . I pretended not to notice. Or exempted myself. 'He's a grown man,' I thought. 'His life is his own to master.' But all I was doing was excusing my own selfishness. The truth is . . ." His voice went raspy, and he cleared his throat, though when he spoke, it was just as rough as before. " . . . it wasn't convenient to me to help him. It got in the way of my pleasure. It meant thinking, really thinking, about someone other than myself. So I let him go."

He turned to her, his gaze bleak. "I could've done something, but I was too caught up in chasing my own gratification to care. He slipped away from me, and I let him fall."

The pain and guilt in his voice—in his eyes, the rigid lines of his posture—cut her deeply. Seeing him hurt . . . it hurt her, too. And while she'd never reveled in the suffering of others, it hadn't ever touched her the way Daniel's agony affected her now. Only Maggie's pain could reach her so intensely. Yet on a different level. Maggie was her dearest friend, but she didn't hold Eleanor's heart in her hands.

What could she say? How could she comfort him? She couldn't offer false palliatives, trite words that neither of them believed. He deserved better than that.

"Whatever sins you committed in the past," she murmured, resting her head on his shoulder, "what matters now is the atonement for them. The will and desire to make a wrong right."

"Perhaps." Yet he didn't sound much convinced.

"Hell," she said, with a little smile, "you marched into my office and offered me a chance to peer into the darkest corners of your life. That's the act of a man who truly wants to do good."

He gave his own tiny, answering smile. "Or one with considerable disturbance of his mental faculties."

"And look where that got you."

"I have looked." He turned, and wrapped her in his arms. Heat filled his gaze, chasing away the pain she'd seen moments earlier. "I've looked and wondered and been amazed."

A tumult of birds' wings pervaded her belly, fluttering and soaring. "You're not alone in your amazement." She gave a small shake of her head. "A month ago, I'd have laughed myself dizzy if someone had told me that I'd lose my heart to a libertine aristo."

"Have you?" He tucked a strand of hair behind her ear.

"Lost, indeed. Never to be found again."

His gaze darkened. He held her close.

In slow increments, he lowered his head. Until his mouth met hers.

It was a silken, promise-filled kiss. His tongue stroked against hers. There was that tobacco taste, and his own flavor, that worked through her like an opiate. Making her pliable yet demanding. Turning her bones to satin ribbons that curled on themselves, while filling her with immeasurable power. What had he come to mean to her, this wicked, rakish earl? This man who felt far more deeply than he ever let anyone know? This honorable profligate?

Everything.

He held her tightly, possessively, and while she desired to be no man's possession, there was something viscerally thrilling about him wanting her so completely to be his. She felt it in the hard, tight lines of his body, growing harder and tighter by the moment. One of his hands cupped her hand, and the other splayed on the curve of her lower back. They stood hips to hips. The long, rigid curve of his arousal pressed into her, and she remembered how he looked, thundering down that narrow, dangerous lane in St. Giles. Coming for her, all purpose and intent. And oh, how it made her head spin, like a falling leaf.

She pulled back enough to rub her lips over the stubble darkening his jaw. Poor man—he couldn't seem to keep his shave for more than a few hours. But she didn't regret it as she felt the rasp of his incipient beard against the tender skin of her mouth, her cheeks. She could well imagine that one of his ancestors had been a pirate, prowling the Spanish Main. It seemed only the smallest push was needed to turn Daniel from elegant aristocrat to wicked buccaneer, as if his wild forefather's blood ran through his veins and eagerly wanted to return to those unruly days.

With unerring instinct, he moved so that he rubbed his prickly jaw over her neck, and lower. Trailing kisses and stubble along her collarbone and the small band of exposed skin above her dress's neckline. She still wore her shabby dress, the fabric thin and threadbare, so that she felt him easily through her clothes.

The flesh he kissed was delicate, sensitive, and with each rasp, fire built in her, centering in her breasts and between her legs. How did he know her so well? What she needed, wanted? Yet he did, and she delighted in it.

Hazed by sensation and desire, she barely noticed when he guided them both from the window to his desk. He kissed her at the same time that he lifted her up, setting her on the front edge of the desk, and stood between her legs. Bringing them even closer together.

Only when she felt the tug of his fingers on the fastenings of her borrowed gown did she manage to surface just enough to ask, "Here?" She glanced around the study.

"Anywhere," he growled. "Everywhere. I can't get enough of you."

This thing between them, it burned hot and fast. She'd read accounts of the Great Fire of 1666, and now knew how the city felt, leveled by flame, becoming nothing but a smoldering ruin. Yet she'd gladly immolate herself in this fire, turning to ash, carried aloft by the wind.

And like the fire, this, too, had to be extinguished. She'd be razed by the flames, charred into nothingness. But she wouldn't give this up, no matter what future devastation came.

"Daniel," she whispered.

"My keen-eyed hawk of a woman," he answered, taking little sips and nips from her flesh. "Bird of prey."

She smiled against his mouth, bittersweet. "How do you manage to make that sound like a compliment?"

"It's meant to be."

Cool air stroked over her skin, and she realized that while he'd distracted her with his words and his lips, he'd also managed to undo more fastenings on the back of her well-worn dress. The neckline inched lower, revealing the top edge of her chemise and more of her sensitive flesh.

His mouth followed, teasing and tasting. He tugged on the fabric, and with his clever, wicked rake's fingers, he managed to inch the garment even lower. Until he'd bared her breasts. Her nipples tightened, becoming even more sensitive, more ready.

"Ah, lovely woman," he breathed. Lowering his head, he took one nipple between his lips. Drew lightly on it.

Arcs of fiery sensation shot through her, pulled forth by his talented mouth. She cradled his head to her. His hips rocked against hers. He understood her so perfectly.

He turned his attention to her other breast as his hand gathered up her skirts. She scraped her fingers along his shoulders and was rewarded with his pleasured shudder. It seemed an outrageous thing to do—make love in a study in the middle of the day—but it felt exactly right. Anywhere he was, that was the perfect place to join with him. Her dark logic knew they only had a limited time together—she'd take whatever she could, to hold close and treasure in the cold, solitary time that lay ahead.

She hooked her heels around his calves, snugging their bodies even closer. Her back arched as he continued to kiss and toy with her breasts, his play filling her with heat and need. He was an irresistible force that knew her body as well as she did.

His hand skimmed up her leg, over her stocking, past her garters. These at least belonged to her, and were of a finer quality than her dress.

Thoughts scattered when he found the opening in her drawers. Then touched her. Lightly, only a tracing, a relearning of her. She jolted from the exquisite sensation.

She was nearly embarrassed at the state of desire he found her in—wet, ready, wanting. But then, she'd seen the evidence of his desire straining within his breeches, so there was no hiding for either of them. She sensed in his fevered touch that he wanted to join with her as much as she with him, in the most profound way possible.

Every moment with him, she fell farther and farther.

There would be no going back. And she couldn't make herself stop. Didn't want to stop. Because this—he—was everything she needed. While she could still have it.

"Yes," she breathed as he delved deeper, caressing her intimately. "Yes," she sighed again as he circled her bud, shaping pleasure, with his mouth against her neck, another hand on her breast. His touch grew more focused, more intense. A madden ecstasy built and built, robbing her of sense. Raw need urged them on. They were still fully dressed, because they couldn't wait. Here he was, touching her as though he'd created her body specifically for this pleasure.

Sensation grew, consuming her. And when he slid a finger into her, she broke apart.

She cried out as the climax engulfed her. Her release became the entire world, holding her fast in its bright grasp. He hooked his finger slightly, pressing into that deep place within her, pulling forth another climax and holding her there for a keen, fleeting eternity.

Finally, she fell back against the desk. Scattering pens and papers. But he didn't seem to care. He stared down at her with a scorching gaze, a look of profound satisfaction on his face. More heat ripped through her as he licked his fingers.

"Yours is the only taste I'll ever want," he murmured. He gave her a heavy-lidded look, replete with meaning. "And I mean to have more. And more. To last me the rest of my life."

Oh, she was lost, lost. And she couldn't make herself care if she was ever found.

Chapter 21

*The sweetest gifts are the most ephemeral. An orange
at Christmas. The first hawthorn flower of spring.
A beloved's kiss. They all pass in hardly the time
it takes to draw breath. Thus we must grab hold of
these prizes and cling to them tightly, before they slip
from our grasp and into the realm of memory.*

The Hawk's Eye, May 18, 1816

Daniel would not sacrifice this moment for the promise of
immortality or the gift of flight. As Eleanor perched at the
edge of her desk, heavy-lidded with satisfaction, the taste of
her on his lips, he realized such gifts would be utterly redun-
dant and unnecessary. He knew them both with her.

He bent forward and kissed her. She returned the kiss
with equal potency.

All her tastes were delicious. He could subsist on her
alone. And the way she kissed him, ravenous and urgent, he
thought she felt the same.

He continued to grip her thighs, sensing the flesh and
muscles beneath his palms tense and release. Her arms
wrapped around his shoulders, pulling him closer. She
held nothing back of herself. She was in all ways bold and
open.

"Want to be inside you so damn much," he rumbled
against her mouth.

"I want you there."

Ah, God, how she changed the shape of the world with only a few words.

He undid the ribbon of her drawers and slid the thin garment to the floor. Daniel allowed himself the privilege of stepping back just far enough to look at her. Eleanor's patchwork skirts were pushed to her waist, revealing her legs, the bare curve of her belly, and her beautiful quim, softly golden and pink in the afternoon light. Eager for him.

"You are making me wait," she murmured in half protest.

"I want to see you."

"Then see me." She leaned back onto her elbows, shameless and delectable. As she gazed at him with ageless power, her knees fell apart, baring her even more. His mouth watered at the delicacy revealed to him.

He sank to his knees.

Her small gasp filled him with gratification. Good to know that he could surprise her, as well as she knew him. There was still much to learn, to explore. Hands on her thighs, he felt anticipatory trembling traveling through her in soft pulses. A shaking that was echoed in his own body.

He bent down, bringing his mouth closer to that secret, special place. She tensed. His whole body was tight and hard, his cock aching. But it could wait a little longer while he gave her this, this intimate, profound kiss.

The first touch of his tongue to her flesh sent a wave of drunken pleasure roaring through him. While she'd tasted wonderful on his fingers, she was even more delicious here. Her breath caught as he stroked her once more with his tongue, tracing her folds. As much as he wanted to bury himself in her, he forced himself to go slowly.

He learned her innermost geography. This beautiful place where he worshipped. Her very essence.

He stroked and caressed her with his lips, his tongue. Feeling her alive and responsive. She writhed beneath him, bringing her hands up to press him closer. The signal he was waiting for.

His caresses grew deeper, bolder. He circled her pearl, took it between his lips and sucked. She moaned and tugged him even tighter against her.

"Yes," she breathed.

Yes, he thought, unable to speak.

He dipped his tongue inside her, in and out. His finger continued to circle her bud, rubbing at it as he made love to her with his tongue, feeling her passage against his own sensitive flesh. God, how shallow everything else had been before this. Now he felt a rare alchemy of physical pleasure and deepest feeling. And the sounds she made were so much sweeter because it was *her* making them, crying out her pleasure, tightening around him as she bowed up. Called his name as the climax clutched her.

His name had never sounded finer.

He would have gone on like this, wanted to, for hours, weeks. Years. Except she tugged at his shoulders, pulling him up to standing.

His legs actually shook beneath him as he stared down at her, splayed beautifully on his desk, all his papers and quills and books awry from her thrashing. Order be damned. She was all that mattered.

"Now," she commanded, breathless.

His fingers scrabbled at the fastening of his breeches. Reaching in, groaning, he freed his cock. The liberation felt wondrous after being so tightly constricted. Aroused as he was, even his own touch was nearly too much, but he had to keep control. Each moment was infinitely valuable.

"Fierce lady," he growled as her heels hooked once more behind his calves, drawing him closer.

He positioned himself with shaking fingers. Groaned again when he felt the touch of her flesh to his. He paused, savoring the pleasure of this anticipatory moment, savoring her as she looked up at him through lowered lids, eyes gemlike and gleaming.

He sank into her. They both sighed. Damn and hell and

everything wonderful in the world, but she felt good. Tight. Silken. Fevered.

Pausing again, he delighted in this first moment, when he was fully within her, gripped by her. But instinct won over. He had to move. He pulled back, feeling the slick drag, the shock of pleasure shooting from his cock up his spine, pushing into every part of him.

He slid back into her. Then out. Again. Each slow glide and thrust white hot behind his eyes. He panted like an animal, bending over her.

"More," she demanded. "More and more and . . ."

Her words trailed off into a moan when he did just that. His pace increased. His hips moved with growing speed. He lost himself in the joining. The desk began to shake with the force of his thrusts. He barely noticed when papers slipped to the floor and a bottle of ink rolled away. All that counted now was her, them. Where their bodies and hearts connected.

She cried his name, arching up, her fingers digging into his buttocks. As they tightened around him, he felt her release in waves through his own body. And it set off his own. He'd just enough presence of mind to pull out, spilling upon her stomach.

The climax harrowed him. He felt drained by it, yet stronger than a titan.

He used a corner of his shirt to clean her. Then carefully, tenderly rearranged her clothing. Once she was covered, he straightened his garments as well. Overpowering tiredness crept through his limbs, yet he managed to keep himself upright enough to gather her up in his arms. He carried her to one of the chairs by the fire. Sat himself down, then arranged her across his lap.

They sat like that for a long while, watching the fire. Lazily, he toyed with the damp strands of hair that clung to her nape and forehead. She rested her head against his shoulder and traced the folds of his disordered neckcloth.

So this is love.

It was strange and terrifying. Astonishing. Wondrous.

He closed his eyes, holding her closer. Amazed that he should be given such a gift.

"**W**hat, exactly, did you plan on doing in St. Giles?" Daniel asked as they shared an early supper in his study. She still wore her shabby dress, even more wrinkled than before. A table had been set up, and two dining chairs brought in, and they sat opposite each other as they dined on simple roast chicken and asparagus. Oranges glowed in a cut-glass bowl in the center of the table, each a miniature sun.

A lavish feast wouldn't be appropriate, not with her. She deserved the best, but indulgence and extravagance were not Eleanor. She would want simple, good food, well prepared, essential. So that's what he'd ordered for her.

He poured Eleanor another glass of wine, the sound domestic and warm against the crackle of the fire. "You wouldn't know Jonathan Lawson. Hell, even *I* don't know him anymore."

Eleanor took a sip, then set her glass down. Her hair was a tangle, slight bruises of sleeplessness shaded beneath her eyes. Yet in the fading light of day, in the firelight, she was as beautiful as redemption.

"I saw a print of him once. And I assumed there was a family resemblance between him and his sister. Besides, I had an excellent plan for learning whether or not he'd been in the area."

He shook his head. "It'd do you little good. He's become a wary creature, Jonathan. Suspicious. The only person he's likely to trust is his sister."

"Thus your need of me—to throw off the scent of your search with her."

He couldn't deny it, but they'd come to an accord on this subject.

"How are we to proceed?" she asked. "In our quest?"

Warmth unfolded in his chest. "I never much cared for the word *we* until now."

"I never had cause to use it." She smiled quietly, softly. "But it does form a pleasing shape and make a good sound."

Damn hard to be seated so far from her. Now that he knew the feel of her, he couldn't stand not touching her, as if to assure himself that she was as real as he hoped her to be. So he edged his chair around the table and took her hand in his. Ran her fingertips over his lips.

"*We*," he repeated against her fingers.

Her mouth opened slightly, and her breathing hitched.

"Yes," he said, rubbing his thumb along her wrist, across her palm. "It's not the biggest word in the dictionary. Just two letters. But they change everything."

A lovely, carnal pink crept into her cheeks. Worldly she might be, yet it seemed she could still be moved with a few honest words. How strange all this was—speaking truthfully, with no objective other than to say exactly what he thought, and felt. Because he could be completely himself with her, no jaded façade to shelter him, no cynical disguises to hide behind.

"And we will find Jonathan," she pressed. "Thinking on it," she continued, "the best thing I can do for you is to keep writing the articles. So no one pays attention to your search. Though," she added, her voice grudging, "I'm rather disinclined to continue to trumpet your rakishness to my readers."

He grinned. "You'll know the truth. All my rakish behavior will be saved for you."

"I'm fortunate, indeed." But she said this with a wide smile, her eyes sparkling. "Where shall we venture next? What adventures await us?"

He stroked his chin. "It's likely known by many that I'm Lord Rakewell. They'll be suspect of any woman in my company." It pained him to say this. His greatest pleasure had become the hours he was with her. Yet now, for the sake of the articles, and Jonathan, their time together—in public, at least—had to be curtailed.

Disappointment creased her brow. "I can't write the pieces unless I'm present," she protested, but he sensed the other argument beneath her words.

"How's this: I'll report back to you at the end of every night."

"But you haven't the eye for detail that I have."

He liked that she affected no false modesty and took proud possession of her abilities. "I'll do my damnedest to be observant, as if you're perched on my shoulder."

"Like a little angel," she mused.

"Devil," he corrected.

"Don't give in to temptation if I'm not there." She pointed a warning finger at him.

He lifted his brows. "Are those the acid tones of jealousy I hear in your voice?"

"You're delusional," she insisted, but then looked thoughtful. Perhaps she was as new to the experience of jealousy as he was. A somewhat cheering thought. He'd always extracted himself from a lover's embrace before the woman could form enough of an attachment to warrant covetousness. The very thought had been an iron cage. Yet it didn't feel that way with Eleanor. He didn't want to rebel from her possession of him. He wanted to revel in it.

Damn, I've changed.

Even that didn't alarm him the way it might have a month ago.

"I'm sure your journalistic powers are great enough to derive an excellent story from my meager offerings," he said.

She rolled her eyes. "Save your flattery for publicans and old women. I know what I'm capable of."

"It won't be the same," he said softly. "Going out without you."

She blushed again, then cursed quietly. "It's unfair of you to be so bloody marvelous."

"I do live to spite you," he said.

"Then you'll live a good, long time."

"Let me taste that viper's tongue of yours." He leaned

close and kissed her. She had the flavor of wine and herbs, and her own sweetness and spice beneath. They sank into the kiss, savoring each other. How had he gone so many years without knowing this, knowing her? It had been a shadow life, mired in the colors of ash and dust. Now the world revealed itself to him in a riot of color. It was almost too much. Almost, but not enough. Never enough. He'd live in their stolen hours and try to learn to be grateful for that. Though he knew his hunger for her could not be easily sated. If ever.

Finally. The last writer and printer had gone home. Eleanor was alone in the office, having stayed late. Like she always did this past week. Bundling up whatever articles she hadn't edited into a leather portfolio—the second gift she'd accepted from Daniel, with her initials discreetly embossed on one side—she locked up.

Outside, her breath chuffed in the cool air, and she began the now familiar walk to Portland Square. She always refused Daniel's offer of sending his carriage for her—they had to maintain some semblance of propriety, nor would she allow him to pay for a cab. On foot it was, then. Until a familiar enormous house rose up before her. Such a contrast from her own small rooms.

Was it better to enter from the side entrance or the front door? The question always came as a challenge. One spoke of too much secrecy and clandestineness, as though there was something shameful about what she was doing. Yet a single woman couldn't very well approach a notorious bachelor's home via the front entrance. There were too many pedestrians out at that hour. Anyone might see her and draw the wrong—in truth, the right—conclusions.

The servants' entrance it would be. The staff knew to expect her. After Eleanor tapped on the back door, a rosy-cheeked maid ushered her into a small parlor. On a table, salad, roast lamb, and potatoes awaited her. Though she felt the familiar needle of disappointment that she was dining alone, she told herself it didn't matter. She couldn't have everything, and shouldn't expect it, either.

The meal completed, she rose from the table and walked purposefully to the desk Daniel had set up for her. She liked it better in here, feeling in the chamber the echoes of his presence, and she settled in comfortably, knowing he was, in his way, close. Though she still couldn't look at his desk without blushing.

A clock chimed once. One o'clock. But he would not be back for many hours. And at last, her work was finished for the evening. After a good stretch and a walk through the massive building that constituted his home, she climbed the stairs to his bedchamber. A bath was in readiness—as it always was, regardless of the hour—and she almost fell asleep several times in the warm water, weary from a long day. But anticipation and expectation always sparked beneath the surface of her skin, knowing what was to come later.

She slipped on a plain cotton nightgown, one of her own she'd tucked into a corner of a wardrobe. Daniel had promised her silken gowns, which she'd refused. Stubborn, perhaps, and unreasonable, but it was already a strain on her sense of independence to dine on his food and use his home as though it was hers.

It wasn't of course. It never would be.

Every night, she shoved that melancholy thought from her head and heart. Whatever they had now needed to be enough. Neither could wish for more.

She climbed into his giant bed, which was becoming an all-too-habitual luxury. Somehow, by some mysterious grace, she drifted off.

Only to waken hours later at the feel of his big, unclothed body sliding into bed with her. They didn't speak then. Not even a word of greeting. Too hungry for each other after a day apart, they were all need. Hands and mouths and voiceless demands, bodies straining and growing slick with sweat. Groans and sighs. Tonight, they went fast and hard, shaking the posters of his bed as they gave and took with equal ferocity. In the low light of that single candle, they did things to each other that would make the Lady of Dubious Quality applaud.

Eleanor had never been so bold, so free. His body was a wonder—his carnal, physical self—and she took greedy possession of it, and every part of him. Just as he laid claim to her. They took ownership of each other in the joining of flesh to flesh. In their ceaseless need for more and still more.

Only after they had exhausted themselves—and this could take hours—did they finally speak beyond erotic encouragements and delighted murmurs.

"Tell me of your night," she said, as she always did, stroking her hands over his long, lean body. He made such a gorgeous picture, stretched out nude atop the covers, slick with the sweat of their desire.

"Very dull without you," he always answered. His eyes were bright but heavy-lidded.

"Pretend I was with you," she said, twirling a finger in the crisp hair on his chest, "and spin me a tale."

So he did. This evening it had been a private assembly. Last night had been the theater. And the night before that had been a gentleman's party, complete with actresses and demimondaines—though he'd assured her that he'd never sampled the offerings. She had believed him, though she hadn't been able to stop the barbs of jealousy at the thought of these satiny, perfumed women draping themselves over him like gaudy hothouse flowers.

"And what of Jonathan?" she pressed. "Any sign?"

His mouth flattened into a hard line, and he shook his head. "It's more and more fruitless. The clues to his whereabouts are drying up. Appearing with less regularity."

"I went to St. Giles again today."

"Alone?" he demanded, always too protective.

"I took Henry, one of the printers, with me."

Daniel relaxed at this, but only slightly.

"Same pretense as before. I told everyone, even Henry, that I was researching a story on the gentry touring slums." Now she shook her head. "No results either, I'm afraid. But I extracted a promise from some of the people in the neighborhood that they should find me and let me know if they had anything to report."

Daniel stared at the fire. "My heart goes cold to think this. I fear either he's left London and England, never to be found again, or, damn it, he might not be alive."

Resting her head on Daniel's chest, feeling the steady beat of his heart beneath her cheek, she sighed. "What does Catherine think?"

"I haven't voiced my concerns to her. She holds out hope, but I suspect she's also losing faith that he'll be located."

"Poor girl," Eleanor murmured. So much rested on Catherine Lawson's young, thin shoulders, which bore the weight of family and dauntless optimism. Even as that optimism faded in the face of grim evidence.

Eleanor burrowed closer to Daniel, absorbing his heat, his solidity and realness. How quickly everything passed. How fragile was this world. She had to hold tight to what she was given for the brief time it was hers.

"Tomorrow night," he continued, "I'm off to Vauxhall."

"Didn't you say that place was dull as a parson's sermon?"

"Some other fellows are going, and they expect me to make an appearance."

An idea quickly came to her.

"Not on your own, you aren't," she countered, raising herself up on her elbows so she looked down at him. "I want to be out in the world again with you."

He looked wary. "We agreed that it'd be better if we weren't seen together."

"But I miss being out in the world with you." She ran her fingers over the curve of his lips. "You're going to Vauxhall. And I'll be there."

Chapter 22

Much has been made in countless other writings of the manifold pleasures of Vauxhall Gardens—the abundant lights, the proliferation of music, the paltry yet remarkable viands one dines upon, the spectacle of fireworks and the greater spectacle still of those promenading up and down the celebrated walks, including the infamous Dark Walk. In truth, Vauxhall Gardens have fallen in and out of fashionable favor too many times for your humble author to count. But know this, dear readers, the pleasure garden is once again in the fullness of its esteem, and one has only to pay the entrance fee to assure oneself of a night of adventure . . .

The Hawk's Eye, May 26, 1816

Dusk fell in a purple curtain over the pavilions and pathways of Vauxhall, suspending the guests in a misty haze. Eleanor pulled her borrowed silk cloak closer, seeking a small amount of warmth. Cold, damp air clung to the walkways and in the trees. It was far too cool for this time of year, yet that hadn't kept anyone at home. The gardens were abundant with those seeking diversion, with Eleanor and Margaret amongst their number.

And Daniel. Somewhere out there, amidst the supper boxes and fountains. He kept himself at a distance, and she'd yet to glimpse him tonight. The idea that he was also here, unseen but present, thrilled her far more than any engineered spectacle.

Eleanor and Maggie stopped their slow perambulation as a whistle sounded. The crowd paused in its collective breath, waiting. Servants stationed at various points around the pleasure garden touched matches to fuses. All at once, the garden blazed with light as thousands of multicolored lamps in trees and hanging from the colonnades lit up at the same time. Eleanor had to shield her eyes from the sudden, dazzling light. The crowd burst into applause at the stunning effect.

"Theatricality and showmanship," Maggie grumbled.

"And yet you clapped along with everyone else," Eleanor said, smiling.

"Theater's my livelihood," her friend countered. "I can appreciate stagecraft. Even one as obvious as this." Yet she smiled, too, and tucked her arm through Eleanor's.

They continued on their walk down a tree-lined pathway, watching what seemed like all of London parade and display itself in its finery. Cold weather be damned—women still wore low-cut, flimsy evening gowns, and men, in accordance with custom, walked bareheaded, carrying their hats beneath their arms. Everyone stared at everyone else. If there was anywhere in this city, in this country, where one was meant to see and be seen, it was Vauxhall Gardens.

The music had stopped for the lighting of the lamps, but now it started up again, emanating from an ornate pavilion. Notes rose and fell from the orchestra, and a soprano trilled out an Italian tune. The crowd only partially listened to the concert, more interested in being a part of the pageantry than standing by and simply taking it in.

Where was Daniel now? Watching her? She'd thought she would be able to see him immediately, though they had agreed ahead of time to keep their distance in public. Yet it seemed that her tall, wide-shouldered lover could hide himself away if he so desired. She had to think it was deliberate.

Keeping her on edge, aware of him at all times but never certain exactly where he might be.

"Let's view the supper boxes," she suggested to Maggie.

Her friend slanted her a look. "Not much to see there besides toffs pretending that paper-thin slices of ham and diminutive roast chickens are worth the extravagance."

"Amusing enough to have a look. The emperor's new clothes, et cetera." She guided Maggie toward where the supper boxes were arrayed. Each of the boxes was constructed like a room with three walls, the fourth wall being open so that the diners within could view the people walking past—and, more importantly, for them to be seen. People and paintings adorned the boxes. Those who didn't have influence or prestige had to make do with dining at tables arrayed beneath the trees. But Eleanor didn't care about them. An earl would most assuredly have access to one of the supper boxes.

"Like miniature theaters," Maggie noted as they strolled past each open-air chamber. Waiters presented plates of food to the elegant assembly within, who made a great show through laughter and exaggerated gestures that they were having a wonderful time, and wasn't it a marvelous shame that this pleasure belonged to them alone?

Maggie continued, waving at the diners. "See how the missing wall turns each box into a proscenium, lit from within?" She smiled wryly. "Couldn't stage it any better at the Imperial."

"And what would you title this play?" Eleanor asked.

"*Privilege; or, Full and Empty Bellies.*"

"Comedy or tragedy?"

Maggie's expression darkened. "It starts out a comedy. Very romantic and full of laughter. Then it turns unexpectedly to tragedy."

Eleanor knew most of the details of her friend's history, yet it hurt her anew every time she saw the lasting pain caused by past betrayals. "Then, triumph," she reminded her.

She peered into the boxes as they strolled around, looking for one face in particular. Every time they passed a new supper box, her heart lifted, then sank again.

"At a cost," Maggie noted.

"Most worthwhile things come at a high price," Eleanor countered.

"Such as the adoration of an earl?"

Eleanor stopped and faced her friend, heedless of the people swarming around them. "I am careful—"

"Not careful enough." Melancholy brimmed in her friend's dark eyes. She took Eleanor's hand in her own. "Oh, darling, there is no use in pretending. Either to me or yourself."

"There's no pretense," Eleanor said. "The earl and I are lovers. I've never hidden that from you. And I certainly know what I do with my own evenings." Heat washed through her body and into her cheeks, thinking only of last night in Daniel's bed. More warmth crept through her when she recalled the time they'd spent afterward, lying in each other's arms.

It was always an agony to leave him in the morning. This dawn was no exception. And though she knew he wasn't an early riser by nature, he was always awake whenever she left, kissing and caressing her and making it so damn difficult to go. Yet she had no choice.

"But what do you do with your heart?" Maggie pressed. "My dear, even if he shared your feelings—"

"He does," Eleanor said immediately, confidently.

"There isn't hope for either of you," Maggie continued gently.

Eleanor glanced away, at the thousands of lights dancing from the trees like distant dreams. A sudden burn glazed the back of her eyes. She blinked it away.

"I'm aware of that," she said, sounding wounded to her own ears.

Maggie gave a dispirited sigh. "I'd hoped to save you this heartache. Warn you."

"You did." Eleanor turned back to her friend. "But all the

warnings in the world turn to paper mulch when presented
with a man such as Daniel."

"Daniel?" Maggie shook her head. "Dear heart, you *are*
far gone. You say his name as if it contains every word of
poetry ever written."

A small, sad laugh bubbled up from Eleanor. She pulled
her hand from Maggie's and gave her friend's shoulder a
little swat. "My God, Mags, don't descend into sentimentality now. What will your critics think?"

"My critics can swallow half the Thames." Maggie tipped
up her chin. "I'm planning a burletta that will be so brilliant,
it will send every last one of them to the madhouse."

"I'd buy a ticket for that."

"I'll reserve a seat for you in one of the boxes." Maggie
nodded toward the supper enclosures.

Eleanor hadn't seen Daniel in any of the boxes. It didn't
mean he wasn't here tonight. She had to remind herself of
that. They'd planned on coming to Vauxhall separately and
enjoying its pleasures, knowing that the other was nearby—
even if they couldn't actually be seen together.

"Someone seems very interested in you, Mags." She
glanced toward a booth, where a company of voluptuar-
ies and their female companions was assembled around a
table, drinking and carousing. One of the men stared right
at Maggie. He was dark, raffish, the sort of man women
steered their daughters away from—then returned to later
on their own.

Lord Marwood.

Maggie followed Eleanor's look. Her gaze seemed to
catch Marwood's. Strangely, instead of returning his gaze,
Maggie glanced quickly away.

"He's always around the theater," she said stiffly. "Flirting with actresses and dancers." She tugged on Eleanor's
arm, and they began to walk away. Yet when Eleanor glanced
back, Marwood continued to watch them. More specifically,
he watched Maggie.

"Have you ever spoken with him?" Eleanor asked.

Her friend sniffed. "Why would I waste my time with some aristo?"

"Because he's rich as the Prince and handsome as wickedness embodied."

Maggie's back was straight and tense. "All the more reason to give him wide berth. His kind are gold-dipped parasites."

"They aren't all like that," Eleanor said. They walked down a long, tree-lined lane, past fountains and statues, tiny panoramas, and even a flower-bedecked goat on a jeweled leash.

"Perhaps your earl isn't," Maggie countered. "But he's the exception to a well-proven rule."

Her earl. Eleanor liked the sound of that. Too much. Because it presaged what was certainly to be insupportable pain when they would have to part. When he wouldn't be *her* earl anymore.

An earl had to think of future generations. He had a responsibility to his title and holdings to keep the bloodline going. That meant marriage to a suitable woman of his own rank. Having a family with her.

This awaited him, as surely as the earth turned and the tides rose and fell. There was no avoiding it. And Eleanor could have no part of this future.

God, how would she withstand it?

She barely saw the wonders around her or the stylishly attired people walking past. She thought only of that inevitable time when she would be working, and a wedding and then birth announcement would cross her desk. *Lord A—d has abandoned his rakish ways and now welcomes his future heir into the world.*

The thought felt as though someone had rammed an elbow between her shoulder blades, robbing her of breath.

No, tonight is about enjoyment. Pleasure. If her time with him was to be limited, let it be the best of her life. Even if he wasn't close by, she knew he was out there, somewhere. Near enough.

She and Maggie walked on toward the Colonnade, a long portico of columns with arched roofs, all brightly lit with more of the celebrated lights of Vauxhall. It was indeed beautiful, and even Maggie grudgingly admitted admiration.

A finely dressed man suddenly appeared in their path, stepping out from behind one of the columns. He was tall, his fair hair shining in the lamps, and handsome, with a well-defined jaw and nicely shaped, if somewhat small, nose. By the way he smiled, it seemed evident that the man knew the catalog of his charms.

Eleanor saw at once that he was no threat to her or Margaret. Though he was attractively formed, she suspected that the width of his shoulders came more from padding than muscle.

"Ladies," he said, bowing.

They curtsied in response. "Sir," Eleanor and Maggie responded in unison.

"A confession," the man said, continuing to smile with the air of a man who anticipated his presence would be eagerly welcome. "I have lost the rest of my party. A shame, though, for the company is unwilling to do anything without my approval."

"And yet," Eleanor noted, "they somehow manage to exist in the hours you spend apart."

"Unless," Maggie added, "his friends lie upon the floor, unable to feed or fend for themselves."

The man laughed in short, sharp barks. "Ha! Ha! Indeed, I would not be surprised were that the case, for I hear always, 'Where are we to venture today, Mr. Smollett?' 'Shall we dine now, Mr. Smollett?' "

" 'Shall I wipe my bum, Mr. Smollett?' " Maggie whispered into Eleanor's ear, causing her to snort.

"Indeed, sir," Eleanor said, reining in her laughter, "you sound nigh indispensable to them. It's a wonder that they managed to wander off without you. Perhaps you aren't as essential to their happiness as you thought."

The man—Mr. Smollett—frowned faintly at this. From this, it seemed clear to him that Maggie and Eleanor were not as enchanted by tales of his importance as he'd anticipated.

He tried another tactic. "Though I ought to locate them, I find my own happiness increased considerably by your company, ladies, and am loath to leave."

"If you must . . ." Maggie said.

"No, no," he said, waving his hand, "I shall play the gallant and remain with you."

"Chivalrous of you to remark upon your chivalry," Eleanor noted.

Mr. Smollett fought a scowl and seemed to struggle to make himself look agreeable. "Of course, I know that you would recognize it without such overt direction. But you possess a finer understanding of grace than most."

Eleanor dipped into another curtsy, though she shot Maggie a look as she did so. "Thank you, sir, for your condescension."

"You are most welcome." He beamed at her, his prized pupil.

Maggie and Eleanor shared a look. Her friend's lips twitched, and Eleanor herself could barely hold back her laughter. Oh, poor Mr. Smollett would find his way into the next *Rake* article, and if he recognized himself, he would not be flattered by his inclusion.

"Though the lamps burn brightly," Mr. Smollett continued, "they do not shine with the same brilliance as you ladies."

"Again, you flatter us excessively," Maggie said drily.

The man made a dismissive gesture with one gloved hand. "Not a bit. I merely speak the truth, though such is the world today that flatterers consider themselves great wits."

"We would never think that of you, sir," Eleanor said.

"And now the kindness is yours," Mr. Smollett replied. "Ladies, would you do me the greatest honor of accompanying me around the grounds? I can think of no higher pleasure." He offered them both his arms.

Maggie shot Eleanor a glance that said she'd rather be

forced to claw her way out of a dung heap than spend any additional time in the company of this *gentleman*.

"I thank you, sir," Eleanor said, "for an offer that is so terrifically gracious and complimentary. Yet I'm afraid that we must demur."

For half a moment, Mr. Smollett looked confused, as though he could not quite believe that Eleanor had declined. Then his smile widened. "Ah, but I understand that as women of refined breeding, you cannot accept a gentleman right away." He gave them a conspiratorial wink. "Fear not, ladies. You may consent at your discretion. No one but we three shall know."

"But *we* will," Eleanor pointed out. "And that is the only opinion that matters."

Warmth suddenly spread up the back of her neck. She felt a familiar, welcome presence nearby. Just behind Mr. Smollett, she caught a glimpse of another tall male figure emerging from the shadows. There was only one man whose presence could fill her with this much happiness.

Daniel.

Like the other gentlemen in attendance at Vauxhall tonight, he wore evening finery. Usually, by the time Eleanor saw him in the late hours of the night, he'd disrobed, so she took this opportunity to admire him. A bottle-green coat fit snugly across his shoulders, and he wore a gold-and-cream waistcoat and snug white breeches. He looked every inch the elegant aristocrat, yet with a decidedly wicked air that shone in his eyes and revealed itself in the curve of his lips.

Her stomach clenched. Good God, *this* man was her lover? It seemed too fantastical, as though she were Psyche shining a candle upon the sleeping form of Cupid. Any moment now, her hand would shake and drip scalding wax upon him, causing him to flee and the whole enchanted interlude to end.

But he was *here* now.

He sent her a look, his gaze darting toward Mr. Smollett in a silent question. *Would you like me to get rid of him?*

She shook her head, the tiniest movement. This she could handle on her own.

"You are all that is modest," Mr. Smollett continued, seemingly unaware of Daniel's presence nearby. "An excellent quality in a woman. Each demurral only increases my opinion of you, and thus I must again request that I attend you both for a stroll through the garden."

"Sir," Eleanor said, more firmly. "I wonder that you speak the King's English without a trace of an accent."

"Indeed, ma'am?" Mr. Smollett cocked his head to one side, like a spaniel trying to catch a sound.

"Surely," Eleanor continued, "this language must not be your first if you do not yet understand that neither I, nor my friend, have any desire to walk with you."

He looked flustered. "Oh, but ma'am, your propriety—"

"It is not a concern for propriety that motivates our refusal. It is our utter lack of interest in spending a minute more in your company. Is that modest enough for you?"

The man's look darkened. He scowled at her. "I have revised my opinion. Surely no woman of good breeding would speak thusly to a gentleman."

"Indeed, no," Maggie said. "For neither I nor my friend are of good breeding. And you, *Mister* Smollett, are not a gentleman."

He drew himself up. "I can assure you, my family is of the highest caliber."

"Your name might be considered estimable by its presence in *Debrett's*," Maggie said coldly, "but a gentleman is distinguished by his behavior, not his blood. I've known too many of your stripe to consider a carriage and country estate to be the valuation of a man's character."

"I . . . I . . ." Mr. Smollett sputtered.

"Good evening, sir," Eleanor said, hardly able to keep the glee from her voice.

"It is most certainly *not* a good evening," the man said, then marched off, muttering beneath his breath about women with too high an opinion of themselves, and they should be *honored* by his attentions, the ungrateful trollops.

The moment he was gone, Daniel stepped forward. He bowed.

"Vicious," he murmured with admiration. "I haven't seen such a thorough evisceration since I saw a gazelle fed to a lion at the zoo."

"The lionesses have dispatched their prey," Maggie said with hauteur, yet she smiled.

"With great efficiency," he agreed.

Eleanor's hands burned with the desire to touch him. Yet she kept them folded at her waist. There would be a time for that later.

"Ellie's been jumping out of her skin all night," Maggie noted. "Now I know why. You've been here the whole time, haven't you, my lord?"

He bowed again.

Maggie looked at Eleanor. " 'Come to Vauxhall,' you said. 'Just us. We've been so busy lately. Let's have a holiday.' "

Eleanor's face flamed. "I didn't mean to mislead. I *do* want time alone with you."

Yet her friend held up her hands. "The truth is all I ask of you. Only that."

"I'm sorry, Maggie." Eleanor glanced down at the ground, then back up again. "I hope, in time, you'll forgive me."

"It's not much recompense," Daniel said, "but might I invite you and Eleanor to supper?"

"In one of the boxes?" Maggie raised her brows.

"Of course."

For a moment, Maggie looked tempted. Eleanor couldn't blame her. It wasn't an everyday occasion—or any occasion, for that matter—that either of them could gain entrance to one of the exclusive supper boxes. But then Maggie shook her head.

"Thank you, my lord, but no. It's time I ought to be returning home. Sadly, my burlettas have not learned how to write themselves, and so I must guide my quill over the pages if they are to have life."

"I'll come with you," Eleanor said at once, though she

was loath to leave Daniel now that he'd finally appeared. Yet she wouldn't neglect her friendship, and it was clear that Maggie was still hurting from Eleanor's subterfuge.

Again, Maggie shook her head. "My characters can't take shape unless I have a good thirty minutes of solitude before writing."

That was the first Eleanor had ever heard of that rule—and she'd known Maggie for nearly a decade.

"I'll go alone," Maggie said.

"Let me at least escort you to my carriage," Daniel offered. "It can drop you off at home—or whatever destination you wish—then return here."

Maggie looked as though she was about to object, perhaps on the basis of sheer pride. But then she shrugged. "Foolish of me not to accept such a suggestion." She gave a wry smile. "Prideful feet are aching feet."

Daniel made another bow and offered Maggie his arm. She took it.

"The Dark Walk," he murmured to Eleanor. "Ten minutes."

She gave a small nod.

Surprising, how Eleanor felt no stab of jealousy at seeing her friend's hand upon her lover's arm. There was no cause for it. She had absolute faith in both of them. Even watched sedately as they strolled toward the exit. It made her smile when Daniel bent close to say something to Maggie, and her friend laughed. The two most important people in her life ought to enjoy each other's company.

But why? To what purpose? It wasn't as though they'd be spending any time together. That would imply a certain degree of openness that could never exist. It was inevitable that all this must come to an end—the book closed and put upon the shelf, never to be read again.

Under the tarnish of these thoughts, the gleam of Vauxhall dimmed, leaving Eleanor suspended in shadow despite the lights.

Chapter 23

It has ever been the object of this periodical to venerate behavior that is upright and virtuous. But sometimes one must stray from the paths of lightness into the realm of the shadows, for even the most moral heart craves passion and emotion. Otherwise, we are destined for a cold and solitary existence, which, while honorable, provides little pleasure or comfort.

The Hawk's Eye, May 26, 1816

Standing amidst the trees in the deliberate shadows of the Dark Walk, Daniel's heart thundered like cannon fire as he awaited Eleanor. It was as if they were new lovers enjoying the heat and anticipation of a first tryst, rather than a man and a woman who had been exploring each other's minds and bodies for half a month. Yet it didn't matter if the time they'd spent together had been a day, a week, or a year—he couldn't seem to get enough of her. And this game they were playing in Vauxhall only whetted his appetite for more.

A couple's low laughter curlicued over the manicured lawn and between the shrubbery. Then a woman's sigh. This was a place for amorous encounters, designed exclusively for that purpose. Daniel was no stranger to the Dark Walk, but it had never held the promise that it did now.

He shifted restlessly, his gaze on the barely lit pathway

ahead of him. When would she be here? He'd said ten minutes, but surely no ten minutes had ever moved with such glacial slowness. Civilizations could rise and fall in the span of these minutes. His own edifices and structures had succumbed to wilderness—the wilds of unrelenting need.

It confounded him. Astonished and terrified and amazed him. For years, he'd been drowned beneath a wicked man's ennui, occasionally coming to the surface when some relatively new pleasure or sensation appeared. But they faded all too fast, and he'd be submerged again in the murk of his own privilege. He had a goal with finding Jonathan, which both gave him purpose and reminded him of how little he contributed to the world.

But Eleanor had truly brought him up, through the depths, to breathe and see and feel. As though he'd never experienced any of these actions before.

At this moment, he'd allow himself the exquisite agony of waiting for his lover in the sly shadows of the Dark Walk.

A woman strolled leisurely past. He didn't move. Even in this darkness, he knew Eleanor's shape, her walk. Knew her as well as he knew himself. Better, because he gave a damn about her.

Just thinking of the scent of her skin and the way she murmured the most wicked, witty things late in the night made him tighten in anticipation.

He'd watched from a maddening distance when that bloody preening fool had approached her and Mrs. Delamere. It had taken all his strength not to race over and plant his fist in the bastard's face. He'd taken two steps to do just that when her words had rung out, clear and cutting. She'd verbally disemboweled the idiot—so cleanly and with such precision that the man hadn't noticed the fatal wound until minutes had passed and there had been no saving him.

Seeing her so effectively defend herself with the blade of her wit had stoked Daniel's hunger to a burning fever. He'd barely been able to keep his hands off her when he had finally approached. Why did some men prefer vapid women?

They were as airy and ephemeral as pale clouds drifting across the sky. But Eleanor was a summer thunderhead—dark and powerful.

Daniel chuckled ruefully under his breath. He'd turned into a poet. Or rather, she'd transformed him into one. The sort of man who compared a woman to a summer storm. Certainly, she'd blown into his life, leveling everything, leaving him standing on the plain of his own identity. Ready to be rebuilt.

God—there he went again. He'd never considered himself a particularly poetic man, yet she kept inspiring him to linguistic heights. Yet it was merely the feeble attempts to encapsulate something huge and revolutionary, something that could be barely bound by the limits of language.

He tensed at the sound of a woman's tread on the path. A figure emerged, glancing around. Without a moment's hesitation, he understood it was her.

Noiselessly, he stepped out from the shelter of the trees and took hold of her wrist.

She seemed to possess the same instinct that he did. Instead of whirling around and slapping him—as she would do with an importunate stranger—she turned immediately toward him and laced her fingers with his.

The barest light from distant lanterns traced the edges of her features. How well he knew her face now. Her sharp angles, her determined chin and full lips. The fiercely intelligent gleam of her eyes. He'd seen those eyes closed in pleasure. But now they looked up at him with happiness and relief. As if she, too, had been bursting with impatience to see him again.

Silently, he drew her off the path, deeper into the shelter of the darkness, to an alcove with a stone bench tucked amongst the trees. They were hidden from all eyes. So he sat upon the bench and gently tugged her down onto his lap. At once, her arms wrapped around his shoulders, and he clasped her waist. They were face to face now, the warmth of her body sweet and vital against his.

"You are impertinent, sir," she said briskly. "Taking liberties with my person like this, when we haven't even had an introduction!"

Ah, so that's how she wanted to play it. He wasn't averse to games.

"The impertinence is yours, madam," he answered lowly.

"Mine! Pray tell how."

"It is the height of impudence to parade such a face and figure as yours about. And your eyes, madam, are most rudely enticing. Sparkling with liveliness as they do."

"Sir," she returned, "I find your reasoning most unsound—for I have no control over my face, figure, or eyes, and if you cannot temper your response to them, then the fault lies in yourself, not me. Besides," she continued, "were I to follow your logic, then I would accuse *you* of insolence."

"What have I done," he demanded, "if not heeded the call of your siren's song, as helpless as Ulysses lashed to the mast?"

"Flaunting your excessive height, for one. Making an exhibition of your own handsomeness. Displaying your calves like the veriest braggart." She tilted up her chin. "It is not to be supported, sir!"

"Were I to own to those acts of audacity, madam," he said, "what should be my punishment? For surely such effrontery requires a penalty."

"It does." She moved her hands from his shoulders to the back of his neck, her fingers slim and hot against his nape. "Some have said I have acid upon my lips."

His heart pounded as his gaze was drawn to her mouth. "Certainly," he agreed, "your tongue is sharp."

"Again with your unmannerly behavior!" She shook her head. "I see no alternative but to subject you to the most severe punitive measures."

God, how he loved this. "So you keep insisting, and yet here I am, entirely undisciplined."

She shook her head. "You leave me no alternative, sir."

Then she brought her lips to his. Or perhaps he took her

mouth. He couldn't tell. Only that in an instant, they devoured each other in a burning, ravenous kiss. She pressed tightly against him as he held her close, their bodies nearly fused but for the clothing that separated them. She tasted of sweet wine, her tongue sleek and searching, as he explored her lips and mouth. It had been only a day since they'd last kissed, but in the chronology of his need, eons had passed.

His hand traced up her ribs, feeling her shape, her living self, until he reached her bodice. Through the fabric of her gown, he cupped her breast. She gasped into his mouth, and he took her inhalation into himself as though it was the air he needed to breathe, to exist.

Maddeningly, she rubbed herself against his hips, rousing him even higher. He was hard as stone, aching, wanting.

"Have to stop," he growled. Yet he couldn't, unable to deny himself the pleasure of her and her own unfettered need. He was drunk with it. With what they created together.

"I know," she breathed. Yet she didn't pull away, either.

Only when he felt his hands drifting up her skirts did he manage to contain himself. She made a sound of protest when he dragged his mouth from hers.

"More," she demanded.

"Not here." His voice was a hoarse rumble.

"No one can see us."

He rested his forehead against hers. "Not going to make love to you in bloody Vauxhall."

"What if I want you to?"

Hell—she would kill him. "I want more with you than a hurried tup on a bench. Been watching you all night, and goddamn it, when I'm inside you, I want to take my time."

Her lids lowered. "Do you think your carriage is back from dropping Maggie off?"

"It'd better be." With supreme effort of will, he removed her from his lap, setting her on her feet. "To hell with discretion. We'll go to the exit together." He stood, painfully.

"To hell with everything," she said, stepping close and once more looping her arms about his shoulders. Yet instead of kissing, they only held each other, wrapped tight in an embrace.

A woman. *This* woman, in the darkness. He felt anticipation and want and the alignment of their selves. He would always count this moment as one of the finest of his life.

Daniel paced in his study, crossing back and forth through blocks of translucent afternoon light. Pacing did no good, except to wear tracks in the carpeting, but he couldn't sit or be still.

He whirled at the soft tap on the study door. "Enter," he said.

The door opened, revealing Eleanor. His heart gave a kick to see her again, though they'd parted in the early hours of that very morning.

A small frown creased between her brows as she stepped into the chamber, shutting the door behind her. They met in the middle of the room, clasping hands.

"I came as soon as I received your note." She looked up at him with a worried expression. "There's been a new development with Jonathan?"

"A message came with the morning post," he explained. "From the tobacconist."

"Someone's made a purchase of the cheroots," she deduced.

"Yesterday, just before closing."

"Was it him?"

He gave a helpless shrug. "No idea. The message only said that somebody bought the same variety of cheroots that he favors. I'm going down to the shop to investigate. Don't know where it might lead, but I have to follow all avenues."

"We ought to let Catherine know," Eleanor noted.

"She's been called away to the country. Won't be back for a few days. But I wanted to let you know because . . ." Because? He knew this mattered to Eleanor. He needed her by his side. She'd become essential to him, and he couldn't think of anyone he wanted with him for this task more than her.

He loved her. The words always hovered close, like swift moths around a flame. Yet he and Eleanor had never spoken of love, and a part of him still feared it, feared revealing this last, vulnerable part of himself. She cared about him—this he knew. But did she love him? He couldn't ask. He'd rather take a stab wound to the chest than learn that the depths of his feelings for her went unreturned.

"Because you said you wanted to help," he finished.

She nodded. The frown creasing her forehead lessened, and she exhaled. "When your note arrived telling me to come at once, I thought . . ." She glanced away.

"Thought what?" he prompted. His chest tightened.

She looked back at him, offering a rueful smile. "A writer's fancy. And seeing too many of Maggie's tragic burlettas."

Something loosened and freed itself within him. As if walled battlements cracked. He couldn't remember anyone worrying about him—aside from his role as the heir.

Her own admission seemed to embarrass her. She couldn't meet his gaze. "If the message from the tobacconist came this morning but the purchase was done yesterday," she said, her tone turning brisk, "each minute that passes means the trail turns colder."

He understood. This thing between them was too large, too bright. Easier to turn their focus to something else, something that could be picked apart and hopefully solved.

"My carriage is already waiting," he said.

There was little to distinguish the tobacco shop from any other. It had its wooden Highlander stationed outside the front door, announcing its intent as a purveyor of cigars, cheroots, and snuff. The gilded letters on the glass-fronted door proclaimed that the shop had been in continuous business for half a century, making it precisely the sort of place where a titled gentleman might go to purchase his tobacco—to his wife's strained tolerance.

Daniel alit from his carriage and helped Eleanor down. She studied the front of the shop, and he watched her take in the details, from the polished brass knob on the door to the large, sparklingly clean bay window. Evidence that it was a well-cared-for establishment that prided itself on appearances. Next door was a boot maker, and on the other side was a tailor, each with samples of their fine wares on display in their windows.

"Doesn't seem like the sort of place a desperate man might come," she noted.

"It could be the one extravagance he allows himself," Daniel offered. "And if he is truly without recourse, he might seek out one familiar comfort."

"We'll know the truth in a moment." She placed her hand on his arm, and together, they went into the tobacconist's.

A rich, toasted aroma clung thickly to the air. Painted ceramic jars and small wooden barrels lined the walls, and a scale sat with self-importance upon the counter. A few top-hatted gentlemen chatted with an aproned clerk, and everyone gave Daniel and Eleanor a bow as they stepped inside.

It was a risk, Daniel realized, to be seen with her in public at this hour of the day. He should have thought of that earlier—but neither he nor Eleanor seemed to have given it any consideration.

"You should wait in the carriage," he murmured.

"Not a chance," she answered lowly.

"Your reputation—"

"Can withstand something like this. If anything happens, if you learn anything, then I want to be with you."

She had the most effective means of disarming him. He could deny her nothing.

A second clerk, older than the first and sporting an exemplary pair of side-whiskers, emerged from the back of the shop. Daniel recognized him as the proprietor, and the man seemed to recall him, as well. His eyes widened, and he glanced over to the other customers, as though concerned that they might overhear something.

"Good morning, Mr. Christchurch," Daniel said smoothly. "I understand that the special blend I ordered finally arrived."

"It . . . uh . . . yes, my lord," the man answered.

"It's in the back of the shop, correct?" Daniel added.

"Oh, yes! Right this way, my lord, and, uh, madam." Christchurch waved them through the door from which he'd just emerged. They ducked beneath a curtain into a storeroom, where the smell of roasted tobacco leaves swirled even thicker in the air, and a single lamp burned.

"Tell me everything," Daniel said, closing the door and pulling the curtain.

The shopkeeper's uneasy gaze flicked between Eleanor and Daniel.

"You may speak candidly in front of my friend," Daniel assured him. Eleanor gave the man an encouraging nod.

"A young ruffian came in yesterday," the tobacconist said after a pause. "Just a boy in ragged clothes. But he wanted those cheroots, and had the blunt—excuse me, the money—to pay for them. I said I didn't have that blend in stock—which I don't, it has to be ordered special—and he told me that when they did come in, to have them delivered to this address." From a pocket in his apron, he produced a crumpled scrap of paper, which he handed to Daniel.

Unfolding the paper, Daniel saw that the address was in Whitechapel. It was the first solid lead he'd had in a long while.

Eleanor, too, looked at the address. "There was no man with the boy?" she asked. "Waiting outside, perhaps?"

The shopkeeper shook his head. "Only the lad, and an impertinent one, at that. Wearing hardly anything but tatters, his accent disgraceful, and acting as if he was Prinny himself. Still," he added, "I had a meat pie on the counter, and he eyed it as if it was more valuable than a fistful of diamonds, so I gave it to the boy. He grabbed it and ate it right on the doorstep. Two bites and it was gone. Then he disappeared."

Was Jonathan also hungry? Yet he hoarded enough money to buy expensive cheroots.

"My thanks." Daniel handed the tobacconist a pound note, and the man's eyes went round again.

"Can I be of any other service, my lord?"

"Have a case of your favorite cheroots delivered to me."

"Yes, my lord!" The man bowed.

Moments later, Daniel and Eleanor were back in his carriage. "We'll take Miss Hawke back to her offices," he called up to his driver.

"No, we are not," she said, loud enough for the driver to hear.

"Eleanor."

"Daniel."

They stared at each other in the small space of the carriage. "By the look on your face," he said, "you have no intention of going back to your nice, *safe* office and awaiting my findings."

"I won't dignify that with a response." She reached across and gripped his hand. With a wry smile, she said, "You were the one who brought me into this."

"Me?" He frowned.

"When you stepped into my office and proposed I write about you."

He expected no less from her. And as he gave his driver the address in Whitechapel, he could only feel damned grateful that she'd taken his life and completely torn it apart.

A child of unknown gender sat upon the stoop of the tenement, watching the street with a cautious gaze. She—for Daniel was able at last to see the frayed, faded ribbon around the collar of the girl's shift—also held a sharpened stick, which she ground into the cracks between the stones. As if she were trying to shove some small demon back into the earth.

The girl didn't move as Daniel and Eleanor approached the entrance to the run-down building, only stared with a look far older than a child her age ought to possess. There hadn't been time for Daniel and Eleanor to change clothing, so the child wasn't the only one watching the newcomers. Women peered out between shutters, and a few men slouched with interest against nearby walls. But no one came near, as though an invisible barrier encircled Daniel and Eleanor. Privilege had a way of holding the world at bay.

Yet there was no way to avoid the fact that this place, Jonathan's last known address, was hardly fit for human habitation. The walls barely held together, and most of the windows were missing their glass. Years of grime and smoke coated the façade. Inside, a baby wailed. As Daniel and Eleanor came closer, faces appeared in the windows. He counted at least seven people crowded into one casement. God knew how many people called this shambles home.

Eleanor's expression was somber as she also took in these details. She shared a look with him—despairing, angry. He understood. No one, from the scion of a genteel family to the humblest laborer, should live like this. In his searches for Jonathan, he'd seen the grimmer parts of the city. Yet it never failed to strike him, the disparity between those lucky enough to be born with a title, and those who were nameless.

He'd have to increase his charitable donations. It might be a futile gesture, but he needed to make it—or else he could never meet his own gaze in the mirror.

"It might be time for *The Hawk's Eye* to write more substantively," Eleanor said lowly. "Devote less columns to Lady H—d's scandal, and more to a different kind of scandal."

"Will your readers object?"

"Everyone needs to escape," she answered, "but sometimes we need to face the truth." Her lips tightened. "We're attracting attention."

More people had gathered to stare at the finely dressed

strangers. So, after tucking a coin into the hand of the girl on the stoop, Daniel escorted Eleanor inside.

The dim interior proved no better than the outside. Paint peeled off the walls, and the stairs listed like a drunkard. A door edged open, but the person inside must have decided they were uninterested in making Daniel's acquaintance, because the door slammed shut. In an open doorway, a woman walked back and forth, a crying babe in her arms and two more children trailing after her.

A middle-aged woman hovered at the top of the stairs. Her clothes had to be decades old, but they were clean and well mended.

"Can I help you, sir?" she asked cautiously, slowly coming down the creaking steps.

"I hope so," he answered. "I'm looking for a friend of mine."

"Not many with friends who live here," she said. He noted that she remained on the steps, ensuring that she stood taller than Daniel.

"He would have spoken like an aristo," Eleanor supplied. "Kept himself to himself."

"I don't know if there's anybody like that here." The woman narrowed her eyes.

Daniel held up a coin, but she didn't move to take it. Surprising. So she wasn't motivated by greed.

"We're here to help him," he said. "Get him back to his family."

"Are you now?" The landlady assessed him openly, from his boots to his hat, then looked to Eleanor.

"He's had others prey on him," Eleanor said. "He's a veteran, and lost his way. But we're only here to make sure he's all right."

Relief and concern took the place of wariness in the older woman's expression. She crossed herself. "Ah, thank God. I'd been so blessed worried about the lad."

Daniel's gut clenched. Was it true? Had they finally found Jonathan?

"What did he call himself?" he asked, trying to keep the urgency from his voice.

"Connelly. Mr. Jonathan Connelly."

Connelly was Jonathan's middle name, taken from his mother's Irish side. Daniel's gut knotted again. Close. He was so bloody close.

"Can you take us to him?" asked Eleanor. "Mrs. . . . ?"

"Irving. And I'd be most happy to take you to him, except . . ."

"Except?" Daniel prompted.

Mrs. Irving frowned. "He left this morning. Won't be coming back."

Disappointment came like acid, burning through Daniel. *Damn and hell.*

"How can you be certain he's not returning?" Eleanor asked.

"Told me so." The landlady twisted her hands. "I'd been trying to help him, too. Fair broke my heart to see him laid so low. Mind, we're all of us here trying to keep afloat. I help everyone where I can. And that lad was in a poor way. Sick and tormented. And him once a soldier, too." She shook her head. "But he'd never let me help him. Wouldn't take the food I left. Wouldn't let me clean. Wouldn't listen when I told him to leave off with that bad company he'd keep."

Daniel frowned. "Bad company?"

Mrs. Irving scowled. "Aye. The worst of 'em. Bad men, the lot. And their leader—never got his name, but I've heard talk of a bloke that finds himself fallen lordlings and sucks 'em dry, like a leech."

"Is that where Mr. Connelly is now?" Daniel demanded. "With that bloke?"

The landlady shrugged. "He never said. Just decided this morning that he'd had enough, and bolted."

Daniel cursed under his breath. They'd been a hairs-breadth away from finding Jonathan, only to have him slip away again.

"Can we see his room?" Eleanor asked. To Daniel, she

said quietly, "There might be some information about him and where he might go."

He nodded. It was a good plan, when plans were in short supply.

"This way," Mrs. Irving said, and started back up the stairs.

Daniel placed a protective hand at the small of Eleanor's back as she followed the landlady. Mrs. Irving was a good, kind soul, and there were many like her in Whitechapel. But the neighborhood's peril couldn't be discounted, either. The men who'd latched on to Jonathan were proof of that danger. He might have lost Jonathan, but like hell would he let anything happen to Eleanor. She was brave, though, able to extract information from seemingly impossible situations. And she moved without hesitation as she climbed the stairs. Upward.

Once Eleanor had come into his life, his quest had altered. Now he knew that his own redemption was something to pursue. Because it had value to her. And that's what mattered.

Chapter 24

We can never understand the heart's capacity for endurance until tested.

The Hawk's Eye, May 28, 1816

Knowing writers, artists, and actors, Eleanor thought herself prepared for an untidy set of rooms. Yet when Mrs. Irving unlocked and opened the door to Jonathan Lawson's flat, Eleanor was entirely unprepared for the squalor. Rubbish lay everywhere in thick drifts. Dirty clothing, greasy wrappers from food, moldy or dried bits of the food itself, and crumpled papers of unknown origin. Cheroot stubs also littered the ground. A few prints, torn from broadsheets, were tacked to the peeling walls. The only furniture consisted of a lone, broken-backed chair and a bare mattress lying upon the floor. A smell of unwashed human body and stale alcohol hung morosely in the room.

She chanced a glance toward Daniel. His face was drawn tight, his jaw granite. She could only imagine what it must be like for him to witness the long, hard fall of his friend.

As she and Daniel drifted into the room, nudging aside debris with their feet, the landlady chattered nervously behind them.

"It's not Mayfair," Mrs. Irving said, "but I run a clean establishment. But Mr. Connelly, he wouldn't let me in here. I said I'd do it for free, in truth, yet he still refused."

"Very generous of you," Eleanor noted. "To donate services most people in your profession charge for."

Mrs. Irving shrugged. "I help all the families in my building. We're all scraping by—working our fingers to blood and bone. I watch Mrs. Farquhar's babies when she has to stay up late to finish making hats, and I tidy up after Mr. Duggan, who's down at the shipyard and no wife to see after him."

She shrugged. "He was a good lad, too, that Mr. Connelly. Dragged one of my boys home from a gin palace and made him promise never to go there again. He kept an eye out for all the local children—making sure they stayed off the street, giving them some of his food when he had any to spare."

A rueful smile curled in the corner of Daniel's mouth. "Sounds like Jonathan. He can't stop himself from helping others." His smile fell away. "Except himself."

"And you said he kept rough company?" Eleanor asked, avoiding a stain on the floorboards.

"Oh, aye. At all hours there were brutes coming and going, especially that one with the reputation. Dead-eyed, he was. Like a wolf only thinking of his next meal." Mrs. Irving wrung her hands in her apron. "I'm afraid that Mr. Connelly was his meal."

A door down the hallway opened and shut. Mrs. Irving glanced after the sound. "That's my daughter-in-law. She'll be back with the mending she takes in. I'll have to leave you for a few moments."

"Take your time," Daniel murmured distractedly, his gaze moving intently over the disordered room.

With a curtsy, the landlady departed, leaving Eleanor and Daniel alone in Jonathan's flat. Though Mrs. Irving had said he'd been there only that morning, the room exuded a profound neglect. A leaden weight sat in Eleanor's chest as she contemplated it.

She placed a hand on Daniel's arm. "It doesn't give much comfort, but . . . I'm sorry."

Daniel gave a clipped nod, yet he looked deeply angry. With himself. "Every turn I take I see more and more how I failed him."

"But you're here now," she pointed out.

"Too late. He's run off."

She eyed the heaps of garbage. "Didn't take much with him."

"He ran off before the cheroots could arrive. Likely he thought he'd come back for them." Daniel stirred one of the piles with his walking stick. "He didn't leave any clues as to his current whereabouts."

"We don't know that for certain." Glad she was wearing gloves, she picked through a heap of rags and empty bottles. "There could be something here that might lead us to him."

In silent agreement, they both searched the flat. Yet after several minutes with nothing worthwhile, aside from the fact that the gin bottles proved Jonathan's drinking habits, it seemed their efforts were in vain.

Until Daniel said, "Look here." He held up a stack of newspapers. She recognized them as issues of *The Hawk's Eye*. "We know he's an admirer of your work."

She approached and studied the papers. "These are recent issues. I wonder that he can afford them."

"Maybe he nicks them from a coffee house."

"He seems particularly interested in the *Rake* articles." She pointed to one of the papers. "Look here. It's been folded so that only the article shows. And the ink is smudged."

"From reading many times," Daniel deduced.

"Perhaps he's not as lost as you might think," she said. "He might know that you're the subject of the articles, and it still draws him—his old life."

Daniel frowned in thought. "We might be able to plant a message to him in one of the pieces. Telling him to come back."

The idea had merit, yet . . . "There's a powerful sense of despair here," she noted. "The kind of hopelessness that logic and reason can't reach." An idea began forming in her mind, coalescing into shape. "What if . . . we put something in *The Hawk's Eye*, something that might draw him out of hiding, yet he won't know that we're luring him out."

She strode to the narrow window, but it only looked out onto a wall. As if he'd chosen the room with the grimmest view. "We know about the cheroots, but that wouldn't be enough. Did he have anything he loved? Something particular that he enjoyed above all else?"

Daniel walked over to the mattress and looked at the pictures tacked to the wall. "This." He tapped one of the images, and she saw that it was of a man and a woman atop a phaeton, driving at what appeared to be a rapid pace. "High-flyers. Racing them. In everything else, he was the mildest of men, but get him in a phaeton, and he became wild. Giddy." Daniel's expression turned contemplative. "Thought about him when we had our race. He would have loved it. I even looked for him in the crowd. But to no profit. If he was there, he'd changed too much for me to recognize him. Ah, damn. Maybe he had been there."

He pulled something off the wall and held it out for her inspection. Coming closer, she realized it was the piece about their race. A slight chill ran along her neck. Had Jonathan been at the scene? But she hadn't known about him then.

The idea that had been fomenting continued to gather shape. "What if . . . we placed an item in *The Hawk's Eye*? Something about a phaeton race. One that's going to happen, rather than one that's already transpired."

Daniel rubbed at his chin as he considered her idea. "We give it a few days' lead time. Make sure that he gets a chance to see it."

"If he's as mad for phaeton racing as you say he is . . ."

"Then he'll be there," Daniel said.

"And so will we," she concluded.

They stared at each other for a moment, mulling over this plan.

"A wild gamble," he finally said.

She spread her hands. "At this point, what's left?"

"Nothing." He stared down at the well-read clipping in his hand, and it seemed he saw what she did. Jonathan was a man who'd given up hope, yet still clung to some small piece of what he'd once been, as if unable to completely let go and sink into the abyss of desolation. "There's nothing left."

Together in her office after hours, they wrote the article. It was a blind item, hinting at the race that was to take place at Hyde Park in two days' time. Rumors were spreading, according to the article, and bets were already being placed. When it was finished, she proofed it and gave it to her typesetters to add to the next issue.

By the time the piece was completed, full night had fallen, and they returned to Daniel's house.

They climbed the stairs to his chamber. Inside, he sank wearily onto the bed. "Damn it, I promised Marwood I'd go to the theater with him tonight." He rubbed the heel of his hand against his eyes. "I'll cancel."

"Don't," she said, sitting beside him. "Marwood plays the libertine, but he's sharp. A cancelation might arouse his suspicion, and we've come too far to let him guess what's going on."

Daniel exhaled. He gave a tired nod. "Marwood or no, I'd give a king's ransom to spend the whole night with you."

Her smile was small, tinged with melancholy. How she longed for that, too, and how distant it all seemed. Perhaps if they did manage to find Jonathan—and she prayed that their gambit would work—perhaps she and Daniel might be able to continue their affair for a little while longer. Perhaps . . . Perhaps many things. But she dared not wish for them.

Future heartbreak already neared. She could hear its slow, dragging steps approaching, inevitable. Unstoppable.

He rose and rang for Strathmore. In a moment, the valet appeared.

"I'm dressing for the theater tonight," Daniel said.

"Yes, my lord." Strathmore didn't even glance in her direction as he prepared a ewer for washing and laid out a change of clothing.

Wrapping her arms around the post supporting the bed's canopy, Eleanor watched him get ready for the evening. The entire process might fascinate her from a journalistic viewpoint another time, but now she just enjoyed simply looking at him. How his athletic body moved in the gleam of the lamps as he peeled off his clothing. How she knew exactly those divots at the base of his spine. Hunger burned to see him in just his thin smallclothes as he leaned over the washstand, cleaning himself. More than desire, she loved the domesticity of the moment. Almost as if . . . they were more to each other than temporary lovers.

The valet tidied as Daniel donned his clothing.

"Unique, this," she murmured as he shrugged into his waistcoat and fastened its silk-covered buttons. "I'm more familiar with getting you *out* of your clothes."

He shot her a hot look. "We'll get to that later."

"I'll mark my dance card," she said.

"A very private waltz." God, how his smile tugged at the very core of her.

"Not suitable for any public assembly," she agreed.

But too soon, he was dressed, and the carriage waited for him. Before he left, they stood in the middle of his bedroom and kissed, hard and deep. There was a particular fire in them both, and they clung to each other. As if some disaster awaited.

No—they would find Jonathan, and everything would work itself out some way. She had to believe that. She wasn't like Maggie, with one eye toward calamity.

Eleanor finally stepped back, breaking the kiss. "Enjoy your debauchery. But not too much."

"Not without you."

Together, they walked out, and down the stairs. In the foyer, a footman handed him his coat, hat, and walking stick. Again, that sense of looming catastrophe swam close, making her eyes hot. She swallowed back words begging him to stay. It was just one night. He was a grown man. He'd be back in a few hours.

Yet as she watched him go, she couldn't seem to stop the chill that relentlessly scraped over her. And she knew she wouldn't feel warm again until they were in bed, safe, together.

To distract herself, she ensconced herself in the study and pulled out a sheaf of articles to edit. Work could always serve to block out the outside world.

Sitting at her desk, a single lamp burning, she reviewed a story about two lordlings fighting over an Italian opera singer. The sound of the front door opening and closing resonated through the house. Her heart jumped. Daniel was home!

A glance at the clock revealed that it was only ten o'clock.

She frowned. Was he ill? Or perhaps he'd found a convincing way to get out of his engagement with Lord Marwood.

Eleanor was halfway out of her chair when the door to the study opened. But Daniel did not come striding in. No, she knew who the striking, silver-haired gentleman was. He'd been touted in the pages of *The Hawk's Eye* as a model of honor and decorum—even if his son was one of the Town's most notorious scandal-makers.

The Marquess of Allam. Daniel's godfather.

Barely encumbered by his cane, the nobleman stalked into the chamber and stared at her. Almost insolently. If an aristocrat could ever allow themselves to be insolent. Well, she didn't have to return his rudeness. Courtesy often disarmed disrespect.

"My lord," she said, curtsying.

"Miss . . . Hawke, is it?" he demanded.

"How do you know my name?"

"There isn't much in this city that I don't know about." He leaned slightly on his cane but made no motion toward sitting down. Was this a sign of strength? An attempt at intimidation? "Including the fact that you and my godson have become lovers."

Heat crept into her cheeks. "My lord, it's really—"

"It certainly *is* my business." Lord Allam's eyes, so like his son's, bore into her. "His head is completely turned by you. So much so that he's neglecting his duty. The continuance of Ashford's line is my responsibility."

"I thought it was Daniel's responsibility."

Lord Allam's eyebrows rose at her impertinence. "I made a solemn vow to his parents that I would see their son married to a *suitable* woman, and that he would bear them *suitable* heirs. You are not that woman, and whatever children he gets by you will never be admitted into respectable Society."

Though his words pierced her, speaking to her deepest fears, she continued to stand her ground. "Again, my lord, all of this is Daniel's decision. And mine. We'll do what we feel is best."

The marquess gave a hint of a cold smile. "Fancy yourself in love, do you?"

She stiffened. "You love your wife, do you not, my lord?"

"You shall not speak of her," he ground out. "And love will not protect you. It cannot. Perhaps you've heard of Lord Fleming, and his reckless decision to marry an opera dancer? They thought love would shield them, but it didn't." He peered at her. "I can see by the ashen color in your cheeks that you know exactly to whom I'm referring, and the ultimate end to their ill-advised union."

Eleanor tried to swallow, but nothing would go past the rock that lodged itself in her throat. "We are not those people, my lord."

"You know I'm speaking the truth," he countered. But his tone was almost gentle. "Ashford will not do his duty while you continue to remain in his life, yet there is nothing in the future for either of you but misery. He will have to leave you eventually. Would you rather you part ways now, before you can truly hurt him, or later, when he'll be devastated?"

She pressed her lips together tightly. Damn Lord Allam. Damn him. He understood her weakness wasn't herself but Daniel. And the marquess was perfectly willing to exploit that weakness.

"I know you care for my godson," Lord Allam went on. "I also know you're a very intelligent woman. Which is why I believe you will do the right thing. Because you understand, in your deepest heart and intellect, that it must be done." He nodded at her. "Good evening, Miss Hawke."

She did not wish him a good night as he turned and left. Instead, she sank down, back into her chair. The clock chimed the quarter of the hour.

In less than fifteen minutes, her entire world had fallen apart.

Hours later, the front door opened and closed again. Voices murmured in the foyer. Then a familiar tread sounded out in the hallway. The door to the study opened again.

Daniel peered in, frowning in concern as she now sat in one of the wingback chairs in front of the fire. "I thought you'd be in bed by now."

She couldn't speak. Only shook her head.

He came inside, closing the door behind him. "Is everything all right?"

"Yes," she managed. But it wasn't. It felt even worse when he came and crouched before her, taking her hands in his. He smelled of tobacco and the night, and all she wanted was to throw her arms around him. She didn't, holding herself still.

"I can see that it isn't," he said softly.

She tugged her hands out of his and clenched them. Fear

had been gnawing along her bones, and she couldn't keep it contained within herself any longer.

"I won't cry," she said, focusing on her fists. "Not in front of you, anyway . . ." She looked at him. Her eyes did, in fact, burn, but she willed everything inside.

He wouldn't take his eyes from her.

"Why would you cry?" he asked.

She shrugged. As she spoke, her words felt like shards of ice. "Ever since we left Whitechapel, I could feel it." She rose and stepped around him. "The chill of a door left open. You on one side, me on the other. And then the door closing."

She could hear him rise to standing. "I don't want this to end."

All she wanted was to rail and rage. Which would only shame them both. If this had to stop, she would try to console herself with clinging to scraps of dignity. Even if she might regret it later. It was like writing one's own epitaph.

"It's time. We both know it. It's always had a limited life span."

He spoke behind her. "I've never said anything like that." He gripped her arms and turned her around, but she focused on the loosened knot of his cravat rather than look into his eyes. "And I won't let you hide in some polished, brittle performance."

"What do you want of me?" she demanded. "Hysterics? Hair pulling and begging?" She now tilted up her chin. "I don't beg." Fractures spread through her. Yet she would wait until she was in the shelter of her own rooms to allow herself to fall apart.

"Then don't," he countered. "You've decided what I'm going to say before a word leaves my lips. And the bloody last thing I want to do is end this."

Relief almost made her sag. Yet her legs held her up as her heart careened toward the ceiling. "Ah."

"Yes, 'ah.'" Wry humor glinted in his eyes. "The least you could do is fight for me."

"And risk looking like a fool?"

His gaze turned melancholy. "Love makes us fools."

Surely she hadn't heard right. Surely he hadn't said—

"Yes, my lady scribe," he said, taking another step closer, until they were chest to chest. "I love you."

All she could do was stare. It was either that, or finally give in to the tears that threatened to burst forth. "How . . . ?"

"The poets say it's the usual turn of events when someone finds they can't live without another. You're the beat of my heart."

Brightness expanded within her, radiating out like the dawn. It was a happiness so severe that she might not endure it. It could tear her apart. Accompanied by a limitless sorrow. She'd never known those two feelings could exist side by side—not with such profundity. "Daniel—"

"So don't tell me you're going to play this cold and noble," he said with vehemence. "Because I bloody well won't have it."

She rose up onto the tips of her toes, then took his mouth with a hunger that surprised even herself.

A long while later, she said, "You've a peculiar way of showing a woman you love her."

"Never done it before," he answered. "Going to make a few mistakes."

"You're forgiven."

He held her closer, his long, lean body enfolding her. "Tell me."

"Tell you what?"

"You know."

She did. And it would ruin her to speak the words aloud—yet she couldn't stop herself. "I love you."

He had the look of a man enormously relieved, deeply satisfied. If possible, he seemed to grow even taller, broader. He cupped her head and kissed her once more. A thorough, delicious ravishing.

She'd never known pain like this. Hadn't comprehended it was possible. Because *they* were impossible. And his declaration of love only made it worse. Love couldn't hold out against the reality of their situation. Lord Allam's visit had only confirmed what she already knew.

Breaking the kiss, she gasped. "I . . . have to go."

"Eleanor—" He reached for her.

But she'd already turned and fled. It would never be far enough.

Chapter 25

*Forgiveness is an uncommon and precious quality,
and its origins begin with the ability to forgive one's
self before it can be extended to anyone else.*

The Hawk's Eye, May 30, 1816

Though he burned to clutch the reins tightly, Daniel was
careful to keep his grip on them loose. His horse was already
finely tuned to the commands he sent through the ribbons,
and he didn't want to communicate his nervousness to
the animal.

But Eleanor, perched beside him on the seat, shifted for
the dozenth time and tapped her foot without seeming to
realize it. She kept glancing around at the small crowd that
had formed in this corner of the park. Others had deduced
the location of the "race" and were eager to join in the fun—
though there was, in truth, no fun to be had. As Mrs. Delamere
might say, it was all set dressing. Pretend revelry in
order to lure Jonathan out of hiding.

What wasn't pretense: the strain between Daniel and Eleanor.
It hadn't abated. A day had passed. Then, last night,
she hadn't waited for him in his bedchamber. Any written
communication that had transpired between them had been
terse, with her claiming to be too busy for anything but an
exchange of a few hastily penned words. And when she'd
appeared in his study this evening, ready to accompany him

to the race, they'd been as stilted as formal acquaintances. Certainly they hadn't acted like two people who'd declared their love for each other.

The churning in his stomach thus had a dual origin as he stewed over the consequences of this trap for Jonathan and also brooded about Eleanor. It felt as though everything hinged on the next few hours. They could be triumphant, or disastrous.

He didn't try to break the fraught silence. He wasn't certain what he'd say. How could he close the gap between them? He didn't even know what had caused it. One moment, they had been confessing their feelings for each other, and the next, she'd fled. Yet every moment with her now was time spent in an unknown country, where he didn't know the language or customs.

And he needed his focus to remain on looking for Jonathan, though everything in his life was in complete chaos.

Glancing over his shoulder, toward a pathway surrounded by trees, he spotted the outline of a fine—but not too fine—carriage. Inside was Catherine, who had returned from the country only that morning. The plan to draw out Jonathan had been met with her approval, and she'd even brought a pair of opera glasses so that, from her vantage in the carriage, she might be able to search the crowd for a glimpse of her brother.

To disguise himself, Daniel wore a greatcoat with the collar pulled up high to cover most of his face. Eleanor needed no hiding from Jonathan, though she was also bundled against the cold. Together, they watched a small parade of phaetons slowly collect in the park, along with two dozen hardy souls willing to brave the unusual chill in order to watch the competition.

"Any sign of him?" Eleanor whispered, breaking the silence between them.

He scanned the spectators. Earlier, Daniel, Eleanor, and Catherine had agreed upon a whistled signal should any of them spot Jonathan amongst the crowd. Thus far, they were silent. "Not yet."

"The crowd is getting restless," Eleanor noted, glancing at the waiting phaetons and onlookers. An impatient, excited energy hummed through them. Money changed hands as bets were placed. "They want the race to start."

"We need more time," Daniel gritted. Damn it, was this whole scheme a false hope? Had Jonathan even seen the announcement of the race? And would he even show up?

Every male face seemed to belong to Jonathan. The more Daniel looked at them, the more they blended together into one endless blur. Those could be his old friend's hollow eyes over on that thin man by the shrubbery. And that chap there near the tree, his drawn mouth and sunken cheeks could be Jonathan's.

Daniel was a powder keg, on the verge of exploding. He'd never known such tension. Eleanor's nerves added to his own. He was certain that he couldn't contain himself much longer and would level the park with the force of his detonation.

"Are we going to run this bloody race or not?" one gingery man atop a high-flyer demanded to the crowd.

A noise of assent rose up from the onlookers. At the same time, a sharp, high whistle sounded.

The signal.

"He's here," Daniel said lowly to Eleanor. "Somewhere in the crowd."

"I can't see him," she muttered.

Daniel jumped down from the phaeton and began pushing his way through the assembled people, staring intently into each face. Frustrated by the collar obscuring his sight, Daniel shoved it down. Where the hell was Jonathan? A moment later, someone cried out.

Whirling around, Daniel spotted a man being dragged down off a phaeton. The assailant was a tall, angular bloke in a set of clothes that had seen its glory come and go. The attacker picked up the high-flyer's reins.

Daniel finally recognized him. Jonathan. Looking like a twisted ghost of himself, pale and worn almost to transparency. He must have spotted Daniel and was now attempting to flee.

Jonathan's gaze locked on Daniel's. A fleeting moment. And in that moment, Daniel saw the shade of his friend. His eyes pleaded with Daniel. *Help me. Stay the hell away from me. I am lost.*

Someone jostled Daniel, and the moment broke apart. Jonathan snapped the reins, and the phaeton shot off. Its owner shouted for the thief to stop, but the vehicle sped off into the dark streets.

Daniel ran back to his own phaeton, where Eleanor anxiously waited.

"What now?" she cried.

He vaulted up into the driver's seat, greatcoat billowing around him. "We give chase."

The last time Eleanor had sat beside Daniel in a phaeton, it had been a mad, thrilling gallop through London that had set her blood afire. Now, they careened through the streets in pursuit of Jonathan Lawson.

She clutched the seat tightly, her knuckles aching, her heart threatening to tear a hole in the front of her dress as Daniel drove after his friend. Glancing quickly behind her, she saw Catherine's carriage valiantly attempting to keep pace, though the larger, heavier vehicle kept falling behind.

Up ahead, Jonathan drove like a man pursued by demons—which he was. The demons of his past. He made reckless turns, almost upsetting his stolen phaeton, and nearly ran down several pedestrians. People leapt out of his way as he rushed down the street, cursing him, then Daniel, then Catherine's carriage as they shot past.

Though the night and the speed made it difficult to know exactly where they were, the quality of the neighborhoods grew rougher and rougher as they sped eastward. Twice,

Jonathan rounded a corner and seemed to disappear, but Daniel managed to catch up.

"Jonathan!" Daniel shouted. "Stop, goddamn it! We want nothing from you!"

But Jonathan only threw one terrified look over his shoulder before turning forward and urging his horse on harder.

Suddenly, Jonathan's phaeton skidded to a stop outside a tenement. He jumped from the driver's seat and ran inside.

Daniel pulled his horses to a halt just behind Jonathan's vehicle. The building into which his friend ran had boarded-up windows and a look of aggressive neglect. But there was no time to consider any of this as Daniel leapt down and ran toward the front door. He tried the knob, but it must have been locked. Then he pounded on the door.

It swung open suddenly, revealing a squashed-faced hulk of a man. Without a word, the giant man threw a punch at Daniel. Daniel ducked and landed his own combination of blows. One to the stomach, which made the big man double over. Another to the chin. The bloke staggered. Daniel pushed him, and the man stumbled backward, dazed.

Eleanor leapt down from the seat, taking the whip with her—just in case she needed a weapon. She followed as Daniel barreled inside. A miserable room awaited them, bare and dimly lit. A door was at one end of the cramped chamber. Jonathan must have fled through it. Then it opened, and another man appeared. He was burly, with a coarse face and shaggy, straw-colored hair. And he looked determined to keep Daniel out of the other room.

"You ain't getting him," the blond bloke snarled, raising his fists.

So this was the "bad man" Mrs. Irving had talked of. The one who fed off men like Jonathan, taking everything until nothing was left. And he didn't seem ready to let his prize go.

"You won't stop me," Daniel growled back.

Without another word, the man charged. He slammed into Daniel, and the two lurched back into a wall. Eleanor could only stand by and watch as the two men exchanged punches, the bully clearly using moves that one learned on the streets, not a boxing salon. But Daniel fought back well, nimbly dodging blows and landing his own so that blood sprayed from the mouth of the blond man.

She whirled at a grunting sound behind her. The big man who'd guarded the door now roused himself, and he looked as though he was preparing to launch himself into the fray. Acting on impulse, Eleanor cracked the whip at him. The weapon lashed his arm. But it didn't stop him. He came at her, and she lashed out again, harder. The whip sliced through his shirtsleeve, and deeper, cutting into his skin. A stripe of red appeared on the giant's arm.

He looked down at the wound and grimaced. Yet he charged at her once more. And once more, she cracked the whip at him. Again and again, fending off his advances. He edged backward, held at bay by her strikes.

At last the giant decided he wanted no more of this. He bolted out the front door, almost flattening Catherine as she approached.

Daniel and the bully continued to fight. A gaunt shadow appeared in the entry to the other room. It took Eleanor a moment to recognize him as Jonathan.

"Stop it, Lyle," he rasped at the blond man.

When Lyle turned his head to snap a retort, Daniel's fist shot out. Right into Lyle's jaw. The man stumbled. Daniel hit him again with a sharp, effective blow. Lyle fell to the floor, his eyes rolling back.

For a moment, nothing happened. Eleanor cautiously approached and nudged the prone form of Lyle with her foot. No movement. He was insensate.

She looked up at Daniel, then at Jonathan. The man they had been searching for came forward a little, stepping into the light. She fought a gasp. Now that she could see him more clearly, it stunned her that he managed to keep his feet.

Whoever Jonathan Lawson had been, it certainly couldn't have been this waxy, emaciated, dead-eyed man, barely kept together by some force of will. Definitely not his own will, for there seemed nothing of any spirit or energy in his gaze. Not when he looked at her, and not when he stared at Daniel—which chilled her a little. But when Jonathan saw his sister come into the room, he gave a sharp cry, like a man seeing his own soul. He backed up, retreating into the shadows of the other chamber, and slammed the door behind him. A click sounded when a key turned in a lock.

Daniel rushed forward and tried to open the door. To no success. He rattled the knob.

"Jonathan," he called through the door. "Let us in."

"Leave me alone," came the muffled, forlorn wail.

"Help," Daniel said. "That's all we're here to do."

"I can't be helped."

His shoulder pressed against the wood, Daniel shouted, "Bloody hell, Jonathan, open this door right now!"

Eleanor closed the distance between herself and Daniel. She laid her hand upon his arm and gave her head a gentle shake. Bullying and demands weren't the way to reach Jonathan. She wasn't certain *how* he could be swayed, but that seemed an unwise strategy. A man's strategy. Of a certain, Daniel was the sort of man who got whatever he wanted, and he thought he could use the strength of his determination to make it happen.

Stepping forward, Catherine said, loudly enough to be heard in the other room, "Jon. Won't you come home? I . . . I only want to take care of you."

"Cathy," her brother said, her name seeming to catch in his throat. "Please go. I can't . . . don't see me like this."

"It doesn't matter to me," she said, imploring.

"It matters to *me*" was the desolate answer. "Your brother died in France. I'm his ghost. You can't take care of a ghost."

"But—"

"I'm begging you. Leave."

Catherine turned her desperate, bewildered gaze to Daniel and Eleanor. They were so close to their goal, but held back by the one man they were here to assist. Frustration and pity elbowed for position inside Eleanor.

"I could kick the door down," Daniel said lowly. "Pull him out and drag him home."

"Then what?" Eleanor asked. "Lock him in a room so he can't run away again? That's a shadow of a life. And he'll only try to escape. He's got to come out on his own."

"I agree," Catherine said. "But he won't listen to Daniel, and everything I say seems to drive him further away."

"May I . . . may I try?" Eleanor asked.

When Catherine glanced at Daniel, he said, "The decision isn't mine to make."

The girl thought for a moment. "We haven't many other options." She waved toward the door.

Heart beating with the strength of her responsibility, Eleanor dallied for time by gently pulling Daniel back and guiding him to stand over Lyle's prone form. "In case he wakes up," she cautioned. Daniel looked grim, but compliant.

"And Miss Lawson," she said to the girl, "you might also want to give a little room."

Catherine obeyed, standing in the farther corner, her hands clasped anxiously at her waist.

Slowly, Eleanor approached the door. She tried to marshal her thoughts. What could she say to make a wretched man without hope have some semblance of faith again? Nothing she had ever written held such significance.

"Mr. Lawson," she said, pressing close to the door. "You don't know me, but I'm a friend of Daniel's. And your sister's, too, I hope," she added, glancing at Catherine.

The girl gave her a small, encouraging smile.

So Eleanor pressed on. "Those two—they care about you very much. You don't know the lengths they've gone to find you. Daniel even had me write about him. You know those articles you liked so much? The *Rake* pieces? I wrote those. So we've a bit of a connection, you and I. Daniel had his private life exposed for all the world to see, using the thinnest veneer of a disguise, just so he could locate you. I can't imagine that was very easy for him. In fact, I think it must have been awful. But he did it for you."

There was silence on the other side of the door. Then, softly, "I liked those articles. They made me smile."

A filament of hope came to life inside her. "There, you see," she said in a matter-of-fact tone. "Ghosts don't smile. They don't read scandal sheets or go to phaeton races, either. I think," she continued, "that you aren't a phantom at all. I think that Jonathan Lawson is still alive. Perhaps not thriving, but alive. And a part of you knows that, as well."

"No," he said flatly.

"Yes," she insisted. Praying for inspiration, she continued. "The spirits of the dead, they don't feel pain. And I know you're in pain right now, Mr. Lawson. But . . . that's good. It means there's part of you that wants to heal. That clings to life. Even in the midst of darkness, that flame still burns inside of you. It's a beautiful thing, that flame. Maybe it's a little dim right now, yet it can be kindled higher. Don't concern yourself with getting that fire back to its full height. Don't worry about that now. All that matters at this moment is nurturing that tiny, flickering light. A bit at a time. That's all. Just a minuscule trace. Just for today. Just for an hour, a minute. Can you try something like that, do you think?"

Another long pause. "Perhaps."

God, was this working? "No one said it will be easy. It'll take hard work. But you'll have an advantage over all the thousands of souls dwelling in darkness right now. Do you know what that advantage is?"

"None," he said lowly. "I have none."

"We both know that's not true." She gazed at Catherine, then at Daniel. He looked back at her, fierce and resolute. And loving. "I'm looking at two advantages right now. Two allies. They both care about you so much. They accept you as you are. Not who you were, or who you might be, but you, in this very moment. And they will be beside you. Every step. Every stumble."

"I can't let them down again," Jonathan said.

"You won't," she insisted. "Because you never disappointed them in the first place. They *love* you. You might think you don't deserve that love, but you do. All of us deserve love. And acceptance." Her throat burned. "But right now, I need you to be strong enough to open this door and take the first step. Not for Miss Lawson. Not for Daniel. But for yourself. Because, by God, you deserve that first step. Is that . . . is that something you can do?"

A very long silence followed. Eleanor looked at Daniel, her heart welling. While at the same time uncertainty spun through her. Had she said enough? Had she pushed Jonathan Lawson further away? She couldn't fail him. She couldn't fail Daniel.

And then . . .

The key turned. The door creaked open.

Jonathan stood in the doorway, looking like a man cast out to sea. Eleanor took a step back to give him room. The man barely looked at her. He'd only eyes for his sister. Slowly, his hands came up, reaching for Catherine.

She ran to him. And in a moment, they were kneeling on the floor, embracing. Sobbing. Catherine kept stroking her brother's hair, murmuring soothing endearments.

Tears pricked the backs of Eleanor's eyes, and when she glanced at Daniel, a sheen gleamed in his eyes, as well.

She walked quickly to him, and he enfolded her in his arms.

"Well done, Lady Scribe," he whispered.

They bundled Jonathan into Catherine's waiting carriage. He seemed weak, shaken, and dazed, but he held tightly to his sister. She wrapped him in a blanket, and he huddled into a corner of the carriage, eyes staring straight ahead. Eleanor could only imagine the road that lay ahead of the girl and her brother.

Daniel shut the door to Catherine's carriage. She brought

her face to the open window, her free hand resting on the casement.

"There aren't words," she said.

"None are necessary," Daniel answered. He covered her hand with his. "I'm only glad to have him back."

Catherine cast a worried look at Jonathan. "I am, too. Only . . . this won't be easy, will it?"

"I wish I could say otherwise." Daniel looked grim. "But whatever comes, I'll be there."

"And me," Eleanor added.

Catherine turned her gaze to Eleanor. "Miss Hawke . . . what you said to Jonathan . . . that was the turning point. If it hadn't been for you . . . I don't think he would have come out. That's a debt I can't repay."

"It doesn't need repaying," Eleanor said, and she meant it.

"If there's ever anything my family can do for you," Catherine pressed, "you've only to ask."

Eleanor nodded, though her own sense of honor would never allow her to ask a favor of Catherine Lawson or her family. There were some things a person did without hope of reward, or even recognition. One simply did them because it was a hard, harsh world, and everyone was in this madhouse together.

"Get him home," Eleanor said, nodding toward the shivering Jonathan. "Give him rest. And understanding."

"I will. God bless you both."

Daniel pressed a kiss to Catherine's hand, then let it go. He knocked on the carriage to signal the driver. The vehicle drove off, carrying Catherine and Jonathan Lawson home.

Daniel and Eleanor stood in the middle of the road, watching the carriage ride away. She wrapped her arms around herself.

"They have a long journey," she murmured.

"They do," he agreed. "I won't let him down again. And Catherine's grown stronger. Whatever comes, Jonathan will not be alone."

"He might have a chance, then."

They were silent, contemplating the perilous path Jonathan must now walk. She didn't envy him. But if there was any mercy in this universe, she hoped a little might be spared for him.

She shivered.

"Let's get you home, too," Daniel said, pulling her close.

Together, they returned to his phaeton, and he helped her up. The vehicle itself was unharmed, which was remarkable, given the rough neighborhood. But perhaps the local citizens had seen Daniel fight, and knew not to tangle with a man like him.

After he took his position with the reins, he snapped the ribbons, and they were off. Much more slowly this time.

They progressed through the darkened streets of London, the city impassive as it rose up around them. No one in any of the buildings understood what had happened this night. No one knew that a momentous chapter was about to close forever. But both she and Daniel seemed to recognize it, for neither of them could break the silence that descended, a silence that was weighted with portent and sadness.

"He's home now," she said finally, as they got closer to her neighborhood. "No more *Rake* articles."

"No," Daniel said, his words heavy. "They're not needed anymore."

The truth of this hit her like a landslide, burying her. If the articles were unnecessary, she and Daniel didn't need to see each other any longer. Their time together was finally, truly over.

It was a physical pain. Edged and cutting. As though she was being cleaved in half. Impossible to endure. Yet she had to. What choice was there?

"This doesn't have to stop," he said, reading her thoughts.

"We both know it does." She looked down at her hands knotted in her lap. They were closer to her home, now. Only a block away. Such a short distance, such a brief span of time. "You can't give me forever, Daniel. An earl and a journalist . . . it can't work."

He growled. "Damn it—"

They pulled up outside her building. "It's the truth." Her voice was rusty, tearing her up from the inside out. "You know it. So do I." She dug the heels of her hands into her eyes. "Prolonging it makes everything worse."

Before he could respond, she jumped down to the pavement. She couldn't look at him. Couldn't see his face, his eyes. All the parts of him so precious to her. It only reminded her of what they couldn't have.

"I love you, Daniel." She didn't face him. Only stared blindly at her front door, her gaze filmed with tears. "If you care about me at all, you won't try to see me. You'll let this go. You'll let me go."

"Like hell," he rumbled.

She heard him leap down from the driver's seat, so she dashed up the stoop and hastily unlocked the door. His boots drummed on the stairs as he followed. But she dragged the door open and slipped inside. Before he could follow her into the entryway, she hastily shut and locked the door.

She leaned against the wood as he hammered on it. "Eleanor! Eleanor, damn it! Let me in."

Biting her lip to keep from responding, she squeezed her eyes shut, feeling the shaking of the door through her body. Or maybe the shaking came from her. Distantly, it amazed her that she could feel new levels of heartbreak, when she kept imagining she'd reached the pinnacle of agony.

"Eleanor!" he shouted.

The voice of her landlady rang out. "Go on, now! Or I'll call the constabulary."

"Do it, harridan," he snarled back.

Eleanor almost laughed.

"Police!" cried her landlady, louder now. "Murder! Thief!"

Daniel cursed. Through the door, he said, "This isn't over, Eleanor."

She heard him stalk down the stairs. Then the clip of his horse's hooves on the pavement as he drove away.

Eleanor continued to lean against the door, her heart lying at her feet, shattered into countless bleeding pieces. The door to her landlady's flat opened, and the frowning woman stuck her head out.

"I don't take kindly to that kind of ruckus, Miss Hawke," she snapped.

"It won't happen again," Eleanor answered. And the pain redoubled. Because she knew it was true.

Chapter 26

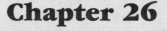

There is nothing as fragile or resilient as the human heart.

The Hawk's Eye, June 13, 1816

Feeling like a caged wolf, Daniel paced back and forth in his study. Late-afternoon sun pooled on the floor. He'd already tried to wear himself out at his boxing studio and with a long ride to Hampstead Heath and back. Nothing worked. He ought to be exhausted. He hadn't slept for days, and he barely ate. But he couldn't.

Two weeks had passed since Eleanor had slammed the door in his face. True to his word, he hadn't given up trying to see her. Yet herein lay the problem with having a very clever woman as a lover—she'd managed to keep herself hidden from him. He'd sent her letters that had gone unanswered. Barring this, he'd gone to her offices, but she'd contrived to never be there whenever he'd been. He'd stalked the Imperial, yet she hadn't been there, either, and Mrs. Delamere had refused to tell him anything. Only looked at him with surprising pity.

He'd even waited outside Eleanor's lodgings. But she must have been sleeping elsewhere, because she didn't appear.

Damn it, he was a bloody *earl,* and this one woman managed to evade him at every turn. What the hell was he supposed to do? He knew she was around somewhere, because issues of *The Hawk's Eye* continued on, though without the *Rake* articles. Was he the only one who detected a certain melancholy quality in some of the articles? Or maybe he was simply seeing what he wanted to see. But he'd heard the heartbreak in her voice, had seen it in her eyes.

He couldn't simply let her go. Yet she seemed determined to keep them apart. Was there a point where he must give up? Her wishes were paramount. If she didn't love him, if she hadn't said how much she cared, if her reasons for this divide came from her heart, he would walk away.

Yet she had some bloody idea as to how the world worked, how things *must* be. And that couldn't be gainsaid.

There had to be something—but what? How could he prove himself to her?

A tap sounded on the door, and it opened slightly.

"What?" Daniel snarled.

"Lord Allam," the butler said.

"I'm not at home." Daniel had never denied his godfather entrance, but he needed solitude.

"The devil you aren't," Allam said, shouldering past the butler.

Daniel fought a growl. But he bowed as his godfather came into the study, leaning more heavily than usual on his cane. It was either bow or throw the older man out, which years of breeding—and respect—wouldn't allow Daniel to do.

Allam immediately helped himself to the decanter on the sideboard, pouring himself a respectable drink. Strange how Daniel hadn't even considered strong spirits to help keep his restlessness at bay. Nothing could satisfy him—except Eleanor.

"An unexpected pleasure," Daniel said.

His godfather threw back his drink, then whirled to face Daniel, his expression irate. He jabbed his cane into the ground. "You deny me entrance and then fall back on meaningless pleasantries?"

"Very well," Daniel answered. He strode to the door and held it open. "Go."

The older man snorted. "The deuce I'll leave." He planted himself in front of the fire, set his cane aside, and crossed his arms over his chest—the action so very like his son that it nearly made Daniel laugh. Except he was in no mood for laughter.

Allam and his son Marwood also had stubbornness in common. By the set of Allam's feet, planted wide as if expecting a fight, he planned on staying.

Daniel could be just as determined. Hands on hips, he demanded, "State your business, then."

"Where have you been?"

"I'm right here."

"None of your equivocation, lad," Allam snapped. "I've got eyes. I can see you. But these past weeks, I haven't seen you out on the Town. Not at the theater, not at any balls or assemblies. I asked my son, and he grudgingly told me you haven't been to the gaming hells."

"You've been keeping watch on me."

"Of course I have," the older man said. "You're my godson. Your welfare is my responsibility."

A drink did sound appealing, after all. Daniel poured himself a strong one and took a bracing sip. "I'm a grown man. I don't require nannying."

"Except when you forsake all your known pleasures and become a hermit."

Daniel stared into the bottom of his glass, but no answers were forthcoming from the cut crystal or whiskey. "I've lost my taste for it."

His eyes narrowing, Allam accused, "There's a woman behind this."

Daniel stiffened. "What do you know of it?" he growled.

"Who is she?" Allam fired back.

Daniel finished his drink, then tossed the glass to the ground, where it shattered. Frustration boiled up, red and seething. "A woman I can't live without. From some labyrinthine sense of how the world works, she believes we can't be together."

Allam gazed at the broken glass and said, "She's unsuitable."

"Depends on how you define *unsuitable,*" Daniel replied.

"She isn't for you," his godfather said flatly. He strode over to Daniel. "You have an obligation, a duty to your name and your future generations. Don't throw all that away on an infatuation. At least this woman understands that, even if you don't."

"You spoke with her," Daniel said with sudden realization. "That night I found her in the study—you'd been here and talked to her. Told her to leave."

"And she was smart enough to do it," Allam answered.

Rage poured through Daniel, searing him from the inside out. He had to forcibly keep his hands from curling into fists.

"How bloody dare you?" he growled.

"I dare because you matter to me," Allam snarled back.

"The Ashford title matters to you, but I don't." Daniel stalked away, too overwhelmed with anger to trust himself around the man he'd known his whole life.

"It has to be this way," Allam said to his back. "You understand that, don't you?"

"So I'm supposed to just forget her," Daniel bit out.

"Yes," the older man answered with brutal candor.

Daniel clenched his jaw. "I refuse to accept that answer."

"It's not for you to accept or deny. It's the truth of our times." A fragment of sympathy glimmered in Allam's gaze. "No matter what your heart tells you, there's no fighting the truth."

"You're wrong," Daniel said, turning around. "The truth is ours to shape as we want it. And I'll have my truth, by God. I'll have it."

The words swam in front of Eleanor like flecks of ash on the oily surface of water. She tried to focus on the copy in her hands, but her mind obdurately refused to do anything.

Except dwell on Daniel. That task, it did with remarkable ease. And frequency.

She pinched the bridge of her nose, trying to hold back the heaviness that always threatened to overwhelm her from moment to moment. Every part of her ached with weariness. She'd been on the run for weeks, constantly evading him. His letters went unread—though she did tuck them into a compartment in her desk. Someday, years from now, she might read them. But for now, she hadn't the strength. Because she knew he would try to convince her to come back. That they could be together. She was so tempted to believe him. Yet she knew reality, even if he refused to believe it.

God, how hard it was without him. Each day a long, colorless struggle. She did everything by rote. Eat, sleep—though both minimally—write.

"You're a shadow of yourself," Maggie had said to her one night. Eleanor had been staying in Maggie's rooms near the theater, but it had hardly been festive. "I think . . ." Maggie had taken a breath, clearly reluctant to speak. "You need to see him."

"I can't," Eleanor had answered, staring up at the ceiling. "You know more than anyone that their kind and ours don't mix."

Maggie hadn't had an argument to refute this, so they had both lapsed into moody silence. Ever since then, her friend hadn't suggested that she contact Daniel again.

Work was her only salvation. The only thing keeping her moving forward. But her old joy was pallid now, with no one to share it. She kept catching herself thinking of things she wanted to tell Daniel. Articles she edited that had to do with acquaintances of his. The scandalous exploits of his friend Marwood, for example. Or something outrageous that happened at Vauxhall.

She'd believed her life to be complete and satisfying before he'd come into it. And that life had been all those things. Yet he'd altered it all. Reversed the poles so that she could no longer find true north.

Weary, discouraged, Eleanor set the article aside and, with her elbows on her desk, put her head in her hands.

A sheet of paper slid in front of her. A piece for *The Hawk's Eye*.

She glanced up to see Harry standing before her desk. The lad gave her a sheepish smile. "It's for tomorrow's edition."

"Give it to Miss Voight," she said tiredly. "I can't look at another article."

"Miss Voight's out covering the veterans' return story. There's nobody here but you to do it."

Seeing as how she had little choice, Eleanor picked up the brief article and read.

> *Has love found Lord Rakewell at last? The dissipated earl has perchance ameliorated his wicked ways. He has been conspicuously absent from all his favorite haunts, and is rumored to have remained within the confines of his own home for over a fortnight!*
>
> *Through this paper's web of intelligence, we have been able to learn that indeed, Lord Rakewell is no longer a habitué of sinful indulgence since he fell in love with one quill-wielding woman. There are those who might believe such a woman would be unsuitable for an earl, but Lord Rakewell has publicly made it known that to continue living without her would be a hopeless endeavor, and one which he flatly refuses to consider.*
>
> *An announcement of happy news is perhaps forthcoming. Depending on the lady's desire.*

Eleanor looked up. Daniel stood in front of her. Impeccably dressed, as always, though his dark hair was longer, slightly mussed. He was thinner than last she'd seen him. His new leanness gave him the impossible, sharp beauty of a saint—though he still had the wicked blue eyes and mouth of a sinner.

The paper slipped from her hands. She wanted so badly

to reach out for him. To touch and smell and taste him once more. Yet she forced herself to keep her seat.

"The staff was to alert me if you were here," she said, impressed that she managed to keep her tone level. Then, raising her voice, she said, "I'll fire every last one of them."

Before Daniel could speak, Harry poked his head in the doorway. "Begging your pardon, Miss Hawke. But the rest of us saw how poorly you were doing, and . . . well . . ." He shrugged his bony shoulders, then disappeared.

"Don't blame them," Daniel said, his voice dear and familiar. "They care about you."

"I'll still sack them all," she muttered. She picked up the article. "We'll need to work on your prose. It's a rather remedial piece of writing."

He raised a brow. "It's not the style of the piece that should concern you but the content."

Abruptly, she rose from her desk and strode for the door. But instead of fleeing, as she burned to do, she shut the door, then faced him. "This changes nothing, Daniel. You and I—"

"Are going to be married."

She stared at him. Her heart slammed in her chest. Clearly, she'd heard him incorrectly. "Married?"

"That's what people in love do. Or so I've heard, and I happen to agree with this piece of conventional wisdom."

"But—"

Her words fled as he lowered himself down onto one knee. "I've heard this is customary, too. When asking a woman to be one's wife. Though rakes are not known for their proposals—except for indecent ones." Despite his light words, his eyes shone brightly, and there was a tremor in his voice. Suddenly, all lightness fled, and he'd never looked more solemn. "Eleanor, everything in that article is true. I can't go on without you. I need you in my life. Now. Forever."

She pressed her fingertips to her trembling lips. Here was a fresh anguish, being offered what she dared not hope for. "We can't," she whispered. "An earl and a newspaper editor cannot marry. Remember what happened to Lord Fleming?"

It took Daniel a moment to recall that unfortunate nobleman and his wife. "He wasn't strong enough. But I am."

"What about—"

All the world was in his eyes. "What's the point of being an earl," he said, "if I can't marry the woman I love?"

"It will cause a scandal we cannot escape," she breathed. "I've seen it. Written about it."

"Scandal sells newspapers."

"Don't jest." She spun away, bracing her hands on her desk.

He rose, and his hands cupped her shoulders. "I'll tease you about many things in the course of our life together, love, but never about this." Gently, he turned her around and tipped up her chin. "Those other scandals, those people you've written about, they could never withstand gossip. But I'm Lord Rakewell. Scandal means nothing to me. I can weather it better than anyone because I'm made for scandal. And I'm rich and influential enough so that no one will deny me. I always wondered what the point was of having so much power—but now I see. It's for this." He lowered his head and kissed her. Tenderly. Sweetly. With an undercurrent of heat that she couldn't resist.

In small fragments, the darkness engulfing her began to fall away. He was here. Anything was feasible.

"I love you, Eleanor," he said against her lips. "Let me wake up beside you every morning. Let me hold you in my arms each night. Let's compose filthy limericks together and ride like demons in phaetons together and grow old together. You have me forever, Eleanor."

"Yes," she said. "Yes. Yes."

He held her close, and their hearts beat in beautiful synchronicity.

It was a beautiful word: *yes*. She loved every word, but at that moment, none was more precious to her than *yes*. Because it opened to her a world of possibility. One that contained him. One that held the potential of them. Life was a blank sheet, and they would write their story together.

Epilogue

*There is nothing which ends which does not foretell
something else's beginning.*

The Hawk's Eye, July 15, 1816

Maggie was surrounded by tables, chairs, sofas, luggage,
mirrors, even a gilded wooden horse and a set of ninepins.
Cluttered as it was, the prop room of the Imperial Theater
remained one place in the madness of stage life where she
knew she could find a relative degree of peace. Upstairs, on
stage, rehearsals were already underway on her next burletta. Which meant there would be an infinite number of
questions. So she had taken the latest issue of *The Hawk's
Eye* and retreated. The only other occupant was the theater's
resident mouser, an orange tabby cat that was busily sleeping upon a velvet-upholstered throne.

The front page of Eleanor's paper was full of new accounts of scandal, but that's not what interested Maggie. She
turned to the third page and began to read.

> *Though this publication reports on the events of the
> Town, and not on itself, there are occasions wherein
> convention must be dispensed with. Perhaps the author
> of this article flatters herself overmuch in considering
> her private life to be the source of public speculation.
> Yet it cannot escape notice that she, that is, I, have*

crossed over the line from one who writes about the lives of others to one who is written about. Considerable conjecture has been hazarded of late, and so I find that I must take to the pages of this periodical in order to ensure as much of the truth as possible.

Yes, the author of this article has indeed married the earl of A—d. It was a decision made by both parties, and not under the duress of any forthcoming natal event. Gauche as it may seem, it was a love match.

A special license was obtained, and the ceremony itself was small and without spectacle. Shortly thereafter, my husband and I journeyed to one of his country estates to pass a most enjoyable honeymoon, the details of which shall not be reported here. We have since returned to Town and resumed our old habits, with the exception of dwelling under the same roof. Yes, reader, it is true. Though I am a countess, I continue to work.

Due to the circumstances of this author's birth, and the fact that she is actively engaged in gainful employment, there are some of the earl's social circle who have declined the pleasure of our association. The loss is not a great one, or so my husband asserts. We are received in most company and find that not a single whisper or intimation of calumny can despoil the singular contentment of our union.

It is my humble estimation that keeping up with Society's opinion can only end in despair and frustration. So I urge you to read this publication with an eye less to the misfortunes of others and more to your own happiness.

Maggie set the paper aside with a sigh. Of all the endings to Eleanor's involvement with an aristocrat, even she, a playwright, could not have predicted so felicitous an outcome. But Eleanor's was a rare tale. One that would not see its repetition. Maggie knew this from punitive experience. But she was pleased for Eleanor. She deserved this contentment.

She remembered how Lord Ashford had made Maggie laugh at Vauxhall. He'd been generous and self-deprecating. He'd said that he was glad the odious Mr. Smollett had been the object of Maggie's cutting wit rather than himself—since Ashford claimed he had no armor strong enough to protect himself against her. Truly, he'd said, if Maggie had been deployed against Napoleon, the war would have lasted days, not years. The Corsican would have crawled away, cradling his masculine pride. The image had been so ridiculous that she'd had to laugh.

Now Maggie gazed at a birdcage perched atop a sedan chair. As elated as she was for her friend, there would be no handsome, gallant nobleman for her. There would be no one. Only her work. She had that, and her freedom. It was enough. It would have to be enough.

"You are distracting me from my work," said Eleanor.

Daniel looked up from reading a book on the exploration of the Amazonian interior. His wife—how he enjoyed thinking that—sat nearby at her desk. They shared his study, their desks on opposite sides of the room. His home was expansive enough for her to have a study of her own, but she'd declined, preferring to keep close. He couldn't deny her. He always wanted her nearby.

"I'm sitting here quietly," he said. "Reading. Silently, mind you. My lips aren't even moving. How, pray tell, am I a distraction?"

Eleanor set her quill aside. A smile tugged at the corner of her lips. "Because I cannot stop looking at you."

That was a reason he couldn't find fault with. "Then the culpability lies with you, my lady. Though I have two possible solutions."

She rested her chin on her interlaced fingers. "I am all attentiveness."

"Horse blinkers might prove an adequate deterrent to looking anywhere but at your work," he offered.

She made a very unladylike gesture. "And the second solution?"

He set his book aside. "Come here, and I'll show you."

Her mouth curled. "Then I'll get nothing done."

"On the contrary, I think we'll accomplish quite a lot."

For a moment, she seemed to seriously consider it. Then she shook her head. "I can't. I have a deadline."

"Let's compromise. I will remove myself from your sight for the next thirty minutes."

She raised a brow. "What happens in thirty minutes?"

"You put down your quill and come to the bedroom. A bath will be waiting. As will I."

That smile he'd come to prize above everything brightened her face. "I accept the terms of your compromise."

He rose from his seat. "Mind, if you're late, I will be forced to seek you out."

"And then?" she asked pertly.

"Then, my lady, you will see what happens when you keep an earl waiting."

"Heaven forbid," she said, though her cheeks turned a delicious pink.

He bowed. "Thirty minutes."

"We shall see," she said airily. Her eyes gleamed wickedly. A minx, his wife. She had upended everything in his life. Torn it completely asunder. Scandal still accompanied them, but he didn't mind, and she didn't seem to, either. Scandal had brought them together, after all.

He'd never been happier. Judging by the smile she continually wore, and the way he caught her sometimes humming softly to herself, she was happy, too. It was all he ever wanted. More than he deserved.

Lord Rakewell had indeed found his perfect match. And her fingers were always stained with ink.

Don't miss the next smart and sexy novel in
Eva Leigh's
Wicked Quills of London series

Scandal Takes the Stage

Coming November 2015

Read on for a sneak peek!

Enter Phoebe, in country dress.
Phoebe: What a task I have set before me!

The Shattered Heart

London, 1816

The curtain at the Imperial Theater fell. The audience rose to its collective feet and applauded.

Standing in his theater box, adding his own applause, Cameron Chalton, Viscount of Marwood was filled with excitement. Much as Cam enjoyed the theater—he went practically every night, and often saw the same work over and over, enjoying it anew each time—half the pleasure came after the performances.

"What say you, Marwood?" drawled Lord Eberhart, one of Cam's companions for the evening. "Gaming at Donnegan's? Shall we away to the rout at Lord Larkin's? He's brought in a whole bevy of beauties from France just for the occasion."

"Why choose?" Cam answered with a laugh. "The night's in its infancy, and we can do anything at all."

"Good point." Eberhart grinned. He wasn't the

brightest star in the firmament, but ever since Cam's good friend Ashford had wed and settled into marital bliss, Cam couldn't afford to be as selective with his company. Besides, Eberhart was always up for a night's revelry. "Let's go."

"Not yet," Cam answered, watching the theater slowly empty.

The Imperial was smaller than the other popular theaters in London, with only three tiers for seats and boxes, plus a smaller pit and orchestra. Yet it wasn't shabby. The proprietors kept its appearance well. Painted plaster friezes depicting scenes from mythology adorned the fronts of the boxes, and blue velvet curtains draped the sides and top of the stage. Gas lamps provided lighting.

The boxes now released their occupants like tropical birds flying free of their cages. In the pit, the younger, wilder set laughed and boasted, jostling one another, flirting, arguing. Orange girls and women of fast reputation circulated freely among the young men.

Cam's status prevented him from sitting in the pit anymore, but he missed it. The energy, the rowdiness. Still, he couldn't complain, not when he'd just watched a performance of a work by the celebrated and mysterious Mrs. Delamere. Not when the evening opened up for him like an endless banquet. One he would sample to his heart's content. But not quite at this moment.

"Tell you what, Eberhart," Cam continued, turning back to his companion. "I'll meet you at Donnegan's, then we'll sally forth from there onto Larkin's."

"Going to circulate?" Eberhart said with a grin.

"This is my kingdom," Cam replied with a wink. "I must inevitably tour my realm. Inspect its crops."

"Of actresses." His friend leered.

Cam tilted his head in acknowledgment. "Merely a part of my dominion."

"Enjoy, Your Highness." With a chuckle, Eberhart slipped from the box and out into the night.

Once his friend had gone, Cam took one last minute to enjoy the theater's house as patrons continued to leisurely make their way. The thrills from the performance still resonated in Cam's body, palpable as electricity crackling along his veins. Though he'd seen this particular work several times, it never lost its excitement—the soaring highs and resounding lows that came from watching characters' love and loss. He especially loved how the heroine thoroughly humiliated the aristocratic villain before gaining her tragic vengeance against him.

Not every work affected him as much. But for a reason he couldn't quite articulate, Mrs. Delamere's tragic burlettas stabbed him through as beautifully and cleanly as a jeweled knife. Her use of language, perhaps, was so much more articulate than other staged dramas. Or the relatable human longing and pain contained within in each work. Whatever caused it, Cam craved the next work from her the way a drunkard needed wine.

Still somewhat tipsy from the performance, he strode from the box. Almost at once, he ran into two young, red-faced lordlings, already listing from too much ale. A pretty courtesan snuggled between them.

"Marwood!" they exclaimed, practically tripping over themselves as they clumsily bowed.

"Gents," Cam answered, a little coolly. He didn't mind being a little disguised from drink, but it was a classic mistake of the young not to pace themselves.

"Come with us!" they cried. "We're going to Vauxhall. Supposed to be quite a crush."

For a moment, Cam contemplated it. The pleasure garden always promised a good time, and delivered. Its theatricality and lurid beauty never failed to entertain, and more than once, he'd taken a female companion to the Dark Walk for an *al fresco* amorous encounter. There was something thrilling about being outside when engaged in carnal pursuits—the fresh air, the possibility of being caught.

The courtesan accompanying the two young men gave him a not very discreet looking over. Judging by the way her eyes brightened, she liked what she saw. Maybe she would be agreeable—if not enthusiastic—about the prospect of a trip to Vauxhall's Dark Walk.

However . . .

"Save me a slice of roast beef," Cam said. "I'll join you another time."

The two bucks looked somewhat crestfallen, but after a quick exchange of further pleasantries, they and their female friend moved on.

Leaving Cam free to head toward his destination: backstage. That's where the real action took place.

As he slowly ambled toward his goal, he passed more and more friends and acquaintances. All of them hailed him. Dozens of invitations were issued. Some to sanctioned Society events, others to more daring, exclusive gatherings. Tempting, every one. He wished he had more than one self, so that he might partake of everything presented to him. Galas, private assemblies, midnight horse races. There was no shortage of amusements, no limit on the pleasures he might experience. Bold widows and bored wives offered their own wordless invitations with their provocative glances and heated gazes.

How could he resist? More often than not, he didn't.

Tonight, however, he had other plans. Specifically, the actress playing the ingénue.

After disentangling himself from another poesy of aristocratic theater patrons, he headed down the stairs. Closer to his objective.

"What a perfectly dismal surprise," someone behind him said wryly.

Cam's heart rose. He knew that voice, almost as well as he knew his own. Now the night could truly begin! He turned to face the Earl of Ashford.

Standing beside Ashford was the earl's new wife, a very pretty blonde, and some of Cam's enthusiasm dampened. It wasn't that he disliked Lady Ashford. Far from it. But ever since she'd come into the earl's life, Cam's own world had been in a state of upheaval. It wasn't nearly as much fun running wild through the Town without Ashford.

"Now the evening's truly ruined," Cam answered.

Both Ashford and his wife were elegantly attired for a night out. Lady Ashford, in particular, glowed in blue. Though she was a countess, she prided herself on being a working woman. Yet Cam felt certain that the substantial sapphires around her neck and hanging from her earlobes were placating gestures to her husband. Ashford tried to spoil her at every turn.

The couple stood unfashionably close. Ashford had his hand on the small of his wife's back.

After kissing Lady Ashford's gloved knuckles and

giving his old friend's hand a shake, Cam said wryly, "I'm older than I thought, since I'm certain that my eyes are failing. This can't be Lord and Lady Ashford actually leaving their home. Joining those of us who haven't found wedded bliss."

"It's not our fault that the female population of London considers you an irredeemable rogue," Ashford said.

His wife smiled warmly. "To women, his reputation acts as a lure, not a deterrent."

"And yet they'll find themselves sorely disappointed," Cam noted, clasping his hands behind his back. "Because this piece of beefsteak is not for sale at Smithfield market."

Ashford shook his head. "Don't tell your father. He comes to me almost once a fortnight, despairing of you ever finding a wife."

Cam rolled his eyes. His father was also Ashford's godfather, and ever since his friend had married, the efforts to see Cam settled and applying himself to the business of getting an heir had redoubled.

"So much labor," Cam said with mock sorrow, "and for so little an outcome."

"You are determined to remain a dedicated bachelor, then?" Lady Ashford pressed, ever the journalist. She used her matching blue fan to cool herself against the oppressive heat in the theater.

"I have a younger brother," Cam noted. "He has three qualities in his favor that I do not." Holding up his hand, he enumerated each aspect on his fingers. "One: he has already taken a bride of suitable lineage and fortune. Two: they have produced a child. And third: he has no compunction about assuming the role of Marquess of Allam should anything happen to me."

Shrugging, Cam said, "There are no obstacles to me continuing to live my life as I so desire it. Free of entanglements." Free of disappointment.

His parents had a remarkably happy marriage. While they didn't show affection in public the way the Ashfords did, at home, it was another matter. His mother and father were devoted to each other, brushing hands, exchanging looks, even—God help him—sequestering themselves in the middle of the day in the bedchamber.

It hadn't been a love match, but it had become one, and Cam knew things like that occurred rarely. What had happened with a seasoned rake like Ashford was the exception, about as common as finding a pearl in an apple.

The only place where love happened consistently was on the stage. It wasn't meant for the real world. Not meant for him. He'd only find disenchantment if he tried for what couldn't be.

Which is why he always kept his amorous encounters temporary.

Lady Ashford raised a brow. "You are quite convinced that you want no such 'entanglements.' "

"As convinced as you are that you must continue to work," he rejoined with a bow, "despite your new social standing."

She tipped her head in acknowledgment. "I yield—for now."

Ashford smiled. "Careful, Marwood. That only means she's taking a tactical retreat. When it comes to matters of significance, my wife is quite tenacious." He said this with obvious affection.

Cam couldn't begrudge his old friend this happiness. A new brightness and life shone in Ashford's eyes now, as if he'd discovered his purpose, the meaning of his existence.

After glancing around to make certain no one listened in, Cam leaned closer to Lady Ashford and said conspiratorially, "I saw a certain Lord V— deep in private conversation with Lord W—'s new wife."

Her smile was wise and knowing. "Already made note of it." Though she was a countess, she continued to own and run *The Hawk's Eye*, one of London's most popular scandal sheets. In fact, a series of articles in the paper about Ashford had actually brought the two together.

Cam bowed. "I see I cannot top you for intelligence, my lady."

"Few can," Ashford said with a grin.

Lady Ashford said, "It appears to this intelligent eye that we're detaining Lord Marwood from some objective. Perhaps he plans on paying a call on Miss Smith, who so delightfully played the role of the ingénue this evening."

Shaking his head, Cam had to admire the countess's shrewdness. "I admit nothing," he said instead.

"A good rake never does," she countered, though she smiled.

"Enjoy the hunt," Ashford chuckled.

"I will."

With that, Cam took his leave of his old friend. A bubble of melancholy settled in his chest at the thought of what he'd lost with Ashford's marriage, and that his friend had found love, when it was such a rare commodity. Given that lightning had struck twice so close to Cam, it seemed even more unlikely that it would strike him. How much genuine love was there in the world? Very little. It was mostly contained within the proscenium arch of a theater.

He wasn't in search of love tonight. Only pleasure.

A tall, broad man stood guarding the backstage entrance. His thick arms crossed over his chest as half a dozen young men vied to be admitted behind the scenes—to the actresses' dressing rooms, most of all. Other theaters had a more lax policy regarding backstage visitors, but someone at the Imperial had years ago instituted a rule wherein all would-be suitors had to be vetted. Clearly, none of these bucks met the criteria.

"Come on, let me in," one lad whined. "She's expecting me."

"I've got a twenty-pound note with your name on it," another pled.

The mountain guarding backstage wouldn't be moved.

As Cam approached, the crowd parted. The noise died down. All the younger men stared at Cam with something like reverence. He tried not to preen. After all, he'd worked hard for his reputation as a hellraiser of the first water. It would be a shame if all that labor was for nothing.

"That's Marwood," one of the men whispered reverently to the other.

"Think he'll take us with him tonight?"

"Did you hear about the party he threw the other month? A masked ball the likes of which hasn't been seen since Ancient Rome."

"I say, Marwood—"

He ignored them. Instead, he stepped in front of the giant man.

"Lord Marwood?" the massive gent asked.

Cam inclined his head.

The man stepped to one side and waved him forward. "If you please, my lord."

Before he moved on, he turned to address all the panting, eager young chaps. "Never beg for anything," he said. "Makes you look desperate. No one respects a desperate man. Especially women."

With that, he strode backstage. All at once, the cacophony started up again. Sadly, it seemed none of the blokes took Cam's advice. Ah, well. They'd discover the truth of his words sooner or later.

Backstage, all was controlled chaos. Still in costume, performers of every stripe milled around—including acrobats, a dog act, a cloud of dancers, clowns, and the rouged, adorned actors and actresses from the final burletta. In addition to the performers were the stage crew, taking away painted flats, gathering up properties, and generally looking put out by the fact that they had to work in the middle of this bedlam.

Cam stopped in the wings and drew a deep breath. It wasn't a pleasant breath, thick as the air was with the scent of paint and sweat, but to Cam it still smelled as rich and heady as a fine perfume. This was the fragrance of the theater, of the magic of make-believe. It was slightly stale and very human. Precisely the reasons why he enjoyed it so much.

Many gazes landed on Cam as he paused in the wings. Within a moment, three actresses in their pretend silks and velvets gathered around him like painted butterflies.

They batted their kohl-lined eyes at him, draping their soft ivory arms around his shoulders, and smiling with pretty little teeth. Beads of sweat that jeweled their hairlines only added to their appeal. Unlike the women of ballrooms and Society teas, these women had a realness about them, grounded as they were in the theater and its work. It was a paradox that, though they invested themselves in the realm of the pretend, they were more genuine to Cam than any debutante. He accepted his own contradictions.

"My lord," a brunette actress cooed. "A pleasure."

"Pleasure is my fondest pursuit," he answered with a grin.

The female performers giggled.

He was gratified to see that Miss Smith was among the actresses' numbers. Tall and willowy, with ash blond hair and gray eyes, she had the figure of a woodland sylph but a knowing gaze. And equally adept hands.

Those hands played across Cam's waistcoat, pressing against his chest. She would've made a lovely pickpocket. No man would have resisted getting fleeced by those pretty fingers.

"Oh, my lord," she sighed. "You're not soft like the other gents that come back here. You're hard all over."

"Indeed, I can be," he replied.

More titters arose from the women.

"Did you enjoy the performances tonight?" Miss Smith asked.

"Everyone was in rare form," he answered honestly. "Tears nearly rolled down my cheeks at the tragic conclusion of the final burletta. And I wasn't the only one in the audience who felt that way. We were all in a swoon." He spoke no exaggeration.

He didn't believe in false flattery. It was a cheap trick used by rogues and frauds who hadn't enough skill to win a woman through the truth.

"In fact," he went on, "I'd very much like to show my appreciation for such a performance by inviting all of you out for a private supper."

The actresses squealed with happiness. Miss Smith beamed at him, and her eyelashes batted so furiously, they nearly tangled. Cam realized that he'd told Eberhart that he'd meet him at the gaming hell in an hour, but he knew the other man wouldn't mind if Cam decided to entertain a small collection of actresses instead. A fellow had to have his priorities.

Cam was about to suggest to the women that they go change out of their costumes, when a movement in the corner of his eye caught his attention. Or rather, the absence of movement. In the sea of commotion, there was a small spot of stillness, and it drew his gaze.

A woman. Petite yet curvaceous, with a mass of nearly black hair piled atop her head, she read over a sheet of paper. Unlike the actresses and dancers, she wasn't in costume. She wore a simple russet woolen gown with a high neckline and long sleeves. Her face was tilted down as she examined the document in her hands, yet Cam could see that she had a small, pointed chin, nearly severe dark eyebrows, and a wide, lush mouth. Not precisely beautiful, but certainly striking.

Within the confines of her small, curvy body, she held a unique gravitas. A purpose and intent. She fairly burned with it. And damn him if that didn't appeal to Cam.

A sudden need to be near her blazed through him.

She seemed familiar to him, somehow, yet he couldn't quite place her. Whoever she was, he wanted to smooth the crease between those arresting eyebrows. He needed to hear her voice—whether it was high and girlish, or low and husky. He wanted . . . he didn't know what he wanted. Only to be close by her side.

"Excuse me for a moment," he murmured distractedly, disentangling himself from Miss Smith and the other actresses. As if in a daze, he crossed the wings, barely seeing anything and anyone.

Only the mysterious woman before him.

At Avon Books, we know your passion for romance—once you finish one of our novels, you find yourself wanting more.

May we tempt you with . . .

- **Excerpts** from our upcoming releases.

- Entertaining **extras**, including authors' personal photo albums and book lists.

- Behind-the-scenes **scoop** on your favorite characters and series.

- **Sweepstakes** for the chance to win free books, romantic getaways, and other fun prizes.

- Writing **tips** from our authors and editors.

- **Blog** with our authors and find out why they love to write romance.

- **Exclusive content** that's not contained within the pages of our novels.

Join us at
www.avonbooks.com

AVON

An Imprint of HarperCollins*Publishers*
www.avonromance.com

Available wherever books are sold or please call 1-800-331-3761 to order.

Give in to your Impulses!

These unforgettable stories only take a second to buy and give you hours of reading pleasure!

Go to *www.AvonImpulse.com* and see what we have to offer.

Available wherever e-books are sold.

AVON**IMPULSE**